WHAT A NIGHTMARE

BERKLEY TITLES BY REBEKAH FAUBION

The Lovers

The Sun and the Moon

What a Nightmare

WHAT A NIGHTMARE

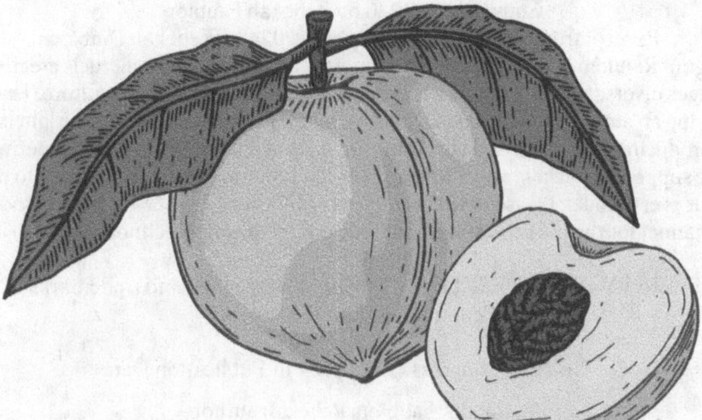

Rebekah Faubion

BERKLEY
NEW YORK

BERKLEY
An imprint of Penguin Random House LLC
1745 Broadway, New York, NY 10019
penguinrandomhouse.com

Library of Congress Cataloging-in-Publication Data

Names: Faubion, Rebekah author
Title: What a nightmare / Rebekah Faubion.
Description: First edition. | New York : Berkley, 2026.
Identifiers: LCCN 2026010169 (print) | LCCN 2026010170 (ebook) |
ISBN 9798217192144 trade paperback | ISBN 9798217192151 ebook
Subjects: LCSH: Revenge | LCGFT: Paranormal fiction | Novels
Classification: LCC PS3606.A857 W43 2026 (print) |
LCC PS3606.A857 (ebook) | DDC 813/.6--dc23/eng/20260608
LC record available at https://lccn.loc.gov/2026010169
LC ebook record available at https://lccn.loc.gov/2026010170

First Edition: October 2026

Printed in the United States of America
1st Printing

The authorized representative in the EU for product safety and compliance is Penguin Random House Ireland, Morrison Chambers, 32 Nassau Street, Dublin D02 YH68, Ireland, https://eu-contact.penguin.ie.

For all the girls they want to silence.
And for me, who they never could.

Content Warning note:

A list of content warnings for *What a Nightmare* is available at the back of the book, following the acknowledgments.

1

THIS BREAK ROOM is where dreams go to die.

I fit right in.

The walls, once painted ecru or eggshell or some wispy-sounding off-white, have soured to a color that more closely resembles curdled milk. My beige button-down and mousy brown hair almost camouflage me from my coworkers Cindy and Sienna, who are enjoying their lunch at the table in the center of the room. I've slid against the wall, let my shoulder blades dig into the plaster in order to avoid small talk. I've done so every day since I started working at Second City Title and Trust over a year ago.

I don't blame them for ignoring me.

My invisibility is by design.

"Roger is such a tool!" Cindy says, her exclamation hopping over the gray linoleum tiles toward me unbidden. She's got one of those chipper, bright voices that usually accompanies sorority girls or cheer captains in movies. Her chestnut-brown hair is cut in a long bob that hits her collarbone with precise straight-edge ends. Not a split in sight.

"You don't mean it." Sienna dips her spoon into her low-fat yogurt and removes it coated. She doesn't take bites; she nibbles and licks and samples.

Elmdale, Illinois, is a suburb of Chicago with a prestigious school system and lots of new money. Second City Title and Trust handles real estate closings for most of the town. We straddle two counties, which puts us in high demand. Sienna and Cindy work in Escrow as assistants. They're starting to do their own closings—their bloodlust reeks. Sienna has a background in real estate, so even though she's been here less than a year, the contacts she brought in with her have ensured a quick rise through the ranks. Cindy on the other hand works hard, stays late, hustles. I can give her credit for that much at least.

"I mean it," Cindy says, with breathy adamancy. "I brought in that contract on Fairfax—1.3 mil. Roger acted like he was doing me a favor letting me clean the title before he handled the closing."

Roger is the lead escrow officer and manager. I work as his assistant, as well as the receptionist for the whole goddamn office. Roger has never offered me a raise, and there's been no discussion of me taking my assistant/receptionist duties to the next level. Not that I want either of those things, not when I know it would require I give more of myself to this job, this place, this life.

I don't have more of myself to give. But Cindy is right.

Roger *is* a tool. This fact is not negated by my appreciation that he seems to see me mostly as shrubbery, just how I like it. And since Roger has an office full of underlings to work his files, he spends a considerable amount of time with his racket and calls it *networking*. We rarely have to deal with him for a full eight-hour workday.

Cindy needs to take her blessings when they come.

"At least that's all he had you clean," Sienna says, using her spoon to mimic a certain phallic activity. Cindy's face tightens—subtle enough that I'd miss it if I wasn't paying attention.

I let out the smallest sound. A groan lodged in my throat like a chip swallowed wrong.

Cindy whips her head around, brown eyes searing. "What's that, Haven?" she asks.

Fuck. Invisibility breached.

"I didn't say anything," I reply, crunching the wrapper of my Kind bar in my hand.

"You laughed," Sienna chimes in. She sets her yogurt container down on the table. Spoon erect.

"I had a tickle in my throat," I say, instinctively clearing it to demonstrate her error.

I blend into the walls. I avoid conversation. I deflect conflict. It's all on purpose.

"Oh my God, is it Covid?" Sienna questions, lifting her hand in a *shoo* motion.

"Allergies," I reply.

"That's what people say when they have Covid." Sienna yanks up her yogurt and moves toward the exit. "I have a date this weekend, can't get sick—"

I'm rooted, shoulders glued to the wall, as I watch her go.

"Don't worry about Roger, Cindy," Sienna says as she moves. "You know he's mostly just a blowhard." I pinch my nose to hold in a snort, and she's gone.

Cindy still watches me. My eyes shift to hers and then divert to the fridge. There's a closing in half an hour, and Roger likes me to have cookies baking when clients arrive. Something about how "studies" show the smell can trigger strong positive emotions, a factor Roger considers tantamount to keeping Second City at the top.

I throw my Kind bar wrapper away and cross the room to the fridge, then yank open the freezer door to reveal a nearly empty cavern. I need to order more cookies and I keep forgetting. Peanut butter. *Shit!* That's all we have left.

Cindy is up, at my side. She smells like citrus and green, sharp and earthy but sweet.

"You're not gonna tell Roger, are you?" Her eyes clamp onto my profile. She's willing me to look at her. She knows she's pretty, and pretty gets you far.

I flick my eyes over, my hand momentarily paused in motion toward the peanut butter balls. "I was just letting off steam."

Our eyes connect. There's a storm of gold that swirls in the deep brown. "You know how it is." She touches my forearm.

I jerk away. She steps back.

It's an overreaction to what can only be described as *friendly camaraderie*. I know it, she knows it, and it's about to get weird if I don't say something.

"I know how it is," I reply. The freezer hangs open, cold chilling the air between us. "I need to make the cookies for Roger's two thirty."

She gives me a weak smile, underscored with how uncomfortable I'm making her, but she nods and exhales a tiny puff of air through her small pink pouty lips. Relief, that we're on the same page. At least that's what she thinks just happened.

"Of course," she says. She takes another step back and grabs the bento box holding the remnants of her lunch. "People come from miles away to close here for the cookies alone."

We both know that's bullshit. But it's a good exit line, and at least she uses it right. She's gone and I'm by myself again, just as I like it.

THE SMELL OF peanut butter cookies fills the air. Salty and sweet, thick like molasses, and nutty rich. I'm trying to ignore the scent and everything it beckons from the past. I know I fail, because the space between the oven and the coffee machine shimmers–a migraine aura, a warning before pain.

I take a breath. I close my eyes. When I open them, it will be there.

The teeny tiny box.

A ding on the oven tells me I've run out of time. My eyelids lift, my vision settles.

The box is made of wood. It has a lid carved delicately with a sycamore tree. The lock is rusty but no less secure than it always has been. There is no key–there never was. And even though I made the teeny tiny box–though I can't remember how, don't know when–even though no one but me can confirm it to be real, I am the only one who's ever used it, seen it, could touch it, though I don't; the sight of it sitting atop that linoleum turns my stomach inside out. I taste acid on my tongue, feel the swish-swash of my vision as it tries to swim away.

I loathe the box, but I would be lost without it.

This much I know: I have somehow designed it to be so.

There aren't many memories from childhood I can still recall with accuracy. Not many I can dust off and admire. Most are inaccessible, locked inside the box. Most should stay that way. But some still stick around, like participation trophies. Little embarrassments or joys, mundane enough that just looking at them doesn't shift the way I hold my body, use my words, sift through my feelings.

These memories remind me that I came from somewhere.

I had a bedroom I decorated with lavender paint and movie posters and a map of the world I would one day see all the way around and back again. I kept my dolls on a bookshelf lined up in a row; my books all had tattered spines and turned-down pages and underlined passages. I hid a black onyx crystal and a set of tarot cards under my bed, along with the necklace my friend Jane gave me to remember her by when she moved away, and a fuzzy pink diary with a lock that I'd stolen from the Kmart a few days before it closed down for good.

The memory about the cookies isn't like that. Still, it never goes away, never changes, despite being unwanted and incomplete. On the days Roger wants closing cookies and the only option in the freezer is peanut butter, it surfaces like a wraith.

My mother was an exceptional baker, but that time she let them burn. The scorched scent cloaked the air and snuck in through the cracks between the two wooden cabinet doors I was hiding behind.

The moments before I climbed in the cabinet and after I was discovered are fuzzy, so I couldn't say what led me to cowering like a kitchen mouse or what my punishment was when I was found. I can remember the way the smoke mingled with dust in the sunlight and the smell of charred peanut butter, rancid and pungent. I can remember eating the edge of a cookie I dug out of the trash, black flesh first.

Mostly, I remember my heart pounding so hard I thought for a second it would break from the walls of my chest and tattle on me as it thumped against the cupboard doors.

Always, I remember her saying, *What a nightmare*, and she meant me.

"Haven?"

My name, called in a question, breaks through the world of my memory, just in time.

I yank the door of the small electric oven open and pull the cookie tray out. Some of the edges are darker than normal, but since people usually just smell the cookies, I can't imagine that being a problem.

A hand slaps the doorframe. Broad with trimmed nails, a pleasant tan, and a very expensive wristwatch.

Seven minutes ahead of his closing, Roger has arrived.

"There you are," he says.

He releases the doorframe to tighten his tie, smooth his shirt. Pinstripe, blue and white. Dark hair is slicked, probably still damp from a shower at the gym. His eyes drop to the table, where the cookies sit.

"Plate those up. I'll be in my office," he says, cutting a look past me to the clock hanging on the opposite wall. "Give me ten and then bring them back."

He means the clients, not the cookies. I bring the cookies when I bring the clients water. I always ask if they would like anything to drink, and with the exception of the people who brought their own from home in one of those big stupid cups, I've never been told no. We offer coffee and creamer (Folgers and Coffee mate, nothing fancy) and water in recyclable cups despite the fact that Roger refuses to put in a recycling bin, so I have to hide the cups in the broom closet and recycle them at my town house after work.

I don't reply to his order; it's unnecessary at best, superfluous at worst. Roger gives orders because he likes to hear himself talk. I haven't needed them since my second day on staff. I stopped giving responses to him when I realized they didn't register. Watching him walk away as soon as my lips opened once was enough.

He claps his hand against the doorframe again and then pushes off the wood in the direction of his office. My gaze drifts back to the cookies. I finger the rounded edge of one before lifting it off the sheet toward my nose. I take a stiff inhale and close my eyes.

"Oh, and *Heaven*?" I cringe at his nickname, which is really unsubtle harassment. Roger is back at the door. This time his eyes don't trail or bounce around, they're fixed on me, my face, my nose pressed into the top of the cookie. I draw it away from the tip, but the toasted scent lingers. "Party tomorrow evening. Everything ready?"

The dreaded schmooze fest. A chance for all the title people and commercial dudes (even the women in commercial are classed as dudes) and real estate agents and assistants trying to get ahead to mingle here at Second City, where quality, service, and accuracy converge.

I bought all the supplies, booked a caterer and a bartender. With any luck, Roger will stay out of my way so I can handle setup without his "guidance."

"Everything is ready to go, just have to set up tomorrow after lunch."

He winks and makes a clicking sound with his tongue. It's disgusting. "You're a dream," he says.

I stiffen.

His eyes drop to my blouse and back up to my eyes. Something unspoken but still violating passes through his gaze. He wants to tell me to wear some color and that I should do something with my hair, that I would look pretty if I smiled, especially with a coat of pink on my lips.

None of it is said out loud. All of it is felt.

The box seems to feel it too.

"Anything else?" I ask him, voice high and thin with a crack of nerves.

He doesn't notice. And he doesn't reply to the question.

He leaves with another smack to the doorframe, and now it's just me, the cookies, and that goddamn box. I hold it in my glare as long as I can, because as soon as I look away, I know it will be gone. Vanished into nothing, leaving no residue except for that dull ache of dread at the back of my mind waiting and watching for it to return.

The cookie I picked up before is still clutched in hand; it warms the tips of my fingers. The fragrance dances out of the break room to the hallway and into the lobby to smack clients in the face with feelings of safety, of home and belonging. I crush the cookie in my fist, watch it crumble over the others and scatter across the parchment like sand.

2

I CHANGED MY last name in Tennessee.

My family had gotten my address from the internet too easily, sent me an invite to my brother Buck's wedding. I was twenty-three and renting a whole room all to myself in a house that looked out over the Mississippi River in Memphis. It had a kitchenette and a bathroom with a shower barely big enough for one. I didn't think they'd come all the way there, try to drag me back or anything. They had let me go freely, it wasn't like I was missed.

I just didn't like the jump scare of seeing "Powers Ranch" on the return address.

I wish they were the only reason I had for leaving almost every other place I've ever momentarily called home behind.

I pull up outside my town house. It's a two-story brick building with white shutters and a cobalt-blue front door. A rental with vinyl wood floors and that thin gray-white carpet stretched over the stairs, in all the bedrooms.

The engine idles for a few seconds longer as I wait. Watch. There is a feeling that strikes me sometimes when I arrive after dusk. It's of eyes watching in the dark as it bleeds around the edge of my building. It's of being hunted, and I hate it, but I can't shake it. There's an alley between this town house and the next few, with dumpsters and a motion-operated light that doesn't work half the time. It yawns like an open mouth.

I flick a glance over at my car door and check the locks.

Rationality should stop me from this line of thinking; it should remind me that they haven't contacted me since I changed my name. Three years with no surprise visits from my big bad wolf. Haven Smith, the new me since Tennessee, isn't their daughter or sister, isn't their property.

Haven Powers doesn't exist anymore.

They wouldn't spend money to track me down, and that's what they would have to do to resurrect this dead girl.

Something moves in the shadow–I think.

I blink, lean forward against the steering wheel to peer into that yawning mouth. It was a trick of my mind.

The first time they found me was in Baton Rouge, Louisiana. I had been gone two months, and I'd had to take such a deep dip into my secret cash stash that I finally realized I would run out within the year, and then what? So I got a job and settled somewhere. I chose a studio apartment with a view of a cemetery and a pantry bug infestation that laid waste to all my dried goods. I got work at the local Piggly Wiggly bagging groceries, and they found me within the week.

They sent me flowers.

This big bouquet of white roses without a card. The delivery guy showed up at the front door and refused to walk up the four flights to get to me. When I told him it had to be a mistake, there wasn't a card, and I didn't know anyone who would send me flowers, he reluctantly checked the order sheet.

"They're from someone named Earl Powers," he said, changing his *Th* to *D*, his words chasing fast one after the other. He refused to take the flowers back, and at the time, barely twenty, I took them in my hands, held them out, arms erect, like they were a baby who had just shit its pants and I was trying to keep my clothes clean.

I tried to give them to my neighbor, an old white lady who made potpourri in her living room and smelled like a candle burning in the dusty attic of a house infested with mold. She told me not to bother her when she was watching TV; she looked at me like a slug she wanted to crush with her shoe. Later on, when she went to urgent care because she sliced her hand open with a knife, I tried to ignore the sinking feeling in my gut that told me that accident and my flare of anger over how she refused to take the cursed flowers off my cursed hands were related.

Mishaps like that had happened before.

I close my eyes. I will my mind to settle.

Get out of the car. You have groceries thawing in the back seat that you need to put away. I swallow the fear and shut off the car engine. With a swipe of the keys and a yank, slam, yank, slam of my doors I'm practically sprinting up the concrete walk to my front door. My motion-activated porch light flicks on, and I slide the house key easily into the lock.

Slam, *twist*, safe.

My town house isn't much better than the break room at Second City Title and Trust.

Two floors. Open-concept living room, dining room, kitchen. Primary. Bathrooms. Guest room. Nothing special, nothing fancy. I don't feel more at home in Elmdale than anywhere else that I've been, but at least the accent is different, and the landscape is different, and it blusters in winter, and it's far enough away that, most days, I succeed in pretending the past can no longer stalk me.

Unless I fail.

I watched a YouTube video once about trauma. It got served to me in that way that all creepy algorithmic suggestions do. I'd been thinking about seeing a therapist, talking myself out of it over a glass of wine in bed, and it showed up like a devil on my shoulder. Or maybe an angel, I can't decide.

All I learned after watching it was that I am indeed a fucked-up little disaster.

I ignored the part about how it wasn't my fault.

I've never had a single therapy session in my whole twenty-eight years alive. You'd think I would have, but my family didn't believe in therapy, just prayer, and meds were never an option. We handled everything the same way: suppress it, and if you can't do it by will, do it with a drink.

I walk to the kitchen in the dark and throw the grocery bags onto the small island countertop. I yank open the refrigerator door, and shove apples and cheese inside as I grab a half-drunk bottle of chardonnay. There's a glass sitting on the drying rack from the night before, ready for a heavy pour. I'm a moderate, but I am not above playing with danger. Booze is a coping strategy. One of many I've adopted over the years.

You're thinking an awful lot about them, and you only ever do that when they're close to: calling, sending an unsigned birthday card, showing up in your dreams.

Or worse.

I leave one frozen dinner on the counter. *Crack crack crack*, I perforate the plastic with a fork, pop it in the microwave, and stand in front of it, just hoping the waves radiate my insides into oblivion.

When I feel like this—my resolve thinner than tissue paper, my mind playing tricks—I wonder again what it would have been like to grow up different than I did. In another universe, maybe, there is a Haven Powers who didn't die slowly, then all at once. That Haven has somewhere to go during Christmas, someone to put as an emergency contact, someone to test for a match if her body revolts and needs help.

It's a daydream, pure and simple. I only succumb for as long as the chicken fettuccini spins on the microwave tray.

At the ding, I wake up and remember.

I am peeling the microwave dinner plastic wrap from the top of the container, my lips pressed to the medically unendorsed, fucked-up-family-advised wineglass when I hear it. In the alley outside, something tumbles. A raucous noise like someone tripped in the deepening dark.

My hand grips the hilt of the biggest butcher knife in the block.

My pulse clips up, a jagged ascent.

There is a war in my brain between rationality and survival, but my body isn't paying attention to it. It's moving to the door that leads out to the alley. It's lifting the knife-wielding hand, ready to slash, slice, sever whatever danger awaits. I tighten my fingers around the dead bolt, turn it, then step outside, ears pricked.

The sound rustles near me again. It could be footfall, but it's sloppy, drunk maybe. And if it's one of my siblings, that would track. They would gather their courage to come ambush me by visiting the bar first. There's one less than two blocks up the road in a strip mall next to a gas station and a burger joint.

I move toward the sound, fishing around in my back pocket for my cell phone so I can surprise them with the flashlight.

The unreliable motion light flickers on above my head.

It isn't a sibling I never want to see again, a parent I wish I didn't resemble.

It's a raccoon carrying loot from the trash bin that one of my neighbors must have left open. The light reflects in his dark beady eyes as embarrassment washes over my skin like tepid water. They didn't find me, and not for the first time do I wonder if I wish that they would, just so I could tell them nothing has changed.

Nothing ever will.

3

THE RED, WHITE, AND BLUE BALLOON arch is objectively tacky, which of course means Roger adores it.

"The optics on this are great," he says with a toothy grin, "for our clientele."

What's more American than the dream of being buried under debilitating debt?

"My thoughts exactly," I reply flatly. If he notices my tone, he isn't bothered by it.

Instead, he looks conspiratorial. *We're in this moment together,* his eyes say. He lays a hand on my shoulder blade. Not quite a smack of camaraderie, but close. It slides to the small of my back, heating it up like a hot-water bottle.

I move away from the unwanted warmth. Uneasy with my back to him, I spin around under the guise of surveying my hard work. "Guests will enter through the main lobby," I say, using both hands like a flight attendant giving a safety briefing to point toward the sliding doors.

His attention shifts like the good boy I know he wants everyone to believe that he is. I take in the swirl of his cowlick at the crown of his thick brown hair. He's tried to tame it, but it still kinks up. A growing patch of skin shows in the center.

"They'll flow to one of the stations—" I cut myself off as I direct his attention to the bar, the buffet, the raffle table, where visitors can leave their business cards in the hope of winning one of our door prizes.

He follows every motion with eager beaver eyes.

"And then they can either mingle in here near the fun or follow the hallway out to the employee lot, where the tent is set up with a DJ and lights."

"Excellent," he says, looking at me now.

Glinting hazel with money green accents. That's his eye color.

The problem with Roger being such a tool is that he's got the look of a guy you might be deceived into dating. I've heard gossip through bathroom stalls, when nobody checked, that almost every woman under thirty-five in the office would "bang him." Forgetting the way he talks down to everyone and how he takes credit when it's not due, all because he's got "good hands" and "broad shoulders" and drives a "new model Porsche." I entertain the concept for a split second. Is there a part of me that likes capturing his attention? A part that is willing even if she isn't able?

I'm snapped back to the lobby by his movement toward me. "And there you have it," I say, stepping back one, two—

"The hair works," he says, leaning as I shrink, "*Heaven.*" His eyes trail over the length of my exposed neck. I put my hair up in a clip because tying up the balloons made me break a sweat. It wasn't on purpose and it wasn't for him, but I'm stuck now. If I take it down, he'll know I'm revulsed. He might get annoyed, and that might be a problem.

I press my lips into a thin smile. He moves off toward the bar, apparently ready to start the party a half hour before the guests arrive.

I may not be deceived into dating him, but I'm not above letting him walk over my boundaries, breach the walls of my comfort zone, take up space he didn't get permission to occupy. Not because of his hands or his shoulders or his car, but because I am a woman who needs this job to survive, and he is a man who holds the keys to whether I keep it or not.

IT IS EXTREMELY unrewarding to clean up after a party you didn't get to enjoy.

I'll deal with the inside of the office in the morning. We have a cleaning service to come through before opening, but they won't do anything about the balloon arch or the folding chairs for extra seating, which will be picked up by the rental service squarely at nine a.m. and must be neatly stacked and ready to go by then. No closings or clients in the office until ten—boss's orders—but that doesn't mean I won't be expected to be here tonight until the parking lot is clear of little plastic cups. I drop another in the trash bag, tamping down the feeling of anxiety that using and trashing all this plastic is taking karmic years off my life. "Sorry, Earth," I whisper to the ground.

In high school, I had the opposite problem, enjoying every party and never sticking around to help with the aftermath. I couldn't, not with my older brother Buck, always threatening to tattle on me to Mom and Dad; he was there around every corner, at almost every party, ready to drag me home if I had too much fun. Buck was a "do as I say, not as I do" disciplinarian. He wasn't my dad, but in every way that mattered, he may as well have been. Earl Prosper Powers II; Buck was the nickname Dad gave him since he didn't like sharing a name, but he was too bound to tradition to "buck" it. It worked on multiple levels as a diminutive, and almost everyone assumed it was chosen because of my parents' affinity for naming their boys after terms associated with money.

Buck didn't rebel out in the open like me.

There was this inherent sneakiness to his rule breaking. He wanted to fuck around, but never did he plan on anyone finding out. A goal all the well-off boys in my town seemed to share.

For a split second, the image of my ex's face slices my vision. That chiseled jaw. Those blue eyes. Thick strawberry-blond hair. He stays locked up in the teeny tiny box, never let out to wreak his special brand of havoc on my mind.

Unable to shove everything away, I go back to Buck.

He would get high with his friends out in the horse pasture, leave the gate open, let a horse loose, and then blame one of the barn staff for the mishap. They all kept quiet because most of them were working at the ranch in hopes of getting a job at one of my family's dealerships.

Buck got away with everything, while he monitored my existence like a nosy cop.

A giggle claps against the concrete of the employee parking lot, ripping me back to the mess I'm way too sober to clean up.

It's Cindy barreling toward me with her hand out, her shiny hair swinging as she moves. I brace to break her fall—almost but not quite—and she slides her body against mine. Sweat turns her palms clammy against my skin. The tinge of mezcal, all smoke and fruit and grass, is strong on her breath as her lips hover near. The red matte color has smudged beneath her chin. Her eyes dilate, trying and failing to focus.

"You really know how to throw a party," she slurs, squeezing my forearm as she struggles to stay up.

"You shouldn't be driving home," I say, and she guffaws. Breath and a little spit hit my face.

I recoil but don't get too far. She may be drunk, but she's got a vice grip. Her closeness isn't about me; it's about not falling over.

"Who knew you had it in you?" she asks, not really asking. "You?" Her awe mixes with a mild disgust in her voice, pushes her nose up into an accordion scrunch. She reaches the hand not clenched tight around my forearm up to move my hair off my cheek.

It's not affection; it's assessment.

"Let's get you an Uber," I say, releasing the trash bag to the ground and fishing in my pants pocket for my phone. If I get it for her, I can track her home at least.

I could take her home. Make sure she gets settled. Be there to hold that curtain of shiny hair back when she wakes up to the world spinning. Then I would be in deeper than I let myself go. In danger of caring, feeling, fucking it all up, like always.

You're a nightmare. Too much. Too loud.

You ruin whatever you touch.

I am jolted by the instinct to step back from her, to let her drop to the ground, find her own way home, fuck herself up so I can't be the one to blame.

"Let me help you." *Roger.* Still here, even though I figured he left already.

I whirl, dragging Cindy with me, and she nearly topples. Her eyes laze closed, her body drooping, limp. He's quick, stepping up, arms out, dress shoes crunching loose asphalt. He has her on one side, but his leg is braced against me, fencing me in to his torso. He shifts and spreads his stance, one could almost say, to gain better footing.

I wouldn't. He's staking a claim.

He peers down at me, half his face cast in shadow by the floodlight we set up for the party. Faintly, I notice a white ring outlining that illuminated nostril. He notices me notice, but he doesn't wipe it away.

"Cindy never knows when to stop." He grins and it has a menacing effect. "I've taken care of this problem more times than I can count."

My mind reels back, back, back to the break room and the conversation between Cindy and Sienna.

At least that's all he had you clean.

The look on Cindy's face as Sienna casually joked about giving Roger fellatio. It was a twinge of shame, in hindsight. Cindy was complaining about something mundane because the truth is much worse.

The thought is cold water dousing the top of my head.

Trickling down my shirt.

Leaving a trail of goose bumps over the whole length of my body.

I can't know for sure, but I can be suspicious, and that is enough right now. Even though it goes against every rule I've set for myself and puts me immediately in a position of danger I have avoided as long as I've been on my own, I can't let him take her home.

He's not sober, but he isn't drunk or high enough to pass out.

He holds all the power.

"I've got her," I say, steady and bright. "You shouldn't have to deal with this mess." It's nauseating to stoop to his level, but it's better this way. When I was young, I didn't get that, or I didn't care. I said it all out loud, never holding back, and I was punished over and over again for it. I can't recall the specifics, but the body never forgets.

He's using one hand to hold her up, but the other is free. At his side until now, it moves up to my bicep and grips. The pressure is light but a presence, a warning without ever saying a word.

"Heaven."

My stomach twists.

Knots.

Knots.

Knots.

That other face flashes. Laughing wide-open mouth, Adam's apple bobbing.

The teeny tiny box appears on the curb behind Roger. There is a thrum of heat in my chest when I see it. Comfort overwhelms me at the sight. I can hide this moment in there just like all the others. Even though the box doesn't do what I tell it to or fuck off, I know it's there for me.

Made by me.

To be used by only me.

My eyes slide back to Roger. "It's really no trouble."

"Even so. You've got *this* mess to clean up." He tosses a glance around the parking lot before lifting his arm around Cindy's shoulder but not releasing mine. "And I'm somewhat of an expert."

"And I'm not?" I question. Immediately, regret causes heat to flood my cheeks. He chuckles, his dark brow knitting together as he glowers. "I clean up messes all the time, is what I mean."

The way his teeth appear, a glint of white, the show of a sharp canine–a threat disguised as a smile. "I insist." And then he tugs her into his side. "Boss's orders." The chipper veneer over his voice feels uncanny, like a doppelganger for cheer. It is a distraction from the tension rolling over his arms to coil all around me.

I move to clutch her by the waist. "I'll come back–"

He yanks me away. His fingers rise to my shoulder, two against the curve, and he presses. His face drops low, right in my eye line. Dilated pupils can't fix on anything, don't try. I am aware of the danger he poses, not just to Cindy but to me. High, drunk, and power drenched, he wants what he wants, and he won't take no for an answer.

His face shape-shifts into another.

Hazel eyes become blue. Brown brows morph into blond. The softer curve of his jaw transforms to a chiseled square.

"Get back to work," he says, voice uneven. He is a rough ocean of energy surging and shifting. "We're not paying you to fuck around."

I am bound.

Tied up and twisted.

I do not move, think, speak.

My legs are lead weight, my arms sand sacks stuck to my sides.

There is no present or past or future.

There is only the box.

It wriggles to life and I succumb.

Caliginous dark smoke—the proof of some long burned-out inner fire—covers my vision.

SHE ENTERS THROUGH *a door.*

Every door is different.

His is painted white wood, the handle a small round classic in polished standard brass.

No lock she would need to find the key to.

The easy access you grant when you don't know to fear break-ins, to question your safety; this is the door, the handle, the mind of someone who knows where he stands in the world.

The knob turns, a single twist, and she's in.

It's a bedroom. Plain in design. A king bed in the center. A window that looks onto nothing. A nightstand, a lamp, a Peloton.

In the corner, a closet.

Inside the closet are shelves. Ten high, ten across. All occupied.

Videotapes, she recognizes them now. Arranged on the shelves like a catalog.

Arranged in order, she senses. Labeled with names.

Women's names, she realizes. She recoils.

All kinds of names.

Long ones, first and last.

Nicknames–Cutie, Red, *others she can't bear to see.*

Places–the bar on Seventeenth, the hotel in Portland, the gym before I quit.

Bra sizes and defining features and signature scents.

Her eyes travel the shelves until they reach the beginning.

She crouches to read the last one.

The label is tattered and worn. There are dings on the plastic from repeated use. He brings this one out often.

Her eye catches something she didn't notice before.

A TV at the top of the shelf. Before, it was darkened. Now the box flickers on.

Fuzzy gray static plays bright on the screen.

The hairs on her neck stand on end. She turns to the room where he sits watching.

Remote control in his hand. He lifts it, not looking at her. He uses one of the strong fingers on his nice hands to push down on the Play button.

His broad shoulders relax. He sits back.

Behind her, a video plays. She looks forward . . . at him.

A woman cries, the sound a punch to her throat. The woman's voice quivers softly, a word with only one meaning.

"No."

She feels the word in her body. Little firecrackers ignite all over her skin, and she's on him.

Knees bearing down on his broad shoulders, mouth wide open, eyes roving in panic. She watches his face, the terror in his eyes fighting with some sick sadistic pleasure in his heart.

Heart, he has one, even if he doesn't know how to think from it.

Her hand travels down his neck, grazing the rise of his chest. She feels the thrum of that heartbeat, the movement of blood in and out of the organ. She imagines its shape, bigger than her small hand, made to manage the life force of this strong man's body.

Her hand hovers over his breast pocket.

It flattens, heat pulsing from the palm. She sees all the arteries lit up like threads connecting the tissue to the vessels of his circulatory system. She imagines his chest and his bones are clay her fingers can easily break through. With a curl of her knuckles she punctures the flesh, digs around in the cavity until she has a grip on the smooth, slick edges.

With a rip, it is free.

She lifts her hand, the sound of his screams a crescendo.

The pump of his heart in her fist slowing, slowing.

A spongy little orb–she smiles, squeezing it like a stress ball. It feels just as soothing. It contracts with the pressure. She releases. It contracts with the pressure. She releases. Softening, softening–

Squeeze, squish, squeeze, squish–pop!

The heart explodes in her hand.

Tomato-red blood all over her face.

4

A CHITTER OF life, joyful in its simplicity, greets me as sunlight slices through my bedroom curtains. I blink, focusing on the windowpane exposed between the panels of blue velvet. Not my choice; they came with the place. I do like the color though. The source of the sound is a wren. Small, squat body, perky upturned tail. The smile on my lips is instant, widening as I stretch my body long, expelling a weird *meow* sound from my lips.

I'm struck by this feeling–like waking up from a delicious dream, like having a craving for sushi and then finally chowing down on a dragon roll, like stretching in the sunlight after days of rain. I languish, considering a cat nap to get back to that dream, but as soon as my lids slip shut–

Gaping mouth screaming. Hands thrashing, grabbing.

I shoot up, heart racing. Willing it to steady, I let my eyes slowly close again.

Dark hair, bushy brows–squeeze, squish, pop.

I dreamed about hurting Roger last night. Not some sweet lovely thing that made me wake up feeling cozy in my chest and safe in my skin. I dreamed about violence against my boss.

And I *savored* it.

Last night screams back. Or, I should say, one distinct certainty and a lot of fuzzy *feelings* from last night scream back. I took Cindy home splayed out in the back seat of my car. I left Roger alone in the lot.

How I wrangled her away from him, I don't know, but I did, and then I must have just passed out from the adrenaline.

The aura appears at the corner of my vision, and I know the box is coming next.

Ignore.

I twist around to my nightstand, yank my phone from the charger, and illuminate the screen. Just after seven a.m. *Okay, this is good.* I can get ready quickly, go back to the office, and check on things.

I open my phone and pull up Roger's contact info. I programmed it into my phone after he tried to get in touch with me during a run to Costco for the office Christmas party.

If I need to call you, I need to know you'll answer. I would have answered a call coming from the company line. I didn't see why he didn't just use that, but I didn't argue, what was the point? He doesn't believe he can be wrong.

I debate just calling him to see if he picks up. If he doesn't, I can assume that he's pissed about how things played out last night. I cringe at my own downplay of what was irrefutably a dangerous situation. But if I call at all, it may open up a discussion of said situation, now in the stark light of day, something my survival instincts would very much like to avoid. Cindy isn't even a friend, and sticking my neck out for her again when I know Roger will be hungover and grouchy doesn't make sense.

The best option is to leave it alone, hope he's capable of something resembling guilt, and that the pressure of shame will compel him to let it go.

I get up from the bed and flop out to the hallway.

The bathroom door is closed, which—I twist the handle. Closed *and* locked. There's a faint sound of a video playing, a chuckle of female laughter, and then a flush, water running to wash hands.

Oh fuck! It's Cindy.

I didn't just take her home splayed out in the back seat of my car. I took her to *my home* splayed out in the back seat of my car.

Jesus Christ.

The door swings wide open to reveal a deeply hungover Cindy. The luster in those chestnut strands has dulled, dark circles punctuate her brown eyes, and she's still in her clothes from the party, all rumpled from the night's sleep. I jump backward and she responds with a burst of a laugh.

"Oh fuck. Split my head wide open," she groans, reaching up to cup her cranium. "Do you have meds for this?" She points a finger to her temple. Her eye twitches.

"Sure thing," I say, and then point back inside the bathroom. "Middle drawer."

She turns around painstakingly slowly and pads sluggishly back to the vanity, tugs the middle drawer out, and rifles around for the pill bottle.

"What happened last night?" she asks. Her voice is hoarse. She twists the top of the bottle, but it doesn't turn. Childproof. Hungover-thirtysomething-proof.

"I brought you home, I guess," I reply, reaching out and motioning for her to hand me the bottle.

She does as instructed. "You guess." It's probably meant to be a question, but the delivery is given without the necessary inflection, most likely thanks to the headache severing her skull in two. I'm not sure how to get out of answering. I wasn't drunk myself, but the exact order of events are fuzzy in my mind. This would be scarier if it weren't something that's happened before.

It's been years.

The thought runs through me, dangerous and chaotic like a

child skipping with scissors on slippery linoleum. In the past, these incidents have been accompanied by the lurking, stalking of the teeny tiny box willing me to crack. Sometimes I think the box enjoys chasing me, taunting me, and other times, it's like it wants to protect me. This isn't the first time, but never–I'm almost certain–has it been accompanied by the delicious, euphoric feeling I had when I first woke up.

Obviously I can't say any of this to Cindy.

"Do you want some coffee?" is what I say instead. And then I press two pills into her palm, and her face falls in relief.

"Injected into my fucking veins," she replies.

BLUE IS MY favorite color. It's a truth I've held as long as I can remember.

Nothing has ever been able to take it away. Not even *his* eyes being the very same shade.

Cindy is looking at me from the passenger seat of my car like I've been body-snatched or something. I get it; I'm wearing color–a blue blouse with pearl buttons and wide cuffs. I couldn't shake the desire when I opened my closet door this morning. It called out to me like a siren, and my weakness for sirens prevailed.

The blouse still had the tags on it from when I bought it last year right after I moved to Elmdale. In a moment of insanity, I thought I might wear it for my interview at Second City Title and Trust, mentally clocking how the powder blue picked up the lighter flecks in my eyes and would make holding focus on my face easier. In the end, I wore a boring white button-down and black pants, like I was a waiter from a catering company or something.

"You're in color," she says, and I'm smacked by the astonishment in her voice. "I mean, like–" She cuts herself off, gestures to my shirt. "Blue looks great on you."

I'm dropping her off at her apartment on my way in to work. This is the most sustained time I've spent in the company of another person that wasn't at work since I moved here. I've held up my end of the bargain I made with myself for a little over a year. It's the longest stretch yet, and I wish I had something to show for it. But it also turns my stomach because it sets off this signal in my brain, hits my adrenals, and sends me into flight mode. Friendship comes at a cost.

Friendship.

Cost.

"Thanks." The word slips out. I can't grab it back. Fortunately, we're pulling up outside her apartment, so in a few short moments, I'll be released from the threat of connection. She grabs her purse from the floor and unbuckles the seat belt.

"Now, for the walk of shame," she says. The coffee, meds, and dry toast I provided did the job to revive her, and now there is a tinge of color that pricks her cheeks, likely from embarrassment.

"Not what this is," I say, despite my mind trying to muzzle my tongue.

The quick lift to her lips sends a *zat* of electricity through my chest. She may not be a friend, but I don't regret helping her last night, no matter what weird murder fantasy dream it triggered in my mind.

"See you at the office once I'm presentable," she says as she opens the door and climbs out. She moves to close the door, then stops and bends down. "Thanks, I owe you."

She doesn't wait around to receive my knee-jerk "No, you don't" or whatever awkward silence might ensue from her explicit gratitude. She expressed it because she needed to get it off her chest. It really wasn't about me at all.

I pull back onto the road and take the shortest possible route to the office. Getting everything in tip-top shape is the best way to assure that I get ahead of a Roger rage monster. I don't exactly know what I'll be coming up against, but at the very least, he'll be hungover and licking his wounds from me taking Cindy home. I think.

Every attempt I make to search my mind for specifics about last night comes up with a *404 error page not found.*

There won't be recovery.

This much I know–have known since I was a little girl with blond hair and a secret to keep no matter the cost.

I owe the little girl this much. I keep the box despite the risk.

I flick my blinker on as I turn into the business complex that houses Second City Title and Trust. There's a shallow hill that leads up into the lot, which sprawls out for visitors, with employee parking around the back of the building.

My foot slams the brake pedal and whips me to a sudden stop.

There is an ambulance in front of the building–doors closing, lights swirling.

This is because of me. I know it in my clammy palms and palpitating heartbeat and swimming, writhing stomach.

Roger is in that ambulance and I put him there.

5

THE OFFICER ON the scene of what they are *not* calling a crime is a handsome woman with a single stud pierced through her left ear. I keep looking at the rectangular diamond as it catches the sunlight on this entirely-too-bright-for-the-mood morning.

"The security guard found him this morning," she says. "At first, he just thought he was passed out, but then he saw the head injury."

Head injury? I blink and turn my eyes to hers. I'm absorbing the information; her expression is inscrutable. I don't think she's judging my reaction, just giving me the time to process. I am the first one of my coworkers in today. Roger has a ten-thirty closing. I should probably let someone know. Another escrow officer, an assistant.

Cindy could take it if she gets here on time.

This sends a thrill through me at the irony. With Roger having her closings, credit and all, this does somehow feel like sweet justice.

"He was tipsy after the party last night," I say, trying to make sense of how he got a head injury.

"It looks like he fell and hit his head on the curb, but we won't know more until they do a thorough exam," the officer says. My eyes drop to her badge: Jensen. The curb beneath the tent. It wouldn't have been caught on any cameras, and because the lot was used for the party, I had parked my car on the street.

"I just don't think he was drunk enough to fall like that." I'm torn about the right type of response to give right now. On the one hand, I don't want to ask too many questions because that might seem weird. On the other, not enough of a reaction is suspicious. My boss was found on the ground with a head wound by the security guard, and I am the first person on the scene to get the news. That's scary and traumatizing! But also, it's not. Because I know there has to be more to the story.

I just hope it's not that I pushed him.

Or worse.

Worse I can't safely consider right now.

"You're his assistant, right? Do you know if he has any next of kin?"

"A mom in West Virginia," I say. Something I only know because he had me send her flowers on Mother's Day. She's remarried, and from what I gathered, Roger hates his stepdad. "His dad died, I think. Don't quote me on that, it's just that on the rare occasion he speaks of him"—when I asked if he wanted me to send his dad something for Father's Day—"he does so in the past tense."

She nods. *This is helpful*, her expression says. "The hospital will be glad to have someone to contact."

Glad? A weird way to put it, but okay.

"As long as it's good news," she says. "Suppose maybe it's too early to tell."

Hopefully this good news also comes with a bit of amnesia. Just in case.

She begs off after that and I follow her lead. I walk over to the office door, pull my key from my pocket, and reach for the door to unlock it. It moves. I am hit by the crushing knowledge that I left last night without locking it, and Roger didn't lock it either. Whatever happened to him must have been sudden enough that he didn't have time.

I yank open the door and step inside. Safely hidden by the solar flow glass they installed in the lobby to keep it cool, the light even all year round. The red, white, and blue arch still stands, though it droops a little after a whole night of trying to stay upright.

Sudden. The word forms a hurdle in my mind, and I can't get over it. What happened to Roger was sudden enough that he didn't get a chance to lock up. What kind of health crisis comes on suddenly? Something that would make you fall and hit your head?

An image returns to my mind lonely and out of context. It doesn't make sense, but there's a knowing in me, a recognition that it's the truth.

A dark red object sits inside my fist.

I squeeze it like a stress ball. It's not an object; it's a gooey pulsing organ. Muscle and tissue, chambers and valves, veins and arteries dangling like loose bloody wires.

Squeeze, release, squeeze, squish–pop!

This is the *404 error page not found.*

Somehow, what happened last night caused a heart event cataclysmic enough to send Roger to the ground, unable to stop himself from cracking his head open.

Something I did, or said, or–

Dreamed.

EVERYONE IN THE office agrees that I should take Roger flowers in the ICU. The hospital didn't exactly tell us what his current health status is, but we do know that he's in serious condition. Everyone agrees that waking up to a big–"not too expensive"–

show of appreciation from his colleagues would be the medicine he needs to get back on his feet. I've gathered cash from them for this show affection—from everyone except Cindy.

She and I haven't spoken since she got in and heard the news about Roger, and frankly, I'm dreading it. I don't know what Cindy remembers. She was passed out for most of the altercation (which is what we're calling it—the best I can do) between Roger and me, but it doesn't make me any less nervous.

"You're the one pooling money for Roger?" Cindy says, startling me from behind. I swivel in my chair to face her. She's holding a crisp twenty in her outstretched hand for me to take.

"That's too much," I say with a headshake. "Everyone's putting in like ten, max. Jolene in Abstract gave a buck fifty."

Cindy's face brightens and she leans in, her voice lowering in a conspiratorial way. "He tried to fire her last year. I believe because she was asking for new chairs for the whole Abstract team." The Abstract plant is vital to Second City's sales pitch. Having one onsite helps with title research, which can drastically cut down on the escrow lengths. I hate that I know that about this job I barely tolerate. "I don't blame her for being stingy."

And what about you? I want to ask her. *Shouldn't you be equally stingy after what he's done to you? Shouldn't you hate him more than Jolene?*

"I don't think Roger is allowed to fire Abstract employees since they aren't part of Escrow," I reply.

"Roger doesn't care about what he's allowed to do," she says, her voice stinging with venom. She hates him, but she doesn't plan on doing anything about it. I didn't either.

Still . . .

She waves the twenty at me, and when I don't take it, she sets it on my desk. "It's all the cash I have. Don't use it all on his flowers. Buy yourself a coffee or something." When I don't respond or touch the twenty, she snorts air from her nose. Not quite a laugh but the sibling of one. "Okay, I better . . ."

She doesn't need to finish her statement. She's thinks I'm a weirdo, and what happened last night didn't change that for her. She may owe me, but she doesn't want to get to know me. Friendship may come at a cost, but having no one has its own hefty price tag.

6

THE ICU AT Elmdale Memorial Hospital is J-shaped and about a half mile long, per the brochure I read in the lobby while I waited for them to approve me to go up. I tried to insist that the nurse take the flowers himself, no need to get a visitor's bracelet or walk me through the double doors. But I am the first person who's come to see Roger, and they swear visitors make all the difference.

"I'll leave you to it," the nurse says. He's a built guy with saucers of chocolate for irises. The rest of his face is obscured behind a surgical mask, but his eyes are kind. "Feel free to stay as long as you like. Visiting hours go until six."

"Oh," I squeak, flicking my eyes to the black-and-white clock hanging on the wall behind him at the nurses' station. Three p.m. I'll be gone before three fifteen.

"Can you tell me anything?" I ask. I'm not family, it's not policy to share information with work colleagues, so I expect a brush-off. But his kind eyes crinkle, letting me know he's smiling beneath his mask.

"Blood tests show a non-ST segment myocardial infarction," he says.

Cardial. Cardiac. Heart.

"A heart attack," I reply. *Squeeze, squish, pop!*

"It's serious, but we don't believe it's fatal. We are more concerned about the head injury and lack of oxygen to the brain." The corners of the nurse's eyes crinkle again, and I nod. He's said more than he should, and I don't feel any better after learning what I learned.

The sound of beeping machines greets me as I move into the room. The light pink painted walls buffer me on either side. There is a TV hanging high up and angled down to face the bed on the opposite side–the view of that still obscured by the blue curtain. There is a shelf that runs the length of the window on the opposite wall, the spot for flowers and get-well cards. I will have to cross the room to get to it, cross past Roger in the bed. No way to leave here without seeing the damage.

I take a few quick breaths in through my nose.

I practically sprint to the other side of the room, willing myself to stay focused on the window, the light, the shelf, and the spot I have selected to set the bouquet down. The smell of yellow roses and lilies mixes with hospital cleaning supplies. My hands release the vase on the shelf and then come to rest on the cool surface. I brace against it, breathing in the sickly sweet tealike antiseptic scent one more time before I turn.

He looks smaller.

Those broad shoulders are lost beneath the white-and-blue diamond print of his hospital gown. Those hands are flaccid, tucked to either side of his hips. They had to shave that thick dark brown hair to stitch up the wound on his head. I watch the monitor lights move. The steady *beep beep beep* of his vitals, the drip of fluids, and I search inside for sorrow, something like regret or anguish, a feeling of remorse.

There is none. Not for whatever role I played in this. Not for the man turned from predator to prey. I'm not broken up about the outcome, even if I should be. I am just scared that it could happen again.

I drop into the chair beside his bed.

I wasn't asleep, and yet I woke in my bed from a dream.

He wasn't asleep, and yet he was somehow part of that dream.

Nightmare. The word sounds loud in my head.

You're a nightmare. Their voices all through my life.

The scar across Roger's skull seems to pulse.

The inside of my head rattles.

He had it coming. I want that to be true enough to make this okay.

It was a nightmare made from my reaction to his predatory grip.

It was justice that otherwise would be impossible.

I let my lids fall closed. My lips twitch up, and a small, desperate laugh escapes them. In the darkness, a memory swims up to the surface.

I don't try to fight it.

My brother Sterling is the middle child, closest to me in age. They liked to say we were Irish twins, which was confusing on more than one level. We weren't twins, weren't Irish, and he looked nothing like me. But I did love him, I feel that now as I hover inside this moment on the porch in a beam of sunlight. I love him and he told me I wasn't his sister. Pushed me out of his room. Locked the door.

I was angry. I lashed out at him—

No.

This is wrong. It was night.

The image squiggles and shifts. I watch it sitting on the ground, legs crossed. My childhood home becomes clear above me. Two stories with an attic, white wood, and a wraparound porch. The sky turns from bright blue wide open space with the wispiest of clouds to night, a blanket of stars laid out over the deep midnight black. The light around little girl me isn't the sun but a porch light. The dolly is dressed in a nightgown that matches my own. I am not supposed to be awake, but I am.

Sterling got out of his bed, walked down the stairs, opened the front door. He climbed to the top of our tree fort.

He jumped.

In the memory, shoe soles scrape against wood and my dad drops to sit down beside me. From here, he looks as big as a monster. His dark brown hair mussed, that red-tinged beard in need of a trim. He wears a flannel button-down and a pair of jeans, with moccasins on his feet.

"You should be in bed," he says. His forearms, thick and meaty, rest on his thighs. He raises a hand to scratch at his beard. How old is he here? How old am I?

"Sterling's arm looks wrong," I reply.

"Broken, but it'll mend."

"I think I did it to him," I whisper.

"Haven, don't be foolish," he answers. He didn't ask why I thought that; he just dismissed it. I wanted him to reach out, to comfort me, to lift me onto his knees and let me rest my head on his shoulder. He wouldn't do that, and I knew it, but it didn't stop the wanting. "You aren't that powerful."

My pulse hitches. *But what if I am?*

The scream of a machine alarm pummels my mind back to awareness.

My nose catches the scent of urine, foul and strong in the air.

My eyes fly open. I'm still in the hospital. Still sitting in this chair beside Roger, only now his body isn't wilted or still as it was before. It convulses, rippling beneath the blue hospital blanket that is soaked with urine. The air is acrid with the stench. His shoulders, his torso, his slack hands, and noodle legs jerk a violent rhythm as if in a flight with some unknown force.

I am up, searching the room for the tiny box, but the typical aura squiggle of warning doesn't appear. The box doesn't materialize in some corner where it shouldn't be.

This furious spasm is Roger's body giving up. It's his last gasp in response to the violence I already inflicted. The monitor attached to him wails, the lines indicating his life force dragging up and down, down, down, flatter and slower as the machine calls for someone to come.

Now I'm screaming too, shouting for help for a man I don't care about, who I put in the bed in the first place, who I'm not even sure I hope makes it.

If he dies, there is only one person to blame. Maybe I should care just a little.

I don't and I know it.

It's vicious, this truth, and I fight to expel it.

I'm not a killer. Not a nightmare. Not the reason bad things always happen.

That nurse with the kind eyes from before is the first to arrive, followed swiftly by another pushing a crash cart and wearing pink scrubs with little cartoon stethoscopes printed all over them. The first nurse looks at me and says something I can't make out because all this screaming rings in my ears, through my brain in flashes of heat, electric as lightning crackling across the sky.

"What?" I ask him, my voice sounding hollow, too far away to be mine.

"You need to clear the room," he replies urgently but still gently. Right, of course that's what he's saying and that's what I should do, but I can't move, I can't look away.

Roger's lids have rolled open, the balls of his eyes spinning back in his skull so that only the whites are showing.

"Miss, please, let us help him." This plea is so genuine, I have to bite back the reply on my tongue.

The nurse with the crash cart runs around to the side of the bed where I stand, and I force myself to move out of her way, stumbling over my feet as I pass the cart on the way to the door. They lower the bed to lay Roger flat and yank down his gown to expose his chest, the furry dark hair shaved in patches where they attached the little white sensors.

I should leave.

I should go.

But the sound of the crash cart warring and the screech of the flatline holds me in place.

"Clear!"

Electricity punches Roger straight in the chest.

For a moment, every sound in the room drops off to silence.

I hold my breath. I don't pray. I don't hope. I don't dare think, because I know it's not the right thing to think, and my thoughts can't ever be trusted.

The screaming machines flood my ears all at once.

"Again, charge to 150," the nurse with the kind eyes says to the other one.

"Clear!"

Again the hit to the chest, the drop-off in sound, and then nothing.

Roger is dying.

I cover my mouth as bile rises in my throat.

Roger is dead.

I lurch toward the door as the nurse with the kind eyes begins chest compressions. It's a formality. Already there's a chill in the air that wasn't previously there. The cold snap that follows a soul letting go of a body. I know in my bones that I've felt that particular chill wash over me before, but when I search for the reason, the impenetrable walls of the tiny box rise to stop me.

It may be there, but it won't let me see.

This is different than the old lady who cut herself with the kitchen knife in Baton Rouge. This is different than leaving in the middle of the night after a hookup because I'm afraid to fall asleep beside someone. This wasn't an accident I can explain away, because that nightmare part of me knew what she was doing, and after years of skulking in the shadows, I'm afraid she's ready to come out and play in the light.

There's chaos at the nurses' station as more rush in to see if they can help. But I keep walking past open hospital room doors, where visitors press into the thresholds, eyes big, ears pricked to eavesdrop on horror that isn't their own.

I hit the metal button on the elevator door, and I don't turn around even when the pandemonium behind me goes quiet. I don't look back down the hallway when I step into the elevator.

When the receptionist at the welcome desk greets me, I don't respond or look up into her eyes. I keep walking through sliding glass doors, down the narrow brick walkway that leads to the covered parking lot, to my car on the third floor, and once I've dropped into the seat, I look across the cement partition to peer at the side of the hospital building. They won't trace it back to me. There's nothing to trace.

But that doesn't matter.

Not getting caught doesn't make me less of a killer.

I go through the motions: turn the key in the ignition, shift into Reverse, then Drive, pay the attendant. But I'm numb to the movement; I'm not even sure that I'm the one moving this body.

Which is why it takes me a beat longer than normal to realize my phone is buzzing in my back pocket. I ease to a stop, pull to the side of the road, and yank it out. It could be Sienna checking to see if I got the flowers to Roger, or if I'm on my way back to relieve her at the front desk since she's got a three-o'clock closing.

But it's not.

It's a number I know in an instant. A Friendship, Texas, area code.

A series of digits I once had memorized in case of emergency.

My brother Buck is calling. And all I can do is answer.

7

"HEY, SIS." HIS voice has gravel in it. There's a deep Southern charm about the way he draws out the letters, but it makes my heart rate speed up. I never wanted to hear this voice again. I keep telling myself that's the whole truth, that it's why, right now, my body is acting like a bronco locked in a pen.

I haven't seen Buck since I was nineteen, the day I left Friendship for good and never looked back. In my mind he's his twenty-two-year-old self still: big aquamarine eyes, his brown hair in a summer cut that isn't quite buzzed but threatening it; he's got a tan already, his toothy smile looking extra white in contrast.

I only see *that* Buck, dressed in a button-down and jeans, wearing alligator skin boots Dad got him for a good first year managing the dealership in Rockwall. I can't imagine what the years might have changed. Or maybe I just don't want to.

"How the hell did you get this number?" My own dumb twang bubbles in the back of my throat like a burp. I swallow, command my stomach acid to dissolve those chewy *r*'s and *l*'s until there's no trace left.

"What? You think we left you alone because we couldn't find you?" he says. I can hear the haughty smile in his voice, see it clear as day in my mind's eye. "Haven Smith? Even with that basic bitch last name, you weren't hard to track down."

I want to ask him if they've been watching, come out here, or sent someone—how often, how long? Mostly, I want to know in case it will make me feel better for all those paranoid nights spent holding a butcher knife, checking the locks, sitting in the living room with the light off.

"We let you be"—he pauses, a held-in sigh tightening his voice—"like you asked."

"I asked y'all to let me go when I left Friendship. Then Dad sent me flowers."

He huffs. "Hell, who remembers shit like that?"

"I do, Buck."

"'Course you do. You love makin' mountains out of mole hills."

"Good to know your general disdain for healthy boundaries hasn't changed."

"Harp on boundaries all you want, we both know only pussies care about shit like that."

My jaw clenches with a pressure I worry might break it in half. "Did you call for a reason?" I'm ready to hang up. Talking to my douchebag brother right after my boss bit the dust—thanks to me!—is *so* not good for my mental health.

A weighty silence follows my question. If not for the subtle sound of his breathing I would think the call had cut out. I wait, unwilling to prod him or show any undue curiosity. I wait, he breathes, a light rain thrums against the windshield. The presence of the box is an electric current tied to my core, just out of reach. Always present even when it's nowhere visible—lurking, waiting to pounce like a cat on the mouse of my mind.

"It's Big Earl," Buck finally says. There is a tremor in his voice like a quaking beneath a dense rocky terrain.

Big Earl.

Dad.

"*What's* Big Earl?" I am steady, no stammer, though there is the threat of one in my throat.

"He's sick."

"Sick with what?"

"Still early days, but we don't know how many days he might have left..." Buck brushes past my question; his voice goes all syrupy. "We thought you should know. We thought you deserved the chance to make it right with him before time runs out."

"Make it right?"

"You broke his heart." Buck lays it on thick. "We all say it all the time. He hasn't been the same since you cut us out–and look, I get it, you needed to go find yourself and you needed us to be the villains. We let you have that one. Gave you what you wanted–Dad insisted."

My eyes rake closed. Heat gathers.

"Your absence–all the stress that brought about–may not have directly caused his health to degrade, but..." he says, voice trailing. I know how Big Earl lives, and I know I didn't matter that much to him to begin with. But insinuating it was losing me that led to whatever health crisis he finds himself in is a sharp knife that Buck wields well. Even with all my logic shielding me, it skewers me through the gut. "You can't understand what it's like to be a dad, Haven. Your little girl, she's your world."

I have to hand it to my brother. He learned to guilt-trip from the best of them. I wonder if Earl gave him this whole speech to say verbatim, or if he just suggested some talking points and Buck came up with the rest. Like it's a test he passes if it gets me on a plane.

"Careful, you'll throw your back out shoveling so much shit," I say, trying to sound unbothered. I don't.

"This is your chance to make it right," he says, using that phrase again. "Don't you want to take it?"

Anger mounts in my chest. I don't want to *take it*. I may not be happy living this life out here all alone, blending in with the scenery of boring fucking job after boring fucking job, moving from one nondescript small town to mediocre midsized city after another on the run from myself and the misery I always inevitably cause around me.

I may not be thriving, but I'm free.

In my periphery, something moves. Teeny, tiny, wooden, carved. The shimmer a craggy shape splitting my vision. It's calling my bluff. *Free* isn't being shackled to an inanimate object that no one else can see. *Free* isn't having a constant reminder of every horror-filled fragment of your life but having no way to access any of it. *Free* isn't somehow dreaming up a nightmare and then waking up to find out it came true.

I'm not free. I can't be.

And worse, I'm not sure I even should be.

I killed a man.

A horrible man who I didn't intend to kill, who earned his punishment—but, no, that's a slippery slope I will not slide down. Next time—because there will be a next time, of that I have no doubt—next time, whoever winds up on the receiving end of this nightmare might not make it to the hospital.

Might not deserve their punishment at all.

I made the box, and it makes the nightmare, but I don't control the box, and I sure as hell don't control the nightmare. But if the box makes all this happen because of something from the past that I can't remember, maybe my family can? If I could uncover that event, it might be possible to stop this violent reaction, stop this nightmare from killing someone else.

Returning to Friendship under the guise of making it right

with my dying dear old dad is the perfect excuse to go digging for the answers I need. It's not a good plan. I don't know if it counts as a plan at all, but it is the only thing I can think to do right now.

And I have to do something.

"Okay," I say, tamping down the electric zap of panic that wriggles across my skin.

Buck is quiet. I wonder if his call script from Dad didn't prepare him for this.

"I'll see you in a few days."

"Well, shit," he says, and I can hear the self-satisfied grin I'm sure is spreading over his face. "Just in time for the Peach Festival."

I jab the red button and end the call without a goodbye.

I'm going back to Texas.

WELCOME TO
FRIENDSHIP!
WHERE YOUR NEIGHBOR
IS YOUR FRIEND.

8

THE HAND-PAINTED WELCOME sign is the first thing I see when I pull off the highway. On a large wooden rectangle, they've stenciled the town's message in front of a detailed painting of the iconic courthouse that presides over downtown. Behind that, they've added a peach orchard and hillside dotted with horses.

"Welcome home," I whisper as I pass the sign and turn onto a route I know better than the back of my hand. Etched in the rabbit trails of my brain, I anticipate every turn before I reach it, even if it hits differently in this midsized gray sedan I rented at the airport. I am the daughter of a car guy, and once, that was a thing we had in common, a shared appreciation that validated our familial bond. Something solid to cling to when everything else turned to quicksand.

"Your first car should say somethin' about who you are right here in this moment," Earl said as he drove his golf cart onto the used car lot. After business hours, just the two of us, so I could pick out exactly what I wanted.

"How do I know what it should say?" I asked him before taking a slurp from my extra large Sonic Diet Cherry Limeade.

"What do you want it to say?" He turned down a row of trucks. It felt like a test, like things always felt with Earl. There was no way to know what the curve you'd be graded on was, and no way to study to make sure you didn't fail. But, make no mistake, you knew if you failed, and there was nothing you could do to fix it. No extra credit, no do-over.

I scanned the field of metal and rubber and glass. The bright colors, muted greens and grays, reds and silvers. My eyes landed on one the next row over from us. A bright orange vintage Chevy C/K with white trim. "That Chevy over there." I pointed.

His eyes followed my fingertip, and as soon as they found it, the corners of his mouth lifted into a crinkly smile. "That paint scheme is rare. The boxy shape is strong but still a little bit girly." It was exactly what he wanted to hear, and not entirely true either. It had a look of freedom about it that made my heart leap. I wouldn't blend in and I wouldn't be stuck. Neither of which ended up being true about my time driving that truck all over these roads, even if I did eventually drive away from Friendship in it.

Now I take a turn onto Main Street and realize I'm making a loop around my old town square. The move is robotic. My hands twist the steering wheel around as my foot presses down lightly on the gas pedal. There is an immediate tightening in my neck muscles that causes my throat to feel constricted. Heat laps up and around my ears, and I open my lips to suck air into my lungs just to prove that I can. My lungs tighten with the move, rejecting the hot air, and I find myself reaching for the controls to turn up the air conditioner to full blast.

The icy breeze hits me square in the face, momentarily freezing out the panic.

The car slogs forward, and my eyes take in the sight.

Unchanged after nine years away, the center of the square is a large grassy knoll where the original courthouse still stands. Its intricately detailed red-shingled roof, cast-iron filigree, and round arched windows are a brutal contrast to the soft sand-colored limestone walls. Erected above the top floor–three floors higher, if I remember correctly from class field trips–is the clock tower with a widow's walk.

The sidewalk that leads from the doors meets up with an arched stone plaque detailing the town's founding. A lot of gloss and pomp to wash out the horror of colonization, a history of agriculture dominates the story, and the proof of its enduring resonance remains when I round the corner to the red light at Main and Elm. A banner hangs overhead, orange and pink peaches clustered on either side of deep green curly letters advertising the annual Peach Festival, a tradition dating back over a century.

My gut churns as I stare at the brightly colored banner, affronted by how happy it looks when I feel so royally fucked. As Buck reminded me on the phone, the Peach Festival starts in earnest in a couple of days, but the town already buzzes with the preparation for it. On the green beside the courthouse, they've set up a display tent to detail the many festivities that will unfold over the next week. They've piled peaches in a wooden barrel, set them atop a haystack, and manned it with some of the town's most genteel-looking ladies. Two girls, now women, from my high school. The march of time hasn't touched Friendship's town square, but it sure has touched them. I can't recall their names, or maybe I don't want to, but my eyes cut across them as I pass by in my car. They don't notice me, thankfully. I wonder if they would recognize me, remember my name even though I can't remember theirs.

With that thought, another wave of panic wrecks me, turns the inside of this car into a coffin I want to escape. The sides slope around my head as heat gathers everywhere my skin touches a surface, coating me in slick, sick sweat.

I roll the window down instead of breaking it with my fist and let my arm fall out. The Texas sun heats it.

The smell of cut grass and barbecue pricks my nostrils, and

nausea writhes from the nostalgic mix. My eyes trail up to the sun and take in its light for a few painful seconds. It's not a different sun than anywhere else, but somehow–just like how the sky opens wide to swallow you whole here–it seems to simmer hotter, stronger, bigger. It bakes the body into submission, crisps the skin up like chicken on a spit. I breathe the heat into my throat, feel it thicken my saliva, nearly choke.

It is a truth I've known always but let myself pretend I forgot: The town of Friendship is preserved in time, just like the peaches they can for jam at the end of the season: overripe and sickly sweet, boiled to oblivion, sealed airtight. The people of this town want it that way. They thrive in this perfect picture of everything that America holds dear.

Historic charm masks just how much this place still values oppression. Gentry's General Store sells everything from water hoses to name-brand breakfast cereal, but it didn't demolish its separate water fountain until the early 2000s. It only did so after a boycott and encouragement from the church to "keep the peace." I remember walking past the debris as a kid on the way to the ice cream parlor, not totally getting why it mattered, but still I noticed the way some adults stopped to look at the change, faces drawn in a scowl even a little kid could understand.

I'm near the end of this row of shops when I spot the coffee shop. Hip-looking, Father's House is really just a church outreach for the youths of the town. The pastor's son, my ex-boyfriend, was the manager there for most of our junior and senior year of high school. I worked a summer behind the counter, even though I was never committed to the cause of winning souls for Jesus.

Some small part of me expected–even hoped–to come back and find that the place had changed, even if only an incremental amount. Hoped to see a small "all are welcome here" sign in a storefront window, or a new historical plaque next to the old one acknowledging the Indigenous people who were the original stewards of this place. There are other towns in this state where that sort of thing exists; it's not an impossible dream.

But it isn't a dream that came true.

Nothing here changes, and I shouldn't expect anything different from the family I came back to see. In a way, maybe it's good, because it's all the more reason to believe the truth I need still remains in the minds of the people who might actually know it.

My car rolls to a stop again at the last light before I exit the square. I flick my blinker and close my eyes for a split second. Even behind the lids, the jagged curved aura shimmers. The teeny tiny box is ready–so ready–to come out and play.

"Haven?" A woman's voice punctuated by the hometown drawl breaks in through my thoughts. My eyes slide open. There on the corner, peering at me through the open car window, is my ex-boyfriend's mother. Strawberry blond with the same piercing blue eyes as his. "Oh my stars, it *is* you!" A toothy gleaming smile cracks, also just like him.

I fight the memory of him trying to surface.

Mercifully, the traffic light changes.

I peel away without responding. My finger slams on the buttons for the front windows, sending them both up with a squeak. My breath hitches, catches in the narrow ridges of my ribs, aching through the too-tight garment of my skin. I pull off the road as panic seizes my chest.

The box has a pulse. I can hear it even without it breaching my vision.

The *thump thump* is out of sync with my own *thumpthumpthumpthump.*

I press my fingertips to my eyelids and hold them down, commanding them not to look for the box, not to look at the live oaks lining the road, the ranch houses all in a row, the Texas flag hanging from the pole in the brown underwatered grass of that yard.

Go home, you thought. Like it would be easy or something.

"Fuck." I breathe out the word, eyes opening. There is no box, just the rest of Friendship fucking Texas vibrating with life all around me.

I refuse to think the name of the boy I once loved. That woman's son. His name is a lance to the tender spots in my brain. Not safe, not ever.

No matter how tightly I seal him away, the residue of him will never wipe away.

But I won't let the appearance of his mother send me into a spiral.

There is danger in being back here. Danger in unleashing the truth of who I am—really am—in all the ways that make me a challenge to the mindset of this place. It's a target on my back, always, no matter what my mind can do if pushed into a corner. Friendship—these people, this place—is like quicksand. The harder I struggle against them, the more constricted I get. Every twitch and tug, all my resistance will drag me further into their mire. There is only one way to fight that won't swallow me whole.

Stay calm and unbothered. *No big deal.*

I turn my attention back to the road. It stretches, heat on the horizon like a wave in the water, Big Earl's domain a siren calling me out to the churning sea.

I PULL THROUGH the main entrance.

Tall and curved over the road stands a pristinely painted white metal sign with the words POWERS PREMIER AUTOMOTIVE secured in human-sized red painted letters.

With dealerships in Texas, Louisiana, and Oklahoma, Friendship is the main headquarters. Right at the border of town, it's the biggest car dealership in Texas (and Big Earl has argued, "the biggest in the US") at twenty-three acres, with new, used, luxury, and vintage car lots situated in a diamond shape that surrounds the corporate offices. I don't presume they're expecting me here at all. I had texted Buck my flight time and refused his offer to pick me up from the airport.

I'm not coming here without a way of escape. I'm also not staying anywhere near the ranch. I'm not even ready to see the ranch, let alone the whole family. Earl is a rough enough start as it is, but at least Powers Premier Automotive doesn't hold any especially shitty memories for me.

Just normal shitty ones.

I turn past the gleaming luxury lot, which is directly across from the main entrance to the corporate offices, a two-story building established sometime in the eighties and never outwardly renovated. The utilitarian design of blocky, bulky concrete and glass feels foreboding in the same way pictures of detention centers do. I park, cut my engine, and stare across the black asphalt lot at the building, trying to work up the courage to get out of the car.

I don't even know if Earl is here. Buck said he'd send along all the info and to come by when I arrived, but Buck isn't Earl. Not by a long shot. There's no way to know if Earl really wanted me to come back to "make amends."

Or, okay, there is a way to know, but I didn't go for it. I have Earl's number seared in my mind, just like the rest of them. I could have called him, and maybe I should have, but once I had made up my mind to come back here to try to fix my shit, I didn't want to risk anything taking the wind out of my sails.

Anything like Big Earl telling me not to bother coming back at all.

It's now or never.

Or later.

Now.

I climb out of the car and slam the door behind me. I'm hit immediately by the impact of standing on hot asphalt with no shade trees and the midafternoon sun beating down from above. My skin practically sizzles. Slick sweat dampens, coating every inch of exposed skin and pooling in the crevices covered by denim and cotton. I put on a simple white tee, a pair of jean shorts, and a set of green-and-white Adidas. Basic and nondescript, not offensive unless you count that my family were always Reebok people.

The door to the office opens and out walks the man himself.

9

HIS WIDE-BRIMMED LIGHT GRAY felt Stetson shields his face from view as he approaches. I can't be sure he's smiling; I can't be sure he's not. He's always been a beefy guy, tall and thick around the middle even when he was trimmer in his younger days. Clad in jeans, a pair of black Caiman croc boots from Lucchese, and a classic polo in deep green, he's put on weight in the years since I last saw him. His gut has that curve men get from overindulgences of all kinds, but especially dark, sweet, heavy liquor.

I step around the front of my rental, tugging my sunglasses away from my face. Closer now, and without the added shadow from my lenses, I can see that his lips open wide into a smile. I hate myself for the rush of relief that floods through my veins, softening the sharp edge of nerves.

"There she is," he calls, stepping from the curb. His arms stretch out, an invitation for a hug.

My body hesitates, not trusting the gesture. I imagine them closing around me, a warm embrace full of long-withheld love, like a balm on sore muscles, soothing me into a lull only true safety can bring. But that isn't the truth. I imagine them tightening until they squeeze the life from my flesh and crack me over the asphalt like an egg to cook in the sun. But that isn't the truth either.

I take too long to step into his hold and his arms drop.

"The prodigal daughter," he says.

"Hey," I say. It's a wholly inadequate response after nine years of silence. "You don't look sick."

His blue eyes spark. They're more like the ocean, more green and yellow mixed in, not like mine, more like Buck's. His skin does have a ruddy tone; maybe it's heart disease. Maybe it's all that aforementioned liquor. He was always prideful, never liked to show his hand before the showdown. In poker, his tell was cracking knuckles. Not all of them, not enough that you'd notice if you didn't know him.

Just the ring finger on his right hand.

I don't chance a glance at it, not with him looking right at me.

"We just got reunited, Jellybean," he says, reaching out to clasp a hand over my left shoulder blade (*Jellybean,* one of his endearments, interchangeable among my siblings and me), "and you're already focusing on the negative."

"I didn't just come here on a whim. Buck called me–"

"Buck told me," he says with a nostril flare. I grew up with horses, so I know what annoyance looks like on a beast. "Even after I asked him to leave it. Never was good at taking orders."

"Not good at taking orders" isn't how I would describe my ass-kisser of an older brother, but okay. I won't defend him, but it's worth mentally noting. The bigger point to acknowledge here is the part about Earl not wanting Buck to call me. My assumption that he asked Buck to call may have been wrong, but that's a big *maybe.* Can't take his word for it.

For anything.

Earl applies the lightest pressure to my shoulder blade. *Time to move.* I step forward, pulling away from his grip in the hopes he doesn't try to maintain contact. His hand drops to his side, his hat goes back on his head, and we take the sidewalk up to the entrance of headquarters.

A blast of icy AC hits me as soon as we enter into the lobby. I tuck my sunglasses in the crew neck of my T-shirt. At the reception desk, centered in the room alongside the dark gray boxy couches in the waiting area, is a young woman with blinding white front teeth, bottle blond by the way her hair's all one tone, and wearing a sweater even though it's well over one hundred degrees outside. She has the look of someone with aspirations of a Dallas Cowboys Cheerleader position.

"Oh my, is this your daughter?" Wow, she's chipper. She comes around the desk, hand out to shake mine. "Tabby Collins!" I know the last name, but right now, I'm not sure why. I also know the last thing I want to do is shake this girl's hand. I want to tell her to run, get out, there's a whole world waiting, but something tells me that wouldn't go over well. It's not her fault she's here. It's not her fault she doesn't know any better. Being young, being online, is not synonymous with being well-informed. I give her hand a shake, which gets a freshly widened grin from her.

Earl beams. "Fresh off a plane from Chicago," he says, sounding proud, like Chicago carries some kind of weight in Friendship. The big city! The bright lights! The deep dish and the mob! I don't correct him that I came from a suburb, and it's really not something to brag about. "She's so cultured." A double-edged compliment. My ears tingle with heat from the attention, my stomach knotting around itself because *culture* is practically a curse word to him.

Tabby's buying the show though, so I just stand there awkwardly.

The elevator dings on the other side of the desk, its shiny metal doors squeaking open to reveal my brother.

"You made it back from the North," Buck says, flashing a grin. It doesn't reach his eyes, but then, I don't know why I would expect it to. He's not happy to see me; he didn't miss me. This is duty, this is family, this is him being a "good man."

Earl used to call Buck a baby face, and at thirty-one, he's not showing much of a change in that respect. His tan is subtle but present, telling me he's wearing sunscreen at least. He's got some faint lines feathering the corners of his aquamarine eyes—a touch more navy in them now, as if getting older has turned them darker. He's tall, trim, and dressed like Earl, only in less expensive boots and minus the Stetson. His brown hair is cut short on the sides, with length and texture on top, and I can tell he's put some sort of product in it to keep it from falling in his eyes. Just enough that it holds, not enough that it glows.

Like Earl, he comes in for a big open-armed hug. Only he doesn't take cues from me about whether I want to give it. Buck always had a way of setting my nerves on edge, subtly prodding at any boundary I ever dared try to set, getting under my skin, and calling it brotherly love. His arms close tight, pressing my nose into his chest. Old Spice: sweet vanilla and cinnamon and orange. He started wearing it as soon as he hit puberty and never changed it. The rough texture of his polo against my nose, the structure of his torso and pecs unyielding, the glimmer of aura behind my lids when I close them all cause my nerves to spike, heartbeat starting to speed.

I press my shoulders back, a subtle request for release. I expect he does it because Tabby Collins is watching and Buck has a reputation to uphold. *Good man.* He wears it like a badge, just not sure who awarded it to him.

Earl claps us both on the shoulders. "Don't wake me up!" he says. "Let me keep on dreaming if it means I get to see you two together."

His dream. My nightmare.

10

WE CARAVAN TO the ranch.

Earl's thick-wheeled shiny silver Ford Super Duty, with all the bells and whistles and painted the deepest navy blue, leads the way. Buck drives a Ranger, which has been voted Truck of the Year three years running (he claims, as if I care). It's a boring gray and it's not tricked-out. "Utilitarian," he called it. They talk about their cars like women. I wonder what they'd think if they found out that back in Elmdale, I drive an electric hatchback made in Japan.

We turn off the main highway that leads southeast from Friendship. Ten miles out of town on two hundred acres sits my family's homestead. I have to pause at the gate. The pipe fencing stretches around the whole perimeter, more for show than security. Galvanized steel with wood beams standing firm every six feet. The gate itself is that same black steel, with the words *Powers Ranch* spelled out in script letters across the top. In between *Powers* and *Ranch* is a huge star, a promise or a warning that the people who live here are Texan through and through.

When I was a child, that brand, TEXAN in all caps, bold, was an identity I was sure would be worth the yolk. I felt Texan in my blood. Patriotic to the land and the heat and the wild promise of this untamed place. There was something ruggedly individual about calling myself by that name. I wasn't American; I was Texan, and therefore I was more. It was a lie, like the lie of Manifest Destiny that drove my ancestors west in the first place. A lie that captures the way all lies like to do.

My eyes drift from the gate to the grounds; my breath catches, tears threaten.

I wanted to believe the lie so bad it still stings.

The dead heat—the kind that turns the whole state brown, the kind that withers up every last vulnerable crop and suffocates flower buds, shrivels delicate fruit—that heat hasn't touched this land. Green rolls over the soft slopes of grazing pastures toward the house and stable. It stretches to the peach orchard, where row upon row of trees stand at attention, their limbs heavy from the weight of their fruit. It is a signal to anyone who crosses through the gate. The Powers family has money, the kind that can afford to keep the grass so green you keel over with envy.

I settle my gaze on the house.

White, two stories and an attic, with a black slate roof on top and a metal one covering the deep wraparound porch. It's like a beacon in this green ocean, sturdy and bright, with a beautiful oak tree offering shade on one side. It faces east so that sunrise can be enjoyed at the front, and sunset can be taken in from the back. If you were to snap a photo, show it to some stranger, they'd think this place must be the happiest home. They would imagine summers playing in the sprinklers on the front lawn, walking down the path to the peach orchard to grab one fresh off the tree for a late-afternoon snack. They would imagine saddling up one of the horses, riding through the grounds into the forest paths and back.

They would imagine the sound of laughter, the sound of home.

And they would be right, except that would not be the whole story.

Not even close.

THEY STILL HAVE seven rocking chairs. One for each of us.

Now, those chairs wouldn't be enough for everyone, not with spouses and grandkids enough to call their quiver full. I haven't gotten out of the car yet–can't make myself. My eyes trace the chairs one by one. They're made of hardwood, stained a deep walnut shade that makes them more weather and age resistant. They may not be the same chairs from years ago, but they are the same style, color, and shape. Mine was on the farthest corner, the in-between place on the porch where you could see sunset and sunrise, with a view of the horse training pen and the green-and-white stable. From this low-sitting sedan, I can just barely see it. The late-afternoon light bursts over the curves and illuminates the memories of myself rocking back and forth for hours, lost in a book or a thought or just trying to make myself scarce from inside.

Get out. Get out. I clutch the steering wheel, resistance coiling around my knuckles. I have to leave this car, stand up tall and ready before one of them comes out here to get me.

I have to get out before the box shows up on my dashboard.

The aura ripples, curving at the top of my vision.

I yank the door handle, and as soon as my feet hit the gravel, a tremor runs through me. The current of my soul tunes to this place, recalling the frequency, sending a message from me to the ground through the soil to the trees of the orchard and the Indian grass like hair sprouted over the rolling back of the earth. I know it's crazy to think it, but when I hear the horses begin to stir in the stable, I believe it's a reaction to my presence, this current. I step around the car and walk along the side of the house until I can see the pen. There's a silver appaloosa and a tan-and-white paint horse in there. One of them has a rider, some guy I don't know. He looks young, with dark hair, tight Wranglers. Earl probably hired him to exercise the horses since Lucky isn't living at home now.

Lucky, the baby, the only one I can say with any confidence I might have actually missed. He was thirteen when I left. Young enough then that he still looked at me like I could be some sort of hero, somehow.

Missing him didn't mean we stayed in touch over the years, but I did look him up before I came home. A junior at UT Austin, he's studying economics and business, he's on the rowing team, and because of a picture in the school's online paper, I know he still looks a lot like me, only his hair stayed sandy blond, where mine darkened to a mousy brown.

I watch the guy on the appaloosa take a turn around the pen, almost envious he gets to ride when I haven't since I left home. And I loved riding, was better at it than Buck, even if he competed in cutting competitions, because Earl never would let me.

"You casing the place?"

That voice. Her voice.

Clear and clean, with the slightest hint of twang, just there in her *r*'s and her *a*'s. It's a voice that rings in my ears when I am scared. It's a voice that tramples through the brambles of my mind when I try to be brave.

I steel myself as I turn to take the first look at my mother.

Olympia Powers was a beauty queen in college, which means even now, her looks command attention. Long-necked and graceful, with thick blond hair she wears in soft waves down below her shoulders, blue eyes as clear as a summer sky. She has a slim but strong build, lean and shapely, always dressed to perfection. Right now, she's wearing a cream linen pantsuit and Tory Burch sandals, and she's looking at me like I shit on her lawn by showing up here in a pair of sneakers and jeans.

Or maybe it's just me on her lawn that's the problem.

"Hi," I say, pausing, unsure if I should add *Mom* or just leave it. I don't know what else to call her. *Mom* feels too casual. *Mother* is just weird. *Olympia* would needlessly piss her off. I'm overthinking myself into a stomachache. My lips drift closed, and her hand settles on the porch rail.

The air between us glimmers.

My gaze latches on to the aura with a threat in my heart. It shivers, warping from the crescent shape I'm used to. For a second I swear it sparks like a match against flint, then twists into the flickering shape of a flame.

Olympia looks down, following my gaze. I hold my breath, because even though I know no other person has ever seen it, for a split second I fear that she can.

"Can't even look me in the eye after all this time?" She already sounds pissed. That must be some kind of record.

"It's a lot to adjust to." I do meet her gaze.

"Your dad wants to toast before Sterling gets here," she says. "He's sober again." Her tone indicates an undelivered eye roll. *Sobriety, how annoying.* She's already turning to leave.

"A toast?" I say, still unmoving. She stops, twists to look at me. Her eyes sharpen. "To what?"

Her glare feels like the edge of a razor grazing over the thin skin of my neck. Deftly, she doesn't break flesh, but with every second that passes, the cool scrape of stainless steel reminds me that she could.

"To you."

The sensation of flesh slicing open, the heat of blood spilling from a fresh wound, is so real I want to scream out from the pain. A tremor runs from my fingertips all the way up through my neck. I resist the urge to reach up to staunch blood that isn't real. I don't look down for fear of the trick my eyes will play on me, making me see the gore spilling down the front of my white T-shirt and jeans.

After all this time, Olympia's disapproval can cut right through me.

"Welcome home."

And she's gone. The clap of her sandals is a slap in the face.

My hands ball up tight into fists that shake. I squeeze until the prick of my jagged fingernails cuts into my palm, then I open the fists and tuck one hand after the other in my back pockets to wipe away the blood that managed to break through the skin's surface. A rush of warmth floods through me at the feel of rough denim over the miniscule wounds. Familiar in a different–though no less horrible–way than Friendship, the ranch, my mother's voice.

I've found all sorts of methods through my life to keep my emotions in check.

The box is the biggest, most gruesome, and dangerous. But there were others. That one, for instance, left calluses in the shape of crescent moons on my palms, a mark of pain, of comfort that went unnoticed by everyone around me. I haven't done it in years, but a few minutes back at the ranch, and it's the first thing I use to regulate my emotions.

Fuck. There's a pulse in the side of my head, rapid and anxious. *Fuck fuck.* I have to keep hold of myself long enough to find some answers. There's no way to avoid triggers, of course, I just have to be better at fighting them off, better at breathing, better at ignoring. Or next time it might not be my own hands that suffer.

It's an opening, and in a flash, the memory of Roger's nightmare breaks free.

My hand buries wrist deep in the cavity of a man's chest. Fingers rip through ribs. Detach a heart. Squeeze until meaty muscle oozes through the crevices between.

Then I am back in a parking lot standing across from Roger.

He drops to his knees, tumbles, cracks his skull against the curve of the curb.

The impact throws me back into my body, shaking.

Control. Get it and hold it.

My safety depends on it.

I shoot up the porch steps, a sense of resignation flooding through me as my sneakers cross the threshold into my childhood home. I can do this. I have to do this. The thought is a warm pulse of hope.

Hope is a weak thing captured fast in a cage.

On the table in the middle of the foyer where a vase of black dahlias and white lilies and sweet baby's breath sits dead center, as if placed there by the lady of the household herself, awaits a box—my box.

I didn't see the aura. I didn't see it coming.

My vision narrows to the area around the edges, where a soot-like film settles over the shiny lacquered wood. My body teeters, feet stuck to a ground that would swallow them whole. I look down, and it undulates, wood turned to mud that I struggle to break free from.

This is the box. The nightmare playing tricks with my mind.

The soot that was inside seeps out into the world. Real in a way that it's never been before. My fingers tingle, my hand reaches. Never have I touched it, never have I wanted to—

"Holy shit, Haven!" comes a voice from above. "It's you."

I jolt back from the box, searching up the stairs to the landing, where Lucky smiles down on me like sunlight.

11

HE BOUNDS FROM the landing, taking the steps two at a time to reach me. I am snapped back into my parents' foyer, standing on thick-planked wood floors. His long arms of lean muscle extend for a hug, and I fall into his grip, shaky, eyes sliding down, down to where the box was just sitting.

To where now only a thin outline of inky black remains.

He pushes me back and peers into my eyes. I don't know what to say to this warm welcome from my baby brother–not with the way that I left him alone here among this den of vipers. The last time I saw him, he was standing on the porch watching me load the bed of my truck with suitcases. I half expected him to ask to come with me, even if there was no way he could. I told him I'd call, but I knew that I wouldn't. I was leaving without any plans to return, and Lucky was going to get lumped in with the rest of them. It was unfair, but I couldn't think about it that way back then.

Self-preservation is funny like that.

"You grew up tall," I say, because it's the honest-to-God first thought that enters my head and feels like the safest thing to focus on.

He lets go of my shoulders and takes a step back. He's got to turn his head down to look me right in the eye. His hand raises up to his hair and tucks into the sandy blond strands. He's wearing it long on top, free of product. The color is no longer towhead blond, now it's almost the same color as the faint freckles on his cheeks. He's got a light farmer's tan on his arms, which I can see since he's wearing a loose-fitting tank, camo shorts, and flip-flops, a style so different from the other men in our family, it's a wonder they haven't hazed him into a pair of Wranglers.

"You've met Dad, right? It's a family trait apparently." He cracks a smile. He's got a small chip in his left canine. I don't remember it from before, but that doesn't mean anything. Still, I wonder if it's new.

"Don't tell Sterling that," I reply.

Last time I saw Sterling, he was almost eighteen and hadn't gained any height since he was fourteen. Could have been because he'd already started boozing, and that can stunt your growth. Could have been he really wasn't related to the rest of us. I may have offered the latter as a reason, which got me in trouble with Olympia. Even if Sterling said the same thing to me as a kid, she would tell me I was overreacting.

"His first sober stint at twenty-one helped him add a couple final inches," Lucky says, his smile turning mischievous.

I cut him a look, twisting my brow up in suspicion.

He cracks. "Okay, he's still shorter than the rest of us, and he's a real baby about it."

"So I'll make sure to mention it."

His laugh bursts out all raspy and loud, this weirdly wonderful, comforting sound. It seems to call Buck, who appears in the doorway looking pissy. He's holding a champagne glass, his eyes cutting back and forth between us. Our levity is suspect, apparently.

"Can you two bring the love fest into the den so we can toast?"

Lucky rolls his eyes before turning to face Buck. "Excuse me for wanting to give her a hug after nine years."

"No, by all means, take your time," Buck replies as Lucky and I reach the doorway. "We're just here to serve." The sarcasm in his voice sounds playful but takes a turn toward resentful and parks there. His face is a smiling mask, lips curved up as he speaks, but the luster of his gaze is flat.

We pass through the archway that connects the foyer to the formal den. Decorated for company, it's got multiple seating areas, with the focal point being the Austin stone fireplace, above which hangs a whitetail buck head with massive antlers. The buck's blank stare presides over the room, fixed forever with that artificial awareness.

Earl stands beneath the dead animal wearing a much more animated expression.

Olympia is fluffing the pillows of two navy-blue armchairs that sit in front of the corner window. She smacks her elbow into the center of one, leaving a tight V-shape.

"The kids are all here," Earl says, eyes drifting over to her. "Come over here, dear." She ignores him and begins fluffing the second pillow. Tension warms the air in the room like someone just turned up the heat, and after a summer, the dust settled into the vents and singed, smelling stale.

"The kids aren't *all* here," she says in a voice so dangerous it sets my nerves off-kilter.

I flick a glance at Buck and immediately hate myself for it. Another old habit resurfacing. Buck wasn't the shield I wanted, but he was the one I had. More often than not, he turned that dependence back on me, twisted it from a hug to a noose around my neck. I know better than to look to him for any kind of protection, but still, old habits really do die the hardest.

Earl shifts his shoulders into a square, juts his chin as his eyes go steely. It's not as effective as it once was since age has softened the sharp definition in his chin, and the roundness in his gut makes his posture naturally bow forward no matter how straight he forces his spine.

Lucky is frozen. His breath and movement still as a deer in a hunter's sights.

I go stiff, all my limbs rod straight and heavy.

It is memory and it is survival. We all know it well, and for a split second we all seem to remember our roles.

Buck is the one to move. A single step in the direction of our mother. He bends to grab up a champagne flute, and as his hand raises, a tremor runs through, causing the bubbles to fizz up through the liquid in a dotted line.

"We'll do one at dinner with Sterling."

Olympia stops adjusting the corner of the animal skin throw draped across the ottoman to look right at him.

I know better than to stare. For me, that was all it took to earn her ire. Not that I cared as a kid. It only sunk in after years and years and years that it was easier to just look away and play docile. I force my eyes to the coffee table where two other champagne flutes sit. Bubbles rise to *pop pop pop* on the shimmering surface. One for me, one for Lucky. *It's my fault this is happening. I need to make it better somehow.* The thought is a knife in my side. This is the shit I left to avoid.

This is the least of it, and you know it.

I reach for the champagne flute and grab Lucky's as well. Lucky nearly fumbles the glass, but his fingers slide around it, and he lifts it from my grip. Our eyes connect for a split second. It's horrible how good it feels to see my own anxiety reflected in his gaze. Horrible because it answers the question, at least a little, of how things have been for him since I left. Good, because maybe I'm not as alone as I thought. Years have passed with him left here, and no matter how healthy and whole he looks on the surface, the truth beneath the skin reveals all the damage.

The brand of being a Powers is burned into our bones.

The set to Earl's jaw is tense, but there is a curl at the corner of his lips. He likes this; he always has. When we were pitted against each other, we would turn on anyone to stay at the top of his game. His game was different than hers, which sometimes meant we had to choose between them. There was a price, always, no matter how you played. There was no good answer, no winning, and the tally they kept was skewed to their constant advantage.

Buck lifts the flute in his hand toward Olympia. Her eyes track from the glass to Earl to Lucky, and then, finally, they settle on me. Not a fucking thing has changed here, and every second makes it clearer that not a fucking thing ever will change. Olympia's lips, still full and pert, drop together in a soft pout. She is the loser this time, and she'll find a way to make us all pay for it later. She reaches for the glass, the three-carat pear-cut diamond on her ring finger catching the late-afternoon light as it slips in through the vast bank of windows behind her.

As soon as the glass leaves his hand, Buck's shoulders drop back to a normal setting.

Olympia lifts her glass. The men follow.

I watch.

She looks to Earl, releasing him to make his toast. His eyes travel over to me. This is not the way any of this is supposed to go. I am here, and that shouldn't be something to toast. Because I left them, and that's an offense I should never be allowed to recover from.

"To Haven's homecoming," Earl says, lifting his glass.

No one responds. Not with a *Hear! Hear!* not with a *clink*. The words just sit in the air, hanging heavily like all those ripe peaches burdening the arms of the trees in the Powers Ranch orchard.

"To Haven's homecoming," Olympia replies.

I am the last to lift up my glass.

12

WE WERE DISMISSED from the den as soon as the glasses were drained.

Olympia wanted to get everything set for the dinner ahead. Buck had to go pick up the girls and the missus. Lucky was wrangled to help Earl with some work in the stable. I managed to escape up the kitchen stairwell to the second floor hallway, even though I was expected to help set the table. Someone else can do it since I didn't want any of this anyway.

I want to see what they did with my bedroom.

I know they didn't leave it as is; there's no way. If Sterling or Buck had been the one to ditch Friendship and the family, they'd have left their rooms as a shrine, created an altar to call them home. They probably stripped every sign of me bare from the walls and had a bonfire with the carcass of my four-poster bed frame.

My door looms at the end of this hallway, closed tight.

I take a step onto the navy-blue-and-tan carpet runner. I half expect to see the ghost of little girl me standing at the end of the hallway, waiting like the twins in *The Shining*, calling out for me to come play. She's not there, but still I feel the chill of her all around me.

The upstairs is divided into two sides, split by the main stairwell that leads down to the foyer. On the other side is my parents' suite and Earl's home office, where he keeps his guns and his trophies from golf and hunting, where the pool table is set up, and where men go to pretend to solve important matters but end up just getting drunk on dark liquor instead.

On this side are all of the kids' rooms, as well as the stairs up to the attic game room, where the big TV, all the video game consoles, and the foosball table are. As I take the hallway one plodding step at a time, my mind supplies memories of the best parts of summer spent up in that attic with my brothers. When the heat was so high that just stepping outside could suffocate you. When we could all play pretend that we were normal kids with normal parents in a normal, not cursed, family tree. One window was fixed with a bench cushioned by soft plush pillows and a sconce in the wall for late-night reading. It was my favorite spot in the house outside my bedroom.

Even as a kid, Buck was horribly competitive with Sterling, who was naturally good at every sport with very minimal effort, and somehow even excellent at video game sports. There were *Mario Kart* tournaments, *Wii Sports* battles, foosball fights, and I would get roped in to watch, judge, or occasionally just to make Buck feel better about beating somebody, even if it was never Sterling.

Every door in the hallway is closed, so I pass each of my brother's bedrooms and the attic door without having to look inside. The box plays games with me as I move. The hallway warps unnaturally out at the end like it's putty stretched thin, and then it contracts to a narrow slip in the world that light struggles to leak through.

Just as I near the end of the hallway, I smell it.

Peanut butter singed air. Smoke mixed with sugar. The same

as that day when I hid in the cupboard. I pinch my nose to cut out the scent. Olympia's not baking cookies; I'd have seen the evidence when I passed through the kitchen to put my champagne flute in the sink. This is another trick of the box. It has to be. Knowing that doesn't stop my pulse from quickening. My palms go clammy. My skin feels thin.

When I let go of my nostrils, the smell will be gone because it's not real.

My brain writhes with a warning.

One finger lifts, then the other. I brace before inhaling.

The air is clear. Relief shivers through me, but the remnants of fear remain, like smoke hanging in the air after a fire.

I'm close to the room when I notice the wall of pictures hanging as a memorial to the Powers family's past. Unlike downstairs, this level of the house isn't for guests. This picture gallery is not uniform in design; it's not here for anyone but the family to see. Rustic wooden, white-painted contemporary, black and basic, antique and distressed—frames of all styles, photos from all the years of this family's life. They start with a small oval frame in metal with vines carved into it and a picture of my parents at their wedding in 1986.

This March was their fortieth wedding anniversary.

Thank God, Dad wasn't dying before that, since I'm sure they had a party, and I fortunately didn't get an invite.

In the photo, Olympia's hair is set in her signature long soft wave. Not even the eighties could influence her into something gaudy. Her dress does have puff sleeves and a lace bodice. Earl is dressed in a suede suit jacket and a bolo tie with a longhorn skull as the fastener. His hair is cut in a shaggy style, longer in the back, and the deep brown color complements his tan. They are the straight, white American dream couple. A strong man with good looks and business savvy paired with a beautiful woman with homemaking skills and a keen sense of feminine responsibility.

From there, the pictures change to show their age and additions to the family. Photos of summer by the lake, first birthdays, portraits from Sears, and Easter Sunday shots next to the church. I am in many of the photos, my image not scratched out or digitally removed. In a lot of these pictures, my expression is more of a grimace than a grin. I squint into the sun, lips open like I'm in the middle of talking. *Probably talking back*. There are a few where I am outright glaring, usually at one of my brothers, and certainly to the great annoyance of my parents.

My gaze settles on one photo in the corner closest to my bedroom door.

It's from *that* year. I know it because Buck is there, so is Sterling, but there is no Lucky to be seen. He wasn't imagined or planned; his appearance in the family came after Olympia had already decided to move on from birthing babies. Here, he wasn't even a daydream.

Sometime before or after this picture was taken, the day with the cookies occurred.

In the photo, I stand between Olympia and Buck. My bony knees stick out from beneath the hem of my denim shorts. My hair is wild ringlets, the white, almost iridescent silver, blond of my early life still a shining light on the crown. I wear jelly sandals. I have a slap bracelet on my tiny left wrist. My fingers curl around Buck's pinky, the grip tight enough that even in the grainy photo, I can see the whites of my knuckles.

My mother looks straight at the camera; Sterling holds her hand and cries. We're in front of the Alamo—this must have been one of our summer road trips. We did that back then, like most families did.

It's not the lie that alarms me.

It's that there in the photo beside me, I see it.

A squiggling line of light right next to my head.

The aura warning. The box was there with me.

I've never been able to set the making of the teeny tiny box in my own timeline. Seeing the aura in this picture is the closest thing to a real clue of when I made it that I have ever gotten. I had it by that summer. It had already breached my delicate reality. Already it was working to keep my horrors locked up. Which makes me wonder, did that day with the cookies have something to do with why I made the box?

I rest my fingers on the curve of my bedroom doorknob as the realization settles over me.

My grip tightens on the handle as I test it—not locked. I twist it to let myself inside.

My mother has turned my room into her private sanctum.

Gone are the movie posters and lavender walls, the four-poster white-painted bed. The walls are robin's-egg-blue with a satin finish, giving it this soft, velvet quality. Offset in the corner is an antique desk, curvy legs and a glossy finish on the rich oak wood. She's hung photos of my brothers, their families, Lucky's high school graduation on one wall. I slink closer to that wall to get a better look at all of them.

Buck's wife is tall, with coppery red hair she wears long. She's kept her figure tight even after birthing their three children, two of whom stand in front of their parents; she has the baby on her hip. They're cute kids; the oldest, a girl, has red hair like the mother, the middle is a boy with darker brown hair that looks like it has some red in it, and the baby is a girl, with wisps of towhead blond hair. I don't know their ages, and I assume this is a fairly recent portrait based on how Buck appears. I'm guessing the oldest kid is maybe six or seven, the youngest probably under two years old.

Buck would have been twenty-four, twenty-five when the first was born. Young, even by Christian family-planning standards.

Sterling, on the other hand, only has one kid, a little boy, the spitting image of him with his red hair and freckles, big hazel eyes and stocky build. The woman pictured with him is stunning, with black wavy hair and a deep tan. She looks young, even for Sterling, who's already pretty young himself at barely twenty-seven.

I shift around the room, passing over Olympia's sewing table and bookshelves to the other large display wall, where she pays homage to her community work in all its varied forms. If Earl is a stalwart in the business and commerce world of Friendship, Olympia is a beacon of community involvement.

A real Proverbs 31 woman.

A wife of noble character, skilled with her hands, and virtuous in all her pursuits. In the center photo, she stands with a group of other community leading ladies, likely business owners, teachers, and of course, right beside Olympia, her plastic smile and strawberry blond helmet hair frozen with hairspray, stands Charity Turner.

They're friends, of course. Still. Even after what happened back then.

In Olympia's hands is a plaque that I have to squint to read: Principled Women for America (PWA for short). I don't need to look it up to know they're probably doing the most to fuck around with the rights of every person they see as undesirably different from them under the guise of protecting the community and the children who live in it.

My eyes scan over the other photos, pausing on a shot of her praying with hands raised, eyes closed, right outside an abortion clinic. It's an older photo by the look of it, and also by the current policies in the state that would make a place like this impossible. She's likely kept it up to remind herself of the role she played in this anti-healthcare movement. It's cruelty masquerading as piety put on display–repulsive but not surprising, which is what I'm thinking when I spot him.

Full color, hanging on the wall in an expensive-looking frame.

My parents stand sentry on either side in the photo.

Acid burns my throat.

His name stings my tongue.

Tate Turner.

Dressed in a three-piece suit and wearing one of those dumb mini microphones in a tone that blends with his skin. Behind them is the church, Fellowship Kind. A modern building designed to be seeker sensitive in its appearance. A contemporary shape with clean lines, mixed commercial use spaces set up to draw people in. Businesses like a hair salon and a day care–things that serve the community.

They beam like proud parents, but Tate isn't their son. That was something they wanted that didn't happen because of me. I ruined their plan to join the Powers family with the Turners, tying the automobile empire to the church and solidifying the reach of both. They hold on to him with a grip that feels desperate, but only elation shows on his face, and everything about it makes my writhing gut boil and bubble and thrash.

The sound of metal shifting against metal comes from behind me.

The tiny hairs on the back of my neck prickle. There has never been sound with the box, but that was definitely hinges shifting ever so slightly. It was unmistakable. There is something about this house that seems to be changing the way the box interacts with my senses. I can hear it move; I can see sooty sludge seep from its sides. It hasn't announced itself with the aura since the moment I stepped inside the house.

I take one more long look at the Tate visage. I swallow, my

throat tight, trying to keep the sick in my stomach down, my eyes hot with tears I want to cry.

I think if I were to close them right now, the nightmare would take that as a cue to paint me a vivid picture.

The box would unlock, and allow the nightmare to pull out its beastly insides.

Metal on metal. *Cling-clang* as if in response to my thoughts.

Bile pools on top of my tongue.

I cup my hand over my lips, taste the bitter, acrid residue of stomach acid mixed with plane pretzels and dry champagne. I hold it there, hostage, and slowly inhale, exhale through my nose, until I can force it back down. When I raise my hand away from my lips, there's a sheen of sweat on my palm mixing with the still-tender crescent-shaped cuts. Slowly, slowly I turn to see that the box has taken a spot on my mother's antique desk.

That isn't the only thing that I notice.

For a split second, the wall behind the desk expands bigger than the inside of this room, the desktop too wide and elongated for the space that it fills. I blink, rub my eyes, and it's back to normal.

Only the box remains.

This is not going well. I am not crushing the whole get-it-under-control thing.

This feels like an escalation. Trigger points punched and exacerbated.

What happened with Roger was a signal of some greater, more horrible scope of power. Even if I am the reason the box exists. Even if the nightmare comes from the darkest parts of myself.

"Go away." My voice croaks the command.

The box seems to firm up even more. The sides sharpen into focus. Viscous black drips like blood down the sides, then unfurls, changing from liquid to smoke. It looks so real there on the desk, in this room, the light from the ceiling fan casting a shine over the top. Energy pulses toward me from the edges, and my eyes roll closed, submissive, exhausted. *Give up, give in–*

The slam of a car door followed by another and another.

Bam bam bam.

I don't give in, though my every raw nerve longs to. Instead, I walk to the bedroom window that looks out on the front drive. My brothers have arrived with their families, here for a dinner that none of us wants.

13

STERLING IS WEARING golf shorts, a polo, and a white baseball cap. Maybe he's coming from the golf course and not work. Not that I know what Sterling actually does. While Lucky is attending college—a couple years late, for reasons I also don't know—and Buck is VP of the dealership, Sterling was never an obvious candidate for a role in the biz or a college path.

Not just because his sobriety never seems to stick either.

Sterling is the spare. The boy that came later because two kids weren't enough for a respectable Christian household. Not an accident, like Lucky; they decided to have him, but admittedly, they didn't do much to steward him into a successful life path.

He's standing in the entry doorway looking up at me on the staircase. His arms are sunburned, so it's safe to assume he was at the course earlier, not wearing sunscreen even though he's got the fairest complexion of all of us. A contributing factor to the mean-spirited joke about him not being related. I do feel shitty about it, but only because it's unfair and kind of an ugly shade on me.

The rim of his hat offers a small shadow over his eyes.

He's not smiling. His jaw is set so hard his muscle twitches.

I lift my hand and wave like an idiot, and before either of us can say anything, chaos descends on the foyer. Buck, his wife, and their three kids shove in through the door behind him. Olympia and Sterling's wife, the pretty woman from the portraits I saw earlier, enter from the den, whispering like they're ladies taking a turn about the room in Edwardian times. Sterling's wife is carrying a set of tall glasses filled with iced tea and wearing a soft pink linen sundress. They continue on to the dining room, pausing only to hand off an iced tea to Sterling.

"Aren't you going to say hi to your aunt?" Buck calls after his kids as they run around the staircase and disappear through the kitchen. I hear the glass sliding doors open as they exit the house to the backyard.

"Violet can't go out there with the pool gate open," Buck's wife says, to which Buck does the *reluctant dad on duty* move and follows after the toddler (Violet apparently) who is running as fast as her little legs can carry her.

Buck's wife turns her gaze to me and flicks on the bright beam of her smile. Picture perfect. I bet she was a cheerleader or a student body president or something in high school. I don't recognize her, but Buck is three years older, so she may have been in his class, which means I may not have noticed her when I was a freshman.

"You must be Haven," she says, voice just as bright. "I'm Clarabelle, formerly Schaeffer, I think you were in my younger sister Hyacinth's class."

Another toothy redhead with a perfect tan flashes in my mind. Hyacinth Schaeffer, of course. She *was* class president, well liked and kind. We partnered up in Chem class, and she was best friends with another important girl in our class.

Or important to me, anyway, not that she knew it.

Winter Reyes.

Lightning fast, her face flashes in my memory. Eyes the color of whiskey, with a quirky crooked smile and the thickest brown hair I'd ever seen, always wanted to touch. Winter was the coolest girl I'd ever met, smart and quick, good at sports, arts, *and* academics. Her parents owned a bowling alley in town and she played drums in a Queen cover band. They never got to perform in Friendship, but I snuck out to watch them in Clover a few towns away and helped Winter load the kit into the lead singer's van afterward.

We weren't exactly friends. By then, I was too far in with Tate, and everything in my life revolved around survival. I had to be careful around Winter, for her sake as much as my own.

"Oh, right," I reply. "How's Hyacinth doing?" It's the polite thing to ask, and Hyacinth really was all right.

A shadow settles in Clarabelle's eyes. "She's"—there's a loaded pause—"finding her way."

On cue, carrying a screaming Violet in his arms, Buck reenters the foyer. "No one wants to hear about how Hy went mental and now she's living in a commune in the desert outside Los Angeles."

I blink, am taken aback, but I'm also genuinely intrigued.

"I mean, I, for one, would love to hear more about that," I reply too fresh and fast. I'm forgetting myself. I'm forgetting where I am.

Sterling gives a snort, the first audible acknowledgment since I walked down the stairs.

I cut him a look but stay silent.

He yanks his cap off, rolling his eyes. "Hi." His voice drops low, and he frowns deep.

"You're sunburned." I point to his arm.

"You're pale," he replies.

"Civility costs nothing," Buck says.

Clarabelle beams, the dark cloud in her eyes lifting.

"Dinner!" Olympia calls.

Sterling and I remain in a standoff. I'm in his way to get to the dining room, where already I can smell something salty and savory, likely a red meat main course, definitely braised, wafting in from the room.

"Welcome home," Sterling practically spits, "Sis." The last word sounds like *cunt*, and we all know that was intentional. He shoves past to the sound of ice cubes smacking his glass. I cut a look toward Clarabelle and Buck. She feigns another overly bright smile.

"It's nice to meet you finally," she says, reaching out to take Violet from Buck's arms. The toddler has stopped crying at least. Now her eyes travel around the faces of the adults with bewilderment. Her face is stained with tear streaks, but the final crocodile drop hangs on the ledge of her lower lashes. "I'll hand her off to Adelaide."

Adelaide must be a nanny. The toddler falls into her mother's arms and they exit the foyer, leaving Buck and me alone. For a second, the sound of the dining room scramble of chairs and conversation fades, and in its place is the rapid rush of my own blood as it races past my eardrums.

My brother looks at me with open concern. Furrowed brow, a frown set in his lips, not a hint of hope. "We're just not sure what to do with you now that you're here."

"I didn't ask to come back," I say, my voice hitching up in an attempt to be heard, to defend myself. "That was you. You called me."

He takes a step closer.

I take a step away. "No need to raise your voice–"

"I didn–" But he's steamrolling ahead. "It was the right thing to do," he says, his voice dropping even lower. I half expect him to reach out and take my wrist, tighten a fist around it and tug me into his side.

My vision narrows in preparation for it, my mind getting ready, gearing up– *No no stop.* I blink. I force a smile. I reach out and pat him on the shoulder. *There now, buddy.*

"You're right, it was," I say with a quirk of my lips. I hate myself for the second time today. I fear it won't be the last time—nowhere near it. Because with Buck, it's all I know how to do. Comply to placate and then loathe my face in the mirror when I do.

His frown twitches; he's suspicious of the change in my tone. "Hope we don't regret it."

He turns and walks into the dining room. I stand there for another beat, hold in a breath, threaten my tears not to dare wet my eyes, and then I'm walking.

The dining room at the ranch is equipped for dinner parties. When I was little, the Powers name was just getting established around the county as one of importance. There was a farm table with benches running along the sides for us to sit at and a chair at each head of the table for the parents. The finishing in the room was rustic family style, comfortable and easy. No paintings on the walls, no linens on the table, no rug beneath our feet.

Later, they began entertaining, and French Colonial was all the rage in decor at the time. They took out the farm table, moved it to the newly expanded kitchen, and turned it into the kids' table. They laid a premium wool rug in an ornate cream-and-navy pattern. They hung a piece of art above the fireplace and redid the mantel in marble. They painted the walls a soft ecru and put in modern sconces for more attractive lighting. Over the new ten-person dining table, they hung a chandelier. It was full grandeur, all finished off by the view from the huge front windows that looked out on their land.

I step up to the table that Olympia has set with eight chairs and formal place settings for each of us. It's just the adults in the room now. They've relegated the kids to the kitchen table. A quick glance in there reveals the aforementioned Adelaide, a twentysomething brunette.

"She's the au pair from Sweden. We adore her," Clarabelle says beside me.

"I'm surprised you've kept her on for the summer," Sterling's wife says, her smile smooth. It's a dig. She's not outright saying it, but she is openly judging Clarabelle for needing help.

"We haven't met," I say, cutting in. I do not need to assist the pretty perfect wife of my fucker of a brother, but this other pretty perfect wife of my other fucker of a brother is already annoying the shit out of me.

"This is Julep," Sterling says, as if Julep can't answer for herself. "Married three years."

"Next month," Julep adds with a toothy smile. What an achievement.

Olympia and Earl enter like the king and queen of Texas.

He carries a bottle of red wine; she's got the basket of homemade rolls. They take their positions at the heads of the table, and now the seating arrangement makes a lot more sense. Julep and Clarabelle are in the spots closest to Olympia, Sterling and Buck are in the seats closest to Earl. Lucky and I face each other in the middle. I look up to where Lucky stands behind his chair and see he's already eyeing me with a mischievous glint. He's clocked me clocking every uncomfortable piece of this puzzle, and it feels like maybe he wants me to know that he's clocking it too, that I'm not alone.

Don't have to be, anyway, if I don't want to be.

Olympia has selected an elegant China pattern, white with robin's-egg-blue trim. She's made braised short ribs and served them on a platter with roast veggies, mashed potatoes, and a summer salad brightened up with peaches from the orchard. There's wine on the table, a couple bottles, one on each end. I glance at Sterling to see that he's aware of every single one of the bottles. My eyes drop to the place setting in front of him to see he's got a wineglass. Every setting has one.

Earl pulls out his chair at the head and takes a seat.

We all follow.

The polite dance of dinner ensues. Plates are served, bread is passed, butter is slathered. Though, noticeably, Olympia passes me a smaller portion of meat and potatoes. I don't have the courage to rebuke her, but I grab an extra roll in defiance. The smell of red-wine-soaked-meat and mashed potatoes and earthy vegetables fills my nose. Olympia is more than an exceptional baker. Her culinary skill extends to gourmet dining. Sure, she does your basic down-home Texas-style cooking too, but executing fine food is kind of her trademark.

"Wine?" Clarabelle asks me, holding a bottle of white in her hand.

"It's just," I try to whisper, "Sterling is sober–"

"We don't walk on eggshells here, Haven." Earl speaks up.

Fuck fuck fuck. I turn to look at him, but he's looking at Sterling.

Sterling has barf face he's trying–and failing–to mask.

Earl smacks him on the shoulder. "You're strong enough to handle a little wine in your presence."

Clarabelle is already pouring my glass even though I haven't said yes. I don't understand why they would insist on a toast before Sterling got here if they're just going to drink around him now.

And then it dawns on me.

The Powers family is nothing if not deeply superstitious.

If we can't all toast with champagne, then none of us can.

"Sterling hasn't even thought about touching a drink since what happened on my birthday," Julep chimes in, leaning forward to look past Lucky and offer Sterling a supportive smile. "It was a turning point, and I'm proud of him every single day."

I am desperate to know what the fuck happened on her birthday, but I'm also not sure I can stomach the bad theater of their happy marriage playing out right in front of me. My appetite is already iffy, and I really need to get something in my stomach with how Olympia eyes my plate like an eagle.

"That's the love of a good woman," Earl says, winking at Julep.

She blushes. Clarabelle prickles beside me. I want to tell her it will never matter how good of a wife she is, how beautiful, how sweet. There is no way to compete with being Sterling's.

The favorite—we all know it.

"Are we sure it wasn't the third DUI that did it?" Buck says, coming in strong.

"I thought it was the Lord's unlimited grace," Lucky says with a snort.

Earl cuts him a dark look, a warning slap without ever lifting a hand. It's one I know well, and immediately my chest heats up like a heavy hot weight just landed on it. I squirm with discomfort, wishing I had the courage to jump in and help him. I decide to fill my mouth with food, hook a piece of braised beef with the end of my fork, and lift it to my lips. As soon as it hits my tongue—*cling cling cling*—my lips close over the meat.

The attention is pulled to the other end of the table, where Olympia taps her knife's edge against a glass. "Now that we're all settled in with our beverages of choice and ready to eat, we can't proceed with this feast without thanking our Lord for the provisions." Her eyes zoom in on me.

I forgot about blessing the food. *How could I forget about blessing the food?* Until I was nineteen, there wasn't a single meal consumed without making sure God got his due. I can't spit out the bite, nor do I want to, not with her watching me. I take one chew, two, and then I force the bite to slide down my throat and hope I don't choke. I'm not sure they'd provide the Heimlich if I did.

I spread my lips into a smile.

She extends a hand to Clarabelle first, Julep second, and they gladly take hold of her palms. Everyone follows suit around the table. Clutching hands, bowing heads. Even Lucky drops his chin and lets his lids slide shut. I look back at Olympia. She's still watching me, waiting for me to comply.

I don't.

This is her game and I just got docked major points. Not that I care.

Right?

Buck takes me by the wrist, palm facing down on the table. I turn my glare on him. His eyes are closed, his face fixed in a neutral expression.

"Dear Lord . . ." Olympia begins.

I squeeze my hands into fists, my fingernails cutting into my palms, finding the same place to dig in as before. I pull against Buck, just enough that he knows I am not sitting here docile.

". . . we thank you for this food we are about to receive. May it nourish our bodies and renew our souls." She pauses, dragging the moment out just for me. "We lift up Big Earl to you, Lord, and ask that you look down on him with love."

Sterling and Buck, who hold Big Earl's hands, lift them now up to the sky in an offering.

"We need him, dear Lord, please let us keep him here with us." It's the first mention of his illness outright, even if she doesn't reference what exactly it is. "And finally, thank you for bringing Haven home to the family."

"Yes, Lord," echoes in agreement around the table.

"We are blessed to all be together again. Your will on earth as in heaven." Her lips spread into a smile.

We are not together.

"Amen" resounds.

I am the only one who remains silent.

14

LUCKY FINDS ME after dinner outside on the porch in my old rocking chair.

"You okay with some company?" he asks before he takes the seat beside me.

I nod without turning to look at him. I'm watching the sun slip low on the horizon line, and already it has started to turn the sky a wash of bright color. Teal and magenta, vibrant streaks of white clouds tinged a baby pink, a light show as it dances over the barn and down on the green grass. Lucky drops into the rocker beside me, stretching out his long legs in front of him.

"On a scale of one to ten, how shitty is it to be back here?" he asks.

I curl my lips up at the transparent honesty baked into his question. "Hard to quantify, but I forgot how much religious guilt fucked with my appetite." I hadn't been able to eat much after all. My mouth felt filled with cotton, and even the wine tasted skunky when I tried to drink it.

"I tune it out for the most part now," he says, easing his rocker into a slow rhythm.

"You mean you don't bless the mess at the UT dorm cafeteria?" I smile and he grins.

"You looked me up?"

"It's no big deal." I shrug.

"It is to me." He's happy about it, and that immediately feels like too much pressure.

"Economics and business at UT. That's quite the double major." I push myself to keep the conversation going.

"After a gap year and then a summer at the dealership working under Buck, I had to get pretty convincing to get Dad's blessing."

"You mean his money?"

"I do mean that, sure, but it's more than that." He's scanning the tree line like he's looking for the answer in the branches. "I don't know how you did what you did, leaving here with nothing. Cutting them out." He looks at me with such admiration it makes my insides squirm.

"It wasn't like I had a choice," I reply, wanting nothing more than to get the pressure off myself. I'm not heroic, and what I did was nothing but survival. "I don't know how much you remember, Lucky, but if I'd stayed in Friendship, it would have done me in."

"Like . . . ?" He lifts his thumb to point at his throat and slices to the right.

I chuckle. "Morbid. And, yeah, in one way or another."

"Then, you're happy out there on your own?"

I didn't leave here to be happy, and I don't think I achieved anything close to it, not even after all this time. I don't think I would be in the mess I'm in if I had. I left here because I realized this place was slowly devouring me, and leaving was the one thing I could do to keep what was left of myself from being swallowed whole.

I got myself away, but I don't have much to show for it. I am not intact; I lived like a criminal until I finally became one.

"Is anybody really happy?"

His eyes travel back to the trees. Quiet falls between us.

I don't know if Lucky's going to be able to keep this up. He's got practically a whole lifetime ahead of him in which he'll be expected to bend, even if it means eventually he breaks. I don't think it's my place to tell him that taking money from Earl never ends well. I may be his big sister in name, but it's not like I've earned any of the perks of that title.

The quiet between us is broken by the sound of car wheels spinning fast on gravel. I lean forward to see past Lucky. It's a black BMW, shiny, compact, and speedy. The kind of car you get when you want to be seen as respectable, accomplished, and important. A statement of success without slapping you in the face.

The tiny hairs on the back of my neck electrify and stand on end like a reanimated corpse even though the heat had plastered them to my skin.

I don't yet know why. But my body sure does.

"No fucking way," Lucky says as he turns back to look at me.

"What?" I ask, my pulse hitching up.

"It's gonna be fine." He reaches out and grabs my hand.

I flinch at the sudden, unbidden contact. He releases me and I hold his stare. He's undeterred but respectful.

"What's gonna be fine?"

"That's Tate's car. I don't know how he knows you're here."

The porch lights flicker, a flutter on and off like a ghost just arrived. An eleven forms between Lucky's brows. His eyes are so like mine: summer sky blue with a deep rim of navy around the iris. They land on the lights and then skitter back to my face. He noticed the flicker; it wasn't just in my head.

"I saw Charity in town," I say, lights *blinking blinking.* Panic seizes my chest as the air thins and it gets harder to fill up my lungs. "Olympia and Earl wouldn't–"

"You want me to lie?" he says in earnest.

Now I almost reach out for his hand, but I don't.

From around the porch corner, I hear the front door swing

open. Earl's cowboy boots shuffle over the wood, and he hoots, "Look who's come to visit!"

"We can bolt around back to the stables," Lucky says. "I know all the good hiding places."

Fuck me. My heart contracts with the knowledge that hiding out is something Lucky has done before. Who knows how many times? Who knows why he needed to?

Who knows if it's for reasons like mine?

The car stops in front of the house. The engine cuts out. The door opens and slams closed.

"Hey there, Captain." Tate's voice cuts the thick heat like a knife.

I shoot up from the rocker, and Lucky takes a step out in front of me. Just enough that it feels like I could hide behind him if I wanted. It's not a nothing move, and it's not too much. Lucky is letting me know with his body and his presence and the way he's whispering quietly under his breath, "You got this," that he's here with me. I'm not crazy for feeling this way. It is an earned response to the years I lived in the grip of that man's cruel hold.

I hear the *scrape* of his shoes over the gravel before he appears.

"I had to bring you this. One of the patrons donated it to christen the new prayer wing, but you know how Dad is about liquor near the altar of God."

If you've never felt this particular fear before, you may not understand how, even if there is no real and present danger, your body believes you are wrong. There is. The warning of it surges beneath your skin. It's the ache of the flu and the rush of jumping from a high building rolled up together. It hurts in your cells, shoots through your stomach like spikes, fires up the muscles of your legs. It radiates into the soft soles of your feet, hot as flames. It makes you feel like ants dance over your scalp.

Tate is on the porch steps looking up at Earl when he finally sets eyes on me. His gaze scans over the rockers and lands on my face. A smile tugs at his full lips.

Blue sparkles.

"Mom told me you came home to Friendship," he says, and his smile breaks out, glittering all over the place. "Had to see it for myself."

Earl turns to look at me now too. His hand extends in a move meant to call me to him.

I turn tail and run.

I'm around the back of the house in seconds, then in through the kitchen, where Julep dries dishes and Olympia sits at the table putting together a puzzle with the little nieces and nephews. They may call out to me. I don't know, I don't care. I can't fit in the cupboard, so I choose the next best thing.

The powder room.

Slam the door shut.

Drop down to my knees at the toilet and barf.

My eyes slide closed. My mind takes me back to a memory, in another bathroom, one of the last times I ever saw Tate.

NOAH FIELDER'S FOLKS had a lake house down a winding road with a bad cell phone signal and no supervision. My parents didn't know I was there since Tate had just told them he was taking me out. Buck had tried to stop me, which only made me want to go that much more.

Buck was right in the end. I never should have gone out there.

It wasn't just the drinking, the way everyone got all sweaty and rubbed themselves up against each other. It wasn't just that I was avoiding Tate as soon as I got there, and I wound up in the lake with a couple of girls and their college boyfriends playing chicken, with one of the girls on my shoulders in a bikini. I was fully dressed in my cutoffs and tank top. I had places on my skin that needed hiding, and I was always careful to dress accordingly.

It was that I got high, and I was sick of everyone, everything, but mostly I was sick of being me.

Tate had seen me across the kitchen, through the sliding glass door, seen red, then came out to get me. Grabbed my wrist, dragged me out of the water, over the rocky beach, slicing up my feet, to a quiet place behind a tree where no one could see.

His breath smelled of skunky beer and barbecue chips. Spit smacked my cheek as he scolded me, calling me "slut" and "cunt" and other things I won't say here, but they were etched that day all over my skin.

"We're going," he ordered. "I'm taking you home."

I wasn't ready to leave. I didn't want to go home with him.

I pulled out of his grip and back into the view of the party. I told him I needed to pee and dry off, promised I would do it quick, then we could go. He bought it; he thought he had me under control.

He thought wrong.

I don't remember getting to the bathroom. But I remember the wallpaper. Black-and-white toile. Up close, the characters printed on it looked like they were moving. The girl and the boy, their little dog, the leaves on the tree standing over them.

It was enough to remind me of a different tree.

The one on my box.

The place I would have to put all this when it was over.

I remember the smell of a storm brewing outside, electric and wet, thunder crashing far off in the distance, and the cackle and calls of a party raging on despite the threat of a downpour.

I remember the sound of the fist pounding the door.

"Occupied," I called out. But I knew who it was.

"Let me in." Tate's voice was so still that it almost went backward.

I closed my eyes. I tried to go somewhere else in my mind.

The handle of the door jiggled. He smacked on the wood. "I don't see why you needed to lock the door." His anger was ice cold. It froze me right where I stood. It wouldn't let me move; it tried to stop my thoughts in their tracks, suffocate them with a chill that burned in my lungs.

"Just a minute." I tried to sound normal, but fear rattled in my throat.

He wouldn't give me a minute. He wouldn't take *wait* for an answer.

The door shot open. The handle hung, broken. He pushed into the bathroom, stood between me and the only way out.

I shudder now, back in my parents' powder room, curled on the floor in the fetal position, my stomach lurching with more it wants to expel. I sit up, grip the toilet, and close my eyes as I vomit again.

Tate Turner is outside somewhere, waiting for me to come find him.

15

IT TAKES ME an unknowable length of time to gather the strength to stand up.

They must be wondering where I ran off to, but I can't bring myself to face the mirror just yet, let alone them. Funnily enough, I almost wish the nightmare had taken control. Even just that small piece of memory brought out in the open in this place threatened to take me out.

Mom told me you came home to Friendship.

I roll onto my back and stare up at the ceiling, blinking.

My skin aches like someone removed it from its frame of muscles and sinew and bone, put it in a dryer on high, and shrunk it. Every move I make threatens to rip it at the seams. My vision is still blurry, but with each blink, it becomes just a little bit clearer. The ceiling of this powder room is painted blue like the sky. There is a pendant light hanging, a gold-and-glass shape that I think is meant to imitate the sun.

Olympia loves the sky. She once told me she was a bird in a past life. She was drunk, loose-lipped in a way Olympia Powers would never be otherwise. I remember thinking then that there was so much I did not know about my mother. Who had she been before she was this God-fearing former beauty queen turned perfect housewife and pillar of the community. She knew Earl in high school, but she did not grow up in Friendship. She has no siblings. Her mother has been in a care facility for as long as I've been living.

I test movement with my left arm, reach up to grab hold of the toilet.

My skin doesn't split.

I pull myself up to a sitting position first, my knees next, and then my feet. Olympia has to have some mouthwash in here somewhere. I yank open the cabinet that's built into the wall beside the sink. There are spare hand towels, soap, lotion, and–yes, an actual win for the prodigal daughter–a bottle of blue mouthwash sitting on the lower shelf beside some Dixie cups and a few packaged toothbrushes and toothpaste. I twist off the cap and pour some of the liquid inside. It smells of peppermint. I inhale the scent before swishing it a few times and spitting it out in the sink.

I knew coming back here would mean more than just seeing my family, but in the couple days between saying I'd come and actually showing up, when I was packing my suitcase and booking my ticket and picking up the rental car, it never actually crossed my mind that I would have to see Tate Turner in the flesh, right in my family's front yard. And it definitely didn't occur to me how visceral the sound of his voice, the feel of his eyes, would be.

I am not in danger anymore because of him. So why do I feel like I am?

I rinse with mouthwash one more time, not because I need it, just because I'm stalling.

I can't smell like vomit. Olympia will pick at it, and she'll try to use it like she used to, and fuck knows I don't need that right now.

This is temporary. I have to remember that being here is temporary. Making nice is temporary. If I can find the answers I need, I can leave again.

I exhale and give myself a hard look in the mirror. "You can be civil to Tate."

My family chose him, I knew they did. They did that before I left Friendship. Still, facing it this early in the trip isn't ideal. I barely have my footing. *Ha! Who am I kidding?* There's no footing to have. I'm in a barbed-wire pit below the tightrope of expectation. The best I can hope for is that I don't bleed out.

If anyone will rip out my guts, it's Tate.

I just won't let him close enough to try.

I turn on the cold water, tear off some toilet paper, and wet it under the flow. I dab at my neck, my lips, pinch my cheeks to get some color back in them. I drop the toilet paper in the bowl right on top of my vomit and flush. I turn back to look at myself one more time in the mirror.

I don't like to admit it, but sometimes when I catch sight of myself, what I see is a hard slap. *Who the fuck are you?* I want to demand, though I don't expect the image to reply. She's just so much more boring than I ever expected to be. Being a child, making hell for everyone, being a tyrant worth naming Nightmare, I really expected myself to grow into a hottie with an impeccable sense of style who stood out from the crowd rather than blending into it. My hair is a boring light brown, waves that hit below my collarbone with too-long bangs. My clothing is nondescript. Even when I'm not at work, I wear stuff like basic tees in colors that practically match my skin. My makeup routine consists of mascara, taupe for my lids, tinted sunscreen for my fair skin, and champagne pink gloss on my lips. I may have once had the kind of aura that made old women clutch their pearls, with the doe eyes, pouty mouth, and strong but still feminine jaw of an actress, but who could notice any of that now with the way I've muted every shade. The only thing I can't subdue is my eyes. Cobalt blue with a deep navy rim and sparks of robin's egg.

All the shades of blue decorating my family home.

My favorite color and my torment.

I stare into the swirling glow of my own eyes until I am ready—or as ready as I can be.

I take a step outside the powder room and am met by Olympia's hand. The pressure of it against my stomach pushing me back into the powder room.

"I need a word," she says, shutting the door behind her. There is a window on the opposite wall, a stained glass peach orchard. The light streams in through the panes, coloring her in shades of orange, green, and shimmering gold. She's aging like fine wine, which I note as another thing to hate her for.

Her eyes slide to the toilet as if she's looking for evidence of why I came in here. As if a few hours back in Friendship would be enough to trigger that particular coping mechanism. As if she isn't trying to trigger it herself. She looks back at my face, her pupils stuttering over it in search of some other evidence. Really glad I used the mouthwash.

Her brow arches, and she takes a single step back. "You saw Tate was here," she says, eyes meeting mine. My mother is taller than me, and I'm taller than most, but that's not the only reason it feels as if she towers above me. It's like her spirit is taller than mine, than even her physical frame, and if the light were to catch it just right, you'd be able to see the true shape of her unnatural shadow.

"I was on the porch when he arrived," I reply.

"Yes." Displeasure seeps into her voice. "You ran from him like he was some kind of serial killer."

I haven't read up on the recent events in Friendship, and I doubt there's a rash of murdered women with unsolved cases, but serial killer Tate Turner isn't the craziest idea I've heard this week.

"I needed to pee," I say, trying hard not to care that she's using her first real moment alone with me since I arrived to scold me about the impression I made with Tate.

My rabid-as-a-rat ex-boyfriend.

I didn't exactly expect a warm welcome from her. Arms wrapping me up in a hug, love-yous whispered into my ear, compliments peppered over my cheeks like kisses. She was never that way with me; there's no reason to think she'd start now.

"You need to remember your manners."

"With Tate?" I cross my arms. Her eyes slide to where my hand presses against my bicep, spreading the bit of excess fat under my arms so it's more obvious. I drop them back down and tuck my hands in my pockets instead.

Her left brow does a swoop up before her gaze returns to my face. "You need to remember your manners with all of us," she says. Then she has the gall to reach out and move one of the pieces of my bangs off my forehead. Her fingernails comb through my hair to tuck it behind my ear. "You broke our hearts, and it's not so simple for any of us to see you back here so different than you used to be."

"It's been nine years. Change is inevitable." Though, to look around here, you wouldn't know it.

She inhales sharply, and her fingers come around to clutch my chin. The tension is light at first, I instinctively flinch, she tightens her grip. Her eyes latch on like fishhooks in a wet gill.

"You left, we didn't." She pauses, digging in with her gaze. "He didn't." I try to pull away, but she won't let me. "Your little stunt derailed more than you even know. It took him years to find love again. I'm convinced your daddy's heart will never recover." There it is, thinly veiled. Earl's heart is fucked, and that is at least some part of what is killing him, and of course it's my fault, not the booze and beef-heavy diet he's had his whole life. "This isn't going to be a quick fix, if that's what you were hoping."

"Buck called *me*," I say firmly, straining my neck to break my chin free of her hold.

She lets me go and crosses her arms. Not an extra inch of fat to be seen.

"In case you forgot." I try to make myself taller, suck in my stomach, lengthen my neck.

Buck may have called me, but I do need this to work, and somehow I think she knows it. Not *why* I do, but that doesn't matter, because she only cares that there is something I need from them now, again, which means for the first time since I left, they once again have power over me.

"Buck called." She lifts both her brows. "You came."

She leaves, letting the powder room door hang open to reveal the kitchen beyond. They've finished cleaning up. The kids have all abandoned the room and the puzzle they were putting together before I came in here. I step out into the alcove that connects this bathroom to the kitchen and leads into the small hallway to the dining room. The hallway feels like the option that leaves me least exposed and therefore most likely to be able to assess before emerging.

When I come out into the dining room, I can already hear that the groups have divided up along gender lines. Upstairs, there's the faint sound of pool balls hitting together and my brothers talking trash to one another. From the den, I hear the women discussing the Peach Festival, Julep talking over Clarabelle about the outfit she's planned for the annual picking party that kicks off the festival every year.

I'm hit by a wave of memory. Lucchese boots in a soft camel brown. Baskets of peaches. Gingham blouse, blue jean shorts. Sweat pooling between my breasts, along my waistband, under my sunglasses where the plastic pressed down on the skin. The picking party at Powers Ranch is a Friendship tradition dating back over twenty years. Families from town sign up for a chance to pick the peaches from my family's orchard, and in return, Olympia and Big Earl donate the harvest to the church. It's all very generous and wholesome, peak small-town charm, and too bad it's a lie. The whole fucking place and everyone in it, lying to themselves about who and what they really are.

"There you are," Tate says, startling me from behind.

I whirl, backing up a few steps, eyes on him. I take in his changes, of which there aren't many.

He has the same strawberry blond hair, thick, combed to one side and back off of his face, showcasing his sloping forehead, his eyebrows dark blond but thick, his slightly hooded striking eyes, with long blond lashes. The blue of his irises is cold, cutting, and captivating–almost vampiric in how they capture you in their gaze. He's got a nice jaw, strong but not square, enviable lips, a big smile, straight teeth. He's tall, he's broad-shouldered, he's got good hands, strong arms that are well defined–definitely still works out. Unlike the photo in Olympia's office, he's not dressed formally tonight; no three-piece suit, no tie. He's wearing jeans, a light gray button-down with the sleeves rolled up, a pair of sneakers–Nikes. He's got an expensive wristwatch and he's wearing a wedding ring.

He fingers it with his thumb. "Just married. Her name's Delilah, but she's not leading me astray like her biblical namesake. If anything, she's been the helper I needed as I find my footing now that I've taken over for Dad."

His dad, John Turner, was pastor at Fellowship Kind. He'd been grooming his son to take over since well before Tate and I ever got together. But Tate and I getting together–well, that was all part of God's plan to marry the two finest families in Friendship. Even if I could have never been the perfect pastor's wife, and everybody who actually knew me, had ever spent any time with me, knew that much. It didn't stop Earl and Pastor Turner from conspiring.

It didn't stop Tate from buying into the idea that we were on God's path together, believing I would just take whatever he threw at me no matter how horrible it got because it was the will of our Lord and our earthly fathers, buying into the idea that I was his property to do as he pleased with.

"Did someone warn Delilah about you, at least?" It almost sounds like good-natured ribbing. He knows that it's not.

"I had hoped that you and I would get a chance to talk, so this is good." His tone is congenial and steady. "God always provides."

God always provides. The thought is derogatory.

"I was just about to leave. It's been a long day, and I'd like to settle in at my hotel."

"I'm surprised you're not staying here at the ranch." How could he be surprised? He's not dumb, just a dick.

"Look, I don't know what they told you, but this isn't that kind of family reunion."

"They didn't tell me anything, Haven. I couldn't believe it when Mom said she saw you"–his eyes trek over my face–"but you're here. She wasn't making it up. You're really here." The sweetness in his voice makes me sick.

"Flesh and blood."

His eyes trail over me, and for a split second he looks like he wants to reach out and touch me. "Yes," he says, looking a little lost. He snaps his gaze back to me a second later. "Yes, and, well, this is an opportunity to put things right."

"Excuse me?" I can't help the way my voice cracks, but at least it doesn't wobble.

"I hate the way things ended between us. It wasn't right–godly."

"Stop," I say, but my voice is too small to hear.

He takes a step toward me, hand out.

"Don't." This time it comes out louder.

"Haven, if you'd come with me outside where we can . . . have some privacy."

"I don't want to go anywhere with you." My voice rises in volume. I don't even mean to do it; it just comes out loud and high, and rippling with electricity.

"Can you please lower your voice? The ladies are talking." He shuffles forward, hand out again, about to touch me.

I take a wide step back, and tighten my hands into fists. *Fight* rears up, ready to strike. "Get back." Now rage threatens, but I can't let it, I have to stop it.

The "ladies" have gone quiet.

"Haven," he says, his voice like a gentle shepherd trying to placate a sheep, "please."

"I'm sorry," I say, swallowing the previous volume back to normal. Swallow, quench, get the fuck out of here. "But I have to go." I sidestep him toward the front door and open it with a quick yank.

My family appears as if summoned. They've been waiting in the wings, it seems.

Olympia, Clarabelle, and Julep are in the doorway to the den. Olympia's face is fixed in a disapproving scowl. Clarabelle and Julep wear differing expressions of thinly veiled pleasure, with only Clarabelle's shaded slightly by concern. At the top of the stairs, Lucky, Sterling, and Buck appear holding pool sticks. Earl is nowhere to be seen. I guess he doesn't care enough to come say goodbye. Or maybe he's just in the middle of downing another tumbler full of that whiskey Tate delivered to him when he arrived, shitting all over Sterling's sobriety.

My eyes catch on Lucky. He looks concerned, at least.

"I'm going to head out," I call up to them. "I'm staying at the hotel in town."

"That's nice. Newly renovated," Buck says.

"Yeah, it looked good online," I reply. Gag me with all this pleasantness.

"Call me tomorrow, we can hang," Lucky says.

I don't nod, but I hope my eyes convey that I want to.

After another strained, overly long pause where no one says anything and Tate still stands way too close to ever be comfortable, I finally say, "Tell Dad"—the name is bitter on my tongue, but I know that using it, or not using it, would be noticed more than I want—"I said goodbye."

16

FRIENDSHIP AFTER DARK has a totally different quality to it. I'm grateful for how it cloaks the scenery.

The roads back into town aren't well lit, just the headlights from my rental car glowing in a curved beam. Every few feet, a broken yellow line swipes past on the asphalt. When I reach town, I have to pass around the square again to get to the road that takes me to my hotel. The square is lively, restaurants doing late-dinner service, a sports bar with all the windows open, sounds of some game filtering into the night. The courthouse lighting is ominous, hitting at sharp angles up the side of the building that make the windows look like shadowed eyes and the door like a mouth nearly disappearing from view.

I take the turn that leads away from the town square, past an auto body shop and a small bakery and a print store. There's a twenty-four-hour diner called the Corral where I used to go all the time to eat late-night meals during finals, and we went after parties because it was the only place open in Friendship at three a.m. The Corral was owned by a busty gray-headed lady named Bess, who liked to work the night shift because night critters (her customers) were more interesting than their daytime counterparts.

She was old when I was young. I wonder for a second if she's still living.

Just past the diner is the sign for my hotel lit up on the edge of the parking lot.

The lot is fuller than I expected, even with the Peach Festival happening this week. Sure, it's a big local thing, which includes surrounding towns and probably some visitors from Dallas–Fort Worth who might book up rooms for it, but I don't remember there being a major influx of out-of-towners in the past. With grape festivals and water parks and antique flea markets within a hundred miles, it's not like the Friendship Peach Festival is uniquely positioned to draw outside crowds.

It's no State Fair of Texas.

I park in one of the vacant spots near the main entrance to the lobby, climb out, pop the trunk of my car, and yank my suitcase out. I packed for a long weekend. I can't imagine I'll need more time than that. Not that I'm planning to go back to Second City after this. Not with what happened to Roger.

The sliding doors split to let me inside, and I am immediately hit by a frigid blast of AC and the thrumming beat of some country-western crooner playing low over the sound system. Across the lobby, there is a bar/restaurant, which is closed even though it's only nine p.m. At the front desk, I spot a man with a perve stash and a rattail dressed in a gray uniform and wearing a name badge that says, "Marshal, General Manager."

"Welcome to the Friendship Inn. Is this your first time staying with us?" He delivers the whole line in a single breath, no pauses. He looks about my age, but I don't recognize him. That doesn't mean anything though.

"First time," I say, and I won't offer more. I hand him my driver's license and credit card, thankful again that I changed my last name. He grins and moves the mouse around to wake up his computer.

"We have a continental breakfast in the lobby starting at seven a.m., and the pool and fitness center are open until ten," Marshal says. "One key or two?"

"Just one. Just me in the room."

He flashes me a smile. "If anything changes, we can always make you some new keys." Nothing is changing. I don't return the smile he's offering. I'm no fun, he realizes, then turns his lips to a straight line. He lifts the cardboard key holder up and places it on the counter between us. "You're in room 432."

"Great, a high floor," I reply. It's not enough to turn this now awkward exchange into something more comfortable.

"Sure," he says, looking ready to be done with me. "Ice machine on that floor. View of the greenbelt that runs behind the property. Walking trails right outside your door."

Walking trails. In the dead heat of summer. In Texas. *Right.*

I take the key, my credit card, and my driver's license.

"Enjoy your stay."

I won't. "Sure."

I'VE BEEN TOSSING around in this bed for over an hour.

I'm nervous to fall asleep, but I'm so exhausted that I know I need sleep. It doesn't feel safe to take melatonin or sleep aids right now. Being here is messing with my whole self. My nervous system is dysregulated more than usual, which means I've gone from freezing cold when I got out of the shower to melting away like ice cream on a hot day while I moved around the hotel room getting ready for bed. I'm out from under all these crisp white linens in nothing but undies and an oversized T-shirt, and there's no way I can fall asleep like this.

I never could sleep uncovered, not even just a foot or an arm. As a kid, it was monsters. The blanket a force field to keep them away. I would cover my whole body, head and all, no matter how hot it made me.

Over time, the phobia warped, turning the monster under the bed into something much more menacing.

Poisoning.

Countless nights of rest stolen. I can't remember where the fear came from, but the reason isn't needed for the fear to remain. Even now, even stale and dried out, recalling it sends adrenaline to my palms, already clammy and clutching the cold sheets.

The first wave of this fixation manifested in an irrational fear of a needle in my arm while I slept. As if the prick wouldn't be enough to wake me. If my whole body was under the blankets, then I would be safe. I would burrow down in bed and grip the blanket so there were no gaps, no air flow. I would fall asleep slowly, eyes drooping with resistance until, finally, exhaustion captured me.

I woke in fits, limbs exposed and needle free. I buried myself back.

Eventually, it escalated to a fear of sleeping open-mouthed. My mind conjured a dark figure slinking in through the window in my bedroom. I got the idea to cover my lips with mouth tape I stole from Gentry's General Store.

A different paranoia led to the crime.

Gentry would tell Olympia about the purchase, it being odd, out of place for a Powers, and it would open up a can of worms she'd spill all over the table, torment until they stopped wriggling. Phobias weren't something Christian folk dealt with. Neither was anxiety, depression, or any other mental health concerns commonly discussed in liberal media.

They weren't something Powers folk dealt with.

I remember the worst of this phobia hitting when I was sixteen, right before I started dating Tate. I had progressed to obsessively guarding my drink glasses, never leaving one unattended, even in an unoccupied room. I would empty the glass if I messed up, wash it out for fear of residue. I wasted a lot of water that year.

In my mind, there was no specific culprit imagined. Just a phantom I never saw who could have been in any room I ever left, hiding beneath a bed, tucked into a dark corner of the closet. I wonder now if it was the nightmare already fucking around with me.

I bolt up in the bed. Now I definitely won't fall asleep.

It's almost eleven p.m. There's at least one place that's guaranteed to still be open.

17

THE CORRAL WAS a mainstay of my youth.

My parents weren't fans, which made it more appealing to me, but that wasn't the only reason. The Corral served breakfast all day, and there was a key to use the bathroom, which felt safer somehow when you were there at three a.m. During finals, my study groups would pile around one of the big wooden tables, order up plates of tater tots and sodas on unlimited refill, and hunker down for long hauls about everything from the Revolutionary War to the life cycle of a cell. It was a spot of normalcy in an otherwise not so normal youth.

I set out for the diner, dragging my hair up into a butterfly clip to get it off my neck. Even this late, the air sizzles with humidity. Steam rises from the concrete walk. When I reach the main entrance, the door flies open as patrons exit the building, sending the scent of the South out into the air all around me, dragging me in through the door before it closes. The Corral isn't a typical Americana-vibe diner. It's not like what you see in movies on the roadside: red-and-white booths and linoleum tiles and waitresses in colorful dresses.

Bess, the owner, took her design cues from her love of barns and the vintage Southwest. Oak wood paneling lines the walls. There are wooden booths with orange leather seats, assorted wooden tables with mismatched chairs. The bar looks more like an actual bar, with a well-worn wooden top and the same orange leather upholstering on the barstools, a full liquor rack on display behind it, and overhead a longhorn skull, horns spreading out wide.

The hostess station is also wooden. And right now, it's empty.

For this late on a random weekday evening, the place is actually still hopping. I wasn't even sure if I'd be able to get a table or if I really need one. There's a sign on the hostess station that reads PLEASE WAIT TO BE SEATED, and then attached to that a Post-it that reads OPEN SEATING AT BAR.

I grab a menu from the shelf on the side of the station and make my way toward the bar.

My eyes travel as I walk, not explicitly looking for anyone I know, just more hoping that if anyone I know from the past is here, they aren't awful or will leave me in peace.

"Haven?" A voice comes in from somewhere out of my immediate line of sight. A woman's voice. Rich, throaty, with a depth and texture that is practically decadent. I turn toward the sound, and my eyes eat up the sight.

Winter Reyes.

She's changed since high school.

The only thing in Friendship so far that has.

Her thick dark brown hair she used to wear chopped off in a bob with severe baby doll bangs has grown out, the cut a lot more polished. Gone are the flare jeans slung low on her hips and the crop tops, and in their place are expensive-looking dark-washed jeans and a tailored shirt with white pearl buttons. She looks well taken care of in every sense.

"Winter." One word, just a name, but it feels like rebellion to say out loud.

I never expected to see her again.

"I can't believe you're back here," she says, edging closer. She's got a beer in hand. Light from behind me at the bar shimmers in her golden-brown eyes.

"I can't either," I say, mustering every ounce of cool inside to douse the embers in my belly.

"After years and years." Her eyes trail to my empty hands. "Did you come here for food or just a drink?" And then she smiles, big and open. "Remember when all the study groups would gather here for exams?"

My lips tug up. "The Corral was the place to be."

"Celia says it still is, as of last year. She's a freshman at Baylor now," she says, looking over her shoulder to where a group sits in one of the bigger booths, watching her with interest. A couple guys who look related to her, one of them her younger brother, Matteo, and her sister, Celia.

"Don't you need to get back to them?" I point with my chin toward the group, who realize they've been spotted and quickly return to chattering among themselves.

"I see those idiots all the time," she replies, reaching a hand out, she presses on my shoulder, touching my clammy skin where it shows around my white tank top. She smells of citrus and fresh cream, sandalwood and cocoa, like summer and s'mores and milkshakes and walks through the forest.

We sidle up to the bar and slip onto two of the stools.

"So, food or a drink?" she asks again. I hadn't actually decided. Wine would probably chill me out a little, might help me sleep, but I don't want to loosen up so much that my resistance completely drops. Not sure if the box would take the opportunity and run with it, but I can't risk it.

"Coffee," I reply.

"Hardcore for almost midnight." She grins. There's a small gap between her two front teeth.

"It's been a long day," I say.

"I bet," she says, lifting her beer up to her lips. Her tooth taps the glass as she closes her lips around the rim.

"You ready to order?" a voice says, pulling my focus. A waitress behind the bar.

"Uh, yeah, I think so." My cheeks flush. "Coffee, tater tots–"

Winter smacks her hand on the counter. "The snack choice of our youth," she says. She wasn't in my study groups, but everyone ordered the same thing for cram sessions.

I grin, can't help it. "And a water." It's overly warm in here all of a sudden.

The waitress nods before ripping the order paper from her pad and confiscating my menu. My eyes trail back to Winter. I don't know what to do, but my lips tug up into a nervous smile.

She returns the expression, only there is nothing nervous about hers. "You were explaining your return."

"I wasn't," I say, furrowing my brow. "You're hallucinating."

She chuckles. "I would like you to"–the husk in her voice brightens into something almost playful–"since I come back a couple times a year to visit my parents, and everyone around here acts like you went to be with Jesus." Bold statement said without a hint of concern.

"Except there's no way he'd hang out with me." I raise my left brow.

"His loss," she says.

"My parents would agree. Getting me back in the fold would be a real win for the Lord."

The waitress is back, setting a tall glass of ice water on the counter and then a short beige mug beside it. She fills it with dark steaming coffee. "Tots'll be out shortly."

I grab for the water first.

"Don't make me ask again," Winter says as soon as I swallow.

I close both hands around the hot coffee mug and tug it toward me. "Big Earl is sick," I say, which gets the exact expected reaction. Pity eyes and then shame.

"Fuck, I shouldn't have pressed you, should I?" She takes a drink to wash down the guilt eating its way up her throat.

"No, it's fine," I say. "I haven't spoken to him in nine years. It's not like we're close."

"But you came back because he's sick." She holds me with her eyes. It's uncomfortable because it's not. There's something about the way she looks at me that makes me happy to be in her sights.

"I guess I wanted to use my vacation days this summer to make amends in case he bites it," I say, a white lie I'm okay with telling. Winter doesn't need to know that I don't believe reconciliation is possible or that the reason I'm here has nothing to do with doing the right thing. Or, I guess it does, technically, if you count preventing another accidental murder the right thing. "But that's boring stuff." I really don't want to waste time talking about Earl, the family, or my sudden return when Winter Reyes is right here. No Tate to get in the way. No Tate, but not nothing. There are other reasons to keep my distance. I know there are. There's never a time I don't know that. I swallow the thought, determined to not make this weird. "Last time I saw you was that party at Noah Fielder's." I ignore the way my mind tries to run back to that bathroom again.

"Fielder, that's right," she says. She tosses another gap-toothy grin my way. "I was supposed to be on a bus the next morning to Austin to intern with a human rights attorney for the summer, and I got extremely high on shrooms."

"Everyone did," I say. "None of us can remember that party." I wish that were the truth.

"You and Tate hid out in the bathroom. I remember that, because he yelled at us to 'go use the fucking downstairs toilet.'" She pauses, eyes tracking over my face. I think she's looking for some sign in my expression. Some clue that can unravel the mystery of Tate Turner and me.

I keep my focus square on her face, force my expression docile.

She doesn't know what happened between us at the party, though she may have heard rumors about what went down after. It made the rounds in town, even with Earl and Pastor Turner trying to squash it.

"I did *not* handle my high well." I tell myself that I'm not protecting him but her. She deserves better than for me to unload about my ex five minutes after reconnecting.

"That's fair," she replies, taking another sip of her beer but not taking her eyes off me. "I vaguely recall walking to Taco Casa barefoot and ordering a dozen super tacos with extra hot sauce."

I laugh. "Damn, Taco Casa. There's a blast from the past."

"I don't know what you mean, we have three in a ten-mile radius. Just had it last week."

"But you made it on the bus," I carry on. "The next day."

"Right on time," she says. "Spent the summer interning, four years at UT, three years at Harvard, going on my third year working with the ACLU of Texas."

It's impressive and admirable at the same time.

"You really did everything you set out to," I say, trying not to sound too awestruck.

"Hardly." She shakes off the compliment, sets down the glass. "My parents would have much rather I take a job at some fancy firm, marry some rich guy, and then, when enough time had passed, gotten pregnant and left the fancy law firm to move to the burbs and be a mom." She makes a hissing sound through her teeth. "I am doing good work, hard work—work that saves lives and rights, but it's not good enough because it doesn't look like them."

Them. Women of Friendship. Principled women like in that photo in Olympia's office.

The kind who married my brothers. The kind my parents wanted me to be.

"I can't believe you don't want that," I say, with a smirk to match the sarcasm in my tone. "They all seem so fucking happy."

She laughs in a burst, firework bright. "You didn't cave in the end either," she says, leaning forward on her barstool so she's closer. There is conspiracy in her tone. "I always hoped you wouldn't."

Something intangible swells between us. Dangerous and dreamy in the same ragged breath.

The waitress drops my order of tots on the bar, the rattle of the plate yanking me back into myself. I look up, catch the cut of the waitress's eyes back and forth between Winter and me, clear judgment written in the expression.

"Can I get some ranch please?" Anger threatens, warming my ears, its flames lapping at my throat.

She moves off without a word.

"Do my eyes deceive me?" The voice comes from behind, warm and kind.

I twist around to find the only other face in Friendship that I'd ever actually like to see.

MATILDA MORRIS MOVED here with her husband, James, a chiropractor, when she was fresh out of college with her teaching degree. She joined the ranks of Friendship High teachers, spent years and years molding young minds for their future. Her kindness was notable, her tolerance saintlike, but it was her willingness to be weird and unapologetically progressively minded that made her a standout educator in a place where every child runs the risk of graduating terribly misinformed.

But my respect for Mrs. Morris isn't impersonal; it wasn't cultivated from a distance. She was my English teacher for both freshman and senior year. She witnessed my slow shriveling and she didn't stay silent. There were small things, easy not to notice and probably done that way on purpose since I was who I was. She suggested an academic summer camp to my parents instead of the youth group retreat I was normally forced onto. She always wrote *Excellent!* in red on every single one of my essays. She asked me to join book club and made sure I knew I didn't have to tell my parents what I was reading. There were a lot of small acts, regular check-ins. There was a letter of recommendation for college, there was asking if I was okay and knowing I was lying, but not forcing me to talk when I wasn't ready.

Her kindness was like air to someone as suffocated as me.

She's taken the barstool on the other side of me and ordered herself a wine. She's wearing a set of worn-looking overalls, black hair laced through with gray and braided.

"Mrs. Morris, it's so good to see you," Winter says. I swallow a not fully chewed up piece of tot and offer my own greeting.

"Matilda, please," she insists. "I haven't been your teacher in years." She smiles.

My lips tug up, an auto response to her expression. "Did you retire from teaching?" I ask, draining the last of my coffee. She sits back in her chair and sighs.

"Not so much retired," she says. "I left after an incident over a book I'd assigned for summer reading."

"Incident?" I say just as Winter exclaims, "You mean the pearl clutchers drove you out?"

Matilda's smile drops. She shrugs. "I've stayed here all these years. I'm never surprised by what it's like." When we don't immediately recant our affront, she adds, "You don't need to worry about me."

Winter is opening her mouth to protest when she stops. Her eyes slip over Matilda's head, and her brows cinch together. A scowl flattens her lips. "My family wants to go," she says, looking back at us. She's annoyed, and I won't assume it has anything to do with me. "Dad is having us come in early to the bowling alley to help him clean balls and polish shoes before the festival this weekend. It's on the pub crawl, so it's gonna be packed."

"I'm sure Earl will be there," I say. Any excuse to gamble makes a place my dad's favorite spot. Plus, he invested in it years ago, which means he probably feels some level of ownership—whether warranted or not. (Probably not.)

"It's good of you to help him out," Matilda says.

"It's obligation." Winter looks conflicted. She stands, pulls out her wallet from her back pocket, and opens it. "I'll see you." She says this looking straight at me before shifting her attention over to Matilda. She hands her a business card. "If you ever wanna talk about how they fucked you over."

"It's years-old news, but thank you." Matilda closes her hand over the card.

"See you around."

I follow Winter with my eyes. I really shouldn't be hoping to see her around. When my eyes trail back to Matilda's, there's a hint of mischief in hers. I brush past it. "If you're not teaching then what do you do now?"

"I finished my masters in horticulture after James passed—"

"I'm so sorry," I interrupt. She offers a sad smile.

"It's been a few years." She doesn't want to talk about it. "Gardening gave me a second wind. I consult with some landscaping companies, work at the nursery some weekdays. And I offer gardening workshops through the church." I scowl openly, which gets a chuckle. "I know, I know, but there's not a community center here. Everything runs through the church."

"That's how they get you," I say, and I only have the confidence to express it so openly because I know Matilda isn't a churchgoer. "Community and purpose."

"No one's trying to get me, Haven." Her voice is airy, almost poignant.

"I'm surprised they let you in, considering the way you left the school."

"It shouldn't surprise you that the–'pearl clutchers'?–aren't as principled as they like to appear. Not when money is involved, anyway. My classes sell out every time, and it's required that I donate ten percent to the church, regardless of whether I'm a member or not." She gives a tiny smile at this, and I don't fight the urge to return it even if I'm still a little leery on her behalf.

"Then, I guess, good for you?"

She laughs again. "It's something to keep me busy. But what about you?"

"What about me?" I ask, hackles raising as a reflex. Talking about my life isn't exactly the safest of topics.

"It's been a hot minute since anyone has seen your face."

"Yeah, yeah. I'm practically 'the circus came to town,' right?"

"'Course we all wanna buy a ticket to the show." I can't tell if she's trying to push my buttons, but I do remember this version of her when she was my teacher. Acutely aware of subtext, intuitive about needs, and never one to back down when she saw an opening to try to help.

Thing is, I'm not a student of hers anymore, I didn't ask for her help, and I don't want to drag her–or anyone–into this mess of mine.

"Earl is sick. I came back to try to smooth things over. It's as simple as that. No show to see, I'm afraid."

She watches me for a few seconds that feel overly long.

I need to get away from the scrutiny. "I better be going." I rummage around in my pocket to grab some cash that should cover my coffee, the tots, and a tip. I drop it on the bar top and shove myself off the stool.

She follows the move. Her hand reaches out, cups my shoulder, her eyes capturing me in their warmth. "If you find you need someone to talk to . . ." She raises two dark brows, and I notice a few wiry grays woven with the black. "I still live in the same place. And I always need help in the garden."

It's too generous an invitation.

"If I have time." I tug out of her hold, but then my stomach twists. I *am* grateful. "It's good to see you." And it really is, I mean it.

"You too."

I make my escape like the liar and criminal that I know I am.

18

I SHOVE THROUGH the door out into the hot night air. My skin is abuzz, my mind filled with ants.

I need to move.

I use a crosswalk to get over to a residential street that backs up to downtown. Well-established yards with big oak trees, some watering their grass in the dark to beat the heat, others with porch lights shining over "This house prays" signs and worn welcome mats. There are a lot of little neighborhoods like this in Friendship, growing denser the farther you get from downtown. They surround public schools and parks, and of course, not too far away from here, Fellowship Kind church sits at the center of a big parking lot with a brightly lit sign telling all to come in and be forgiven.

My feet carry me, and I don't think too hard about where they are going. Friendship is the kind of town where not too much happens. No one locks their doors, no one has Ring cameras, and no one expects the worst because they know their neighbors and they all have guns. It's a fallacy, of course, but don't try to convince them of that.

My mind drifts as my blood pumps away the feeling of nostalgia that threatened to take me in while I was inside the Corral.

Okay. Focus. Walk. Think.

It's clear to me that the power in the box could help me dig around for the truth. It's just that I've never tried to traipse around in someone's head on purpose, so I'm not sure how to do it. When I attacked Roger in the parking lot, I wasn't asleep. When the thing happened in Baton Rouge with my neighbor, I was nowhere near her. I walked outside in the middle of the day to find my landlord rushing her to the urgent care for stitches.

This thing isn't new. Every time I've left a town behind, there was some reason or another tied to the box and some nightmare. Moments piled up all around me, but I couldn't recall them. Running hasn't worked to keep the nightmare from turning full killer.

So maybe I stop running from it.

I made it. I can control it if I try.

The thought clears my brain of its fog, and my sight sharpens with the new clarity.

I stop in my tracks. This isn't some residential neighborhood I've never been in. This is the Turners' neighborhood, and somehow I think I've been tricked into coming here. My body keeps a record, and while I was distracted, it walked me right into the lion's den.

At the end of this cul-de-sac, behind a white iron fence, stands the Turners' house: Creamy Austin stone. A tin roof. Two stories. Understated but expensive.

Prosperity gospel certainly found them.

I spent countless hours behind that fence: On the back porch sipping Sonic Diet Cherry Limeade Slushes, watching Tate and his friends do cannonballs into the pool. In his bedroom with the door open, playing board games and sneaking kisses. In his car in the driveway, getting yelled at for some thing or another before walking inside to play nice with his parents.

Mom told me you came home to Friendship.

Charity Turner knows better than anyone that my breakup

with Tate came with some choice expletive-filled terms and conditions, one of them being my desire to gouge out my eyes rather than ever see his face again in this lifetime. She didn't forget. She sent him to the ranch in spite of it. I know it in my bones.

And it pisses me off that she's getting away with it.

THIS MIND HAS *a locked cage door. The way in, the way out.*

Thin slats up and down, up and down, a small latch that gives the illusion of captivity but doesn't hold anything in.

A birdcage door. For a canary without a thought in her head.

She lifts the latch, steps right through.

Inside is the rest of the cage. The curves more defined than outside. The bars rise up up up until they disappear; they line the space all around in a circle.

A rope toy hangs from the top of the cage out of sight.

A swing made of wood dangles too, and a hammock, a row of ribbons tied up in tight little knots.

In the center there is a mirror.

In front of the mirror sits a woman.

She watches herself in the mirror, eyes fixed on her own face, her lips moving in rapid motion. Her mouth opens, her laugh echoes across the empty expanse.

She, the one who doesn't belong here, walks toward the scene.

Spots herself in the glass. Her face contorted with rage.

Her form, she notices, isn't solely her own. It rises high above her shoulders; it wriggles out in pillars of smoke around her body.

This catches her and she stops to watch herself. She feels bigger than her own body, she feels power in the stance, and she remembers how this woman talking to herself in the mirror has tried to make her feel small.

This woman doesn't notice her. She's too busy with her own reflection. Jabbering away at herself, her one constant companion. She is enamored. She is vain. She is a lie told to all the other women in this town.

This is who they want to become, and she is nothing more than a bird in a cage.

The smoke moves.

It scuttles across the newspaper-covered floor until it surrounds the bird woman. She follows slowly, watching the smoke as it tests the space around the bird woman's body.

It loops around her hands.

Rises up to get lost in the strands of her strawberry blond hair.

Drifts into her ear canals, runs through the paths of her mind.

Gathers at her feet.

Curls around her neck like a noose.

The bird woman pays no attention to any of this though. She chatters and preens–a lovebird who loves only herself.

The she who doesn't belong here, her blood boils up.

Hot, viscous, and hate-filled.

Her eyes clamp onto the smoke tying up the neck of the bird woman.

Smoke turns to rope.

Rope tightens taut, taut enough to deliver tension.

The bird woman swallows.

Tighten.

The skin screams as the rope burns the delicate flesh with its threads.

The bird woman's lips drop open. Her eyes latch onto the her in the mirror.

All at once, she reaches for the rope.

Wraps fists around the frayed end until her knuckles turn white.

She yanks. The bird woman lifts from her spot in front of the mirror.

Her body rigid, her arms stiff at her side.

She drags the bird woman's body off its perch and throws her face-first into the mirror.

Glass shatters. Shards drop to the ground all around her.

Again. It's a hungry, delicious, and decadent thought.

The bird woman reaches hands out to stop her.

Smashes her palms into sharp shards of broken glass.

Again, again, again–

A sinister smile spreads over the other woman's face.

The bird woman lets out a scream, like Caw, *like* Help.

But she has never helped. She has never heard a cry and come running.

So she lets her suffer.

Her face turned to hamburger meat.

Her blood all over the floor.

19

I WAKE IN a hallway barefoot and panting.

I recognize it as a hallway because of how it yawns out in front of me, light beige painted walls and door after door after door is all I see at first. My vision is slow to sharpen, still gripped in the blur of the nightmare.

It was a nightmare and I can remember it all.

I am soaked in sweat, wearing only my tank top and underwear.

My hands find the fabric.

A birdcage.

The image flashes back in front of my eyes.

A mirror. A woman. Blood everywhere–

Fuck, fuck, no.

Not just a woman. Charity Turner.

I don't know if there is a literal translation to the dream, as with Roger, or if it's going to play out more subtly somehow. But right now, I have another, arguably more immediate, problem.

I am standing half naked in the middle of this hallway. I look over to the door closest to me. Room 411. Great, so I am at least still on my floor, and at least I didn't get on the elevator, where they might catch me on camera.

Cameras. The thought hits my gut like a punch. I am almost thrown back by the impact.

I look up to where the wall meets the ceiling, scan all the way down as far as I can see and then back the other way. There's no sign of cameras on this floor, which isn't great for security reasons, but lucky me, at least.

I run back to the door to my room, knowing already what I will probably find when I reach it. Hotel doors are designed to shut fully closed behind you when you leave as a safety precaution.

The door is locked. I don't have the key. Or my wallet with ID.

I look toward the window at the opposite end of this hallway. I can tell it's night still. Dark veils the glass, though it's not deep. A purple haze mixes with the black, telling me we're not as far off from morning as I would like because–*fuck*–I am going to have to go downstairs half naked and try to convince whoever is manning the front desk to make me a room key.

Fuck the box for doing this to me.

Fuck me and the nightmare. That is not what I meant when I thought I should try to use it on purpose.

I close my eyes for a brief moment to gather the courage to move.

I'll take the stairs down and just–housekeeping. There may be a service room I can sneak into and grab a towel to wrap around my waist. I rush over to the stairwell, where there is a fire escape map affixed to the wall, and scan it with my finger. This floor has an ice vestibule and a housekeeping station right next to it. It's back toward the elevator, only instead of a right, I'll take a left.

I don't have time to overthink it or worry I won't be able to get inside.

If anything, the cleaning staff will probably be arriving soon, so if I have to wait around hidden between the ice and soda machine, I can.

Anything to avoid walking downstairs in the current state of undress.

My feet burn against the carpet as I run and turn down the hall. A small gray sign sticks out from the wall that reads ICE. On the other side of the hallway is HOUSEKEEPING SERVICES.

Please. Whatever governs gifts and good luck, please let that door be unlocked. My hand closes around the handle and turns. I exhale audibly when there is no resistance. I don't give myself time to think about who might be behind this door with eyeballs ready to perceive me.

I shove inside. The room is long and narrow with a row of industrial laundry machines at the back, all spinning in varying stages of their clean or dry cycles. Fluorescent bulbs line the ceiling, flickering, the buzz of their electrical current popping in the quiet. There are metal shelves on one side of the room stacked high with supplies. Toilet paper, cleaning solution, paper towels, travel-size shampoos and conditioners and lotions that they leave in the room for guests who forgot stuff at home. And, blessedly, there is a whole shelf of neatly folded sheets, pillowcases, and towels.

I run to the shelf and grab a towel from the top of a stack, careful not to disrupt the rest. I wrap it around my waist and tuck the corner in so it stays up. I'll have to come up with some reason why I am out of my room, dressed in a towel, and keyless. I went to get ice and forgot the key? They may wonder where the ice bucket is, but I can just say that in my panic, I left it behind and came immediately down for help.

I walk back to the door, pleased to pieces this is working out so far when the door swings wide. A young woman dressed in a uniform steps into the room and yawns so wide her eyes have closed. I freeze. Her eyes peel open and immediately land on mine.

"Oh my god!" she yelps, and clutches her chest. "How did you get in here?"

Don't panic. "I was locked out of my room." Her eyes narrow. She needs more. *Think fast.* "Went to grab a soda and got locked out. I'm such an idiot. I *should not* drink. I do dumb shit."

The best lies are the ones with a little truth to them. Something relatable that distracts the person being fed the falsity and makes them feel empathy because they could see themselves in the situation.

When her brows cinch and she smiles pityingly, I know it's worked.

One skill I picked up as a Powers that has yet to fail me.

"I know how that goes," she says, blushing beneath a spray of light brown freckles. "You said you're on this floor?" She lifts what I assume is a master key card and waggles it.

"Yeah," I say, letting out a tiny exhale of relief. "I have my wallet in the room with my ID if you want to check."

"Sure, lead the way," she says.

There is nothing wrong with little white lies. I've told myself this time and again. Every time I moved to a new city, had to start over from scratch, when just saying the basics and trying to keep to myself didn't cut it. When I was interested in someone and wanted connection. When I thought hooking up was worth the uncomfortable feeling of dishonesty and secrecy.

I got good at faking a backstory, trying out a different version of Haven, putting on the skin of a woman without all these bruises. If making myself small and unimportant was too hard, I made myself someone else instead.

It always caught up to me, and eventually I would have to move on. Leave the friends and the carcass of that fake life behind. I got good at not creating much of a footprint, at being forgettable enough that no one was too broken up. Sure, it was all a facade, but it was a facade I could live with.

"Room 432," the maid says as we come to a stop at my door. She lifts her key card, swings the door open, and I run inside.

The room is a mess.

The bedding is discarded haphazardly on the floor. My bra is thrown over the lamp. Other clothing scattered. The bathroom light is on, the door hangs open, my shoes on the ground in the way of it closing. The faucet trickles a slow *drip drip* because I must not have turned it all the way before I flopped into bed.

I don't remember coming back here.

I do remember the nightmare and the reason it happened.

I don't know how long I was in the state I was in. Nightmare time warp–that feeling you get during a dream, like time is sped up or slows down, or years go by, or it's only seconds–is real and I am not immune to it.

I run over to my bag, cut my eyes back to look at her. She's warily taking in the room, probably rethinking her decision to help me. "Let me grab that ID." I reach into my bag, my hands trembling. I clench a fist. *Get yourself under control, goddamn it.* My fingers fumble as they unclip the wallet clasp, slice between my ID and the leather.

I clutch the plastic in hand, ground myself to its solidness against my palm, and walk back to show my face. She looks at the ID. "I'll be just a sec." She steps away to walkie downstairs, I assume, but her voice is muffled, low.

My stomach tightens in a million tiny knots. I look insane, this room is trashed, and by the look of it, the sun is starting to come up, which will only make this scene appear much worse.

She glances at me over her shoulder; her lips twitch from a flat line to a small smile. She drops her hand holding the walkie back to her side and approaches with my ID outstretched.

"All good," she says, still smiling. The wariness hasn't totally evaporated from her expression, but it's mostly fumes left now.

"Great," I say, taking my ID with two shaky fingers. "Don't drink so much!" I give an awkward chuckle.

She shakes her head, leans in. "We've all been there."

I walk her to the door, thank her again, and will myself not to hurl in her hair. When I close the door, hear the click, I drop my forehead against its solid slab.

The coolness is a relief.

It's the only relief I get.

20

UNFORTUNATELY, THE QUESTION of what happened to Charity Turner last night looms like a spotlight over the dark alleyways of my brain as I head into the day. The hot shower didn't do anything to wash away the concern that the memory of that nightmare wasn't just a wish-fulfillment dream, just the exhaustion taking my subconscious hostage and running it off a bridge.

Lost time is never that innocent. Not for me.

Even though I woke up in the technical sense of the word, I don't actually feel rested. With the exception of Roger, I've never left a nightmare vibing and high on life. The anomaly of Roger had to have been the result of my conscience taking a back seat to the sense of justice I gave the man.

I exit the elevator and emerge into the lobby. Yellow sunlight bleeds in through the sliding glass doors, bleaching out the gray-and-navy welcome carpet that covers the tiles on the floor. I walk over to the coffee station, grab a cup from the table, and position it under the dispenser nozzle.

My eyes slide closed as it pours, the throb of hot liquid into the paper cup lulling me. The sandpaper scrape of my lids over eyeballs that are dried out and bloodshot does nothing to comfort me.

It's a flaw in the design of coffee that the caffeine can't be absorbed through inhalation. Too bad I've never been a fan of cocaine. I bet that would do the fucking trick.

Jesus. My lips spread into a grin and I instinctively shut off the nozzle.

My eyes rake open to see filmy dark liquid rimming the edge of the cup, ready to spill over. Careful as a surgeon, I move the cup to the table and fix a plastic lid over the top. A little of the hot liquid sloshes out, but overall, I manage to keep most of it inside. I pull it up so that the cutout where the steam escapes is directly under my nose. I take a deep inhale, savoring the burnt tar and chocolate notes.

I'm used to feeling on the run. It's almost comfortable to me now. Stalked, frayed at the edges, glancing over my shoulder to make sure I'm not being followed. I can do it in my sleep. I snort, suck hot coffee through my teeth, and let it singe my tongue. But the idea of getting caught in Friendship, held in a cell where my family can come visit whenever they want, sends a shot of adrenaline through my stomach. I promised myself I wouldn't be trapped with them ever again.

I can't get caught, so I have to cover my bases. Cover my tracks back in the direction of the Turner family home. It may not yield any immediate answers, but there's no way I can go about the rest of this day without at least trying to unravel the events of last night.

I remember leaving the Corral. I remember walking to burn off the spikes of anxiety that gripped me after seeing Winter and Matilda.

Winter.

Her gap-toothed smile flashes in my head.

I take a gulp of coffee to burn the sensation of yearning away.

IN THE STARK light of day, the Turners' house looks obnoxiously inviting, like the kind of place you'd want to visit. The flowerbeds are full of thriving marigolds and Mexican bush sage and lustrous Penta grasses, the lawn is a hearty green grass that's well maintained and thick. The porch is covered, the swing appointed with brightly colored throw pillows.

No sign of the violence in my nightmare has breached the outer walls.

No cars in the driveway makes me think they aren't home.

This doesn't mean I'm off the hook, but at least I don't see a trail of blood across the smooth concrete drive. At least there's no ambulance or a squad car with spinning lights. I turn down the air conditioner. As my heart rate starts to even out, I don't need it blasting me directly in the face. It's going to be another blazing hot day, but the adrenaline and caffeine fueling my current state has thrown the temp into dangerous territory, and it's not even nine a.m.

I reach for the coffee, lift it to my lips, but it comes up empty. *Fuck.* I need more caffeine, but I also need to cover the rest of my bases. There's another place Charity Turner might be. Maybe nothing horrible happened to her, but I can't believe I'd be so lucky for it to be completely innocuous. Not with how I can still hear her screams puncturing my eardrums, not with all the red that fills my vision when I draw up the nightmare from memory.

The changes to the box since I arrived back in Friendship seem to be seeping into the way I experience the nightmare. I've never remembered before. It's deeply unpleasant, but I guess I sort of asked for it. I wanted to work with the box, but I wanted it on my own terms. I did not want it to go rogue and then bring the remains to my doorstep like a dog with a squirrel carcass in its jaws.

I shift the car into gear.

There's an advantage to driving a nondescript sedan rental with Texas license plates. No one pays attention to your car when it's this boring. Every turn is automatic, the roads a ripple of memory I ride toward a destination I have no choice but to reach. It arrives nonetheless, seconds or minutes later.

There is no nightmare time warp at play here. Just the time warp of a small town.

Fellowship Kind is exactly what you'd expect for a modern church in America.

The building is all straight lines, with big glass windows running along the front and a tall double-door entry. The parking lot spreads out in all directions. The sign at the corner of the lot is fixed with the name in a gaudy, angular font. It's been renovated since the last time I saw it, but it's not a new build from the ground up.

I pull up to the curb at a spot that has cover from the building thanks to the row of manicured hedges, and my eyes scan the lot. There are always people at a church during the day, but if I remember correctly–big *if*–the staff lot is around the back of the building where the same greenbelt that winds behind my hotel sits. It serves as an actual belt through the waist of the town, dividing the main areas, like downtown, the church, the nicest residential neighborhoods, small businesses like the inn and the Corral. On the other side are more neighborhoods–less prestigious ones–a newer strip mall, the middle school and high school, and your basic grocery stores and less aesthetic stores, the kind that don't tell the small-town story Friendship is so hell bent on telling.

Back when I used to be a congregant, John and Charity had designated spots. Tate got one too, which was weird to me since he wasn't officially anything besides the pastor's son at that point. The actual junior pastors and office admin didn't get the same respect.

I won't be able to see if the staff parking has any of the main vehicles from here, which means I'm going to have to actually drive my car onto the lot. It will be less conspicuous than if I walked up from here. The lot is dotted with trees for shade, but it's also mostly empty, which feels exposed. As I pull around and turn into the lot, I drive in the lanes, hoping to not look any weirder. I could be anyone driving up to grab a brochure from the welcome box hanging outside the entrance doors. They keep it stocked year-round, rain, shine, or holiday, because they are always open to new seekers.

It's in this deliberate pursuit up the main row of the parking lot that I notice they've expanded the building on the side. I turn in the direction of the expansion and make a slow crawl around the front. The former recreation center once stood here. A squat building that was left over from the previous owners. It looks like they tore it down, and in its place, they've built a new two-story building more in line with the redesign they did on the main building. They've even given it a snazzy new sign.

THE GATHERING PLACE.

Corny names are like a requirement for these people.

All these improvements are telling: the business of Jesus is thriving in Friendship.

After taking in the building, I finally notice the small red crossover SUV backed up to the front of the community center entrance and see Matilda unloading a bag of potting soil onto the sidewalk behind it.

She's going to spot me.

21

"I NOTICED YOU unloading when I was passing by," I say. Thinking on my feet isn't always my strong suit, but thinking on my feet when it's a lie comes a little more naturally. I slam the driver's side door. "I was on my way to get a better coffee than the stuff in the hotel lobby."

"And you decided to detour here for what?" Matilda asks, yanking her wide-brimmed straw hat from her head to wipe her brow. "Old time's sake?"

"It's changed," I say, and my use of the word rings surprising. "The only building so far that has."

"That's what happens with a flourishing congregation," she says, pressing her hat back on her head. "Got a sec to help an old woman out?"

I shake my head. "Old isn't how I'd describe you." I step up onto the curb and shove my car keys in my back pocket.

"Then you'd describe me wrong. Everything creaks."

I walk around to the open back of her SUV. I'm not being a Good Samaritan here, though I don't mind helping her. She's here at the church and she's a townie; she may know if there's any gossip about Charity, or may have even seen her if she's come up to the church today.

"Grab that pallet of herbs," she says, pointing to a five-by-five plastic carton full of spring-green plants. "We're learning how to make an indoor kitchen garden to beat the heat this afternoon," she says, explaining the supplies. "If you want to join."

"I flew here," I say, bending over and grabbing the pallet. "And I imagine the *we* is your group of Fellowship Kind members, so no thanks."

"It's mostly that," Matilda says, grabbing the other pallet. "But not solely. There are people in Friendship who don't attend the church, ya know, and the classes are open to anyone." She starts walking into the building. "We'll take these to the courtyard and then come back out for the rest of the supplies."

As soon as my foot crosses the threshold, the tiny hairs on my arm stand at attention.

It's not the church, I tell myself. It's just a building with four walls . . . a bunch of which are decorated with overtly Christian decor.

Jesus walks on water in one print, framed and hung on the left side of the hallway.

A rustic wooden cross with pressed metal details hangs on the other.

Farther in, to the left, there's a big community space, open and airy, and over the entryway is a chalkboard sign with a quote from Corinthians.

"It's awful, isn't it?" Matilda says, her voice noticeably lower, like she's afraid God himself will overhear. I want to judge her for teaching her classes out of the church recreation center, but I know that's unfair. Once, way before I met Tate, and Fellowship Kind grew into the space it is today, there was a Catholic church on the other side of the square. I don't know when it closed its doors exactly; I just know that now it's a thrift store and food bank owned and operated by Fellowship Kind.

It's like a fungus eating up the town. It's hard not to get it on your clothes.

At the back of the building, there's a wall of glass sliding doors. One of them stands open. "This place has Charity Turner's fingerprints all over it." I don't know if just mentioning her name will get Matilda to spill if she's heard anything weird about Charity this morning, but it's worth a shot.

We cross through the sliding doors. Matilda's voice is soft. "She's the one who designed it." In the courtyard, there are long wooden tables already set up with other supplies I assume are for Matilda's class. Stacks of different colored pots. Clippers. Hand trowels. "Sorry, you probably hate Fellowship Kind more than anyone."

It's hard to keep secrets in Friendship, but it was especially hard for a Powers and a Turner. What happened between Tate and me made the rounds all through that summer. Or, I should say, the story our parents made up, fed out, made the rounds. There was a lot of misinformation. Whispers that stopped every time I entered a room, stares I felt though never could catch. It's hard to believe Matilda didn't hear some of it, didn't draw conclusions after I skipped town and never came back.

"What's that saying about how you can never go home again?" I ask.

"I wouldn't have pegged you as someone all that interested in nostalgia." She sets her pallet of herbs down on the table.

"Oh, I'm not," I reply, following her lead. My hands come away with bits of damp soil on the palms. I close them quickly to hide the crescent-shaped scratches from yesterday. This is my opening. "But the Turners' house was like a second home, and it *also* looked like a Hobby Lobby threw up all over it."

Matilda snorts. "And you don't miss it?" Her voice is all mock shock.

"I sure as hell don't miss Charity Turner."

"Well, then I guess we can thank whatever higher power we do believe in, because Charity was supposed to meet me here to drop off a key, but she had to cancel."

Heat spreads over my chest. "Did she say why?"

"She didn't." Matilda's expression twitches. She wants to spill, but she's also too good for gossip.

"Glad you were able to get into the building, then." It's a more subtle push.

Now she looks downright ill. It catches me off guard.

"What is it?" I ask, a reflex.

"She sent her only son in her stead," she says.

I stop in my tracks.

She inhales sharply, rushing forward to grab my hand. "He left pretty quick after, didn't stick around. Don't worry."

I'm in the same town as Tate Turner. There's no avoiding worry.

"No, that's good–" I'm nodding a little too emphatically, the rush of adrenaline making me lightheaded.

"I wouldn't have asked you to help if he was still here." Her words have an immediate, surprisingly calming effect.

Our eyes connect. There is a kindness in hers that I haven't seen in anyone else's in such a long time: transparently caring, gentle, absolutely nonabrasive.

Compassion like a shiv, a wound straight to the gut.

"Thanks," I say, the buzz to flee heightening. But I still need more info, and I know I'm close. "I imagine she was pissed she couldn't make it." I somehow manage to smile. I don't know if it totally lands. "If I remember her correctly, she likes to be seen as reliable to a fault."

Matilda nods, moving back toward the front of the building now.

I follow.

"Oh, she sure does. But Tate said she woke up with the most awful headache and a ragged sore throat."

In my mind it appears again—

I draw a noose around her neck.

I smash her face-first into a glass mirror.

"Hope she's not coming down with something," I say. It sounds thin.

Matilda cackles and cuts me a smirk. "I don't," she says, snorting. "A few days without Charity Turner's presence skulking around making judgments is my own personal version of heaven."

She laughs all the way to the doors, and I can't help my own small smile.

In a sick, twisted way, I guess we both owe the nightmare a debt of gratitude.

22

I DROP MY car back at the hotel and walk over to the good coffee shop on the square for a desperately needed cup. I gotta stay moving or I'm going to crash, and driving in a warm car wasn't helping. Now that the adrenaline of uncovering what happened to Charity thanks to the nightmare has dissipated, my limbs have turned to jelly. Grit gathers behind my lids. The tightness like a vice around my head is brutal.

That was too close. A lucky break that what I dreamed about her only manifested in a headache and a sore throat. It's all the more important to me that I figure out how the fuck to use this demented thing my brain can do now.

The town bustles around me as I make my way toward Main Street Coffee. Innocuously named, and owned by a former cop, it's not without its moral issues. But it's not a church business, and therefore it meets my barest minimum requirement today.

I left my phone in the car while I was helping Matilda, and when I got back in, I saw there were some texts from a Friendship number that I don't immediately recognize. I'm pulling it up to see if the caller left a voicemail when I hear an angry car horn from an angry car with a pissed-off driver. I've stopped in the crosswalk.

Jesus Christ, I could take a bath in coffee.

I look up and over to see there is a whole line of cars gathered, all watching me through windshields, others starting to blare their horns.

I wave—*Sorry*—and rush across to the sidewalk. Embarrassment warms my cheeks, or maybe it's just the sun, but my eyes are down and looking away so I don't see him until he's right up on me.

"Haven Powers, as I live and breathe!" Beefy hands close around my shoulders, stopping me dead with their weight. My eyes land on a gaudy belt buckle, then fancy alligator boots clapping the sidewalk. I lift my eyes to meet his gaze. Small and lashless, a murky sort of green-gray, with a face round and red.

Keller Collins. The name swims up from the depths of my mind.

He yanks me in for a hug that immediately makes my skin feel like it's crawling with bugs. Tiny scurrying legs zip-zap over my arms, up through my hairline, across the lids of my eyes, which snap closed.

This man is not a stranger. I know him, though I don't fully remember him or know why he gives me the ick. But the sensation that I never liked him, don't like him now, and don't want his hands on me is a jolt of electricity that wakes me up fast. I push out of his hold, forcing myself steady. He chuckles, uncomfortable at this show of resistance. The kind of man who hugs a grown woman—basically a stranger—on the street and thinks she should take it is the kind of man who does worse when no one is looking.

"You may not remember me," he says, removing the thick hairy-knuckled man hand he just had pressing me into his body and scratching at the nape of his neck. His shirt is collared, short sleeves with pearl buttons. He's wearing a bolo tie. It's got to be over one hundred degrees outside and he's got on a polyester-blend shirt buttoned all the way up with a bolo tie. The lift of his arm reveals a patch of dark sweat beneath his pit.

"I remember," I say. And I do. Memory prods at my mind like a bunch of tiny fingers digging in the squishy soft gray matter, scraping along the ridges of neural pathways. Keller Collins is a friend of Earl's, and I have never, ever felt comfortable around him. A business associate in the sense that I believe he invested some funds in some of Earl's ventures over the years, and this capital got him a seat at our dinner table whenever he wanted, invites to barbecues and pool parties and riding lessons for his daughter at the ranch.

And that's when I see her face. Younger and smaller with a big smile of crooked teeth and dirty-blond hair. Not my age, closer to Lucky's, she came over often to ride Princess–my pretty paint horse with auburn patches. Now she's a bottle blond who got her teeth fixed and flash-whitened. She works for Big Earl at Powers Premier Automotive. Her name is Tabby Collins, and I met her yesterday. Felt some kind of way about her then.

Realizing she's his daughter is making me pity her in a whole other way.

"You and Earl go way back," I add. He grins at me. He's got a silver tooth showing in his smile.

"That we do. I knew Earl before he was Big Earl." Keller is still grinning, but something sinister lurks in his eyes. "I know where all the skeletons are buried."

Sickness swims in my stomach.

The box drops onto the sidewalk behind him. That sooty black seeps from the edges, stark against the bleached-out gray of the sun-drenched sidewalk. A warning bell dings alongside its appearance.

You wanna know why? It's my own voice in my head but somehow more sinister.

A nightmarish pleasure runs through me with a shiver.

I have to get away from Keller Collins before something batshit happens right in the middle of downtown.

"I'm sure that goes both ways," I reply, offering him what I hope would be described as a winning smile and is good enough to distract from my revulsion.

"That's what friends are for." Keller is thick-necked and thick-headed.

"Speaking of Earl," I say, already moving around to the other side of the sidewalk, where I can slink past him by way of the grass in front of the old courthouse, "I have to meet up with my family in a few. Lots of lost time to catch up on."

"I know your daddy is glad to have you home. It was all he talked about this weekend when we went up to the casino in Marietta." The casino right on the border of Oklahoma and Texas. I only know about it because there are full color ads all over the airport. It wasn't open when I was last here, or at least, it wasn't on my radar then. I don't know if Earl was going up there back when I was in high school. "I think it cost him a win at blackjack, but he'd probably say it was worth it."

I show him my teeth in a nonsmile, and it's the first time he's realized that maybe I don't like him all that much. His grin falters, a frown nearly cracking the folds of skin.

"Then I better get going," I say with a wave. I can feel his eyes follow me like hot lasers searing over my skin. The teeny tiny box still sits there, leaking dark sooty something onto the ground around it.

It rattles as I pass by.

I ABANDONED MY quest for coffee after my interaction with Keller. Instead, I stock up on every source of caffeine I can find in the mini market of my hotel lobby.

I get into an uncomfortable spot on the stiff love seat in my hotel room, crack open a Diet Coke, and rip into a dark chocolate bar before taking my phone out of my pocket. There was a missed call from that Friendship number I don't know, and I wonder if it was Lucky trying to get in touch. He didn't leave a voicemail if it was him, but there is a text message from the same number. My phone setting requires me to actually open the text to see the message, so I swipe to open my lock screen, click into my texts, and confirm. It is from Lucky. He must have gone through the trouble to wrangle my number from Buck, which means he had to stoop to ask Buck for help. The realization sends a swift chill from the base of my spine to my neck and down my arms.

It spooks me, but I'm also honored he went to the trouble.

His message runs together.

> Got your number from buck I'm bored as fuck at the ranch since officially the festivities don't start until tomorrow but there's a new Tex Mex spot just outside town where supposedly they also have an old school arcade
>
> wanna go kill some time and get drunk

If I want to try to work with the nightmare, I think I should start by trying to interact with a mind I'm not terrified to enter: Lucky's mind. Of all of my siblings, Lucky is the one I am the least uncertain about. He seems less entrenched, and there was always something about the way he thinks that felt relatable—way more than Buck or Sterling.

This is the perfect chance to get close to him. To see if I can create an opportunity where I can slip through the door of his mind safely.

Gently.

With care and purpose.

With control.

Count me in, I write.

He texts back right away.

> Thank god meet me downstairs at your hotel in ten mins

23

THE FUZZY CACTUS is a family-owned cantina and old-school arcade, with a patio where they have live music on weekends and a mariachi band that walks around all hours of the day serenading guests.

We're a pitcher of margaritas in, sitting on the patio, back in the shadiest spot, where we have a view of the fountain. A young mom and her toddler daughter giggle atop the brightly colored tiles as the girl tosses penny after penny into the water.

Her voice ricochets: "Abracadabra!" The penny *plops*. She seals in her wish.

"Okay, you gotta come straight with me," Lucky's saying, eyes focused on the paper napkin he's folded into a football and is prepping to launch over his sweetener packet field goal.

"Come on, Lucky, you know that isn't the Powers way," I say with a sly grin.

I'm a little buzzed, a little retraumatized, and weak-spirited, but there is something about my little brother that makes me want to let the guardrails come down just a smidge. He stops midway through positioning the paper football, fingertip holding it erect, to look over at me. There's a spark, subdued but still distinguishable, in his deep blue eyes. It ignites the lighter shade near the pupil, making the whole iris seem lighter. He grins back.

"Fair," he says, refocusing on his finger's position against the little paper football. His eyes drop back to it, and he uses the fingernail side of his pointer. It doesn't go through the goal. He groans. "Dang."

"You wanted me to 'come straight'?" I say.

He gets distracted easily, which could be a good thing for me. I hate the idea of breaking into his mind without permission, sure, but it's for the greater good here. I think anyway.

"Oh, right." He picks the paper football up again and positions it to shoot. "What really happened to make you leave town like that?"

That's not at all what I was expecting. Not ideal subject matter either. But I guess I owe him some truth, even if I water it down. It's a way to level the moral gap between going into his mind without permission and lying to his face about everything from why I'm here to how I actually feel about all of this.

"What did Earl and Olympia say happened?" I want to know what level of propaganda I'm up against.

"Blamed you and the liberal media," he replies.

I guffaw. "What the fuck does the liberal media have to do with it?"

"Gave you ideas about what women can do," he says, raising his sandy blond eyebrows. I can't tell if he bought it back then, even if now he's playing like it's totally absurd.

Heat kisses the ridges of my ears. It isn't true, but still, I understand why they would say that, and it stings. Saying the liberal media put ideas in my head serves a twofold agenda: it removes my agency and discredits any outside voice with a different opinion. It's clever in a way that doesn't surprise me. Earl and Olympia are a lot of things, but dumb isn't one of them.

Growing up, they were especially skilled at sending mixed signals about my worth as a daughter, as a girl in the world, as a woman who would one day be the wife of an important pastor. Tie our family to the other great power in the region and expand the good we could all do together. I was never good enough, but I am also a prized possession. I was precious to their hearts and something to repeatedly break apart. I was a girl, which meant I was always a danger unless they could get me to do what they wanted and keep me under control.

Lucky may not buy their story about me now, but that doesn't mean he never did. It also doesn't mean he didn't accept the other lies they would have spewed about me over the years. There is a surge of energy that crackles in warning. The box is near, called in by my anger. I need to calm down, to keep it under wraps.

The nightmare is mine to control. I'll keep telling myself that until I start to believe it's true.

"I told them I wouldn't marry Tate and they couldn't accept that," I say. This isn't the whole truth, which feels way too dangerous to say out loud.

"They said you broke his heart."

"He tried to break me. It wasn't as easy as he thought." I try to come off with a cool, self-contained air, and it feels claustrophobic. "We got into a car accident at the end of the school year. Tate was driving, was drunk, but no one actually believed me when I told them how it played out. They raked me over the coals." It's not the whole story, but I can't imagine that Lucky wants the gory details. And I can't be sure dredging them up from inside the teeny tiny box is something I can even safely do right now.

Or ever.

Everything that happened that night, from the bathroom on, is a dangerous trigger. Tate is the memory that paralleled Roger's assault and activated that murderous nightmare in the parking lot. I can't risk that happening again.

Lucky crushes the paper football in his palm. Anger flashes in his eyes. Unmistakable in its fury. "You should have told me—"

"You were thirteen, what could you do? I told Buck, thought stupidly he'd give a fuck because he was my overprotective big brother even when I didn't need to be protected. But he went the other way, as if what I said about Tate was somehow a threat to problematic, dangerous guys as a whole."

Maybe I hoped they all felt threatened with the callout.

After the spiral in the bathroom when I saw Tate at the ranch, I really don't want to go over the story in my head. The rest of the story is a lot worse than that first part. But that can't stop me from feeling the truth in my bones, body, and soul. The body never forgets.

Lucky looks like he's conflicted over what to say next, so I decide to rescue him from the pressure. I can't have him distressed over my shitty backstory and how he never saw it, even though he was right there with a front-row seat.

I need him chill. I need this *all* to calm down.

"Whatever. Look, I didn't come here to rehash old stories," I say, pushing up from the table. I grin. "I came here to get to know you all now." Not really, but maybe him. "What do you say to losing a game of air hockey to your fucked-up big sister? We can bet on it."

Powers boys love a chance to gamble.

It takes him a weighty beat to shake the pall, but finally he stands, grins a little, though the color of his eyes is still muted.

"I say you better be ready to pay up."

We abandon the table, Lucky's laugh ringing in the air as we go. It's enough for a second to make me regret that I may have come here seeking redemption, hoping to fix this broken thing inside me, but it will mean breaking the trust of someone I want to protect.

It may be the only way, and for his own good, but it doesn't mean I have to like it.

LUCKY IS SACKED out on the sofa in my hotel room.

A little tipsy when we left the arcade, flying high on beating me at three out of five games of air hockey and me winning the jackpot on the Skee-Ball machine and buying him a stuffed pink teddy bear with the tickets. We left after dark, and I asked him if he wanted to go back to the ranch, which got me a growl and a "Please let me crash with you. Just one night, and I'll be out of your hair."

I almost feel bad about how easy it was.

I sit on the edge of the bed, hugging a pillow for support. Just like how Roger had a door, and Charity had a cage, the mind always has an entry point.

Even mine.

On instinct, I know that's where to go first.

I close my eyes, willing my thoughts to settle. I imagine the waves of my brain smoothing out, from jagged peaks and valleys, uneven and rigid, to a more rhythmic flow. A soft curve up and an easy descent. There is a place inside my mind that makes this connection to other people's. It's not just the box and its nightmare that holds the power, it's tethering myself to what has been stored in there and using the rotting, smoldering ooze to trap my target.

But for this, I don't want to use any of that rage. I want to use the power that made the box in the first place. Power I must possess for this to be possible at all. As much as I can, I want to try and leave my trauma out of it.

I see the box as it once was.

I see me as I once was. Blond hair in ringlets. A daisy-print T-shirt.

There is a tree stump in a meadow of tall grass where the newly formed box sits.

The wooden sides are smooth, not weathered as they are now. The lid is carved with a sycamore; the hinges and lock aren't rusted.

There is no slithering figure of darkness, no soot-covered horrible memories.

In this moment, the nightmare knows its job is not to terrify, do harm here that shows up out there. Its job is to help me connect, and on that thought, the image begins to change.

The box shivers and twists, swirling until it liquifies, streaming down like waxy goo until the whole thing melts away.

A door appears in its place.

THE FIRST THING *I notice is that I am in my body and aware of every move, though I don't move at all.*

The next thing I notice is the door.

Painted blue. The frame white.

Written on a plaque hanging in the center are the words LUCKY'S ROOM.

The door handle has a key hanging around it. I remove it, hold it, examine the edges, my finger tracing over them. Small, dark metal, simple. I bend to see that there is a lock on the door that looks about the right size. The key slides easily into it.

I twist and it opens.

The space is cramped. Four walls with a window lit up. There is a twin bed covered in Sonic the Hedgehog *sheets. There is a small wooden desk and shelves of books and posters of* Super Smash Bros. *and a beanbag chair.*

Lucky's childhood room.

I enter it, take stock, and walk over to the window to look out and find that the backdrop is painted. Rolling hills of green. Hay bales dotting the scene. Cows and horses that look like little toy figurines. The sun is a circle with lines for sunbeams spraying out.

A kid's drawing. Something about it unsettles me. The uncanniness of the valley rolling, or the way everything feels a little disproportionate, or the idea that Lucky needed to surround the room of his mind with a child's drawing, a fantasy so far outside reality that anyone who looks at it can immediately tell.

I turn away from the creepy drawing of the ranch and fix my attention on the nightstand, where a lamp fashioned to look like a baseball glove sits. The light switches on. I focus on the framed photo sitting beside it.

The boy in the photo is small and fair and thin–wiry, all arms and legs–with dark circles beneath his eyes. He holds an ice cream cone that drips over his small, grubby hand. He does not smile; the expression on his face dips closer to a frown, uncertainty shadowing his every feature. This is the only photo in the room. Of Lucky or of anyone else.

He has to be around eight, maybe? The baseball cap on his head is from the Little League team he was on for a couple years in a row. I don't know how I know that, since it would have been smack dab in the middle of high school when I was knee-deep in my own fucked-up soap opera.

I wonder what it is that made him choose this photo, this memory captured this way. Why he keeps this room intact, frozen in time, and what that says about him. My finger grazes the glass covering his face and an electric pulse zaps the tip, rips through my arm, and bolts into the center of my head.

My vision blurs as I drop to the floor.

The scene in my head changes fast. Like a movie queuing up, only the images it passes over can't be distinguished, the static on the screen too jagged, the images degraded and discolored.

It stops abruptly, comes into focus slowly.

The little boy sits on the edge of a park bench eating an ice cream cone. He is alone, or so it seems at least. I approach him from behind and feel my lips try to open, to call out. I don't want to scare him or startle him, though that inclination does seem irrational.

My lips won't open; all sound refuses to leak out.

Not even a trickle.

When I am close enough that I can reach out, he looks up. Not at me, he doesn't notice me. He doesn't see me. His eyes fix on the person who drops down beside him.

Our mother. Younger, clad for summer in a soft yellow dress, her tan golden.

"You didn't want to go join the other boys?" she asks, leaning back on the bench beside Lucky.

"They told me not to," Lucky says. He doesn't look too broken up about it. He does have his ice cream after all. It is starting to melt down his hand. "They said I'm not like them."

Her expression softens. She nods and turns to look somewhere off in the distance. I can hear the sounds of boys playing, but the images of it aren't filled in. What is important about this memory is contained right here on this bench.

"You have to try," she finally says. She lifts her arm to rest it over the back of the bench. "It will be too hard if you don't."

A lump forms in my throat, an emotion expands, getting trapped in the narrow canal. I try to swallow it back as I'm dragged away from the paused image of Lucky as his tongue touches the ice cream drip on his hand.

I am in the room of his mind where I lie on the ground. My neck is tilted to the side, my eyes pinned to the closet door that stands slightly ajar. I should go back the way I came. I have learned what I need to know from this, but then . . .

The light in the closet flicks on.

I push up from the ground, and my feet carry me over to pull back the door.

The closet is simple, cedar lined, and full of boxes. They are stacked high, well beyond where the natural ceiling to this room should appear.

"Storage," I whisper. It sounds muffled and strange. My jaw all tight and weird.

I am just about to leave the closet when I notice a faint line in the wall in the back; it's out of place with the rest of the panel lines. I move closer and reach out to touch it when I hear the soft sound of someone crying. A low, wispy whimper.

I try to use my voice again, but again it comes out garbled.

I touch the wall, but I cannot do anything to help whatever–whoever–*is trapped inside.*

24

A RINGING FILLS my ears.

Alarm bells and blood pumping. Adrenaline screeching a warning signal.

I am thrown from Lucky's mind, but it takes my eyesight a while to clear. When it starts to, the popcorn ceiling appears first, the whir of the air conditioner rushes in next, and my knees ache and throb.

From where I lay on the ground, there is a rectangle of white light that is visible. I blink and realize it's the light I left on in the bathroom.

It flickers. A stutter to black, then back on.

Putrid stink fills the air. Rotting organic matter. It reminds me of the garden outside the church a week after Easter when the last unaccounted for eggs begin to spoil.

The box drops beside me.

Hinges jostle.

The light in the bathroom flickers off. I swallow, my head spinning.

My eyes prick with tears against the scent.

My skin has gone icy, and I don't know if it's the temperature in the room rapidly dropping, if I'm imagining it, if I died and am a ghost, my spirit stuck like glue to the carpet in this shitty hotel room, but I do know that I am scared. My body frozen, breathing ragged, like when I used to lay in bed waiting for my poisoner, my monster with no face or name, to come and finally take away my life.

Inside me, there is a crispy sound. Crackling like fried chicken skin. I can't escape it.

My own laughter turned terrible, filtered through a loudspeaker, amplified over the din of my thoughts. I think this is funny, sick fuck that I am. I think my own fear is delicious.

I roll my head to the side. The box is close.

You could touch it. A taunt, but it's just me teasing.

I never have before.

Do it, I dare myself.

Pain hardens my muscles when I move my arm, but I breathe fast through it. I extend my reach with a gasp, sooty black substance turning to smoke when it touches the air, but I don't stop until the pad of my finger touches the hard edge of the box, then sinks into the substance oozing from the sides.

Cold spreads up, up, up, tightening the muscles of my forearm, like ice shards hardening on the side of a gutter, and I begin to seize up.

My hand drops to the ground as my eyes roll back in my head.

I AM BACK *in that meadow from before.*

The box is there but the girl is not.

I look for her, as if she's planning to pop out from the tall, tall grass and surprise me.

As far as I can see, there's rolling land, no defining structures, but it is bigger than it was the last time I was here.

Instinctively I know there is something wrong, off, but I can't place what, and I don't know why, and I'm not sure where, so I begin to walk.

My feet decide to move before my mind. Or maybe it's the other way around, mind ahead of body, body not real at all. As I move, the landscape becomes clearer. Distant trees dance. At first it looks like wind blowing them back and forth, swaying rhythmically, their limbs lifting up toward sky, their trunks yielding to the steady gust.

Except there is no wind. There is no rustle of leaves.

And as I draw closer, I realize that the trees don't actually dance.

They glitch.

A signal broken. A misfire.

The trees become horse stable walls.

The me becomes a little girl.

Then back.

Trees, woman, walk.

Little girl, stable walls.

There is a strong urge to close my eyes, to shut this out. There is pressure on my chest, the panic of the real body woman, the real me who I left lying on the hotel floor in a state of dream paralysis.

This is all in my head.

This is all real.

The stable walls solidify around me. There are jelly sandals on my feet. Tiny hands with painted nails of pink. Heat blooms over my chest as my skin bumps up into gooseflesh.

Because . . .

This is the peanut butter cookie day. This is real. This is a nightmare of memory.

This is the day the box was made.

My body glitches back to its grown-up self.

Like in the nightmare I made for Charity, I sense a presence surrounding me.

Hot and dark, it curls around my body. It comes out of my body.

Black rims beneath my nails.

Soot stains my hands like blood.

It is inside me and all around me, blistering and dirty and bleeding.

Sick swells in my stomach, acid in my throat, and then my body shifts back into the little girl me from before.

Together, we move.

We approach an open stall door where some of the hay has been kicked out from inside. Most likely an animal had done it, one of the horses annoyed with the ranch hand coming to take him out to the pen.

But the way the light around it pulses, dimming and brightening tells me the truth: this is a lie.

This is the distortion work of the box. This is the something.

The something that started it all.

I don't want to see what it is. I know I said that I did, but I don't.

There is no way to know what will happen if I don't.

I am not doing this just for me.

The little girl me has already seen. The thought twists around me, pulling the fear from my grip. I can do this for her. I must do this for her.

We step up to the stall door.

There is no breathing in a dream, no reason to inhale or exhale, no body function needed without a body. Still, I go through the motion, steeling little girl me for the sight.

We push the stall door open, the creaking sound of rusted hinges in need of oil squirms through our ears.

Little girl me does not close her eyes, so neither do I.

Our scream shakes the world off its axis.

I AM RIPPED back to the hotel room, gasping.

My head pounds like the side is a drum someone beats in a steady, obnoxious rhythm.

I close my eyes, press my hand to my crown, will the image to come back to me. I want to pat myself on the back for my bravery in this moment, but I really don't have time for that now. I can feel how the memory already tries to scamper away, even as I grab at its heels and try to drag it back. It squirms in my grip, but I manage to make it succumb.

It was a man's body.

A wound on his head, blood congealed beneath him. Stained hay clumping up around the outline of his frame.

He was big, with a white shirt, sneakers, a baseball cap cast off to the side, discarded.

He is familiar. His splattered skull and bloody face made it hard to make out what he had once looked like for sure, but as I stare at the image playing over and over in my mind, a knowing settles deep in my bones.

I'd seen him before that day.

Who he is, how he died, and why I made the box that day aren't just fuzzy.

They're blackout-curtain opaque.

But somewhere behind them is the truth.

The answer.

That might finally set me free.

25

I'M WILLINGLY ON the road to the ranch with my suitcase in the trunk and my baby brother leading the way. I'm running on no sleep, buzzing from all the caffeine and nerves buzzing through me.

Last night, I was scared of what would happen if I let myself lose consciousness, and with Lucky close by, I just didn't want to risk anything. I didn't think there was a way to mark someone as "not a threat" to the nightmare, but I wanted to make sure Lucky wouldn't actually get hurt. I dosed myself with enough caffeine to spike my heart rate to alarming levels.

It did the trick to keep me awake. Then I was alone with my thoughts in the dark.

I couldn't get the sound of whimpering out of my head. Whatever it is he has walled in behind the storage boxes in his mind terrifies him. The nightmare could rip that wall out. It could drag the thing crying and into the light, but the real-world consequences of that could be dire, fatal even.

Then there was the memory from inside the box. Trying to work with the nightmare must have some effect on my access to the contents, and even though the nightmare may not be trustworthy, that memory must be true somehow. The only way to find out would be to unravel the rest. I just wasn't sure how.

I needed to focus on something that wasn't just thoughts, so I spent the rest of the night looking my parents up on the internet to see if there were any clues to who the man in the stable was.

The internet search wasn't fruitful—no surprise. I wouldn't expect that Big Earl would allow himself to be pictured with a man who died mysteriously. And at least in the case of my father, there were no articles, no police reports, nothing that points to anything overtly nefarious. In fact, most searches for things like "Earl Powers murderer" or "Earl Powers scandal" or even "Earl Powers criminal" provided the same sort of results as simply searching for his name.

Earl Powers, the company, and his beautiful wife and family are shining beacons of philanthropy and goodwill. In the Texas sense of the word anyway.

Sure, Earl is a member of the NRA and a swanky country club between Friendship and Dallas, where he does business on the green, he invested in a whiskey company that went nationwide a few years back, and he gambles in Oklahoma at the big casino, but he's also one of Fellowship Kind's most gracious donors. Hell, they even named a bench in the garden after him! And through Olympia's work with the PWA, his money has helped get legislation against abortion voted into law, driven out clinics that would provide them, and just last week, they were both photographed at the governor's mansion in Austin—a party that was attended by every shithead you can imagine, and probably a number you don't even know exist who'd like it to stay that way.

To anyone without discernment, Earl is a God-fearing, good man.

Even with all the gambling, golfing, guns, and heavy drinking.

The internet search proved that if Earl had any skeletons to find, they'd be buried so well not even a cadaver dog could get to them. I flick the blinker, turning onto the long drive that leads back to the ranch. My goal isn't simple, and I don't have a plan except this: find out who the man in the stable was and give the little girl who saw his body the closure she needs once and for all.

26

OLYMPIA IS VISIBLY perturbed about this new development.

She's sent Julep to make up the guest room for me since my former bedroom is her current office, but I can tell that having me back in her home isn't sitting well with her. We're standing in the kitchen while event staff bustle around us, cleaning and prepping food for the evening's festivities.

Earl and Olympia Powers aren't just town participants in the Peach Festival: they're two of the main sponsors. Not only does the annual picking party officially kick off the weekend of events, but the night before–this night–they hold a Texas-style barbecue featuring traditional smoked brisket, juicy pork ribs marinated for forty-eight hours, spicy sausages, gourmet sauces, potato salads, macaroni and cheese, jalapeno-cheddar cornbread, an array of beers, and peach-themed cocktails made with a small ration of Powers peaches reserved just for the event so as not to interfere with the picking party. The kids swim in the pool or play horseshoes and cornhole in the pasture, and the most influential families in town show up.

"We're elbows deep, as you can see," she says, stirring a Sweet'N Low into her iced tea. The metal spoon clanks against the glass.

She crunches the wrapper in the other hand and sets it down in a neat little ball.

"I won't be in the way," I say, wondering if she plans to offer me a glass or just taunt me with hers.

"You could take that one step further and offer to help your sister-in-law in the den," she says, lifting the spoon from the glass and setting it neatly on the paper napkin folded beside it on the counter. "It's not like you're really a *guest*." The word has bite.

I think about the guest room I'm about to inhabit and consider a retort. A member of the event staff appears as if from thin air to whisk away the wrapper, napkin, and spoon.

My family doesn't normally have staff at the ranch besides the stable hands, horse trainers, and the usual workers in a place this size: groundskeepers who maintain the yard, the fields, and the orchard, with a supervisor, and probably a housekeeper inside. Olympia cooks; she'd never outsource it. So this event staff must be under her watch, like the staff in a kitchen at a restaurant.

I flick my eyes over to where an apron is draped across one of the island barstools. There are barbecue smudges visible on it.

"What's Clarabelle doing in the den?" I ask as my eyes rove back to focus on Olympia's face. It couldn't hurt to spend time with Clarabelle. I definitely got the impression the other night that she pays close attention to everything that happens in this family, and not just what directly affects her and her kids.

If there was a dead man in our stable when I was six, there's no reason to think there weren't more dead men or shady dealings over time. And Buck is the most likely candidate to help with cleanup. He wouldn't necessarily tell her, but she might hold her own opinions or suspicions.

"Don't play the idiot," Olympia says. "You've been gone nine years, but you were here for nineteen. You know we always offer our guests goodie bags at the barbecue." Olympia crinkles her nose. She's perpetually forty-seven in my mind, because that's how old she was when I left town. She's still got the toned arms and taut face of a much younger woman, with full cheeks and high cheekbones she insists she inherited from her Chickasaw great-grandmother.

From a distance, I still look like a mini version of her, only fairer skinned, with bluer eyes, with browner hair, with a slighter build, and with less shapely legs.

Her gaze is fierce and unwavering. "Or I could send you out to the stables to muck."

The stables. A chill slinks through me.

My fingernails cut into my palms.

The stables are the last place I want to go. Somehow, I think she knows it and that's the reason she said it. She twists her lips as she pinches them closed, but it doesn't fully hide the ghost of her smirk. She's savoring this and only barely trying to hide it.

"Happy to help Clarabelle," I say, pressing my lips back into a smile.

"Then quit staring at me and go on." She shoos me away with a wave of her hand.

As soon as I start to move away from her, my equilibrium tilts. I barely manage to reach the hallway before I brace my hands against the wall, let my forehead fall to the cool plaster, trying desperately to get my breathing under control. This feels like more than normal panic. The room is hot, like the inside of an oven.

Like *I want to rip my clothes off and jump into the pool* kind of hot.

Nauseating, head-spinning hot.

Out of the corner of my vision, there is a glimmer.

Not an aura. Not the box.

Something metal and shiny, acting as if it's caught the light, which makes no sense because there is no light to catch. The hallway pendant light is turned off; there's also no window. I press the back of my palm against my mouth, turn toward the shiny thing, and inch my way over.

The object is a small rectangle, silver. A card box with hinges and some letters etched into the top. Not just letters—no, on a card box, the letters are usually initials.

AGL

It isn't Earl's, not one of my brothers, not Julep or Clarabelle. Could be a member of the event staff, though that seems kind of unlikely given the location. There's really no reason for them to use this hallway to get from front to back, back to front, since the kitchen has an open archway that lets you in from the foyer. I know they didn't come this way for the toilet. I spotted a porta potty out front, which I assume is for staff use.

The silver box is out of place, awfully bright. I reach to pick it up...

It's not really there at all.

My fingers graze baseboard.

But still, the image of the card box remains like a blip.

I rub my eyes, close my lids, immediately soothed by the darkness. What the fuck though? I know I'm exhausted, but I'm not to the point of hallucination. Maybe you could argue that I'm actually quite primed for it, and all things considered, it would be a surprise if I wasn't fabricating images all over the place, considering the whole nightmare thing.

I press my fingertips hard into my eyeballs and rub.

When I open them, it's the same.

My back goes cold, like someone opened the refrigerator behind me.

The hairs on my arms and the nape of my neck raise. The card box is gone as if it were never there at all. But I know what I saw. Don't I?

I whirl around, back to the wall now, looking for a sign of the tiny box in the hall, expecting this to be its handiwork. But there's nothing.

I take a few steadying breaths. Okay, fine, maybe I had too much caffeine.

That's all this is, all that it could be. *You sure about that?*

Shut up, stop trying to argue.

I carry on through the hallway to the den, leaving the minor mental breakdown behind me.

Thankfully, the den is bright and warm. The plantation shutters are all open to let the midday light in. The big fan overhead is on, its thick wooden blades spinning to spread the subzero AC around the room. Clarabelle sits on one of the couches with gift bags piled neatly around her. They cover the coffee table and the floor, and beside her is a pile of what looks like beer Koozies that she's placing inside.

She's absorbed, doesn't notice me entering. Her lips are set in a straight line of hard focus, a small eleven between her brows. The expression gives the impression that this is the most important work she could possibly be doing and not at all the kind of thing a robot on an assembly line could master.

"Olympia sent me to help," I call out, breaking her focus.

She looks up, face still fixed for a second longer before she unclenches, her bright-toothed smile spreading all the way to her eyes, which crinkle just a little at the edges.

"Haven!" She pops up from the couch, still holding one of the beer Koozies in her hand as she walks over to fold me into a hug. "Thank the Lord." She pushes back to grin at me. "Julep abandoned me—"

"Olympia has her making up the guest room," I say, cutting in.

"She left half an hour ago. Please. I bet if we went in there right now, we'd find her napping." She snorts, tugs me into her side, and pulls me with her over to the couch. "At the Christmas party prep day last year, she said she was going to hang mistletoe in the stable, and Buck found her in one of the pool cabanas a few hours later, with a full bag of mistletoe. She said she'd sat down to make a call to her mom, but then why was her mascara smudged like she'd been sleeping?"

We drop down onto the couch. Koozies spray like geyser water.

I flick my eyes over to the bags in front of me. Brown paper with light brown handles and each guest's name written on the front in calligraphy.

Written in real ink, not printed from a print shop.

I recognize the handwriting immediately.

Olympia taught herself how to do ornate calligraphy. She's employed the skill to the admiration and envy of women in town for years. Every party has handwritten place cards. Every gift bag too.

"This is the last of the bags. They all need Koozies, and then we just need to tie them up with this." Clarabelle leans forward to fish out a spool of twine from the middle of the table. "I already did the batch in the dining room." She looks past me through the opening in the wall where we can see the dining room table burdened with the other gifts bags. Pride turns her cheeks pink.

"I could load, you could tie?" I ask, reaching for some of the Koozies that fell on the ground. I hoist them up onto the couch beside me.

She grins and it's such a nice expression. Clarabelle has these deep mossy-green eyes, her tan is pristine, her copper-red hair is carefully coiffed and clearly babied.

She's also not the type to sit silent for long. *Perfect.*

"Buck would never tell you, but he's glad you decided to come home."

"He was the one who called me, so I would hope so," I say, dropping a Koozie in a bag and handing it to her to tie.

"Because Big Earl told him to," she says. "And Buck does everything Big Earl says, no questions asked." It hangs between us for a second. I don't think she realizes how what she's just said could be interpreted. "I mean," she says, jumping to smooth this over, "we all do. We're so grateful for all your daddy does." Her eyes cut over to mine, locking in. "Such a wonderful father."

I have to hand it to her. Clarabelle has to know I left town and cut all of them out. She has to know at least a little about why. Calling Earl a good father may not be intended to rile me up, but it's not entirely innocent either. What Clarabelle said also contradicts what Earl told me the day I arrived, that he didn't want Buck to call me, that Buck made the choice on his own. So which one is the lie?

I am unfortunately interrupted from this line of thought, and any follow-up prodding I might try, by Julep entering the room and slicing us apart with her death glare.

"Your bed's ready," Julep says with a surly tone as she strides to the armchair near the coffee table. She flops into it and crosses one long leg over the other. Where Clarabelle is all sweet tea and summer, Julep takes a different approach. She's more like whiskey in a crystal glass. Her denim cutoffs are a suitable length but a tad too tight, she's wearing a pair of turquoise Lucchese and a halter top in crimson red.

"I thought Olympia told you to change clothes," Clarabelle says. She's wearing paisley, perfectly demure.

Julep groans and sticks out her tongue. So when Olympia and the boys aren't watching, the truth comes out. Catty and callous. I have to admit it makes me like them both a little bit more. Even if they are part of the problem and not the solution—to the patriarchy and its stranglehold, that is, not really to my personal thing.

"I will before tonight. I brought a dress." She lifts one of her dark brows. "Get your panties out of a bunch, will you?"

"Don't say 'panties.' It's vulgar." Clarabelle cringes.

"It's an item of clothing, but okay," Julep says, barking a laugh at Clarabelle's disgust. She cuts her eyes over to me, where I'm trying to stay out of it and just load Koozies into gift bags. "Don't let her fool you, Haven. She plays precious, but she's got crazy running through her veins."

Clarabelle stops midway through tying up the bag in her lap. Her cheeks flush so red I fear they'll catch on fire. This must have something to do with her sister. I remember Buck saying—distastefully—something about Hyacinth going mental and moving to a commune.

"There is no reason to bring up my mentally ill sister just to land a dig at me," Clarabelle says, her voice hoarse with held-in emotion. She blinks, and this close, it's easy to see a sheen of moisture form over her eyes.

"I'm not." Julep grins so big I can see her molars. She uncrosses her legs and leans forward, propping herself up on her elbows. Her wavy black hair falls forward. "I'm just making sure Haven is up-to-date. She's missed out on so much while she was away." The loose cannon is Julep. I wonder what other info she has stored beneath those big pretty black waves of hers.

"Haven doesn't care about what happened with Hyacinth," Clarabelle says, then looks at me for confirmation. And normally, I wouldn't care, except that in order to get Julep to spill, I have to act like I want in on the tea.

"Only in the *concerned former classmate* kind of way," I say.

Clarabelle rolls her eyes and Julep yips, pleased.

"Well, Hyacinth had this boyfriend whose identity she kept secret," Julep says, launching into it. "But she talked about him like his *you know what*"—she waggles her brows—"was made of pure gold or something."

"Yikes," I say.

"Crude," Clarabelle interjects.

"Never showed us a picture of him, never told us his name. And then one day, she shows up at the hospital all black-and-blue, and the nurse asks her who did this to her. How did it happen? You know, normal questions to assess her properly."

"Gosh, I hate the way you're telling this story," Clarabelle says, tossing the twine at her so that it smacks her square in her pretty, rosy mouth. "Let me tell it. You tie these."

Julep grabs the twine up from the floor, and she looks ready to protest, but Clarabelle steamrolls right over whatever she was about to say.

"Hy wouldn't tell them anything, but the sheriff and a lawyer my parents hired both tried. It was hard on her mental health, I think—all the scrutiny."

And not the physical abuse? But it's clear that neither of them are going to comment on that part. As if her showing up at a hospital in need of help was just some mistake that they could all sort out if she'd just tell them who the guy was.

Boys will be boys.

Fuck. My pulse is pounding. My upper lip sweats.

"She left not long after that. It destroyed my mom, as you can imagine." Clarabelle isn't dense, so I don't know how she doesn't see the similarities between Hyacinth's story and mine. What happened to me, the way I left. Maybe she does, and maybe she's actually more ruthless than I thought.

Hy went mental. Those were Buck's words. They come screaming back.

It isn't even that they didn't see the danger she was in; they just didn't care. And Hyacinth probably knew that, just like I did back then. She knew they'd hand her right back over to him if they had a chance. She was damaged goods, nothing worse for a woman to be, and the fact that she wouldn't go back and try to fix it made her "mental."

The temperature in the room inexplicably drops.

Julep lets out the tiniest shiver.

I gotta get out of here. Right. Now.

I shoot up, dropping a Koozie to the ground, where it flops over my tennis shoes.

"Oh my goodness! Haven, are you okay?" Clarabelle exclaims.

"Yeah, sorry, I just suddenly feel a little nauseous," I say, swallowing, swooning wobbly to sell it.

Clarabelle reaches out to steady me, but I don't need her help.

I hold out my hand to deter her. "I'm good, I'm good. Maybe I should just go lie down–" I cut myself off, cut my eyes from her to Julep, who looks suspicious of the show. "I'm not used to the Texas heat anymore."

This gets the exact response I hope for. Clarabelle's shoulders release their tension, Julep goes back to looking bored, and the room returns to a normal air-conditioned temperature.

"Well, of course you aren't," Clarabelle says.

Texans think everything is bigger and better here, but one thing that isn't grandstanding is when they talk about the heat. Of course, I can handle the heat just fine. I grew up here and that power stays in your bones. But it tracks that they would believe the lore that I couldn't.

I make my exit. I would love to pick my sisters-in-law's brains for info, but not with the nightmare's help. The likelihood it would take my metaphor literally and go to town on the gray matter with a set of tweezers is too great.

Now that I'm up, I can double back to the stairwell that goes from the kitchen to the landing outside Earl's office upstairs. He may not have anything in there about the dead man in the stable, but who knows what else I could uncover. Right now is probably my best chance since he isn't home, but he will definitely be here later tonight and a lot more tomorrow, with the picking party happening first thing to beat the heat.

It's worth taking a look. Even if nothing turns up.

Tonight, after he's asleep, I'll try to break into his mind and see what I can find.

Find.

Not *dig up.*

Nothing gruesome. Just a gentle tiptoe through a dangerous minefield.

27

EARL'S OFFICE HAS deep oak wood paneling with a thick lacquer to give it some shine. There's a glass gun case displaying his rifles and handguns, trophies from shooting competitions back in the eighties and nineties before he shifted away from that to strictly being a seasonal hunter. I wasn't alive then. That was the Earl who existed before he became a car dealership mogul.

There are other signs in this room of his previous life, an hommage to his family history in the region. A photo hangs in a thick wooden frame of Big Earl when he was young, flanked by the three previous generations of the Powers patriarchs. Buck looks so much like Earl's dad, it's wild. Same blue eyes and dark brown hair. Same athletic build, tall and broad-shouldered, tanner than any of the rest of us ever dreamed we could be.

Earl Prosper Powers I was born into oil and gas money. His great-grandfather was somewhat of a tycoon, his grandfather a bit of a local legend who supposedly had ties to the Texas Mafia, and his father, Judd, was the one to put their money into developing Friendship and the surrounding area, including buying up the land that eventually became Powers Ranch. The house, stable, and all those rows of peach orchards were built by my parents, but the land came to them through an inheritance. Like most of Big Earl's startup capital for Powers Premier Automotive.

I did meet Judd and Rita, Earl's mom, but I didn't really know either of them. Judd died of lung cancer when I was barely four, and Rita didn't take it well. For years, my parents talked about her like she was dead, but then when I was eleven, we went to her funeral, so I'm not sure what the hell happened there.

God, is there any part of this family that isn't totally fucked?

Maybe Lucky, I think, a bit wistful. But even he's got some kind of secret.

I turn away from the gun and trophy case to survey the rest of the room. There's the pool table my brothers were playing a game on the other night. Thick wood, ornate carving detailed along the corners, with maroon felt for the play area and tapered legs. Hanging on the wall are a set of polished cue sticks and chalk. In the center of the table, the balls are all racked and ready.

On the other side of the table is Earl's desk. Also heavy wood, his chair a plush leather executive style. Beside his desk is a rustic bar cart outfitted with every kind of dark liquor you can imagine. I spot the bottle Tate brought him, opened with about a fourth of the liquor gone already.

I cross to the cart like a moth to a flame. On the lower shelf are crystal tumblers, clean and polished. The liquor sparkles, my mouth waters, and not because I want a drink. I want to hold a glass in hand, sit in his chair, and feel for a second what it would be like to be a man with nearly unlimited power. A man who can get away with almost anything. A man who can look at the world and see only possibility.

And so I do it.

The whiskey smells of caramel and wet wood and cloves. I swirl it in the glass, fall back into the rough leather chair, and put my feet up—one, then the other—on top of the desk.

My eyes drift closed. I'm so fucking tired.

The kind of tired that makes your teeth ache and your skin constrict.

Tired in that way that isn't simply about a lack of sleep but runs deeper.

When I was a little girl, I wasn't allowed in Earl's office. This place was his sanctuary after a long workday, and for him, that meant he didn't want to be reminded of his messy, emotional, live-wire daughter when he was trying to unwind. Buck was often invited, even when he was too young for it to be appropriate. I could hear through the doorway even when it was closed. They'd shoot the shit, usually with some of the guys who worked for Earl or sometimes just the two of them. Buck had Earl's ear, always had his attention, and he did everything he could to keep it.

Sterling was next to be pulled into the boys' club. Though, back then, he was never in it as thick as Buck. Younger, for starters, and not as hard of a worker, Sterling liked to hang with the big boys, which is what led to his teenage drinking problem, but he didn't really have a head for much else. Boy did he have a taste for debauchery. Alcohol was everywhere in our house. Always wine at the dinner table and nightcaps in Earl's office and beers for game day.

It's not an excuse; it's conditioning.

This is tradition.

The Powers family can hold their liquor. We drink and we don't talk about the dark shit we've all buried deep. The only reason Sterling is doing the sober thing again is because he's had another DUI. Big Earl can make a lot of shit go away, but Texas is a three-strikes-and-you're-out state. I'm not sure even Earl could fix that.

I've been on the run for nine years, but it's like I never left.

I don't know how much I actually changed about myself in the time away, or if all I managed to do was lie convincingly, construct the story of a woman who was living on her own terms, when really, I've locked so much in the box that it's turned a part of me into a monster.

It threatens to take me over every second, the creep of it crawling into more of my brain. I wonder if that is the price for my escape. The bounty so I can keep on living. The one thing I've always had, the thing that protects me from other horrible things I could do. My survival instinct. My desire to live and not die.

I don't know if I'm different from them or if the only difference is that I'm more aware.

I know I'm a monster, but I don't want to be.

My eyes are closed, lids heavy as my lashes brush over my cheeks.

Then I slap my face hard with the palm of my hand to wake back up.

28

I STARE AT myself in the guest bathroom mirror, trying to muster the courage to join the barbecue, which I can tell by the growing rumble of chatter outside the small frosted window is already in full swing. I've been hiding out in the guest room, pacing, playing games on my phone, sucking back so many Diet Cokes that I have a triangle stack started on the dresser across from the bed.

"Pull yourself together," I say to myself in the mirror, running palms over stray hairs, taking a few centering breaths. The concealer I put under my eyes is barely doing the trick of hiding my dark circles. "There's practically a whole town outside the house. You have to go out there."

I try out a smile, show off my teeth, tilt up my chin.

"You look psychotic."

My eyes drift behind me in the mirror, searching for the shadowy smoke thing from the nightmare. I don't see it there, but I wonder if someone took a photo of me today, would I be able to identify the smudgy outline that's too big for the shape of my body? Like how in the image from when I was a child, there was that aura light just past the spray of my ringlets.

I straighten, apply a coat of nude gloss.

Red would be better. Red would draw the eye from my sallow cheeks and exhausted sunken gaze.

I don't want to go to this barbecue, but I can't very well come back to the ranch instead of bunking at the hotel and then not play Haven Powers, good prodigal daughter. Olympia is already suspect of me; I don't want to push it. The fact that Olympia is suspect is a question for another day though. I know she low-key hates my face, but she's treating me like a cop would treat a perp, questioning them about a disappearance they most definitely know something about.

I flatten my hand over the fabric of my tank top.

I don't have a dress. I don't think I even own one, but I definitely didn't pack one. The best I can do is a pair of black jeans with a ribbed dark brown tank top. I wear sneakers because that's all I packed. One pair of shoes, what a dumbass. I'm sure this outfit will still piss Olympia off, but at least I've styled my hair with some loose waves, so the ends hit at my collarbone and are nice and smooth. With this much skin showing, I can see how close my darker freckles match my hair color. If I had stayed in Texas, I probably would have highlighted my hair into oblivion. I definitely would have considered a boob job. There's a look that gets traction here, and my natural mousy brown hair color and tiny tits aren't it.

With one more glance in the mirror, and an internal plea that the nightmare stay in the box, I shut off the bathroom light. Ready as I'll ever be.

OF COURSE, EVERYTHING is picture fucking perfect.

The backyard, where the giant outdoor kitchen is a focal point on one of the elevated decks, is the centerpiece of the event. The sun won't set for a few more hours, but they've already lit the rows of lights strung up in zigzags covering the whole space.

The pool is a large kidney shape and sparkling blue. The cabanas are opulently decorated with plush seating. Tables are erected in different stations: one for sides and breads, one for sauces and meat, and then a bar where drinks are being made by an army of bartenders. My eyes scan, searching the crowd for familiar faces. Buck and Sterling stand over toward one of the cabanas talking to a group of men in cowboy hats. Sterling looks bored. He's holding a glass bottle of Dr Pepper in hand, eyes sliding surreptitiously over toward the bar.

Earl is up by the outdoor kitchen, where an open grill smokes with hot meat on top. It's all for show since the meat table is already loaded up with mains, but I imagine he likes to give off the impression that he's the grill master, when in reality, Olympia and her event staff are behind the food. I was holed up in the guest room whenever he came home, and the fact that he didn't come say hi shouldn't piss me off, but it does. He may not have even noticed my car since Olympia had someone move it "out of sight" for the event parking.

Speaking of Olympia, she's making her way from group to group, greeting, smiling, wearing a baby blue eyelet mid-length sundress. She's set her hair in soft waves, and she wears the big diamond on her all-important left finger.

Lucky is over by the cornhole boards with some of the nieces and nephews and other town kids, probably trying to avoid as much elbow rubbing with the creeps of the town as possible.

I tuck my hands in my pockets and serpentine through the crowd, trying to get an idea of who else showed up and who might be worth pretending to care enough to talk to. I spy Tabby Collins, the young woman who works for my dad–the daughter of that dickhead Keller–talking with some college-age adults.

I assume if she's here, her dad's skulking around somewhere too.

"Some party." Winter's voice crackles behind me like an apparition through a radio speaker.

I wrangle my face to a neutral enough smile before I turn around to face her. It's not lost on me how pretty she looks, but it really should be.

She's dressed in a denim skirt, dark cowboy boots, and a leather vest. Her dark brown hair is pulled up in a clip, showing off her warm brown eyes and sharp cheekbones, and the glow of her tan in the late summer evening sun is a rich light brown. I should have figured the Reyes family would be here, what with her dad owning the bowling alley and her mom being in the PWA with mine.

She's got a beer bottle in her hand that looks almost empty by the way she holds it.

"Want another?" I ask, flicking my eyes to the bottle and then the bar behind me with a twist of my neck. When I face her again, she's downing the last drops. A thick film of beer coats her lips. We start walking, me catching glances as I wind through the crowd. No one approaches, but I feel them see me, and I know as soon as I'm comfortably out of earshot, they won't be able to resist the urge to gossip.

"I don't usually come back for the Peach Festival," she says, "so I haven't had the pleasure of joining your family's barbecue before."

"It's like everything else the Powers family does: over the top with pomp and circumstance."

We reach the bar, and she grabs another beer from the metal bucket. I order a chardonnay because I am more confident in my ability to keep track of wine than liquor, and I never really liked the taste of beer. Winter takes a deep swig.

We keep ourselves moving, and I tell myself it's because if we stay in one place too long, then anyone around us could get the full context of our conversation. But it's also because I'm tracking through the crowd for someone else. Someone I haven't spotted yet, but who I know will be here.

"I remember when I was in middle school, when we first moved here," Winter says. She's got a thick metal ring on her middle finger, which she lifts and lowers to tap the bottle a few times. "My family was treated like outsiders. 'Latinos from where?' Even though we were born in Texas for generations back." There's a heat to her words, the fire of anger that hasn't gone out even if she gives the impression that what she's about to say comes with a positive twist. "Your parents welcomed us. Your mom came over with a basket of local goodies and invited mine to the PWA. Your dad rented lanes every Wednesday, brought buddies in, encouraged mine to start a regular league, and then joined it."

"They're really good like that. Good at wrapping you up in rope and then getting you to thank them for tying the knot."

"I know, I know, and I don't love how wrapped up they still are, but at the time, I was grateful. The Powers family approved of us." She chuckles, but it's a thin sound. "It helped me not feel so terrified of this place."

"I think you deserve an apology, and I also get the feeling you want to say thank you but aren't going to?" I smile, even if I'm not sure I'm supposed to.

"Oh, well, *you* don't deserve a thank-you," she says, her tone turning more playful. "You never gave me the time of day."

"Ohhh!" I exclaim, and she cackles.

We've reached a cabana corner with a small love seat tucked as far back as it can go. She drops down into it.

"I see, so you're grateful to my problematic family *and* calling me out on my bullshit? Awesome."

She's smiling, pleased. I glance down at the spot beside her and she scoots just enough to let me know she wants me to sit there. I do.

"You had your own problems, I quickly discovered."

"I didn't start dating Tate until the summer between freshman and sophomore year."

"I didn't mean just him, but noted. He *was* a problem." Her eyes leave my face to search the crowd. "I hear he still is." Her voice drops low, so quiet I have to lean closer to hear her. "I can't say how I know that, of course–lawyer shit–but if it's true, and I'm inclined to believe women always, then I can't even imagine what kinda problem he was back then."

I have to deflect this line of conversation away from Tate. I'm still not sure I can control the box if my emotions get worked up. It wouldn't be all that hard for me to go full Carrie, considering everything.

I would just hate for Winter to get caught in the flames.

But I can't ignore what she said about Tate, not completely, no matter how much I want to pretend the idea that he's still hurting women–maybe even his new, good Christian wife, Delilah–has nothing to do with me now, or the way the nightmare has changed since I've been back in Friendship.

Being near him is almost as bad as being near them.

"It's been nine years, and I'm not the same person I was back then." I *am* a liar, though, with a psycho-killer ability trapped in a box of horrors.

"Oh yeah?" She smiles, showing me the tiny gap in her front teeth. "Tell me all about the changes, Haven." My name sounds pretty when she says it. My body feels electric, buzzy with the energy between us, and I read it as a warning signal. Danger comes from all kinds of big emotions.

"It's boring. I was always pretty boring," I say, pulling back. I set the chardonnay on the side table. It's chipping away at the wall I built with caffeine and anxiety.

"You were town royalty–"

"No, Earl was, and Buck was popular–"

"And you were dating the pastor's son. Everyone watched you." She pauses and it feels deliberate. "I wasn't immune to watching you too."

"What did you see?" I almost choke on the words.

Her hand twitches, lifts a little, and then drops back to her lap. "Same thing I see now. Someone who tries to hide but who I wish wouldn't." Her gaze is heated. It burns through the layers and layers of ice I keep around me for safety.

"I shouldn't." The words drift out a statement.

"You wanna get outta here?" The light of the mosquito tiki torch dances in her deep brown irises, pulling out the gold flecks.

"And go where?" A spark of mischief, deep and long tamped down.

"I know this place outside town"–she smirks–"where they check judgment at the door."

Leaving sure sounds good.

I look out into the crowd and catch sight of–if not the last person I want to see walking toward me–the second to last.

Buck wears a dark expression. His hooded blue eyes are pinned on the space between Winter and me. He's making a beeline straight for us. Of course she notices the change in my energy and the shift of my body language. The bud opening up shrivels beneath Buck's gaze. He slows his speed as he nears us, painting on a smile as he lifts his beer-holding hand and nods his head toward Winter.

"Hey, there, Winter," he says, turning the charming twang on full blast. His smile is stiff. "Good to see you back in town."

She hesitates only a second before she paints on her own too-wide saccharine grin. "Been a few years since I came to the festival," she says, lifting her beer toward her lips. "I'm really looking forward to the picking party tomorrow."

"Oh yeah," he replies, blue eyes sparking. "Well, better bring your A-game. You know us Powers come to win."

She nods, closing her lips around the rim of the bottle.

"It's not like there's a prize," I chime in. Why I do, I have no idea, but it draws Buck's attention right back to me. His clear target in the first place.

"Winner takes home the spoils," he says. "I know it's been nine years, but there's no way you forgot."

"Oh, I didn't forget," I say, and my left brow hooks up. "When we win, we're just keeping our own harvest. I've always thought it was ridiculous that we participate."

"It's tradition," he says flatly, cutting a glare back to Winter. "You mind if I steal my sister for a quick second? Got some family stuff to discuss."

The words drop like lead in my stomach.

Before Winter has a chance to reply and I have a chance to decline, he's leaning down, closing his hand around my bicep and tugging me up with enough force that it pinches my skin. I stop resisting so it doesn't leave a mark.

He draws me into his side, hand releasing my arm to lift up and drop down around my shoulder, pinning me in. We start to move back through the crowd, Buck's attention outward, his smile wide, but he speaks through his teeth in a voice only I can hear.

"Just what do you think you're doing over there?" he says.

"Catching up with an old friend," I say, moderating my own volume to match his.

"You and Winter Reyes weren't friends," he says. "Do you think my memory is as shitty as yours?"

It's a deep cut, and I don't know how he's got it so right, that it also catches me off guard. What the hell does Buck know about my shitty memory? I never talked to him about the box or how things from childhood were fuzzy.

"You don't know every person I was friends with in high school, Buck."

We're at the edge of the yard, where the fence opens up to the path that leads out toward the stables.

"Oh, is that right?" he says, dropping his bottle in a trash can and pushing me through the open fence. The path slopes downward in the direction of the stable, so a few more steps, and we'll be out of sight and earshot of the party. "Well, I know Winter is a muff diver and always has been."

"Wow!" Even for him, it's a nasty insult. "What century are you living in?" I try hard to break free of his grip on my shoulder.

"Now you're defending queers," he says with a scoff.

I use my elbow to dig into his ribs.

"Shit, Haven!" he exclaims, smarting in pain and releasing me.

I whirl on him. "Did you actually have something to talk to me about, Buck, or was that just a lie to get me away from Winter?" I cross my arms.

Buck's shoulders droop, only a little and only for a second.

Behind him, the sky is lit up with a sunset that could rival a masterpiece painting. Orange and teal streaks wash across the canvas, bleeding into pink and purple and the lingering blue.

"Clarabelle said you came back to stay at the ranch."

"And?" I don't know why Buck would be suspicious of the decision. It's not like he knows I killed my boss with a nightmare and discovered that when I was six years old, some dude went toe up in the stable and it didn't look like natural causes.

The memory is like a feather on wind, the way it drifts down into my awareness and catches on the branches of my mind.

Buck's small face. Big aqua eyes and dark smack of hair. Peering at me through the space between the cupboard doors.

Buck was there that day. He was the one who found me in my hiding place.

"You haven't been here in ages, and suddenly you want to come back to the ranch for some close-knit family time." He shakes his head like he's trying to shake a Polaroid clear. "What game are you playing at?"

"You said this was my last chance to make amends because Earl is sick," I reply. "Earl doesn't look very sick to me. Can you explain that?"

There is no winning against another Powers. The best and only way to stay afloat in a fight is to play your own game and not the one someone presents you with. Buck wants to corner me, to press me on what my real intentions are in being here, so I have to do the same thing. Never answer the question directly. Never cave, no matter how much you want to be done with the fight. That is the Powers way.

It becomes a battle of will. And mine has always been strong.

"Dad doesn't want to talk about it. Can't you understand that? Have some sympathy," he says, dismissive, reductive. Classic. "But if you came here thinking you could play black sheep with freshly dyed wool in some attempt to get a handout or weasel your way back in—"

"I don't know why I have to keep reminding you that *you* called *me*. I didn't come here with some master plan." Gaslighting the gaslighter. "I came here because I didn't want to live the rest of my life with guilt hanging around my neck like a noose."

Buck takes a step forward and presses his lips together in a shush sound.

"Oh, they can't hear m—"

"I remember what you said when you left town. That day you packed up your shit in the car our dad bought you—"

"Gave me from the used lot on his dealership," I interject.

"You never saw this family for what it was," he continues, talking over my snark. "You never saw your place in it for what it was either. The only daughter, the little princess—"

"Princess my ass, you all treated me like a chore–"

"You were one. Holy shit, Haven! You don't remember what it was like to try to keep you under control. You don't remember all those times I had to drag you out of church or apologize to your teachers or make up for your mistakes with Mom and Dad." His voice cracks, and it breaks something inside me.

A little piece of my heart chips off but I don't feel sorry for him. I don't feel bad.

Rage flares. All I want to do is slam the heel of my shoe onto that little glass piece of my heart and grind it into shards I can throw right back in his face.

"I remember," I start, even if–no I don't. Whatever he's referring to, it's still all locked up. "And I never asked for you to do that."

"I didn't have a choice," he says, reaching out to put hands on me. I step back, widening the space between us. "I was trying to help you. Just like right now, I'm trying to help you."

"Then don't treat me like the bad guy," I say.

"Prove me wrong," he says, his voice dropping into that signature Buck tone. Too even, too controlled, with a charming drawl delivered through a gritted smile.

29

FUCK BUCK.

The idea takes hold a second after those words scorch through my mind.

It's shitty of me to throw Sterling under the bus in this way, but the desire to screw around with my older brother's ego is bigger than my desire to be a good person. The whole lot of them hate a scene they can't easily spin, but Buck hates it worst of all.

Sterling is supposed to be sober.

Anything to the contrary will be undesirable.

The Powers family doesn't need to impress anyone. What they need is to remind people they're in control. Of them, of the industry in town, of the leaders of the church, and especially of the Powers family themselves. Buck, who, if Earl is actually on his deathbed, is set to inherit the whole thing and will want to make sure to use every opportunity available to project power.

Losing control of Sterling in a public way, well, that would fuck with his head, and by extension might fuck with the rest of them. It might make breaking into Big Earl's subconscious later even easier.

And it will really piss off Buck.

Wins all around.

From this upstairs window, I have a view of the whole party and all the players.

Earl and Olympia, now both with drinks in hand, are standing over by one of the high-top tables they had brought in for the event, talking to Pastor Turner (the original, Tate's father, John) and Charity. For a second I'm stuck on her, looking for further signs of damage from the nightmare. She looks like she's got a stick up her ass like always, but otherwise normal. Disappointment flashes through me. Tate is physically John 2.0, right down to the small dimple in his left cheek, but he got his strawberry blond hair from his mother.

Nearby, I spy Clarabelle and Julep—who did change into a pretty summer dress with a modest pink floral print—chatting with other young wives, among them quite possibly Delilah, though I don't know what she looks like.

From there I track back across the crowd until I see the three of them: Sterling, Buck, and Tate.

The latter two nurse Coronas with lime, but Sterling has a glass of something. By the look of it, club soda. He's the only one with food, which makes me wonder if he's eating to mask the smell of liquor in his glass. Sterling was never picky about what booze he drank as long as it did the job. Jaeger, gin, schnapps, on and on. The horrors persisted but so did the shots.

Unforgiving as it is to think he's already fallen off the wagon, if he has, it will make this whole thing a hell of a lot easier to execute. And I've done this before, once, to him—the time I made him sleepwalk off the treehouse edge. Theoretically, I already know how to get through the door in his mind.

From my experiment with Lucky, I know I can stay aware within someone else's subconscious as long as I stay in control of the nightmare. The idea I have is simple, really, even if nothing about controlling the nightmare is predictable. The nightmare part of me does seem to be aligned with my desire to engage my family members' subconscious. It seems to want to help.

Or something that looks like help anyway.

I take a deep breath, steadying myself to begin. No one's upstairs, and the only people going in and out of the house are the event staff Olympia hired. I am alone enough and out of sight.

I drop down to the ground and turn around so that my back is against the wall. I curl my legs up, hugging them, dropping my face to tuck in between the crook of my knees. If anyone does come up, it will look like I'm hooked in an upright fetal position crying and they probably won't bother me.

My tears never got me much sympathy here.

I close my eyes and go back through that same process to settle my brain waves and sync up my breath with my thoughts as when I entered Lucky's mind. A slow in and out, a steady rise and fall of the waves, growing less erratic until they even out and I am in that space where the box appears. I wonder for a moment if the box comes first because that is the habit my subconscious is used to. *Here is the box to store all your most horrible memories.* How many times have I come here and not remembered it after?

After a few seconds—or so it seems, though time is wobbly in this place—the box melts away. A door appears. With a deep knowing, pulled from some long ignored, dusty space in my own subconscious, I recognize it.

STERLING'S DOOR.

It has a sleek handle of brushed metal. With a piece of frosted glass in the center. Instinctively, I understand it to represent escapism, an easy-to-penetrate entrance into his mind, but as I draw closer to the door, I realize that it already stands open.

Ajar only slightly but enough that anything can slip right inside.

Including me.

It's disorienting at first. Unlike Roger's mind, a cavernous sterile apartment of a meticulous creep, unlike Lucky's mind, the thoughtful curation of his childhood bedroom, or Charity's, that weird-ass birdcage, Sterling's is set up like the game room in the attic of our house, but it doesn't stay that way. As I move farther into the room, it begins to change. The outer walls crumble, opening up to reveal other locations.

The golf course at the country club.

The casino floor.

A kitchen with a fancy stove and a sign reading THIS HOUSE PRAYS *in swooping scroll letters hanging overhead.*

The ground is unsteady; it feels more like walking on a rocky dirt path, the kind that would come with a falling rocks warning attached. It's hard to maneuver even if I'm aware that I'm not really walking. There is no sign of the nightmare here, which makes me think this is all me. It didn't follow me into this room, and it isn't going to try to do something worse to my brother than I have planned for him myself.

I keep moving. Past his gym full of weight machines. Past the playground I assume is near his house, where he must take his son. Past what looks like an office at Powers Premier Automotive. Each of these spaces gives me a different feeling: confusion, joy, anger, pride, obsession. This is simple, straightforward.

Just like Sterling.

Finally, I see it.

The backyard at the ranch, the sparkling kidney-shaped swimming pool and the comfortable cabanas lining the fence. When I walk into the space, it surrounds me, and the rest of the locations–the attic game room, even–drops away.

Sterling is there, dressed in a set of swim trunks and a loose-fitting Shiner Bock T-shirt. In his hand, he's holding a cold one of the same brand; the brown bottle and yellow label are immediately recognizable. Condensation drips down the neck to land on his finger.

In Sterling's mind, he's still a drinker.

I approach him slowly, unsure how he will react to me here, unsure if he will even recognize me. You know how it is in a dream: you don't necessarily know who someone is when you see them. It's only once you wake up that you can put names to faces, remember snippets of dialogue and themes.

I call out to him, my voice that weird dream sound, like it's coming from underwater.

He turns, eyes grazing over my features, and lifts his beer toward me like he's waving.

I don't know how long I have in here, or what he will think of the suggestion that he jump into the water. I have no memory of how I made him get out of bed, walk out of the house, climb up in the treehouse, and jump.

The most obvious solution is usually the safest bet.

"Wouldn't it be nice to walk over to the pool and jump in?" I ask him, and he doesn't seem bothered by the garbled noise of my voice because he nods and looks from me to the pool. His grin is slow as it curls up his face. "You're even dressed for the occasion."

He looks down at his swim trunks. He looks back up at the pool.

When he sets his beer down on the ground, I know that I've done it.

I walk out of the backyard. The space dissolves back into the attic game room amalgamation. It is primal, the instinct to go back out the way that I came, stumbling over the treacherous terrain as I move. I launch into a run, and the ground rises and falls like roving waves of green carpet.

I grip the handle and yank.

I fall through the door.

THE SCREECHES OF chaos are the first thing I hear when my ears open back up.

Then the splashing of someone struggling in the water.

I stand and turn to look out the window. It didn't occur to me that Sterling might not have a chance to take a breath, hold it in, or that he might jump in the deep end and sink to the bottom.

It didn't occur to me that this might be dangerous. That he might get hurt.

It's hard to see from up here in the chaos of guests gathering around the pool, but the ruckus is undeniable. Sterling isn't taking a lap in the water. Something is wrong. I run back to the stairwell that leads down to the kitchen, taking it two at a time as I do. Fuck, I hope he's okay. But an even bigger fuck, I hope he can't remember what happened.

The kitchen is predictably full of event crew, some of them–the younger-looking ones–have stopped the work to watch out the back window at the commotion around the pool.

"What happened?" I ask them, breathless, hopefully not sounding suspicious. (Though, suspicious of what, I'm not sure.)

A guy with stubble and a single silver earring in his left ear replies, though he doesn't drag his eyes away from the spectacle. "Sterling Powers just deadass walked right to the edge of the pool and fell in."

My eyes widen. *Shit shit.*

"It looks like Buck had to fish him out," another staffer chimes in, this one an older teen who looks like she just graduated high school and this is her summer job.

I press forward, closer to the open door but not all the way out, where someone might see me.

Buck has Sterling by the waist as he hoists him out. Sterling looks to be alert, hacking up water he must have swallowed when he dropped in. I can see Lucky and some of the kids standing on the other side of the fenced area where they were playing horseshoes. He's covering his lips, but by the squint of his eyes, I can tell that he's laughing.

My eyes skate over the crowd and land on Earl and Olympia.

To his credit, Earl looks to be taking the incident with humor. His smile is that self-possessed businessman grin. The *boys will be boys* expression that assures he still has everything under control, that he's up for some fun, even if heads will roll later.

But Olympia's expression could curdle milk.

She searches the scene.

I have a sinking feeling she's looking for me, even if there is no reason to believe she would peg me for this. But if I stay in here, out of sight, something tells me she'll come looking when there's no one around to watch. I step through the door and walk to the edge of the porch to take a relaxed lean against one of the posts.

Buck wipes water from his clothes. His face beet red, nostrils flared with anger. He wants to let Sterling have it, but he's also critically aware of the audience and how losing his temper will look. It's the opposite of being in control, not the image he or the rest of them want to convey, not the image the people of the town have come to expect.

I revel in the way eyes cut away and over the scene, the way they slide closer to one another to whisper, the way they wait to see what happens next.

"What was that?" Buck asks, the tremor of anger running through his voice a fault line colliding. Sterling still sits on the ground, soaked to the bone, bewildered. I can tell he's not sure how to answer, but it looks more like he doesn't really understand what the problem is. Julep runs up with one of the big beach towels they keep in cabinets in the cabanas and drops it over Sterling's shoulders. He clutches it around himself.

"It is hot out here, Buck. Who could blame him?" Julep says, cocking out her hip in a defiant stance. I have to admit, I'm a little surprised at this display of loyalty.

Sterling finally stands up, whipping his wet hair around so it splashes Buck and Julep. She giggles. Buck fumes. Nervous chuckles travel over the crowd.

"I guess I just thought, 'Wouldn't it be nice to take a swim?'" he says, a chuckle in his voice, a shrug lifting and lowering his shoulders.

"And why not?" Earl calls out, lifting his hands up in a clap. "Life's too short, after all." It feels like a nod to his struggle against mortality, and it seems to hit the mark.

Buck snaps out of the rage spiral he's resisting, the light of anger extinguishing as if someone just dumped a helicopter of water on top.

The whole crowd follows Earl's cue, snapping out of their stupor to laugh the weirdness away. Murmurs of "I wouldn't mind a dip" and "Well, with a pool like that, who can blame him?" fill the air, but it's not enough to shake the suspicion etched openly in Buck's eyes when he looks back over at Sterling.

It has unsettled the waters just enough to put every single one of them on edge.

My skin buzzes, a restless energy bubbling up through my veins, fizzy like champagne. It's thrilling, even if my nerves still sit on a razor's edge. With every success, Lucky and now Sterling, the urge to see what else I am capable of grows more potent.

That isn't the only thing that I'm thinking though.

I can't shake the feeling that Olympia was looking for me in the crowd. Even if she was, she wouldn't have been looking for me for the reason she should have been. She doesn't know about the box. How could she? She can't be aware of the nightmare. If anything, she was looking for me to make sure I wasn't standing close enough to Sterling to have been the one to push him.

God, all this lack of sleep and caffeine and trippy brain shit is making me even more paranoid than normal. I have to get out of this house for a few hours without it drawing too much attention.

I step off the porch, moving back through the crowd in search of Winter. She mentioned leaving earlier. With hours left before Earl falls asleep and no interest in sticking around to witness more ass-kissing from the town, there's no reason not to take her up on her offer.

I find her talking to her mom over by the dessert table, a mini mason jar of banana pudding in her hand. Maria Reyes spies me first, and I can tell she's not any keener to see me approach her daughter than Buck was to see us talking earlier.

Her smile is tight. I wave and greet her anyway.

"Hi, Mrs. Reyes." I smile, extend a hand to shake. "I'm Haven. I used to come to the bowling alley all the time. Best lanes within a hundred miles." Out of the corner of my eye, I can see Winter smirking. Her mother takes my hand rather gingerly, gives it a swift shake.

"I remember you," she says, eyes trekking from me to something over my shoulder. "Back then you ran with Pastor Tate, before he was Pastor Tate of course. You were attached at the hip. We all expected you two to marry." Mrs. Reyes is part of the PWA. She's definitely a member of Fellowship Kind. She would have been tracking the developments between Tate and me back then, and she may have bought the story my mom fed her.

"I didn't," I reply, my smile thinning.

Mrs. Reyes purses her lips.

I turn my attention to Winter. "Could you show me that thing you mentioned?" I lift my brows, a swift up and down.

Two small lines form between hers, but then she grins in a sick sort of way that fills me with glee. "The *thing*, right." She flicks a gaze to her mom and then back. "Absolutely, let's do it."

"Nice to see you," I say, waving again at Mrs. Reyes, who looks ready to protest my coming over here to steal her daughter away. Winter leans in, plops a quick smack on the woman's cheek, and whispers just loud enough for me to hear: "Don't wait up, Mamá."

We're out of the gate before anyone can stop us.

30

WINTER HAS BROUGHT me to a honky-tonk in between Friendship and Fort Worth.

Coyote Crossroads looks like an old-time saloon with its low-sitting tin roof, deep front porch, and rustic wooden beams. I can practically imagine it with a water trough for horses and a dirt road running past.

Inside, the vibes are immaculately Texan. The sawdust on the boot-beaten wood floors. The neon beer signs and wagon-wheel tables scattered around the dance floor that floods right up to the stage, where a cover band belts out some vaguely familiar country song in an accent so thick it's hard to understand the words.

Winter has taken me by the hand as we snake through the crowd toward the bar, where she presses up against the wood to order each of us a margarita on the rocks. One thing about Texas, everywhere you go serves some version of a margarita.

"So, what d'ya think about this place?" She's reaching over the bar to grab a couple of pickles with a toothpick while the bartender isn't watching. She hands me one.

"It's a honky-tonk outside town," I reply, taking the pickle. She taps her pickle against mine.

Her eyes trail up to something behind me. Her finger points

when I don't immediately turn. I crane my neck, spotting an LGBTQIA flag hanging alongside the US flag and the Texas flag, a proud display of both patriotism and allyship.

It's like we time-traveled. Left the past in Friendship and blipped into a present-day dimension. My shoulders immediately untense from their tight position. I turn back to look at her, and our eyes immediately connect.

The bartender places our drinks on the wood.

"Should we toast?" she asks, her voice smoky.

"You got any suggestions?" I reply, my voice carrying a quiver of nerves.

"To old friends?" she says. A dark brow lifts, along with the corner of her lips.

"I wish we were that," I say.

"We can pretend." She raises her glass toward me, and the invitation feels like more. More than pretending we're old friends who reconnected. More than pretending this place is the real world and Friendship is the illusion. For this span of minutes, we can pretend to be falling for each other and not be afraid.

I lift my glass to cheers her. She clinks hers, smiling big, so I can see the gap in her front teeth, before she takes a long swig of her drink.

"Lots of people from surrounding towns find their way here to do what they do," she says, twisting around so she can survey the scene. Her eyes are dark jewels reflecting the light of the neon signs.

I follow her lead, watching the crowd, noticing couples hiding in plain sight within it. There are men dancing with men, some in cowboy boots and Stetsons, some dressed like city folk in shorts and T-shirts, in tennis shoes and backward caps. There are men and women kissing, twisting around and all up in each other, some with wedding bands on only one of the members of the pair.

There are all kinds of people here, and all kinds of lies and truths being told.

"I like it here," I say, sipping my drink. It burns the back of my throat, and I take another deep swig before I add, "I like it here with you."

She keeps her eyes on the crowd when she says, "I like it here with you too."

It's part of human nature to hide away pieces of the truth: parts of yourself, secret desires, the hurt that's happened and the pain that's marked you. You show some parts off only in a certain light, keep other bits tucked out of sight, no matter how much you love, trust, or want others to know the whole truth.

I could never tell Winter what I can do.

Not about the box or the nightmare or the way I can hurt people through their subconscious and pierce reality.

Acceptance can only go so far, even for someone with the level of empathy and openness Winter clearly has. This honky-tonk is like one of my subconscious spaces. Not quite real, but still, it can affect reality. This flirtation, connection–whatever it is–lives here, can be real here, but it can't ever be more than that out there.

I know this, but it doesn't change the fact that I want to take her by the waist, to pull her against me as we move around the dance floor, to feel the heat of her skin and the damp puff of her breath on my neck.

She turns her sparkling eyes on me. "You got secrets, don't you, Haven?" Her tone is playful.

"Everyone has secrets." I try not to sound too bogged down in mine.

"I'm an open book," she says, setting her margarita down on the bar.

I snort. "Oh, really." I set my margarita down too.

"For sure," she says, edging closer. I fight the instinct to step back. "I asked you to come with me because I'd like to dance with you, and not because I'm being nice or friendly." Her breath has the tangy scent of lime and tequila, more intoxicating than the drink in my hand. "But because I want to see what it feels like to have your body pressed up against mine."

This isn't real, I tell myself. *It's okay to say yes.*

"I'm not stopping you," I say.

Her hand cups my waist. I exhale when the mound of her lips taunt the curve of my own. "Can I have this dance?"

I'm already folding my fingers with hers. I'm saying yes despite knowing I'm not safe for this woman.

Not safe for anyone.

But desperate to be loved all the same.

We slide together, kicking up sawdust, and we move into the crowd of people. It feels like this song has been playing forever, but that could just be the monotony of this beat, the drone of the voice crooning on about home and his truck and how apple pie tastes like the Fourth of July. But just as she spins me, sending me out and drawing me back fast, the melody changes, slowing down to something more like molasses. Her hands tighten around the small of my back, tugging me into a tight embrace.

We are lost in the moment. Our bodies sliding together. My senses filling with her. Deep brown hair and warm tan skin, a fragrance sprayed on and soaked in that reminds me of summer: salt air, and ocean brine, and juicy watermelon running down my chin. She is strong, this body she uses to do good work. She is kind. She is too good for me, and I know it.

Her lips press light to my forehead. "It's okay to like it," she says in a low voice.

If only that were true.

But here, until this dream is over, I can pretend that it is.

My muscles unclench, the tension unfurling like buds in spring.

I melt into her grip, feel lost in her warmth. My eyes drift closed, my mind wandering to a sandy beach by an ocean somewhere far away from Friendship. Winter is there, wind smacking her hair against her cheeks, whipping them pink. We eat watermelon from the rind. I am not on the run, not a nightmare with a vendetta and an affinity for pain. I am just a woman who is allowed to want something, someone, some life. There's no box ready to open up and remind me why I can't, shouldn't, won't, and because of that, for the smallest, purest second, I believe I can be free.

OF COURSE, ALL that is a lie.

I'm reminded as soon as we step out through the doors.

Winter leaves me at the entrance to go get the car.

That's when I see him.

Through the throng of people forming lines for dancing. Wearing an old band T-shirt and a pair of loose-fit jeans. His hair is tousled. His skin is damp, shiny in the Coors Light sign hanging near his head.

It is in this moment that for just a split second, I remember why I was in love with him.

Because I was. The problem with Tate wasn't lack of want.

Or it wasn't that at first, anyway.

I chose Tate Turner. No one forced me into it. In fact, at first, Buck didn't approve at all. Tate is a year his junior, so he knew him, and he tried to turn me away from the start.

But I liked him.

I liked his meaty shoulders, his ski-slope nose, his blue eyes that were the perfect shade right between a bleached-out summer sky and bluebonnets in the middle of spring. He was smart—the kind of smart I wasn't used to. The kind that wasn't normal, wasn't like the boys I grew up with, the boys who went to Friendship

High, who came to work out at the ranch on weekends, who were buddies with my brothers and popular in school.

Tate was a good speaker, he read books, he played music—guitar at the church in the band—and man, he could sing. And when he looked at me, I didn't feel broken, like a girl who was unwanted for all the ways she was different.

Like a nightmare. A problem. A horror.

It started out that way, and then before I knew it, Big Earl had hung his hat on it, made plans about how to use it for the future, and the fact that I chose Tate became a small piece of the bigger story. The Tate I thought was mine became someone else entirely.

I chose Tate Turner; there's only me to blame.

It was the worst choice I've ever made.

I'm staring at him now as the thought dawns on me that this is the place people go when they don't want to be seen. When they have a secret the folks in Friendship wouldn't understand. And then his secret steps up beside him.

Bottle blond hair, a too-white toothy smile, a pair of teeny Daisy Duke shorts.

She holds a beer in her hand.

Tabby Collins is twenty.

And she's not Tate's wife, so why the fuck does he have his arm around her in a bar?

31

I WAS QUIET on the way back to the ranch in Winter's car, unsure if I should bring up spotting Tate with the Collins girl when I don't know what it means and don't really want to get involved, even if I do have my ideas and none of them are good. I came here to deal with my issues, uncovered a memory that needed to be seen, and I really don't have time to stop a twenty-year-old barely woman from fucking up her young life.

But I stayed quiet for more than my own trepidation. I was afraid that if I brought Tate up in the car, the box would bring the last horrible moment between us back up in my mind like a film reel. That I would lose myself in the story, in that space in the box where I can now tread, and somehow I'd take her with me.

Winter pulls up outside the ranch and not a single light is on in the house; just the porch light beams warm gold out onto the gravel drive.

"You got a key?" she asks, leaning her head back to peer at me. The moon is a sliver of silver in the sky, but still the light finds her, causes shadows from the big oak branches to dance on her skin.

"They never lock it," I say. I wish I could stay in this car looking at her face, caught in a gaze that doesn't make me want to run away. "Thanks for taking me there."

"Anytime." Her eyes drop to my lips. But we left the dream already; out here is nightmare territory.

"See you tomorrow," I say.

Her eyes flick to the clock on her dash. "Today," she corrects and taps the clock–**2:00 a.m.** "Picking party is in seven hours."

"Seven hours." I breathe the words.

"Whole town will be vying for a win."

The whole town.

Seven more hours until the yard fills with vans bringing people from Fellowship Kind out in droves to watch the festivities unfold. Until the mayor and the pastor and every person selected by lottery to participate gets into position to play. Until *he* arrives with a smile that menaces, and there won't be any escape from his eyes.

I yank open the door as my heart rate pitters and patters in an unsteady, erratic rhythm.

I climb out.

The door slams behind me.

Did I say goodbye? Did she think I seemed weird? I try to move and I find that I can't.

My feet are rooted, stuck, like I've dropped into concrete that's slowly drying.

I am steps away from the porch, but when I look up, it spreads out and contorts, gets further away until it's drawn out long, stretched at an extreme angle that warps and twists, the peak of the roof distorts into a sharp point, draws the wide house thin, and turns the dark window eyes into slits.

The smell comes next. Rank eggs forgotten in the sun. Earth mixed with shit turned over. Then the air thins. My lungs seize; my vision clouds.

Panic captures my body, rooting me to the spot, and when I try to move from it, I can't. I drop to my knees on the ground.

"This isn't fair." I gasp out the words. "This isn't real."

But I, more than anyone, know that what happens inside your mind is as real as anything else.

I AM SHUT *in the bathroom and the world spins, spins, spins around me–*

I am in a body that's mine, only younger.

It keeps score on my inner thighs and the soft, malleable skin under my arms and with emptiness, purging everything inside me back out just to feel totally hollow.

I wear cutoff shorts long enough to hide my scars. I wear sleeved shirts to cover my bruises.

I wear chipping nail polish and dirty sneakers, and I'm wet . . .

From the lake. That's it. That's where I was when he found me, claimed me again as his property. He does all sorts of horrible things with a smile, but he is the one who turned this body into a jail cell.

He is one of the ones, anyway.

He is the only one I can fight back against.

This thought shivers through me–new in its certainty, claiming some truth of a life I know little about anymore because I turned those truths into knickknacks I store in a box in my head with a lock and a top and four sides I can't see through.

For now, I am in this bathroom with toile wallpaper pasted up behind and before me.

I hear a storm. I know the night I've wandered back into.

I took something into this body, some drug I've never had before or again, hoping it would make me feel anything but horrible.

Shrink down the inside of this body so it fits in the confines of my own thinned-out . . . bruised, broken, crusted-over . . . suit of girl skin.

In a moment he finds me.

The door shakes with his anger. The handle twists and shudders against his grip.

He's going to claim me. I'm his after all.

Not after tonight.

I am not in that body, not anymore.

I am a woman. The scars on her body have faded. The meat on her bones is fleshier, curved, solid muscle and strong sinew.

I bend to look at the other me. She doesn't notice.

"I'm sorry he's going to take you," I whisper.

I stand and move out of the way as the door flies open.

Hinges clang to the floor in an angry metallic sound.

He is angry, but he doesn't know her body contains the heart of a monster.

He doesn't know she is done playing the punching bag.

As weak and as feeble as she has become . . . she still possesses the sharp teeth of a predator.

She would rip through his skin and tear them both out of the world if she could.

He drags her–hand around wrist burning the flesh as he twists–down stairs, out a door.

He tosses her into a car.

I am in the car with her, stuck in the back seat, calling her name in a whisper.

"Haven, don't be scared."

But she is. Her body shakes with the fear.

Her thighs stick to soft leather seats. Her nose inhales the smell of air freshener in pine.

He climbs into the car. He turns on the ignition. His radio blares country music through its speakers.

Her seat belt is unbuckled. Her head spins, and the world speeds past.

I lean up to whisper something nasty into his ear. In the rearview, my face reflects, the truth of what lives inside me lifting up like an oversized living shadow. Smoke shifts around me.

I smile.

I try to move and I'm back in her body.

Fear courses through me like drugs in my veins.

Pulse rapid. Sweat dripping. Skin slick, and not just from lake water.

My heart beats the warning, radiates through my ribs, twitches in the skin beneath my eye.

My hand reaches out to steady his. It won't work and I know it.

He speeds up.

"What the fuck were you doing back there? What the fuck was that with the girl? Why the fuck are you high? Why the fuck are you so fucking stupid?"

Every word is a bullet jabbing holes into my body. It's a wonder I don't bleed out.

Tap tap tap–*I am numb to his ammo, so tired of this fight.*

I wanna give up, I wanna give in.

Let him kill me, just let him get it over with, please.

He slows down the car, lifts his hand from the wheel. Reaches, searches until he finds my flesh and can fit a small chunk between the pads of his fingers.

No one will notice the mark.

But I notice. And I want to scream:

"How will they ever heal if he doesn't stop making them?"

"How will the palms of my hands be smooth if I don't stop pricking them?"

"How will my life go on if I can't breathe or dream or even believe there is something worth going on for?"

No, *I think, and then I say it out loud.*

"No!"

I slap his hand away.

He jerks the wheel to the side.

My head slams into glass.

Crack. My skull or the window–

My vision bleeds, mixed up with dark smoke.

He swerves again, slams his fist to the car horn, beep beep beep, *and then–*

"Open your eyes. Open your fucking eyes!" He grabs my hair in his fist, yanks me forward.

My hand grips the gear shift. I slam the car into a low gear.

He loses control.

I brace for impact.

He lets go of the wheel to smash his fist into the side of my skull.

The squeal of tires, the crash of glass is the last thing I hear.

32

I COME TO with my face in my hands, and they're wet.

I savor the loneliness of this darkness before I open my eyes to see where I am.

There is no stopping this murderous menace inside me without facing the one horrible thing I held on to long enough to use it to leave.

That night with Tate in the car, I wasn't faultless, and he made sure everybody knew it.

But I wasn't the one behind the wheel. I wasn't the one inflicting the violence.

And I don't have to be afraid of him.

I'm something he should be afraid of.

I pull my hands away from my face to examine them. The crescent-shaped cuts I've left behind since I got here line up with the places once calloused from repeated injury. The bruises on my skin have long healed, turned back into watery milk. Somewhere beneath my hair is a scar from the stitches. The body still knows the score. It can never be fully forgotten.

When I try to stand, I find that though my legs are wobbly, they do provide support.

I walk toward the house, a little woozy but alert. It's slow, but I scale the steps into the golden porch light. Maybe I take tonight off. Even if I can't actually sleep, I do still have to be up early.

As expected, the door is unlocked.

The house is dark, cool even though outside is still muggy from the high heat of the day. My eyes adjust quickly to the lack of light, but still they feel like they are in cahoots with my mind, playing tricks with the shadows in the corner, the deep darkness that looks almost as if it's moving, living, breathing.

"Haven," comes my father's voice from the den.

I am sixteen again, and he's waiting up for me after I missed curfew and Buck told him he didn't know where I was. I am sixteen again, and he's going to punish me even though he wouldn't punish my brothers. I am sixteen again, and he is the monster from under my bed who's supposed to love me.

But I am not sixteen anymore. I don't have to be scared of him either.

A light turns on, casting over me in the foyer so my shadow stretches long, as if reaching for the nightmare hidden just beyond its reach.

"You're still up," I say, turning my voice to something more peppy, twisting around to face him. He's on the couch dressed in plaid pajama pants and a T-shirt. He waited up but got ready for bed. Did he lose a coin toss or something?

"None of us knew where you went," he says.

"My phone works," I reply. They didn't call or text, not even Lucky. This isn't about concern; it's about control. They feel slighted and I should have known they would; it's my mistake to fix.

Earl's eyes shift to mine. They are hooded like Buck's. Aqua like his too, but Earl's have more of a grassy undertone, making them paler. He turns them to the chair across from him.

"Why don't you sit a minute?" While it does come out a

question, there is only one response he'll accept, and my robotic reaction, feet shuffling in the direction, scuffing the wood floors and brushing the thick carpet, proves the point. I drop into the chair; all the lightness that lifted me earlier grows dense under the weight of his gaze.

I refuse to be the one to speak first.

"There's not a lot of places in this town where I can go anymore and just cut loose," he says, bringing his elbow to rest on the arm of the love seat.

We're sitting over by the window, where there's a small couch and two armchairs that make an arrangement. Nesting tables between the chairs, a low marble-topped coffee table in front of them and the love seat. When I was a kid, this room was two rooms, a more formal den and then the family room where we had a TV and played board games. Now it's one big room, scrubbed of the memories of all those years we grew up scratching floors with our shoes and dinging walls and living and pretending we were just a normal family.

"It's hard, being who I am. It draws eyes. Always has," he carries on, bringing his hand to his scruff and scratching. "When Antonio Reyes bought the bowling alley, I came in to invest in the remodel not because I wanted a cut–it wouldn't turn profit for years. I did it because I wanted a place away from prying eyes. Where I could find fellowship." He pauses, lets out a sigh. "So hard to come by back then."

He's working his way into something, and I am not making it any easier on him by offering prompts. I cross my feet at the ankles, drop my head back against the chair.

"It's good that you're connecting with folk back here. You and Lucky went out last night, he stayed over, you decided we weren't the bad guys, and came back here instead."

"I don't know why I would spend money on a hotel when I could stay here for free."

The lower lid under his left eye twitches. "Winter Reyes has her own ideas about how things should be, and she's made it hard for her parents. Antonio and Maria are good people, solid, reliable. I hate to see them struggle because of her."

I narrow my eyes, the furrow in my brow deep. "Are you trying to tell me who to hang out with?"

"You came back here to reconnect–"

"I came back because Buck said you were dying."

"I am." It's almost deadpan. I swear to God there's a smirk hiding under the wiry gray of his mustache. "I'm also trying to talk frankly with you. We were never very good at that in the past, and I don't want to make the same mistakes." His eyes have rounded in this way that cosplays concern but doesn't quite nail it.

"Then tell me what's wrong with you."

Tell me who the man in the stable is, I want to say. But I can't show my cards too early. I learned that from him. "Don't waste your breath on stuff that doesn't matter. It doesn't matter what's killin' me. I'm dying, no way around it, and I wanted all my kids here for as long as possible."

"I'm not staying here. I have a job, I have a life–"

"Haven, we all know you don't have a life."

Tears prick in my eyes as the harshness, and the truth, of his words hit me. He leans forward as I stammer, my mind stumbling for a response to throw him off balance like he's trying to do to me. This is his playbook. Meanness couched in fatherly guidance. A path of control rendered through confusion, with lamps gaslit, casting your eyes only where he wants them to stray.

"We never stopped wanting you here with us."

"No, I won't do this with you again."

"Do what? I'm trying to have a conversation."

"You're trying to convince me that all these years I spent away were my stupid decision done for no good reason. Not because of the shit you put me through, not because you didn't believe me about Tate."

He waves me off, rolls his eyes, and sits back. Straight up, ready to counter. "What happened with Tate was an accident, and all we wanted was for you to see both sides of it, see from our perspective and his. You had both been drinking that night—"

"I'm not talking about the accident. I know what you *think* happened that night, but I know what really did happen."

"Do you? I seem to recall you were fuzzy on the specifics."

"I wasn't fuzzy on the literal *years* before where he tormented me and you did nothing to stop him."

"What happened between you and Tate was between *you* and *Tate*."

"I was barely seventeen when he started abus—"

"That's an awfully strong word"—which he won't even say out loud, fucking coward—"when I know how hard it is to handle you."

"You don't get to do that again, turn this back around on me," I say, shaking my head, a fresh heat at the back of my eyes. I can't cry in front of him; he'll use that against me too. "I needed help, I needed *out*, and I needed a dad, but I didn't have one."

"I was a good father to you—"

"Keep telling yourself that." I stand. I have to move before the dam breaks. Tears are dismissed, they're too much, too loud, a feminine reaction that gives him the right to discredit everything else. "You wanna be honest, *Earl*." I let the use of his name slap him in the face like it should. "I came back here because I can't move on and I'm sick of it. I don't want to keep running from this place, from what happened here."

He's opening his mouth, gas on his tongue that he'll light with the flick of it over his teeth. He doesn't even know what all I mean, and still he's ready to fight me about it.

"You want to fix things before you die, start there. Start by admitting you were wrong." I spin on the balls of my feet, walking as fast as I can toward the foyer and the guest room beyond.

"You're just like her," he says, voice low, cold.

I stop, I shouldn't take the bait, but I do. "Who?"

"Who?" he spits back. "Your mother. It took me years to get her under control."

"And you think she is now?" If there is one thing Olympia Powers is, it's in control of herself.

"You have no idea, do you?" There's a shift in the air around me, hot and electric, the smell stale and metallic. The taste of pennies when I breathe it in.

"I'm tired," I say, not turning. I'd rather dig into his subconscious, or even hers, to figure out what that means anyway. Somehow, I think it would be more reliably truthful than anything that would ever come out of his mouth.

"Picking party starts at nine," he says, not pressing me more though the accusation hangs in the air between us, like a body on a noose. "I left you a gift in the guest room for the occasion." There is a loaded pause. "Breakfast is at eight."

The light goes out behind me, and I don't wait for him to pass by before leaving.

33

I HAVE BLATANTLY ignored the boot box Earl left sitting on my bed.

His gift for me to wear to the picking party tomorrow.

LUCCHESE written on the side.

But I'm in a staring contest with the dress hanging on the back door of the bathroom.

Collared, belted at the waist, light blue, with tiny white daisies printed all over. My fingers can't resist touching the soft, lightweight fabric, which I know without trying it on would be cool in this summer heat. It's my favorite color; it's probably the exact right size–Earl prides himself on knowing women's dress sizes.

The thought turns my stomach, but I can't look too closely at it.

Instead, I push the boot box to the side, crack open a Diet Coke, and immediately lose myself in a search for Tabby Collins's social media.

It looks like almost every other young woman's her age: a mix of cultivated photo shoots and candid drops with out-of-focus images and half-eaten food and random pics you'd have to have been there to understand. She is basic, and I have to fight the instinct welling up to judge her harshly.

I don't know what I would do to help her, or if there is anything I can do.

With Tate's reputation more important than ever, now that he's a full-blown pastor and not just second fiddle to his pop, his new wife, his flock to tend, it doesn't surprise me he's glommed on to a vulnerable girl who probably has her own daddy issues to work out. I remember Keller Collins in the way I remember all the men my dad brought around the ranch: vaguely with a sense of ick. As far as I know—and I know I could be wrong, considering the box—he never outright did anything to me, but I have the feeling he could have.

Tabby has a few innocent pics of Tate on her feed. The most notable—most unsettling—is from a few years back at the church car wash fundraiser. She can't be older than seventeen in the shot, dressed in a skimpy bikini, tanned to oblivion. Her blond hair is damp, she wears big sunglasses, and she's flanked on either side by Tate and her father. The men's hands look to be in competition for prime real estate on her still-adolescent frame.

I taste metal staring at it, eyes burning holes into the faces of the men.

Fuck, this is not my problem.

I let the phone drop to my lap. I rub my lids a little too vigorously, causing little swirls of light to twist around in the dark. When I open them, my vision is blurry. Exhaustion tries to tempt me, tug me down into the lush bedding, cocoon me in sleep I can't trust and won't learn from. I drag the Diet Coke to my lips and suck back another gulp of the dark liquid.

I need sleep, I know I do, but I need to learn what I can from Earl too. And I'm not sure sleep is totally safe anyway. I was tempted to try Olympia first since she was already out, but logic says the man in the stable is connected to Earl somehow. And Olympia is scary in a whole different way.

It's hard to know when I realized she was dangerous.

The memories of childhood, foggy as they are, their sharpness softened to a glow, make it hard to be clear on when she stopped feeling like a safe place to hide and became someone to hide from. But being in her presence is like standing outside in a thunderstorm, the pressure dropping its weight over my shoulders, buckling my knees so I can't move. It's been that way so long, it's hard to believe it was ever different.

There is a rustle of something coming from the closet.

I lock my phone screen, listening for it to happen again.

Everything feels so thin here. The air, my skin, the line between reality and insanity. Every second, I am more in danger of tipping over that line, bone breaking through flesh, lungs collapsing like deflated balloons.

There it is again–*scrape scrape*–like fingernails on a hardwood surface.

A hard lump forms in my throat. I shove up from the bed to inspect it. The creak of my socked feet moving over hardwood floors momentarily masks the sound, but when I reach the door, lay my palm over the handle, it sounds again: *scrape scrape.*

"It's probably a mouse," I say in an attempt to psych myself up. Even my scalp prickles with an awareness of something to fear. "Mice are scary," I lie. The handle is cool, my hand is hot. I twist it open and find that the closet is empty. Well, not empty. There are some hangers free of clothes, a vacuum leaning against the back wall, but the light streaming in from the pendant lamp on the ceiling of the guest room reveals no small rodent scurrying, nothing to warrant that sound. I tug at the door to close it when, over the creak of the hinges, I hear it again.

Scrape scrape.

The sound reminds me of something. It sits right at the edge of my mind, scratching at the soft squishy curves.

All at once it screams through me.

Lucky's closet.

From the corner of my eye, I see something move at the back of this closet. Not mouse-shaped. This form is taller–tall enough to be a small person. Its form off, the head not head-shaped, the shoulders stooped.

A child shape. A child shape with a ball cap.

I fling my gaze to the spot, but it's already scampered away.

The *scrape scrape* comes again.

I wait in silence, breath held in.

I wait, rubbing the sides of my temples, which ache from exhaustion.

I wait, sliding lids closed and open slower and slower and slower.

I wait until my legs hurt from standing.

"I have work to do," I say to rouse my body from the stupor it's trying to drift into. As much as I want a break, this house isn't built for me to relax.

I sit cross-legged on the ground beside the bed and close my eyes, focusing on the way my brain rocks and rolls, the waves slipping over a crest to fall *down down down.* As my mind begins to settle, my heart rate calms, the pump of blood throbbing through the veins in my neck eases from a *thumpthumpthump* to something more like *thump beat thump beat thuuump.*

There is the box in my mind's eye. The meadow. The tree stump it sits atop.

As I rest my thoughts on Earl, the box begins to quiver.

The hinges rattle like a storm comes from the inside, tries to break the lock, shatter the sides with gale-force winds. The sound is loud even though it isn't in my ears. One of my hands presses up to the cartilage, holding the flesh down against the side of my head.

It stops as fast as it starts
The box drops out of view.
A door stands in its place.

AT FIRST THERE *is no obvious way in.*

The rustic wood is weathered, and the chunky metal handle is old. The lock appears to be one that you need a big ornate key for. I don't have a key, but I remember the junk drawer in the kitchen. Over by the back door, it held everything from spare rubber bands to staples, from pens and pencils to Post-its, and a whole bunch of skeleton keys they found around the property when they laid the foundation. Keys from some previous something that existed here before, was bulldozed down, forgotten.

One of the keys materializes in front of me on the ground. The memory the answer to the riddle of his door.

It fits perfectly.

The lock opens with a click.

I enter to find I'm not in a room like the others, not a cage like Charity; I'm in the peach orchard at Powers Ranch. Rows and rows of trees stand rigid beneath a blistering hot sun.

The other thing I don't see here is Earl. Maybe he's hiding somewhere and I'll have to find him.

Dust rises from the earth, dancing. The wind at my back urges me forward.

Boots scuff–boots? I look down to inspect my feet to find I wear boots. The reddish tan and deep brown heel immediately familiar. These were my boots when I lived here. I wore them to ride Princess and pick peaches and play perfect, pretty country girl.

I walk through the orchard now, overcome by the sweet smell of fruit and almond, the honeyed scent of ripening as new blossoms sprout and open.

But it isn't fruit on these trees.

These trees are burdened with objects: a baseball glove, a broken watch, a belt buckle.

On and on and on, as far as I can see.

"Trees sprouting memories." I breathe out the words. I know in my gut they are true.

Earl's life is laid out like an ample harvest, ripe for the picking.

I begin to walk, taking turns around each tree in search for the one I came here to find.

The man was dressed in a ball cap.

Tennis shoes on his feet.

Something about him must be here.

As I move back and forth between lines, branches kissing my cheeks, I find myself filled, surprisingly, not with horror, not fear but . . . with wonder.

There is a prestige to his mind, an aura that this man holds his life with a certain regard.

Fruitful and lush and growing.

He isn't trying to mend anything. How could he? When he doesn't see any one of these things as flawed. His life is an orchard, carefully cultivated, always rising up toward the sun. If his illness torments him, he's found somewhere that isn't here to lock it away.

And that may be where he's put the truth about that day.

Where he's put all his horrible truths he can't look right at, just like me.

As soon as the thought materializes in my subconscious, doors appear in the ground a few rows over from where I stand.

A storm cellar built into the earth, closed and padlocked tight.

I move with dream speed, coming upon it as soon as I have the thought that I want to.

My hands grip the lock, yank, and pry. I use the heel of my boot to slam against the metal. But nothing is working.

"Help me," I whisper-plead to the smoke that makes my shadow look bigger in here. "I need to break in. I need to break through it somehow. I need to–"

Manic energy rips through me as I bang my fists on the door, beat the wood until the edges of my hands look raw, but the material of the door doesn't yield. It doesn't even really feel like wood.

I rise and start to stomp. The doors bob and billow like waves, only solid and unreal.

"What is this?" On the second, third, fourth kick, I am screaming for the nightmare.

My voice takes on a primal tone. My hands ball into fists and unfurl and then–

The smoke that fills in the shadow shape around my body, that I can see in mirrors when I'm here, begins to bleed from the ends of my fingers, spiders up my forearms through the veins beneath my skin. In awe, I come to a standstill as the smoke twists a long hooked shape around the curve of the padlock. Hungrily, I watch to see what it will do.

A force grabs me by the waist, yanks me back through the orchard, the smoke trailing behind like blood.

I fight, my feet scraping the earth, turning up ruts in the ground as I dig in my heels.

I reach for the branches, but my fingers find no purchase, the leaves slip through them, wood slicing my skin.

I bleed ribbons of red that mix with the stream of smoke, and I scream and I scream until my throat is ragged and my body is tossed over the hillside, back to the ranch front porch.

34

I WAKE ON the porch on all fours.

My knees are ruddy with burns from crawling.

My fingers ache, stuck through with splinters.

My pulse pounds in my throat.

A scream dies fast on my lips.

I flip over onto my back and ease up to a seated position, tugging my knees up to examine the burns forming angry red marks. My palms ache, but the sting of tiny shards of wood in the soft pads of my fingertips is even worse. As my mind still emerges from the layers between here and the trek through Earl's mind, it's hard to even see the splinters yet. But I know they are there. I can feel them.

My eyelids rake closed. Something did not want me to go inside that storm cellar. But it wasn't my nightmare that stopped me; the nightmare was trying to help.

It was some other force that interfered.

The thought chills me deep in my core.

"What in the world are you doing out here?" My mother's voice, another force, chilling in its own silky, sweet, sickening way.

My eyes open.

She stands in the doorway, a straw-headed apparition.

"Sleepwalk." My throat is raw. I was screaming in there. I was screaming in there, and now my throat is raw.

"Come on inside. Let's get you cleaned up."

WE SIT AT the kitchen table.

Spread out on the wooden top is antiseptic and some cotton balls. In her hands is a pair of sharp metal tweezers she uses to pluck at the splinters.

This close, her scent consumes everything else.

Like a flower that blooms at night, dark violet mixes together with sweet vanilla and some sharp green smell that reminds me of lying in the grass after it's been cut.

This close, I can map the lines of her face.

They form ridges in her forehead and a bridge between her plucked blond brows. They hang on the corners of her lips. They tell the story of a woman who has spent much of her life disappointed in something.

"You do that a lot?" It's the first thing she's said to me since she started plucking. "Sleepwalk."

"Sometimes," I reply, staring, determined to catch every nuance of her expression.

"Sterling used to as a kid," she says, "Do you remember that?"

"Not really," I lie. I want to know what she remembers.

Her eyes flick up to my face. Same blue. Me and her and Lucky.

"We had to start locking his door from the outside because he kept getting himself hurt or making a mess, which wasn't as bad, except for the time he filled the toilet with paper and flooded half the upstairs."

I laugh, surprised, as an image of Sterling–couldn't be more than five–in pj's, hair mussed up, stands in the middle of the bathroom crying.

"He woke up with wet feet," I say. I remember it, or I supply the image because it makes sense.

"He did." She laughs. It's small but audible at least. "Your daddy was big mad." I don't recall that. I don't even try. Her voice drops off, her focus sharpening on the last few splinters still stuck in my hand.

"I remember when he fell off the treehouse," I say, and it feels risky somehow. For a breath, her hand stutters. She carries right on, right after, but I saw it. She knows something about that night. "You remember?"

"Of course," she says, exhaling and dropping my hands. "All cleaned out." She grabs a cotton ball and douses it in alcohol. It's cold when it hits my skin. Her eyes find mine. "Do I need to lock you in too?"

My eyes widen and I purse my lips. "I think I'll be fine. Almost time to get up anyway."

She looks at the clock to see it's close to six a.m. The sun will be up soon.

"Don't be late for breakfast." She drops her gaze to my hands. Small red drops bloom on a few of my fingers. "Those should close up fast." I think she's gonna leave it at that, but instead she reaches out and brushes her hand against my cheek. "There's a hydrating mask in the guest cupboard, if you want it." She pinches my chin congenially. And she's gone.

As her perfume fades, the aroma of burnt peanut butter dances in the air all around me.

35

LIGHT CAME WAY too fast.

The smell of bacon frying in a pan turns my stomach, already sour. Exhaustion grips my eyelids, but my will is stronger. The coffee in this mug helps. I hover in the kitchen, my back to the windows overlooking the pool, and watch Olympia buzz around like a bee, putting finishing touches on the breakfast spread for the whole family to enjoy before the picking party commences. There's a platter of homemade buttermilk biscuits, sausage gravy staying warm on the stove, fruit salad, and a pitcher of OJ.

She hasn't said a word to me since I walked in. That singular bit of tenderness last night was all I'm allowed to get. Lucky flops into a chair beside me, dressed in a polo, jeans, and boots.

"He got to you too," I say, kicking the toe of my boot against Lucky's.

His eyes drag down to stare at my boots, which I've tucked my jeans into, and paired with a white T-shirt. "Those look new," he says, "and expensive."

"Earl," I reply. I debated putting them on. I debated throwing them in the horse's trough. I decided that wearing them would give Earl the illusion that he'd won a battle, which may aid me in the war.

I debated putting the dress on too. But that felt like too large of a concession, even if I am technically wearing the same white T-shirt I wore that first night again because I am out of clothes. This one had the least offensive smell and no stains.

Earl enters the kitchen, also dressed in his cowboy boots, jeans, and a crisp peach-colored polo. His eyes trail over the space, take in the breakfast spread, see Olympia at the stove removing the bacon from the pan, and then finally land on Lucky and me.

He realizes I'm not wearing the dress but sees that I am wearing the boots.

It gets a smile at least. "Good morning, children." He sounds tired. He trudges across the kitchen to pour himself a cup of coffee.

"Buck, Sterling, and the girls will be here any minute," Olympia says as she turns around from the stove to set the plate of crisp bacon on the counter. She looks up, meets my eyes, and it's the first time I notice how exhausted she looks.

Did no one sleep well last night? Is this somehow connected to me being here?

"Y'all dig in," Olympia says, flicking her eyes between me and Lucky. "We have a full day ahead."

With a groan, Lucky rises from the table. "I need coffee."

"God, I need more," I say.

"Don't take the Lord's name in my kitchen," Olympia says.

From across the corner of the island where she has set the plates, I catch Lucky roll his eyes in response. Earl bops him on the crown of the head, and he straightens up his face. Then grins as soon as Earl turns his attention away.

"This smells amazing," I say to kill the giggle in my throat. It should smell amazing anyway, but my stomach wants to revolt. I can feel it. "Like home."

There's a quirk of Olympia's lips, and it doesn't turn into a smile, but she also isn't openly frowning at me anymore. I sidle up beside Lucky as she passes me on her way around to set down another plate of sausage. "Pace yourself," she says under her breath. "You know how the heat makes you nauseous."

It's a subtle dig at my past. Her reminder that once, I was so fucked up I couldn't keep food in my stomach. That's not fair, or true even, but that doesn't matter to her.

Lucky begins piling his plate, and I follow his lead, even if my anxiety is spiking off the charts now.

"You two need to get your game faces on," Earl says, taking a deep drink from his novelty mug that reads TEXAS SIZED HEART, a laughable concept for him. "We don't always win—"

"Except that every year since I've been playing, we have," Lucky says.

"And when I used to play, I remember you saying, 'Powers are winners, especially at their own games.'" I lower my voice in a shitty Earl impersonation.

Lucky snorts, I smirk, and Earl grunts.

"Y'all always were two peas in a pod," Earl says, but he doesn't actually sound happy about it.

And a quick glance at Lucky's face reveals a conflict in the expression that I didn't expect. Like he wants to be two peas with me, but he also knows the risk that comes with being lumped in with his black-sheep big sister. A wave of grief hits me, and I'm surprised he feels that way, surprised I want Lucky to want to be lumped in with me. I want him to be on my side, but I don't want that to be a bad thing for him.

I internally shake off the feeling but can't shake the truth. Whatever happens from me unraveling the story of the man in the stable and how it ties into my box and my fucked-up nightmare brain, Lucky may get caught in the crosshairs. He might wind up hurt by it, and I desperately wish there was some way to prevent that from happening.

We take seats at the kitchen table as Earl and Olympia grab

their food. There's noise from the front door opening, the sounds of my brothers' voices, Clarabelle and Julep sniping, the clomp of four pairs of boots on the wood floor. They all enter the kitchen dressed in festive, decidedly Southern garb, and for a second I let my guard drop just enough to acknowledge that this is my family.

These brothers, those parents—they are my blood. They carry the same history inside them. We share traits, mannerisms, and a past that we may try to bury but can never erase. There is no way to change where I come from, no amount of running, no new name, no boundary drawn—nothing will ever be strong enough.

This is why I have to try to understand that history instead of smudging the pictures and ignoring the truth, why even if it tears this family apart, it is worth doing.

It's worth becoming their nightmare if that means I—we—can also be free.

There is a clamor as everyone makes plates and passes around the kinds of polite compliments that you would expect from people who don't know how to be honest with each other, let alone themselves. It's easy to read the mistrust still permeating the air between Sterling and Buck, brought on by my influence on Sterling's subconscious last night. But that's not all I notice in Buck's posture, the deep purple smudges beneath his eyes, or how his voice cracks a little at the back of his throat like it's raw. Weariness pulses from every move he makes. He's uneasy, overly tired. I haven't done anything to his mind, so this can't be because of me, even if my conditioned response is to always think I'm the problem.

The rest of them take their seats around the kitchen table, all except Earl, who stands to draw all our attention to him. Buck drops into the seat across from me, his eyes skating over my face, to my T-shirt, and I almost want to show him the boots on my feet just to wipe the look of judgment away.

Clarabelle does it for me. "Oooh, gorgeous Lucchese, Haven."

"They were a gift," I say, then look at Earl.

His lips settle into a smile. Sterling's glare goes nuclear, but he fills his mouth with biscuit and gravy to hide the immediate scowl.

"Let's powwow," Earl says, and I immediately cut my eyes over to Lucky to see that his have gone wide and are pinned right on me.

"Dad, you can't say that," Lucky says.

"I can say whatever I want in my own house," Earl counters.

"Dude, get out of here with your woke Austin shit," Sterling interjects and reaches over to slam his fist into Lucky's shoulder.

"Ow, fuck—"

"Language." Olympia draws her napkin up to wipe at the corners of her lips. She doesn't chide them further though. "Eyes on your dad, y'all." Hers rise to meet Earl's, and there's an exchange of energy that seems to say, *The floor's yours and always will be.* If there is one thing I have never doubted, it's that my parents see the value in each other and will do everything in their power to make sure others do too.

"Thank you, dear," Earl says, a renewed command in his voice. "Now, you all know the rules of the picking party. Each member of the team has a basket to fill up with as many ripe peaches as they can handle. I think it's a good idea we do like last year: fan out across the rows, with the boys taking the limbs, climbing ladders when they can get access, and the girls scouring the ground for ripe fruit, but not overly so." He looks at me, looks like he half expects me to argue with his plan.

I press my lips back into a tight smile but don't say a word. Everyone else chimes in with varying words of affirmation and agreement.

Soon, the festivities will begin. There will be a local news crew outside to capture it all. And the whole time, whether we win or lose, the Powers family name will be front and center. A reminder of who puts this town on the map and the debt of gratitude they are owed.

36

I STAND IN the center of the group, hands tight around the curve of the basket handle, and survey the setup. The mayor, a man I don't recognize, stands at the entrance to the orchard, flanked by the local camera crew on one side and his helmet-haired brunette wife on the other, wearing a pearl-buttoned blouse and her own pair of too-tight Wranglers.

The teams consist of many of the same people from the barbecue yesterday. The Turners, both John and Charity and Tate and . . . Delilah. Has to be her, because she stands beside Tate with her hand clutched in his. She's pretty, with platinum locks she's twisted into two pigtails, tied with red gingham ribbon to match her dress, and boots in a soft, supple white leather. My eyes trail over her profile as she turns to say something to him, a secret that makes her scrunch her button nose, her dark lashes fluttering, a silent giggle on her red lips.

She was there last night among the blonds. I remember her now, though at the time, I didn't know who she was. In a lot of ways she is the more prim and proper version of Tabby Collins, who is basically the bleached-blond, fake-tanned version of me when I was dating Tate all those years ago. I scan across the crowd until I spot Tabby and her father far away from Tate and Delilah.

I notice the way Tabby's eyes are pinned right on Tate's mouth.

I notice the way her lips are tight and her gaze tracks to Tate's hand as it comes around to clasp Delilah at the waist.

I notice other things about Tabby that I didn't before at Powers Premier Automotive or the barbecue or with the brief glance I gave her in the honky-tonk last night. Like how her shoulder blades protrude from a back with no extra meat, how her shorts are long, hiding a lot of her thin thighs, how they hang loose, her belt working overtime to keep them on her hips, how her pointer finger scratches at the skin around her thumb, picking it raw.

And then, because noticing all of that is a threat to the calm I barely control, I force my attention away from Tabby, track over other faces, stop on one that has an entirely different effect.

Yearning is torture, but at least it's the good kind.

Winter stands in between her younger siblings, Celia and Matteo, and in front of her parents. It's just her and her siblings holding baskets, leading me to believe they will compete for their family while their parents look on. Something Earl and Olympia would never do, because that would mean they trusted us, which they most definitely don't. Winter must feel the weight of my gaze on her, because suddenly she's looking right at me. She waves, but there is a tentativeness to it. I definitely was weird when I got out of her car last night. I'll have to try to smooth things over later.

Buck presses into my side. "Get your head in the game," he whispers, elbow digging into my rib cage. "They're about to fire the starter pistol."

And sure enough, the mayor has reached the end of whatever speech he'd been giving, and he's raising his hand, gun at the ready to start the show.

"Game face," Sterling says, edging up on the other side.

"Y'all keep saying that, but I was born ready." This is Lucky, behind me.

And despite everything, I smile, because there is a certain kinetic spark that comes with being part of the Powers family. Inside the huddle instead of looking on from a distance. For this split second, I let the fire ignite within me, empowering all my muscles and bones, lighting my mind up in all the right places.

The gunshot cracks the air, the sound echoing all around as we move in the direction of the orchard.

My feet move before my thoughts catch up, scraping across the earth and underneath the thick cover of tree leaves. Bodies scatter, fanning out to all corners. Sterling breaks to the left, Lucky the right, alongside Buck. Olympia, Clarabelle, and Julep split off toward a cluster of trees, where the ground is covered with peaches in varying states of decay. Earl moves to a ladder, one of the many that stand erect around the orchard for people to fight over in order to get the higher hanging fruit. I launch out onto the path straight ahead of me, eyes trained on a tree about halfway down.

The ground below it is laden with peaches.

As I approach, I'm hit immediately by the sour smell of fruit gone bad. Sweet booze mixes with pungent earth. I bend to search for one that isn't overripe. Flesh gives under my fingers as I fondle the voluptuous bodies, rolling them over to reveal a minty green coat on the fuzzy skin.

Finally, I spy one, unbruised and still tight. This discovery gives way to others, and soon I'm gathering fruit from the lower branches as I make my way meticulously around the trunk. The weight of my basket grows heavy. I round the side of the tree ready to move on to the next one, where Tabby Collins stands a few rungs up on the steel ladder.

My body tugs me toward her without permission.

Words cling to the back of my throat. My skin is slick with sweat that I want to attribute to nothing but the heat. Even here under the cover of all this green, it swelters, cooking more than the peaches. It cooks the bodies beneath.

Tabby spies me and grins. "I got this one practically picked clean," she says, sounding proud of herself. Her voice has a soft twang with a girlish brightness to it that makes her seem younger than twenty.

"Well, then you won't mind me grabbing the ones you missed down here?" I say with a laugh, competition almost getting the better of me. I don't really care about the party, the prize, or the prestige of winning. None of that's real to me, none of it matters. But it would be a lie if I said some small, stupid part of me–the same part that wants Lucky to *want* to be lumped in with me and wishes there was no box and no nightmare and no ulterior motive for me being back here–didn't want to show up at the end of the party with a basket full of perfectly ripe peaches to make my family proud.

Which is why I don't realize what my eyes are showing me until it's too late.

They travel the length of her leg.

My stomach swims.

From here, I can see that Tabby's inner thigh is dotted with plum-colored bruises. Bruises I once had on my own inner thigh and on the soft underside of my bicep from years of Tate Turner gathering flesh between fingers and pinching hard until he left a mark.

"What happened to you?" The words leave my mouth in a burst.

Tabby freezes, her hand midair above her head on its way to pluck a piece of fruit. I move toward her like I'm going to reach out and touch her legs, skate fingertips over the marks as if trying to wipe them away. She flinches back, her feet shifting over to one side of the ladder and causing it to teeter off balance. I reach for the ladder, trying to steady it, but she's already climbing down, boots scraping and then slamming one after the other on solid ground.

Tabby is about my height, but with a smaller frame, bigger head, the proportions of her body more like a lollipop or a bobblehead, and this close, I can see that even a little bit of exertion has her panting.

Tate Turner's desire is a wasting disease.

A parasite that consumes from the inside out.

"I don't know what you mean," she says, adjusting her basket so it's hiding her thighs behind it. Her eyes are like a prey animal: wide pupils blown out with fear.

"You probably don't know about my history with him, but I know how he is," I say. Already this feels futile. She's in a relationship with her pastor, a power imbalance even without the fact that she's barely twenty and he's thirty, a community leader, a man in a world made for men.

"I don't know what you mean," she says, a weak lie repeated. She probably believes it's worth a shot. She doesn't know that I saw her with him at the honky-tonk. She doesn't know that even if I didn't, I would recognize his handiwork anywhere. I would put the pieces together. I would know the truth because I lived it.

"Tabby, I know what's happening with Tate."

"Pastor Turner?" she says, the crack in her voice on the end of his name an easy tell. She swallows hard, hoping to fix it. "He's my pastor." She narrows her brow, scrunches her lips. Her eyes roll. "He's married."

"Why would that matter if he's just your pastor?"

"There's nothing going on—"

"I saw you two." I stop her because, why let her waste more energy trying to convince me? "At Coyote Crossroads. Outside town."

She blanches.

"Last night."

"I don't . . . I . . . um." She lets the basket drop to one side, her single-handed clutch precarious. She shakes her head like she's trying to clear it and her gaze momentarily drifts. She looks lost in the maze of her thoughts.

I'm not a hero. I have never wanted that for myself.

Not when I figured out how to get away from this place. Saved up money, plotted a plan, asserted myself all the way out the door. That was survival, rebellion as a necessity, strength that was self-serving. I didn't do it so others after me would know that they could.

I did it so I could keep on living.

I didn't want it that night outside Second City Title and Trust when Roger stepped into my space and acted like I should just let him. It wasn't about Cindy, what happened next, and I don't think vigilante justice was served at my hand. I don't get a badge of honor for killing a man who hurts women.

I don't want to save Tabby Collins; I can't even save myself.

"You don't have to do this." There's a fight in my voice, something almost righteous, something easily confused with concern. I don't know why it's there, where it comes from, and I wish I could shut the fuck up.

Her eyes snap to mine.

"You can't say anything. He'll get angry." She takes a step toward me, a fresh urgency in her voice. "I have this whole thing under control."

I don't mean to, but I laugh. It's a cutting sound.

"You know that's how women end up dead, right?" *Stop arguing with her, just back away.* My voice, but not totally. My voice, but from somewhere deep inside and hollow.

"Look, I know some women can't handle a strong man—"

"He's married and your pastor and a decade older than you—"

"You don't know anything about us, so why don't you just mind your own business?"

Indignant little shit. I reach out to grab her, hold her in place, force her to listen, but something's not right and I know it.

The world twists and teeters around me.

37

IT TAKES EVERY ounce of my will to turn around and walk away from her.

Inside my head, a rumble of thunderous thoughts collide.

Tabby is in danger and I could help her.

Tate is a threat and he will never be stopped. I should stop him.

Stay the fuck out of it. This is not your problem, you have enough problems, you don't owe anyone anything. This one is in that weird me-voice from the depths of some hollow dark place. The nightmare part of me.

I whirl around and press my back against the smooth bark, inhaling the heady green scent. The box feeds on my emotions, uses it to conjure the nightmare inside me and the minds of others.

Tabby could end up dead at Tate's hands. He will use her up until all that is left is a shell of the girl she once was, and no one will understand what happened. No one will see it for what it really is. She'll keep on giving the best parts of herself away while he goes on playing the good Christian man for everyone who tithes ten percent to the church. She won't learn, he won't change, and one day he'll discard her for somebody else.

Hyacinth.

Clarabelle's story comes screaming back. Her sister dated a

man she never named, he hurt her, he broke her, and when it was all over, she got branded as a woman gone crazy because that is a lot easier to ignore. I'm not certain that man was Tate, but I don't have to be.

If it wasn't, it was some other man.

Some man Hyacinth protected, some man who never faced the consequences for what he did.

Some man who never will.

They never pay for the wrong things they have done.

That's why they keep doing them. Over and over and over–

You can't let them get away with it, my nightmare thoughts whisper-hiss.

I shake the thought away. What can I do? In the end, I'm still just a little girl with a box of horror.

"Haven." His voice is a lance. I open my eyes. Tate has a serial killer's smile. He exudes the charming ease of a man who fears nothing, like Roger, like so many others. He's reaching his hand out to touch me–*a good pastor comforts the weak.*

I shift out of his reach. "I'm fine." There are so many things I want to say, but this isn't the place, and now isn't the time. If I lose control and kill him right here, the whole town would bear witness, and what then?

You're not plotting a murder, I instruct the psycho inside my head.

"You don't look fine," he says, dropping his hand to his side. The basket in his other hand is half full. His grip on the handle tightens, causing the exposed muscle of his forearm to ripple. "Let me get you some water. You're overheating."

"Fuck off with this Good Samaritan bullshit." I straighten. It feels good to spew curses right in his face. "I need to get back to the competition."

There's a twitch to his upper lip. The snarl of an angry beast. "Give me a break," he says.

"Not on your life," I say as I move.

His free hand grabs my forearm, wrapping it up in his grip. "We need to talk."

I yank, trying to break out of his grip, but he reverses the thrust of my pull and drags me closer to him.

The temperature drops. Goose bumps rise on my arms, pricking against his hold. His arm hairs stand on end. There's a flutter of confusion that runs over his face, he loosens his grip momentarily, and I break free of it.

"For your sake, I wouldn't bother me again." I could threaten him with what I know about Tabby Collins, but something tells me that would be the key to unlock the box all over him. I can't be doing that, no matter how much I'd love to see that shit-eating grin of his wiped off his face.

I bolt around him, not waiting for whatever response he might give.

I keep walking until the temperature returns to normal.

I don't bother gathering more fruit, don't want to risk slowing down. The nightmare part of me sure does hunger for free rein to do her vigilante shit. The more I use the box on purpose, the stronger, more volatile it seems to become. It's been changing ever since I arrived back at the ranch, and with every use, it seems to gain more access to my mind.

The more I try to fix this–fuck–the harder it gets to control it.

The further away I get from safety.

The closer I am to insanity.

I weave through the trees, not sure what I'm searching for but just wanting to put more distance behind myself, Tabby, and Tate.

I reach the area closest to where the crowd that's come to watch is gathered.

My eyes graze over the faces and bodies, looking for something to ground me–Matilda. Maybe she came here; maybe I could hide out beside her until the game ends. There is a sinking in my stomach when I realize she didn't come, and I guess I should be glad. She's probably not in support of this free labor masquerading as fun. She's not a shit person, even if she's living in a shit town.

Now I turn my attention to the players.

They've morphed into similar shapes, skin suits moving around in a frenzy. Vaguely, I hear the mayor announcing a warning. It crackles from a megaphone and sends the frenzy of the zombies picking to a feverish pitch. I take a spot next to one of the unoccupied trees near the front. Already picked clean, leaving behind only unripe fruit and the sickly sweet smell of rotting discards on the ground.

Winter. She takes shape in my vision. Then her siblings. They compare the haul in each other's baskets. I remember from back then that families often register with other families to up their chances of winning. There can be a total of ten to a team, but because there are only so many peaches and because people have to register for the lottery as the team playing with all members included, smaller teams wind up throwing in their names and—when chosen—also wind up outnumbered.

It feels rigged from the start.

The Reyes siblings are all smiles. The easy way they talk to each other, the lightness in the air around them even as the rest of the picking zombies rush to gain just a little more harvest. It is a knife in my guts twisted incrementally with every single breath.

I want what they have.

I want to be good enough to have it.

Haven, we all know you don't have a life. Earl's shitty words.

Of course I don't. This family made sure that I couldn't.

Not directly, maybe not intentionally, but neither of those things turned out to matter. There's a lot I let happen to me, even more that I did to myself, but I don't believe any of that is coincidence.

I grew up as a Powers. I was a foal to be broken.

When I find Earl in the crowd, he looks winded. His skin overly ruddy, sweat coating his brow, dripping down to stain the collar of his shirt. Buck moves up beside him with his overfull basket in one hand, the other outstretched—an offer of help. Earl doesn't take it, anger flashing in his eyes. Cold spreads though the blistering heat.

Crack! The gunshot to end the game shatters the frenzy.

Shatters my thoughts.

Shatters whatever was left of my hope.

MY PARENTS HOLD their peach baskets up in the air like trophies.

We are the runaway winners, even with my fairly poor showing, and even though the rest of the participants fought hard. We keep our spoils while everything they picked for us today is turned over to be cooked into preserves and sold to raise money for the church. Not philanthropy, more like some kind of fruit-based money laundering scheme.

Earl steps up to address the crowd before they disperse. Right about now, the festival will be starting in full swing. The bulk of the setup is downtown on the grass surrounding the courthouse. They added a carnival in the parking lot behind the antique store a block off the square this year, per the pamphlet I now hold in my hand, given to me by a young, peppy volunteer.

"This year, Olympia and I considered pulling the picking party from the festival—"

The assertion is met immediately by an outcry of dismay and disapproval.

Earl waves them off, turns his eyes to Olympia, and offers her a sad sort of smile. It's his *be strong for the cameras* moment, and he milks it for all it's worth.

"Oh, Lord have mercy–" Olympia steps in, taking Earl's hand in hers as she moves. Her smile is blinding. I almost look away from the sheer brightness of it. "We didn't, and we won't. As long as we're both here, the picking party will be too," she says with the smallest tremor in her voice. A little earthquake of held-in emotion. Both of them, not just her. Olympia has built her whole life around Earl, and if he's gone, that life crumbles right along with it.

I don't need to get inside her head to know this to be true.

This house may be her home, with her fingerprints on every surface, her sensibilities hidden in the nooks, the crannies, the throw pillows on the couches, and the paintings on the walls, but that is where her ownership stops. She helped him build his dealership empire, birthed his heirs, but her life is a legacy to his.

"We're grateful to this town for holding tradition at its heart for another year running"–Earl looks at the mayor, who glows like a lamp with a brand-new bulb–"and Fellowship Kind for keeping the hearts of the people trained to the Lord."

A cacophony of agreement in the form of hoots and hollers dances around the crowd. A few of the men closest to Tate reach out to pat him on the back: *Good ole boy, well done.*

I can't help it. I search for Tabby in the crowd, and with so many blonds–including Delilah, who is in her place right at Tate's side–it takes me a minute. All that straw hair and tan skin, it's a sea of beige. When I find her, she's standing in close proximity to her dad. Keller has her wrist in his grip, keeping her pinned in beside him. Her body peels away like wallpaper coming unstuck. Thick hairy knuckles are a vice she can't escape. I hate myself that I want to help her, as if I could change anything without also ripping through her father's throat like a wild animal tearing a carcass to shreds, as if my help wouldn't cause her more trauma.

"We're a blessed *body*," Earl says, using the biblical meaning of the word.

"Now, y'all go on and enjoy the festivities!" Olympia finishes.

Earl wraps an arm around her shoulders, tugs her in tight, and plants a kiss. Never ones to disobey an order, the crowd quickly begins to disperse back to the buses that brought them here.

My skin chafes against the leather of these boots even though there's a layer of denim between them and the inside. I want to change back into my regular shoes and splash cold water on my face and tie my hair up in a ponytail to unstick it from the thick coating of sweat on my neck. I want to wipe this whole day away and try to put what I've learned behind me.

I want to store it in the box, but I know I can't anymore.

"Hey, Sis." Lucky comes up beside me. "Was thinking I'd go check out the festival if you wanna join." He shoves his sunglasses up, pushes back his sandy blond hair.

I throw a glance to where Buck, Sterling, Clarabelle, and Julep are all gathered.

"I think it's just us." Lucky tracks my gaze. "The others want to bring their kids, so they'll show up whenever."

"Even better," I reply, not fighting back the smile that wants to show up on my face, not popping the bubble of hope that forms in my chest.

I want him to want to be a pea in a pod with me. This is a chance to bond with him without the added pressure of trying to break into his mind afterward. This is a chance to be someone to him, someone he might even think of fondly, even when she's gone.

"Give me five minutes to freshen up first?"

He gifts me the biggest grin. It's mine now, forever, to carry with me no matter what comes next.

38

FRIENDSHIP PEACH FESTIVAL turns the already quaint historic downtown into a scene right out of your favorite movie. Maybe a Hallmark one, a summer romance you can watch when the heat is too high and the drinks are ice cold.

Too bad it's all a lie.

I park in one of the pay lots they've set up at the edge of the town square. It's usually a free public lot attached to the civic center and the public pool, but with everything converted for the festival, this lot now requires a purchase, another economic boost to the town.

The Romanesque courthouse rises from the center, green grass sprawled all around, now hedged with rows of booths selling peach-related food products, local artisans and artists hocking wares, and even a few food trucks along the road. The carnival rides peak over the tops of the buildings to one side of the square. The antique store has a sign on the shut-down street advertising that you can walk through the maze in the store to exit through the back, spilling you out into the carnival entrance.

"Wanna go halvesies?" Lucky asks, pointing across the grass to a booth promoting their funnel cakes and frozen drinks, all different variations of peaches and other summer fruits. My stomach whines inaudibly. I didn't dig into breakfast. Eating hasn't actually been all that easy since I got back here in general. Not super surprising either when I'm trying so hard to maintain control. Not eating too much keeps me from receding back to that other coping mechanism. Utter lack of sleep and vats of caffeine also have a way of making me nauseous with no end in sight.

Lucky doesn't dredge up the same stress inside me.

My mind shows me the image from his, the closet with the something scratching from behind the wall. I blink–fuck, I'm tired–and then remember the weird thing from the guest room closet last night. There's no way they are connected, right?

"Sure, but I could use the sugar rush, so I'm getting my own peach-blackberry slushie," I reply, and then I add, almost as an afterthought let out by the previously mentioned exhaustion, "Texas wild blackberries are peak nostalgia."

The forest that creates the back boundary to the ranch, and forms one of the wild areas on the two hundred acres, was one of the playgrounds of my childhood. Memories of picking and then immediately eating the unwashed blackberries from the bushes that grew out of control at the edges are some of the few sharply focused ones I can recall.

Safe from the box, preserved like jam.

"Peak nostalgia," Lucky agrees, though his voice is shaded with some deeper emotion. Suddenly, not casual or nostalgic at all.

"You remember picking the wild blackberries?" I ask, prodding at him now to try to understand the change. We make our way over to the booth. "It was my favorite thing to do when school let out for summer."

"Yeah, it was fun," he says, gray-toned, though still with a smile.

For a second I imagine him there again, his mouth stained by the deep rich purple juice. The image slips away too fast.

"There was this one time, after you were too old to take me," he says, his voice bruised as he rushes to pretend he's not injured, "I followed Sterling out there even though he'd told me not to follow him."

I raise my brows. Lucky mimes flipping him off.

"Sounds right," I say.

"I got turned around because it was dusk–you know how the forest is that time of day," he says, and I do.

I remember the velvet lavender light, the way it softened the edges of tree trunks and branches, a cloak to call wild animals out from their hiding places to claim the night for themselves. None of them ever harmed us, but that didn't stop us from making a game out of our fear.

"I wound up over at those old house ruins," he says, "you know, the ones from whatever was there way back before Friendship was formed." I nod, remembering the crumbling frame of the house overgrown with weeds and poison ivy. "I had stupid tennis shoes on with thin rubber soles, and I thought I heard a coyote, so I went running to the ruins to hide. Stepped right on a rusty-ass nail and sat there scream-crying. It was night before Buck came and found me."

I don't remember this, not in the *pulled from my mind and played like a movie reel* way. But as he tells me the story, I supply all my own images for details. There is the sound of his scream, his running feet, the sharp prick of the nail. Then another one swims up to replace the one I conjure for Buck.

My brother looks at me through the opening of cabinet doors. Hand outstretched.

Sent to find me.

The smell of burnt peanut butter cookies still lingering in the air.

Buck was always coming to find us. When did he stop feeling like my own personal chivalrous knight of a brother?

"Two peach-blackberry slushies and a funnel cake," Lucky says, and I'm tossed back into myself, present and accounted for at the festival. He pulls out his wallet, drops some cash on the counter to pay.

"You don't have to get my slushie," I try to say, but he waves me off. I stare at the side of his face, watching the small inflections as he pays, the smile that spreads as he says thank you.

He starts to move away to wait for the order and I follow, but there's this weight of yoke around my shoulders now. I don't have to know his whole story, ask him about his horrible secret that he's locked away in his head to be there for him now as a sister who cares.

"I'm sorry, Lucky," I say.

He looks ready to protest.

I push forward. "I'm sorry I stopped being there for you."

His brow twitches. The corner of his lip edges up, but it doesn't turn into a smile. It won't reach his eyes. Some other emotion resides there. Maybe relief, or gratitude, something hollower than hope but still shaped like it.

"It's okay, you had your own shit—"

"That's not an excuse." I reach out, take his hand, and even though I don't deserve it, he turns his palm up and squeezes mine back with affection.

"Well, okay then." He grins now. "You're not off the hook."

I laugh through a sob trapped in my throat.

LUCKY AND CELIA are friends, it turns out.

I'm sitting at a picnic table just inside the fairground entrance, lips coated in a thin layer of powdered sugar, fingers licked clean, with Winter across from me chowing down on a corn dog. Lucky, Celia, and Matteo hover nearby.

"They're scared of you," Winter says. "You're kind of a legend."

"I don't bite," I say.

Winter laughs. "I know that," she replies.

We both watch the three of them chatting happily. It's good to see Lucky at ease with somebody. He looks more comfortable in his skin, I realize, like a weight is lifted. If that's where that feeling came from before, his weight—just a little of it—shifting to my shoulders, then I'll take it. It's not too much to take if it helps him.

Careful, you're almost sounding heroic—the nightmarish sound of my own snarky voice.

Winter calls to them, saying something in Spanish through cupped hands. It gets them to move in our direction, even if Celia and Matteo do trail a little behind my brother.

"Who's up for some carnival rides?" Lucky asks, lifting a handful of red tickets.

"I could stomach the Ferris wheel," Winter says, cutting her eyes to her siblings in a very *big sister, don't embarrass me* way.

"Let's do it." Matteo caves to the pressure.

Lucky walks between Celia and Matteo as they make their way to the Ferris wheel. Winter and I hang back just enough that we almost lose them in the swarm of the growing crowd.

"So, you decided to be friends with one of your family members after all?" She bumps me with her elbow. It's casual, this contact.

Too casual. I try not to make it obvious as I put space between us.

This isn't the honky-tonk bubble. *Reality is a nightmare, remember.*

"Lucky's different," I reply.

"Because he's still basically a big kid?"

"He wasn't part of the shit that led to me leaving here. It was unfair that I cut him out with the rest of them."

"Maybe, maybe not. You did what you had to do at the time." She tugs her eyes from me, back to the pack of them walking ahead. "It's not like family stuff comes easy to anybody, and I'm not comparing my shit to yours. I pay attention, and it's obvious your family is different from mine."

"What gave us away?" I have to chuckle because otherwise I'll cry.

"Daughters don't leave like that without a good reason."

Her words are heavy between us. I don't know how to respond, so I stay quiet. The whirring sounds of rides, the throngs of voices, the call of winners and losers and prizes and fun surrounds us, but the silence from me is the loudest.

"Sorry," she says quietly, but she's close enough that I can hear her.

"No," I say. I make myself look at her. "Thanks. It's hard to explain, but thanks."

Her smile is just a little bit sad.

39

LUCKY AND WINTER'S siblings met up with some other townies, so it was on me to take Winter the short drive back to her family home.

Her parents live on a quaint street near downtown. Mostly ranch-style houses with well-maintained yards and big oak trees, established and a little dated.

"This was fun," she says, and then she rethinks her words. "I hope you had fun. I can't tell."

"It was fun," I reply, making my voice bright, hopefully reassuring.

"I'm still around for a few days," she says, the trepidation mostly evaporated from her voice. "If you wanna hang out again, let me know."

In another life, I would kiss her right now.

Maybe next time.

"Sure thing." It feels like a lie, but I wish that it didn't.

I watch her stride up the concrete sidewalk, damp from the sprinklers that must have just turned off. The light above the red front door flicks on, casting her shadow back down the path toward me in a long distorted shape. When she reaches the door, she pauses, half turning to look back over her shoulder. She still smiles, still hopes, and I wish I could snuggle up with her confidence, let it soothe the slippery sickening voice inside me that whispers the truth.

You will never be happy, safe, loved.

The smell in the car is rank. Suddenly all-consuming, it fills every crevice with a suffocating, stomach-churning decay. That telltale chill raises the hair on my neck, turning the hot humid air in the car frigid. The box is with me, even when I don't see it.

It never leaves.

And the nightmare inside it, she's always watching every smile and frown, every fuck and freak-out. There's a sense of it filling the space all around me. Smoke spreading out in a shadow that's shaped like my own, but bigger and scary and not of this world.

Revulsion washes over me.

I let my eyes travel to the rearview mirror.

A part of me fears the truth reflected back to me in the glass.

The shadow is me.

Mine, always, not the other. Not something different. Not a monster.

There is no girl trapped in a box in my mind that isn't me.

We are one in a way that can never be parted; we're tied together but prevented from taking over each other by the walls of the box, by the veil of consciousness and what lies beyond.

There is no shadow in the mirror.

There is only the empty back seat.

No smoke show swirling around me.

Just light and my own desperate blue eyes.

I TAKE THE only open road back through downtown. It brings me past a row of shops and bars, many still lively with the after-dark activities of the festival. Country music plays loud enough that it breaches my car's closed window. Probably from the rooftop of the burger joint advertising a live band tonight. I roll my window down to let it stream in, pretend for a second I'm a woman who didn't have her heart broken by this place and the kind of people who write country songs. The front woman croons in a twangy alto about heartbreak that only a horse ride can heal, and I buy it for a second, because I remember when that was almost true for me.

I was a girl who loved her horse more than almost anything.

Then the horse died when I was sixteen. A twisted stomach that led to Earl putting her out of her misery, with the help of the vet and a whole lot of morphine. I stayed with her all night. I remember the feel of her mane in my hands, braiding it, stroking her velvet coat. I remember the fear in her eyes.

And then somewhere in the night, the image fades out. Like the camera cuts away from it and comes back later on me crying in the stall with her bridle in hand.

My mind trips back to reality, to the slow ebb of this car as it stops at a red light.

The door to the sports bar opens, the noise of a rowdy crowd spilling onto the sidewalk like beer from a solo cup. A man stumbles out into the green neon light of the sign.

Not a man.

Keller Collins.

Face ruddy from drink, smile plastered over cheeks glossy with sweat, he's stumbling on boot-covered feet over concrete, heading in the direction of the parking lot, and I'm thinking how someone should stop him from driving. It's not safe for him to be on the road in this state. Where are the cops who used to be so vigilant about pulling me over, Sonic cup in the partition between the front seats, music blaring Miley, hair whipping in the wind from my rolled-down windows?

They are nowhere to be seen.

And then it doesn't matter anyway, because Keller stops in his tracks outside the ice cream shop. He's looking in at something I can't see from here, but the change in his expression makes my stomach swim. *Lascivious*–the word slithers, oil slick, over my brain. Beady eyes like hot coals. Tongue practically wagging out, ready to lap up whatever it is that he sees.

The door to the ice cream shop opens, and two teenage girls step out.

They're dressed for the summer weather. In short-shorts and tank tops, hair tied up in braids and twisted on their heads to let the air onto their necks. They're tan, taut with youth and that special kind of sensuality that men love to pluck before it's ripe.

Keller's hands are primed to pick.

He reaches out to pinch at their thighs, a swift swipe of delicate skin. They bounce away, twisting around to look at him. Ice cream drips down waffle cone shell to coat the tops of their fingers. The girls know it's wrong–what he just did. A look passes between them, disgust mixed with fear, but instead of speaking up, putting the old creep in his place, they chuckle. Quick flashes of smiles, they wave him off, and he says something I can't hear from where I am.

One of the girls grips the other's hand. Her smile falters.

None of the adults sitting outside the open restaurants notice or care about this old man's lewd behavior, or the fear in the girls' eyes, or the fact that their fun summer night of ice cream, of innocence, is now tainted by his hands on their bodies and his tongue licking his lips, wagging for a taste. Hungry for fruit still maturing on the tree.

None of them care. None of them ever care.

But I do.

And so does the nightmare inside me.

The light must change to green, because a horn blares from behind me.

Too bad I'm no longer driving. It's not my hands on the wheel or my foot on the pedal or my eyes that follow Keller all the way home.

THE CAR SITS *on the darkened street corner, headlights off.*

Inside it she waits, her hands on the wheel holding tightly, so tight that her knuckles go white, palms ache with the pressure against her tiny, crescent moon–shaped cuts.

She waits and she watches.

From here she can see that the house is lit from inside. She can see how his car, which wove in and out of lanes all the way home, ran up on the curb and onto the grass, and finally came to a stop right in front of his closed garage door.

From here she has seen how he entered the home, left the door ajar, didn't lock it behind himself as he stumbled through the house, flicking on lights as he went.

From here she can sense that he still moves about in the house as if his pulse is an audible, restless, belabored endeavor.

As if she is a hawk tracking prey on the ground through the brush.

Is it she who can sense it? She who is predator?

From here she can't tell.

Because sometime, somehow, somewhere, she lost track of where she stopped and the other her started. She can see through the eyes and feel through the fingers and know through the pump pump *of the heart that she's here, but it's like being underwater in a swimming pool, watching people above walking around. Separated and suffocating slowly.*

Her hands release the wheel and unbuckle.

Her pulse is rapid, her eyesight sharp. The predator is ready to move.

They climb out of the car, slink slowly down the street, up the sidewalk to the front door and . . . push.

It falls open. The metal handle hits the wall, bounces off it.

She and the other her, they take the first step inside. Rubber soles on tile floor squeak.

But it is no matter; they know it because the heartbeat has settled, steady and even, the rhythm of sleep.

The playground this predator craves.

They make their way over the carpet, past photos on walls of a small unhappy family.

A mother, a father, a girl with blond braids.

The photos follow the years from baby to child to youth to teen.

Sometime in the midst, the mother goes absent.

They notice; they don't wonder why.

They walk past doors down the hallway to the one that stands open.

A light beams over a room made of darkness, cast through a doorway tucked deep inside. It touches the edge of the mattress, where a single socked foot dangles over.

It shouldn't surprise them that the man doesn't care about monsters.

Doesn't worry that one will emerge from beneath the bed with claws ready to claim him.

This man is the monster. He has no reason to fear.

But he is wrong this time.

They slip through the door, move up to stand beside him.

There are so many ways they could do this–

With bare hands.

Make it look like he suffocated sometime in his sleep.

Easy, clean, quick, and painless.

"That is the problem." Their voice sounds strange, tastes bitter, rings sharp.

"Pain is part of the punishment." They whisper the words to the room.

He stirs.

They watch his lips mutter, twisting around the sound, forming nearly inaudible words.

But they hear it.

Begging, the daughter's name, a plea for her silence. They close their ears, hands cupped over lobes and locked around drums. Shut it out, shut it down.

"Pain is the punishment," they say together. Melodically sounding as one.

It is quick work from there to find the door to his mind.

Rusted hinges, weathered wood. It is battered and beaten, poorly maintained.

Easy to break from its purchase.

It hangs wide open for entry, and so they trample right through it.

Inside, they find a replica of this home.

The hallway, the entryway, the den with its couches and big-screen TV, but inside, every single item, from pillow to portraits, is covered in bubble wrap.

Surrounded, protected.

Every inch, every step–pop pop pop–*they follow the sound down the hallway again, push into the room, where they find him.*

Standing.

Naked except for the sheet of big plastic bubbles wrapped around and around his whole body.

This is his armor.

This is what guards him.

Every inch of his mind is covered in packing materials, preserved, designed to ensure nothing gets broken.

Fragility fine-tuned and unearned.

They can feel rage boil up until it spills.

They run.

Their body overpowers him, drags him down to the ground. Fingernails turn from manicured beds–short, polish-free–to smoke, then the claws of a monster.

Long curved black talons grow out from the tips of their fingers.

Rip rip ripping *the bubbles to shreds, tearing layer after layer after layer away until his face is exposed–his neck, his torso, his thighs.*

They don't stop there. They rip through his skin, unwrap it like a banana peel.

Inside is soft gooey red muscle.

They dig in, through the sinew, slicing it clean like a steak.

Blood spurts, sprays across their face.

Touches their tongue.

"Pain tastes like cherry."

Juicy, sweet, sour.

His pain is dessert, the center gooey red decadence.

She peels muscle from bone, picks them clean.

Her claws find purchase, clasp curved bones hiding vital organs.

Lungs, heart, stomach. One by one, lacerated until–

the stomach seizes up, the lungs deflate, empty.

The heart pitter-patters, then goes out with one final ferocious, frenzied life-ending gasp.

40

I WAKE ON the floor. Drooling. My body stiff.

I am undressed right down to my underwear and bra. I feel this rather than see it at first, my eyelids weighed down, my mouth full of cotton, my memories of the night before swimming slowly from the depths of my subconscious.

Kicking, screaming, bubbles–

Bubble wrap.

The words come to me accompanied by flashes of color, still blurry.

I inhale, I exhale. Breath wheezes, throat raw as if I'd been screaming. I roll onto my back, the sound of all my joints cracking rips through the silence. On my back now, I let my left hand rest on top of my bare stomach, lift the other to arch over my head. As soon as my hand touches my stomach, I flinch.

The whole thing is rough on contact. I suck air through my teeth. I will have to look, even if my instinct tells me the answer that my eyes will find. I peel my lids back ever so slowly.

Caked on, baked on, rusty red brown that crusted over and separated into little patches all over my hands, up my arms–*blood.*

I bolt upright, extend my arms to see the gritty dark rust brown.

My hands move to my face and hair, discover more crusted patches clinging, sloughing from the curve of my chin and the corners of my lips and the fluttering lashes on my left eye.

It's around my ankles, a rim of red so dark it's almost like it was painted over the edges of my socks. The scales of deep cherry ridge over the small flexing bones beneath my skin.

Cherry.

The word screams and I taste it again.

His blood on my tongue, not like pennies. A cherry syrup, like my former favorite slushie.

Blood on my lips and in my eyes and all over my body.

A man's blood.

I suck air in through my teeth, grip my head as the memory slashes through it.

At first, it's just flashes. Reels of film broken into snippets.

I enter his home, move down the hallway, climb on top of him passed out on the bed.

Flash.

In my hands I hold a mandoline. The dial turned to a thick setting.

Flash.

I take his skin off in strands. Slide the sharp edge of the tool over the curves of his flesh.

Flash.

He begins to scream. The sound leaves his lips for no more than an instant before—

Flash.

He's gasping. Strangled. But my hands don't tighten around his throat.

Flash.

He writhes, his face turning colors, his hands grabbing at the phantom holding him hostage.

Flash.

I drop the weapon. I turn to my fists and my fingernails.

Tear at the skin I've already shredded.

Poke at his eyeballs, blot out his vision.

Flash.

His heart stops. His lungs stop. His life stops.

Flash.

I move back through his house, out the front door, down the sidewalk–

I shake my head, slamming my fists on the cold tile floor.

This is wrong. It's not what happened. Because I couldn't have done this, not all on my own.

It was the nightmare. It was the nightmare me.

It wasn't me. It wasn't this body.

I was in a car on the street, far away, far away.

My fingers were claws, its claws.

We were in his subconscious; it was all bubble wrapped. And what we did would have hurt him, stopped his heart, stopped his lungs, but I didn't actually tear him to shreds. We didn't actually do any of that.

It was you!

The thought screams in my head.

There is no we.

It's not in my ears, not in my brain. This thought is attached to some place deep down inside me. I shoot up from the ground and face myself in the mirror.

I was drenched.

I must have hit his carotid artery, because the caked remains coated my face, soaked and then dried in the whole front section of my hair. The blood streamed down my neck, pooled in the curve of my collarbone. I don't recognize my face for a second. I can't see my freckles, they blend with the dark rusty tone, lose themselves in the caked, baked grit coating my skin.

The color brings out the blue in my eyes.

Makes the cerulean look like it's glowing.

It's not just the color that's complemented; it's like the fire that lights me is brightened.

Ignited and living and burning with . . . satisfaction.

Fuck it.

Keller deserved it.

My teeth show themselves in a smile.

It starts slowly, the glimmer, twisting and sparking and dancing, caught in the mirror.

A halo around my head that turns smoky.

It curls up and around in the shape of my body, only bigger than the frame, taller than these bones have grown me.

The killer is taking me over, and goddamn it, I think I might like it.

But that doesn't mean I want to get caught.

I turn on my heels to survey the bathroom. My shadow shape slinks away.

Washing comes first. I can't do anything when I look like a psycho killer on a walk of shame.

I reach over to the shower curtain and tug it back.

"Fuck me." My voice grates, rough and strange to my ears.

Lying in a pile at the bottom of my parents' guest room tub is the blood-covered heap of my clothes.

"Jesus Christ." I grab them up.

And then immediately drop them back. The blood has dried, but clinging to the fabric are rubbery bits of Keller Collins's flesh.

I spin around as puke surges up my throat, and I barely make it to the toilet bowl.

I must have come straight home last night, stripped off in the bathroom, and then passed out on the ground.

As I lean against the bowl, my eyes finally begin to fully take in the rest of the room.

Smears of dried blood on the tile.

The yellow bath mat is stained dark ruby red.

Fuck. Fuck. That's ruined, no way I can wash it without Olympia seeing it. No way she wouldn't get suspicious even if I feign a period mishap and played like I had cramps. I'll have to throw it out and hope she doesn't notice it missing before I leave town.

This thought brings up the other pressing issue—though admittedly less pressing than covering up a murder!—of solving the mystery of the man in the stable.

"Not now," I hiss. God, what a fucking mess—literally. I almost have the urge to laugh, but my head pounds too hard and my stomach is still writhing. I'm struck at the irony of me trying to solve a decades-old crime that might have happened while committing a fresh one and hoping not to get caught.

And, possibly worse, the box convinced me that I was dreaming a nightmare.

I believed it, no question.

What else could it make me believe? I shake my head, fear springing off me like water droplets from a dog's mane.

That doesn't matter right this second. I have bloodstained, flesh-bedazzled evidence to clean up.

My mind races.

Gotta clean the room. Clean myself. Check for a trail in the house.

Dispose of this evidence in a way that won't immediately tie back to me or be quickly discovered. Burning the clothes would work, but I have no idea what the rest of the family is up to today. It's morning, still early, but already light out. I glance through the door to the clock on the nightstand—6:07 a.m. Okay, so likely a couple hours still before the whole town is up. Earl might be awake already, but it's doubtful.

I have a thin margin to fix this.

Razor-thin and narrowing.

That's when I notice the window's ajar in the bedroom.

I don't run over to it, because I'm still covered in gross peeling blood chippings, but it dawns on me that it must be how I got inside. The Powers family doesn't lock doors or windows, just their cold steel-vaulted hearts.

I dip down and open the cabinet below the sink. I have to rummage, but at the very back is some bathroom cleaner and a half-used roll of paper towels. If there is one thing you can count on Olympia to do, it's make sure the bathroom is fully stocked with all the amenities.

Including a makeshift murder cleanup kit.

I'M OUT OF clean clothes. My one pair of shoes is ruined.

My fingers slide the last button through the hole at the top of the dress, buckle the belt, flatten the collar.

My feet slide into the supple leather boots.

My eyes find my image in the mirror.

I wear the gifts my father gave me, and even though I hate him, and even though his gifts scream of tradition, modesty, history, and duty, I don't hate the way they feel.

I am soft. Clean. Even a little bit pretty.

It's the lie juxtaposed with the glint of rage in my eyes.

The same blue as the dress, as the sky, as the eyes of my mother and brother.

Mine are the eyes of a killer.

My mind is my weapon of choice.

I hate the dress because he gave it to me, because it is demure and polite and delightful, with its happy daisy print so much like the ones I loved as a little girl. And I love that it doesn't blend in.

Neither do I.

Something that terrified me for so long. Made me twist myself small, run away, hide all my horrible pieces, hide who I am, because I'll never be loved.

Love isn't all a woman can need.

And if love isn't possible, at least there's revenge.

41

POWERS PREMIER AUTOMOTIVE is supposed to be closed to the public today on account of the festival, but there is signage that advertises the "bonanza blitz deal extravaganza" at the end of the whole thing. No one should be at the dealership.

No one, that is, except Buck.

I recognize his Ranger immediately. Lonely in the crisp morning light.

It doesn't change my plans, but it does give me pause. I can't risk Buck looking out his window to see my rental tooling around the back of the building, where the only thing to do is dispose of garbage. He wouldn't be able to leave it alone, and if he caught me, he wouldn't be game for a cover-up.

I stowed the trash bag of bloody clothes and sneakers in the trunk. It's safe to leave inside until I can make sure Buck isn't around to see me toss it. I park my sedan beside his truck, cut the engine, and step out. The heels of my boots clop against the asphalt.

As I walk to the double doors that lead into the offices, I try to convince myself that I can use this to my advantage, pick Buck's brain about the past that I know he has to remember. He was there that day; he's the one who found me hiding in the cupboard.

Buck isn't going to spill easily, no matter how much he thinks he wants to reconnect for the sake of our dying father. I'll have to be cunning if I want this to work. The man in the stables was murdered, covered up somehow, and as far as I know from my internet searches, I don't think anyone ever came looking for his corpse.

It doesn't mean he was forgotten. There's no statute of limitation on murder.

The secret of that day is still a threat.

Same as the secret of this one.

I have a bag of bloody clothes and shoes in my trunk and no idea what I did with the body, but there is an inkling, a gnawing in my gut that the amount of blood on my skin, my clothes, my sneakers, the windowsill and floorboards means the corpse of Keller Collins is likely to raise some suspicions when it's discovered.

I can't worry about that right now.

One thing at a time.

I still need to figure out how I created the box. Without that knowledge, there's no way forward. No path to redemption. No stopping what happened to Roger and Keller from happening again. I want to leave town, put as much distance between me and this place as possible, but I want the truth even more, and if there is one thing I'm starting to believe, it's that redemption sure as fuck doesn't mean no one gets hurt.

I've tasted violent justice. It's as sweet as dark cherry juice coating my tongue.

It's not as bitter as I thought it would be.

I yank open the door and step inside the dimly lit lobby. Buck came down on the elevator that first day when I showed up here to meet him and Earl. Logic says his office is up on one of the higher floors, and that's where he'd be now, so I take the elevator to the top. I'll just tell him I came to apologize about the other night at the barbecue. I overreacted; he was just trying to watch out for me. His ego may be big enough that he'll actually believe it.

The elevator dings. I step out to silence.

The perimeter of this floor is cut into boxes of corporate office space, with the center gaping like one big open bullpen. Desks are arranged in rows, spaced evenly, with matching chairs and desktop Macs.

"Buck?" I call out. "You here?" I wait a beat and listen, but no reply comes. It doesn't mean Buck isn't here, so I start around the perimeter, walking past offices with nameplates on the doors.

Sterling has one—no surprise—even if I am still not entirely sure what he does here. The title below his placard reads CHIEF BRAND OFFICER, and then right next to his office resides Vance Polk, Head of Marketing. If a job title could be an embezzlement scheme . . .

There are a few more offices before I reach the door to Buck's, which is right next to Earl's corner office on the other side.

VICE PRESIDENT EARL PROSPER POWERS, II

Beneath it: BUCK.

I lightly rap my knuckles on the door before twisting the handle. I ease the door open just enough that I can see the lights aren't on. "Buck?" I ask the air. I push the door all the way open.

There's a desk facing the door with windows banking the whole back wall. There's a drink cart fitted with brown liquor, a putting green practice pad, and a couch with my brother fast asleep on it. I stop in my tracks at the edge of the room, surprised by the sight. There's a real pillow, not just a couch cushion, under his head. There's a blanket messily covering the lower half of his body. He's wearing gray sweatpants. One of his socks hangs halfway off his heel, his foot dangling over the edge.

He didn't just fall asleep while working here late, or pass out because he came in too early and hadn't had enough coffee. Buck is staying here. His cosplay of a God-fearing churchgoer with a perfect family, dream-girl wife, and respectable job is at least a partial sham. And not just in the obvious way–not just because he's a prick. He's also a prick whose life might be falling apart.

He's asleep.

He's asleep.

This is the perfect opportunity to get into his mind, find answers.

But, no, no, because I don't exactly have calm or nonviolent feelings toward my big brother. No, no, I can't trust that once in there, my conscious nonviolent side will be able to stay in control. Not after last night.

This may be the only chance you get. That thought from the hollow den deep inside me insists.

I walk over to where he lies sleeping, crouch down beside him, and extend my hand right below his nose. Steady breathing; he's in deep sleep. The erratic shifts of his eyes beneath his lids tells me he's in REM cycle.

If I am able to break into his subconscious, I may also be able to manipulate the dream he's currently in to change course, to show me the story of that day in the stable, to solve this mystery without ever having to ask him what happened.

TALL, DOUBLE, PAINTED *white and green, the doors to Buck's mind is the same as our stable. Buck spent countless hours there as a child learning to ride, training for cutting shows, training us on horseback; it shouldn't be a surprise.*

The door to the stable has never had a lock.

Not even here in his mind.

The wood heaves as I pull one of the doors back, half expecting to see the yawning expanse of the stables twisted and contorted by Buck's perspective.

I step into a deer blind instead.

His dream.

Buck is beside me loading a rifle with two red-and-gold bullets. He's dressed all in camo: hat, jacket, pants–only his hands and his face are exposed. There is a thick beard growing in over his chin, and I have to bite back a chuckle, because even at thirty-one, Buck is still pretty baby-faced. Can't imagine the guy could even grow in a beard.

He closes the barrel with a metallic click, leans up to the open edge, and positions the rifle on the shooting rest.

I move up to look out, expecting to see a prize buck, a bear, some kind of fantasy big game animal stalking past caught in his sights and about to be slaughtered.

That is not what he hunts.

Across the field, taking a stroll by a riverbed, is our father.

Buck moves his eye to the sight to aim. He waits, and my pulse grows jagged.

A shot rings out, reverberates all the way through me.

Earl's side explodes with the impact, guts spilling onto the ground. He falls, twitching, as blood pools, soaking into the dead leaves blanketing the ground beneath him.

Buck sits back and smiles. "We'll feed on him all winter."

"Buck," I say in that weird underwater dream voice.

Then suddenly, we're in the stable, in a stall I recognize immediately as the one from my memory of the dead man.

Earl's carcass hangs by his feet from hooks attached to the ceiling. There is a nasty slice taken out of his neck. Blood streams down the curves of his face to drip drip drip *into a metal bucket already full to the brim with blood.*

Buck stands beside him, face emotionless, chilling me all the way through.

Behind him is a gun case. Black iron and steel with a stamp painted on the front in thick gold letters: OFF LIMITS.

I reach out a hand as if I could touch it from where I stand, and then

I am right beside it, palm flush to the cool steel, ear pressing in as I try to turn the handle.

The door to his mind may have been open, but this gun case is sealed shut, and whatever Buck has stored inside it is something he doesn't want anyone to see.

Not even himself.

I lean back, eyeing the mechanics. There has to be a way to break in. This isn't real.

I imagine that the iron turns liquid in my head.

My hand presses down on the surface.

It remains solid, impenetrable.

I open my eyes, hear a gurgling slurp coming from behind me. I'm scared to turn, to see what is making the sound of something sucking, chewing, and right below that grating.

Hard against hard.

Teeth against bone.

Slowly, like cold honey poured into a spoon, I turn around.

Earl's body is laid out on a table.

Buck hovers over him with a handsaw in one of his fists and one of Earl's arms hacked clean and held firm in the other.

He tears flesh from the bone with his teeth, like a turkey leg at the fair on a hot summer day.

I am overcome. Something feral within me lashes out of my skin.

Black oil bleeds from the ends of my fingers, turns to smoke when it touches the air, reaches out, swirls around him and tightens, constricting his movements, holding him back from consuming our father.

I have to get out of this nightmare.

We . . . have to get ourselves free of his grip.

I run for him as the smoke envelops us both.

42

I WAKE WITH my hand wrapped around my big brother's wrist and shake him back into consciousness. His lids flutter, showing me the whites of his eyes as they roll back in his head. His chin lolls forward with no control. I use my other hand to stop it.

"Buck." I say his name loud, with enough force that I hope it'll break all the way through the layers of sleep and my own interference. "Wake up!"

He startles like a newborn baby.

I shoot to my feet, step back, hope my face looks less alarmed than my body feels.

His eyes are dilated, he's blinking to clear his vision. His hands lift, fingertips to lids for a good hard rub. Fuck, I really shouldn't have done that. It's so obvious this whole subconscious walking thing isn't safe anymore—if it ever really was. My eyes settle on Buck, and I wish to God I could scrub everything I saw in that dream from my mind, even if I know now—on trend with me and my box, and Earl and his storm cellar, and even Lucky with his wall in the closet: Buck has built himself something to hold a horror he cannot accept.

I wonder if it's the same horror as mine.

"What the hell are you doing here, Haven?" Buck spits, sitting upright on the couch and yanking the twisted blanket back.

"I came to apologize," I say, trying to sound as self-righteously angry as I possibly can. "What the fuck are you doing sleeping here?" I yank my phone from my pocket to check the time. "It's almost nine."

His eyes narrow. "How did you know I'd be here?"

"I didn't." But why is he all suspicious? It's weird that he's here, sleeping well into the morning, and I need to make sure that I shame him really good so he won't pick too hard at the threads of my story. "I went by your house and didn't see your truck parked outside. This is the next logical place. I figured you came in to work with the office quiet since everyone else is off."

"Shit," he says. It's clearly dawning on him that he's the one who's been caught, not me.

Thank God.

"You can't tell Mom and Dad."

I have to swallow back bile as the image of him chowing down on Earl's arm swims in my vision.

"What's going on, Buck?" I say, sliding around to sit on the cushion beside him.

He scrubs his face in his hand. "Clarabelle and I have been arguing," he says, sounding more defeated than I expect. "She's been pressuring me to get Dad to step down and let me take over running the day-to-day."

"Because he's sick?" I ask.

He grunts, cuts me a look I can't quite read. "Sick and losing his touch."

"Aren't you already doing that though?" I say, pointing around the office as if to illustrate his prime position.

He falls back against the couch and groans. "You'd think that, wouldn't ya?" he says, voice hoarse. "Dad ties my hands at every turn. He's the face of the company, an image that bleeds into everything else he has his hands in around town. I half expect he'll have to croak before he actually eases off."

It's a little surprising to hear Buck talking about Earl dying in such a cavalier way, but then I did just see him chowing down on his fucking bicep, so what do I know?

"Did you explain that to Clarabelle?" I manage to ask, despite my line of thinking.

"She's worried Sterling got sober and is making a move for my position. Ever since he married Julep, Clarabelle has had a burr up her ass. Paranoid we're being phased out of our spot in the family."

Jesus, it's easy to forget what it's like to care about your place in the hierarchy when you haven't been part of the family plan in almost a decade.

"Sterling may not actually be sober," I say. I hate myself even more for how the smirk spreading on Buck's lips sends a thrill of camaraderie through me.

"You mean because of the other night?" he asks. "His whole 'It's a nice time to take a swim' or whatever? I called bullshit on him, but he denied he was drinking, and his breath didn't smell of it either." Buck runs a hand through his board-straight hair, but it just falls right back down to hang in front of his eyes. "Weird behavior though. Maybe he's switched up his drug of choice."

I refrain from offering any of my own insights. I just remember Sterling was drinking in his subconscious, which makes me feel his sobriety is held together by duct tape at best. Buck grabs his phone from where it's charging, and there are a bunch of notifications from Clarabelle visible on the screen.

"Looks like the fight with Clarabelle is still going," I say, before he darkens the screen.

He shoots up, stretching his arms overhead and cracking his

back. "She'll deal. I just wanted to get some space, so I came here. Dad put in a gym in one of the garages a few years ago when Sterling was using exercise and diet as a coping mechanism for not drinking," he says. "Didn't work. But at least there's a locker room where I can shower."

He stares down at me, an expectant expression on his face.

"What?" I ask, turning younger sister indignance on full blast.

"I'm going to shower, and I need to lock you out downstairs," he says.

"You know the door was unlocked when I got here, right?" I reply.

All the color is leached from his face. "You're fucking with me."

"Buck, how would I have gotten in here otherwise? I don't have a key."

He grabs me by the arm as he walks briskly toward the door. "That means either I left the door open last night, or someone else with a key has been here while I was asleep."

"Chill out." I wrench my arm from his grip. "You were distracted–"

He cuts his ice-blue eyes over at me, the feeling like glass slicing skin.

"I don't get distracted," he says. He opens the door to peer out on the empty office. "Wait here. I'll just be a second." He shoves me outside the door, slamming it closed.

Buck's paranoia runs deep. It strikes me that this is something we have in common, that hunted feeling. That *always looking over your shoulder* type of anxiety. The creeping sensation that makes you walk around your kitchen with a butcher knife looking for an intruder to stab.

He emerges a couple minutes later, fully dressed, carrying a backpack. He must have stowed the pillow and blanket somewhere in his office. His hair is still product-free, and the skin under his eyes is dark from exhaustion.

"Let's go," he says, shoving past me.

I have to run to keep up with his pace. "You don't think Earl would understand?"

"You *can't* think he would," he says, looking at me just so I can see his eyes roll. "Did living up north make you stupid?"

"Jesus," I say. "Asshole."

"Language," he says with a mischievous grin.

A chuckle bubbles in my throat.

It's the tiniest moment of shared camaraderie, but it's not nothing.

We take the elevator back down.

"Where'd the dress come from?" he asks.

"You don't think I brought it from home?" I grin.

He looks sideways at me. "Earl."

The name lands like a boulder between us. Silence expands as we travel the rest of the way down, until the lurch of the elevator stopping.

"It doesn't suit you," he says. "But the color looks pretty."

The doors slide open. He steps out, I follow, shaken. Because he's right about both, and that's quite the curveball.

He holds the front door open for me to exit and then steps outside, shutting it behind us both. When it's locked, his body stills. He doesn't look at me.

"You said you came here to apologize," he says. It takes me a second to catch up with the train of thought. He's waiting for me to do it.

"Oh, yeah, I'm sorry I was so defensive at the barbecue," I say, even if I don't feel all that sorry.

His expression softens. I'm almost thrown by how much he looks like the boy I once saw as gentle, caring, and ready to step in between me and anything trying to cause harm.

"You had your reasons," he said. It sounds almost like his own apology. The gentleness doesn't last long. His jaw clenches, eyes go glacial. "This is just between us." He holds me in his glare until I finally realize he wants me to promise.

"Sure thing," I say, hoping it's good enough.

He walks off toward his truck, not giving me another look and not waiting to see if I leave before he peels out. I assume he's going to try to confirm who came into the building and left it unlocked. My guess is no one, and it really was just him, but he can't admit to himself that fighting with his wife could unnerve him so deeply that he made a mistake.

And for a full fucking minute, I let myself pity him.

43

I'M DRIVING BACK through town after stashing the trash bag of bloody clothing in the garbage dumpster behind the dealership when I notice red and blue swirling lights behind me.

That putrid smell fills the car. My temperature plummets. My pulse skyrockets.

They've found Keller. I know they have. And somehow, somebody must have seen me.

They've found him and now they've come for me.

I'm ready to pull off the road, unbuckle, climb out of the car, and surrender. I'm ready to call on the box and transform, leaving the carnage of blue-clad cop bodies in my wake as I drive for the border.

I'm ready for it to be over.

They blare on their horns, and from the loudspeaker fixed to the top of their vehicle come the words "Make space. We need to pass by."

Not *Pull over, hands up, you're under arrest.*

This caravan isn't for me.

It's on its way to somewhere else. It's for someone or something else. I pull to the side of the road to let it pass, waiting for my own panic to subside.

It doesn't.

The box appears on the top of my dashboard.

Sooty smoke excretes from inside it.

How do I kill a whole part of myself? Because that's what it feels like I'll have to do. Stopping the nightmares will mean killing *me* in the process. A bigger part of me than I've ever been willing to admit, let live freely, validate, or readily name. If there is one thing I've learned for sure from being back here in Friendship, it's this: They were right. I am a nightmare.

Me, Haven Powers. Not just a part of me, but the whole woman.

It's always been true.

The tug of my eyelids is relief. They drift, sealed shut, until all I can see in the dark is the smoke of my nightmare shadow. It seeps through my skin, pours through my nostrils, twists up and swallows me whole.

Wrath is not wrong. Vengeance is sweet.

There are people who've earned punishment and warrant being ripped apart with my claws. They deserve what they get, but so often, they do not get what they deserve.

Comfort seizes me slowly.

My mind scampers off as my muscles move my hands back to the wheel.

I WAKE TO the hot late-afternoon sun beaming right through my windshield.

I'm no longer on the side of the road where I'd pulled off to let the cop caravan pass.

My vision is watery, blurred, and I have to rub hard to clear it.

I'm parked at the edge of the Fellowship Kind staff lot. Behind me is the greenbelt, a dense cloak of cool leafy trees protected with thick poison ivy. In front of me is the lot, small, mostly empty, with the exception of two lonely cars. One of them is definitely Tate's BMW. I don't recognize the other.

My car is turned off. I realize it all of a sudden. Even with the shade, it's blisteringly hot inside; I have no idea how long I've been sitting here with the windows rolled up and the air conditioner off. I scramble to crank up the engine. I probably shouldn't be parked here.

I'm sweaty, but the cotton of this dress is surprisingly breathable; however, my feet feel swollen and trapped in the leather casing of these cowboy boots. I shove open the door to let some fresh air in, only to be hit by a horrible blast of humid heat. I grab my phone from the center console. It's a little after four p.m. I have a few texts from Lucky and Winter, which makes sense. I haven't seen Lucky since I left him at the festival last night, and Winter . . .

I open the text from Winter.

Yesterday was fun. And then she's sent a photo of me taken from a distance. The background is blurry behind me, what's in focus most is my face. I'm smiling, lips curved up but open, and maybe it's just a trick of the light, or maybe I'm imagining it, but a blooming dark aura distorts the image all around me.

Like a shadow, my shadow, the shape undeniably mine.

Bigger, menacing, morose.

The nightmare all around and inside me.

And *me me me.* All me.

I can't reply. I can't tell her how much it's meant to me, these few stolen hours beside her. I have to leave the photo alone, her alone, let her go live a life far away from me. She'll get it, I know she will, and in the end, I hope she'll easily forget me.

I flip into my text thread with Lucky.

hey you awake yet

That one was from this morning, then around ten.

> your car's gone wanna meet up for breakfast at The Corral

Then twelve p.m.

> Holy shit balls they just found Keller Collins's body
>
> They think he was attacked by a wild animal cause his skin was like . . . shredded
>
> his back door was wide open
>
> cougar maybe they won't know until the coroner sees him

Then just before I woke up

> are you okay I'm kind of freaking out

I darken the screen and let my head drop back against the seat. I'll have to come up with some explanation for Lucky. I need water and something to eat and space to gather my thoughts, and I really should get the fuck away from this parking lot because Tate is inside and—

Just then the doors that lead into the church offices slam open.

Tate emerges with his hand around Tabby Collins's tiny wrist. He's dragging her violently across the asphalt.

44

RAGE FLAMES THROUGH me like a wild forest fire.

Tabby's face is tearstained, with lines cutting through her thick makeup, dripping onto the front of her white eyelet button-down. Pity smacks me in the face.

Her father is dead. I killed him.

He was a creep. He was a monster.

I did her a favor.

Her hand raises up to grab hold of Tate's shoulder as she struggles to wrench her wrist free of his grip. He whirls on her. I can't see his face, only hers. But I don't need to see his face to know how it distorts in rage. I still have plenty of memories myself of exactly what that looks like.

He slaps her straight across her face.

Pain warps her features. She touches the red, angry skin. She is frozen, her body, her expression, she looks afraid to blink, to breath, as if she fears any movement might set him off again. There is the slightest quiver in her lip. That's it. A fresh tear drips down her cheek.

Tate's shoulders relax just a little. "I told you not to come here," he says. "Delilah is starting to get suspicious already." She doesn't take his words as an invitation to respond. "And now with what happened to your dad, I have to keep my distance. Can't be associate–"

"I just need to feel better," she says, but her whole body quivers. "I need someone to hold me." She tugs on his hand that has a hold of her, but her body language is all kinds of submissive.

He pulls his body away, causing her to lurch awkwardly forward.

When she regroups, she grips the sleeve of his shirt to hold him in place. New desperation surges; her eyes gleam bright. "I need you, only you–"

He yanks her straight into his body. His arms pin her to him. "You *need* me?" he taunts. He laughs, and it makes me feel sick to my stomach.

He draws her tight, squeezes, lifting her up until her feet struggle to find purchase, flip-flops skimming the ground. She's featherlight in his arms, her body whittled down, pinched and poked until it's practically nothing.

"You're hurting me!" she cries out.

"You think you don't hurt me when you do this." His voice is metal and fire and pain. "You disobey me, you always do, dumb little cunt." His spit splatters across her face.

"You're all I have now." A whimper. A plea. She begs to be seen as something more than trash he's already discarded.

His hands release from around her, and she falls back, slipping to crash ass-first onto the concrete. She crumples like a baby doll, limbs unable to hold her, head too heavy to stay upright.

But he's not done punishing her.

He grabs her by the crown of her head, yanking her up by the hair. He opens the door to her car and tries to shove her inside it. She's fighting him. He slams her into the seat, twists her arm, one then the other, until he's got them tied at her sides. What is he hoping to do? Beat her unconscious, drive her somewhere, and abandon her.

The smack of a fist pounding flesh, *thwack*, her screams are muffled, but I can still hear them. I have to do something, I have to. I can't just let this happen.

One of her flip-flops falls and she uses that foot to kick him, but he sidesteps. She doesn't have the strength to try it again.

And then she stops fighting. Stops screaming.

Stops.

I run.

Boots clap loud against concrete.

A feral noise rips from my throat. Beast-like and birdlike, ancient rage and wild survival roars through the air to pelt into his back like a fist.

He jolts, whipping around with eyes wide in terror. Until he sees the source of the sound. A sick smile twists over his face. I am a joke to him. My ferocious eyes flaring, my vicious hands reaching. He foolishly thinks he is safe. Why should he fear me? I was his very first victim.

The one he cut his teeth on. The one he used to sharpen the blade of his tongue.

"Let her go," I say, my fists clenched and ready.

"Just calm down there," he chides.

"Calm down?" I scream out, the shrill echo of my outrage pops over the concrete. She's motionless, legs dangling at an awkward angle. Her face is bloody, eyes shut, and everything limp, almost lifeless. "She's not moving." My breath catches on the ridges of my ribs; heat swells through me.

I am no longer thinking. I grab him by the collar, mustering strength I didn't know I possessed to rip his body back from the car and send him stumbling. In the second I have before he regains his footing, I check her for breathing. It's there, but faint. Her left cheek is already bruising, lip split, eyes shut and swelling.

His hand slaps down on my shoulder and tightens. "This is none of your fucking business," he spits, applying force to try to uproot me.

But I am not the eighteen-year-old girl he was once able to torment. I twist around, my hands open and searching. They clamp onto the slope of his neck, thumbs covering his Adam's apple. I squeeze. I can't keep the hold for that long, but it's long enough to make him start gagging.

As soon as I let go, he doubles over, hacking. "Holy shit, Haven . . ." His voice sounds almost broken.

I lunge for him, slam the heel of my boot over the toe of his loafer and grind. He screams, rearing back with his fist, but I'm faster, and this dress is made for movement. I kick him right in the dick.

I draw my fist back and hit him square in the face.

He falls to his knees on the ground.

I don't have time to savor this moment. It's not a moment to savor, not when this girl could be in serious danger. I turn back to face Tabby in the car. I lift her legs up and scoot her in just enough that I will be able to close the door. Before I do, I take her keys from the floor of the car where they fell.

I slam the car door, feel a small bit of relief knowing she's at least got metal between her and Tate Turner's fists. My senses tingle, little prickles of awareness calling my attention to the predator behind me. He's pushing himself up from the concrete. But every woman knows that keys can be a weapon in a pinch. I place Tabby's car key between my pointer and middle finger, and hold it out like a knife.

"Stay the fuck back," I order, as I feel around behind me for the driver's door handle.

He lifts his face up. His lip is bleeding.

"You haven't changed, have you?" he says, his voice gravel. "You're the same bitch who never understood her place." He tries to laugh, but it winds up a wheezing cough.

"I'm taking her with me," I say.

"Go ahead." He shrugs, voice still gritty, though he tries to sound nonchalant. "She'll come to, and she'll be just like the others." He smiles, splitting his lip open even further. "She'll come crawling right back in the end."

I yank the car door open and drop into the driver's seat.

As I speed off, I half expect to see him follow me, realizing that letting me go is the fool's move, but he doesn't. I guess it shouldn't be a surprise.

He believes he's safe. He's never been given a reason not to.

45

I TAKE SIDE streets, avoiding traffic lights that might have cameras to catch me.

Tabby needs medical care, but I can't be seen with her. I can't be tied back to this incident, have it used to hold me in Friendship. As long as Tabby stays knocked out, my plan should work. There is one place I can go. One person I believe will do right by this girl in need of real help.

I remember the way to Matilda Morris's house because I went there for book club in high school. It's a small yellow frame, white shutters, white door. It always had hearty flowerbeds and healthy green grass. Now I know that's because she probably always loved plants and took pride in her garden even before she became the town garden lady. It's also right across from a neighborhood park with a big sturdy playground and plenty of places to hide.

Ideal, hopefully, to make a quick escape.

When I pull up outside, it's almost dusk, but I can still see the porch pretty well.

No Ring camera. I scan the surrounding homes, looking to see if any of her close neighbors have cameras. It doesn't appear that they do, and I have to believe that like everyone else in Friendship, the people who live on this street also buy into the notion that this place is safe. Nothing bad happens here.

Though that perception might change after this week.

All thanks to me and my nightmare.

I park the car in front of Matilda's. Her vehicle is in the driveway. I expect that she's home. Even though Friendship is pretty walkable, the heat makes doing so in summer a mostly prohibitive venture. Though, I'll have to deal with it in order to get back to my rental at Fellowship Kind. I turn around in the seat, and I press my fingers to the inside of Tabby's wrist. There's a pulse, rapid and erratic. She's breathing. I lift her lids, revealing dilated pupils.

Matilda was the one teacher who saw my pain and didn't wholly dismiss it. She tried to help me, and I know she will try to help Tabby too.

I climb out of the car, walk around to the other side, and open the door. When Matilda comes out to check on the sound of honking, she'll see Tabby lying in the back seat.

It's not safe to linger. At any moment, Matilda or one of her neighbors could walk by their front living room windows and see me out here being shady with a girl's broken body in the back seat of a car.

I run around to the front, inhale sharply, and slam my hand on the horn a few times before bolting.

Clap clap clap–the sound of my boots as I race away, chewing up grass across the playground, kicking up mulch that's been laid as padding. It's empty, not surprising in the heat, and at dusk. There is a small climbing wall dead center in the main play structure. I duck behind it, panting, hair sticking to the sides of my face and the nape of my neck.

I wait and listen. When I don't immediately hear anything, I turn. There's a small hole in the wall where a screw has pushed out of its place. I peer through it.

I don't believe in any god, but that doesn't stop me from making a plea that this will work.

This is enough to save her.

Even if nothing will ever save me.

I let out a gasp of relief when Matilda's front door whips open.

46

THE FELLOWSHIP KIND welcome sign is planted in a bed of gray gravel.

I come up on it as the cool gray light of late dusk blankets the empty parking lot.

On the marquee, they've placed black block letters. The weekly bible verse and the ever-present ALL ARE WELCOME HERE bullshit. I finger the letters of the marquee and trace over the curve of the last *S* in PSALMS as a wave of exhaustion washes over me. I wish I could run into the arms of the Lord, trust him to cover my sins, wipe away all of my sadness. If that were the truth, if that worked, I wouldn't be in this fucking mess to begin with.

Blood doesn't wash away shame and make you white as snow. Blood is the flow of our life force. Blood is spilled in acts of violence. Blood stains instead of cleanses.

My hands are covered in it.

Roger's blood.

Keller's blood.

Even a little bit of Tabitha Collins's blood.

I didn't know when I drove away with her that I would come back here to face him. In that moment, I was only thinking about getting her to safety, holding him back from doing more harm, but as I cross the parking lot and come around the side of the building, I realize this was always how it had to end.

There is no running from him, not this time.

I did it before. Look where it got me.

Tate believes he's immune to consequence. That there will never be anyone to punish him for all of the horrible things he's done. But he shouldn't feel safe when I can't. When Tabby can't. When no woman who's with him can. He wasn't my first captor. He isn't the only reason I've trapped horrors in a box in my head, but he went on tormenting long after he broke me. There's no end to his violence. No one who cares that he isn't the good man he claims to be.

They praise him.

Bow beneath him on Sundays.

Drop their hard-earned wages in the tithe buckets, and he takes a profit.

I step into the shadows at the back of the building, scan the greenbelt for signs of people walking on the path. There won't be. Still, I check just in case.

There's only my car and his in the lot. This is just between us and his god now.

My feet move before I give them the order.

From somewhere inside me, a lock comes undone.

Hinges creak.

Skin stretches.

Mind reels.

Filling me with power I've held at arm's length until now.

I stretch out my fingers, crack every knuckle, step in front of the glass door entrance. My reflection is feral. Wild hair flung out in unkempt waves. Mouth taut, teeth bared, skin slick, dripping with sweat. The skirt of the dress flutters gently, not because it's touched by the wind. It's the shadow, made physical. It breaches the walls of reality, free of the box tied to my soul.

No longer merely an aura, a sinister concept. Now it's a promise.

The nightmare is in me.

It *is* me.

It always has been *me.*

I slip through the door into a dim, narrow hallway, then turn a corner into a waiting area in the lobby.

The carpet is worn down from foot traffic. The offices must not have received the same makeover as the rest of the place. The walls are faded beige. The welcome sign on the desk is bulky wood painted yellow. It's just as pathetic as the break room at Second City Title and Trust. I savor for a second how far away that place feels from me now, and how different a person I was just a week ago. Blending into the wall, eavesdropping on coworkers' boring, inconsequential conversations.

My eyes trail over the desk to the other side, where a door stands open.

The sign reads PASTOR TATE'S PLACE.

How fucking ridiculous. Like this man is normal and gentle and kind, a caring leader of a thriving community, here to give counsel and shepherd the flock in the way it should go. I cross to the door, peer through the gap. He's not aware of me yet.

He sits at the desk. Hair tousled, tonguing his split lower lip. His Bible lays open, papers of what's probably next Sunday's sermon spread out on the desk in front of him. Behind him is a bookcase full of theology texts, modern Christ-centric titles, a row of photos dead center: Him and his wife. Him and his parents. Earl and Olympia.

I linger on that one, a wave of nausea washing all the way up my throat. It's hard to know how to feel about the claim he has on their hearts. It isn't as if I want them to love me; I gave that up a long time ago. I'm over it now. Their love would be a lie and I know it. My nightmare thoughts blend in with my own. Close to my heart, right at the edge, ready to tip over. The truth is so grotesque that looking right at it is torment.

I want them to love me.

They never will.

Rage wells up fresh inside me; evidence seeps from my skin.

Black ink-like liquid coats the tips of my fingernails and turns to smoke as soon as it makes contact with the air. It is a wonder, something almost like witchcraft. I relish the sight of it on my skin.

I know in the way I think all predators must—

He's mine.

He won't see me coming.

I am the smoke that slips in through the windows, fills your throat with black sludge, and glues your tongue to the back of your teeth until you choke.

You can scream, but nothing comes out.

The nightmare moves through me, flies like a dart to a target.

Tate's throat.

My smoke fills it up, spills back out into the air.

Horror twists his face.

His fingers claw at the skin of his throat.

Eyes searching, confusion narrows them to slits in his head as his mouth gapes open, trying and failing to pull air into his lungs. Fear contorts his features from cool and collected, the patriarchy's mask of charming oppression, to that of a stalked, scared, small, little man.

My laugh makes a mockery of his mounting fear.

I step into the room so he can see the face of his killer.

He drops out of consciousness.

I drop into his mind.

—

WE ARE IN *his office. Me at the open door, him behind his desk.*

Some of this is different. On the shelf behind him, instead of theology books and Bibles and photos of family, there are photos of women. I have to squint to make out their faces, but slowly, sickeningly, they come into focus.

Tabby. Hyacinth, who I recognize from high school. It was he who abused her, in the end. There are also others I don't know, never will recognize.

And right in the center is a photo of me.

Not me as I am now. Not a woman. Not a monster.

A girl wasting away and ready to break.

Grief swells, violent inside me. Smoke bleeds out into the air.

I take a step closer.

Tate doesn't look up as I move. Doesn't see me.

I *am an apparition and that is almost poetic.*

The ghost of his past come back to kill him.

But how will I do it.

I–this is mine.

I want to make sure that he feels it. Pays for it all as much as he can.

I move farther into the room, pace back and forth across the blue carpet like a big angry cat in a cage. He is the human on the other side of the fence, a delicious, decadent prey. But then I hate to see him as victim, and I won't give him pity, and there is no reason to make this quick or painless.

What matters more than how bad it hurts is that when they find him, they'll know that he is not a good man, make no mistake.

Not godly–whatever the fuck that actually means.

Not faithful, not pious, not clean.

There on his desk, an object draws my attention. Golden, sharp, not a knife.

A letter opener. How fucking pretentious.

How perfect.

Tate will help me make sure they get the message. I'll use his fingers and blood to do it.

I grab the object, slide my finger over the cool blade, touch the sharp tip, and then slam it down into his wrist.

He jolts, head smashing into his chair, but he can't move.

His eyes widen. His wrist is fixed to the desk.

His scream is violent and visceral.

With my hand on the hilt of the letter opener, I begin hacking away.

Cutting through tendons, slicing at veins that spring out from the skin like live wire.

I grind the bones.

Blood flows from the wound.

Tate sobs, but he cannot see me.

He never could; it makes sense.

I am not done, but I have to hurry. I have to finish before he fades out all the way.

I draw the smoke through my other hand, send it shooting to wrap around his fingers.

I drag that hand over and dip the pointer.

A pen in a blood inkwell staining . . . the leather cover of his Bible, the scattered papers of his sermon, the oak top of his desk.

Now he is up with a tug of the smoke's grip. I move him over to the wall, hand outstretched. Blood drips back down his arm as he presses his finger to the wall and begins to write . . .

For I have sinned.

The words cascade in loose, jagged writing across the beige wall.

I step behind him, holding the letter opener in my hand.

The image begins to distort. He's fading, but I am not finished yet.

I lift the blade in my hand and stab him straight through the neck.

I'M DRAGGED FROM the nightmare to find Tate bleeding out in his office.

He's almost fully unconscious. In a few minutes, he'll be nothing but matter.

I shake with adrenaline, my body temp dropping, my heart racing.

His eyelids flutter.

Blink. Blue. *Blink*. Blue. *Blink*.

"Haven . . ." He tries to speak, but his voice box sounds broken. "Help." Blood spills from his lips.

But just like my pleas were ignored, tossed aside, and made smaller than nothing, his will not be acknowledged.

I stand rooted. I watch as his life drifts out of his body.

His skin color goes sallow, he clutches his wrist, but it does nothing to squelch the flow of blood that covers the desk, soaks all of his papers.

His eyes search for me slowly, can't land, fall closed, strawberry lashes grazing his cheek.

His chest stills.

He is gone.

Tate Turner is dead.

I am his killer.

The thought sends me down to my knees.

I took his life. I don't feel remorse that he's dead, but why does my chest feel like it's splitting in two? My head falls to my hands as a sob rips through my throat, spit and tears filling the scarred flesh of my palms. Killing is ruthless, a horrible, terrible thing. This violence inside me, it's become something inevitable, desperate, impossible to escape. I am a monster born of monsters, raised in a world where girlhood is stolen, victims ignored, and nothing is sacred or good anymore.

Gently, the kiss of smoke surrounds me. Envelops to hold me in an embrace.

How can I stop this cycle of violence? How can I heal the little girl who locked all her horrors away in a box?

Killer–it's not what I wanted for her.

For me and this one fleeting, finite gasp of existence.

Killer is what we are.

And there is a reason.

The thought settles; the smoke warms all around me. This is the beginning, a piece of the truth I've long tried to forget.

It's instinct that tells me where to go next.

I have to finish what I started.

Write the ending of this story I've been telling the teeny tiny box since I was a child.

For better or worse, it's all about to be over.

47

THE WHOLE LOT of them have gathered at the ranch.

Three trucks for Earl, Buck, and Sterling. Lucky drives a Land Rover. Olympia's Denali gleams closest to the porch. It's a gaudy display. I don't know why they've gathered, but I have my ideas. Buck may have told them he saw me this morning. They may have gathered to shit-talk me, because that's what this family is good at. Drawing uncharitable conclusions about each other.

I guess, to be fair, I'm doing the same thing right now.

I park my rental horizontally behind the three trucks, blocking them in.

As I take the steps up to the porch, I am caught by a chill. My blood icy cold, my skin slick as if coated in condensation. The porch is a warp, momentarily turning me sideways, a trick I know now cannot contain me.

I am the nightmare; I have nothing to fear from my family.

Not even the truth.

My eyes catch on the sight of the stable right before I enter the house. I can't say if it was intentional, not going inside since arriving back in Friendship, or if I knew somehow that there was horror lurking there, ready to claim me. Memory is maybe the only real ghost that there is.

The door handle twists in my hand. I walk inside to a dimly lit foyer. Their voices sound from the kitchen, a low hum calling to me. I take the path from the dining room, listening to them talk as I move closer.

"And I'm telling you, I don't think she left town." This is Lucky, his voice laced with fight. He's trying to defend me, which tells me the others haven't been so generous.

"You're just saying that because you don't know her like we do," Sterling spits. I don't know why he's so adamant. The dude has barely said three words to me since I came home.

"You know nine-years-ago her. I'm the only one who's actually spent any time with her," Lucky says.

"Not true. Haven and I have talked plenty," Buck says. "There's something off. I could tell today. She's skittish."

"Haven has always been skittish," Olympia says. "She came home and we all assumed she was here to reconnect, but the only one she's made a real effort with is Lucky. The easiest."

"Why am I the easiest? Just because I'm the baby?" He sounds genuinely annoyed. "I was hurt just like the rest of y'all when she left the way she did. I was barely thirteen. She was my big sister and I didn't get it. I didn't understand what was going on, and you guys made it seem like she just ran off for no good reason."

"Hell, Lucky, she did just run off for no good reason," Sterling says.

"She didn't though. She told me what happened with Tate, or at least, sort of what happened and how you guys acted."

"Not this fuckery again," says Sterling. Again. Jesus Christ, this is the most he's ever talked in his life. Good to know he's practically verbose when he's shit-talking me.

"She and Tate got into a scuffle in his car," Buck says, cool and collected. "It got out of hand. They were drinking—both of them."

"I looked it up, you know," Lucky says.

"What did you look up?" Olympia asks, her voice threaded through with mistrust. She's preparing a counterargument before she even knows what she's arguing.

"The accident kind of went viral. It's a miracle that Haven didn't die, that both of them didn't die."

"The miracle," Buck says, "would have been if Haven could have seen that it was an accident, not malicious, and dealt with it like a grown-up."

"To be fair, she was nineteen," Sterling says. That's probably more about him and some youthful indiscretion he made than actually defending me.

"Oh, now you're gonna be fair?" Lucky snipes.

"Fair or not," Buck says loudly, "she blamed Tate for what happened, and then she started telling all of us that he'd been abusing her for years, quietly, and none of us had ever seen any evidence of it. Were we just supposed to *believe* her?"

"Yeah!" Lucky says. "Haven't you ever heard of the concept that we should believe victims?"

This is met with uproarious scoffs. Because of course it is.

"Okay, boys, that's enough. We're not going to get into the nitty-gritty of this nonsense story again."

"Come on, Mom. You can't be okay with this," Lucky says. There's a long pause. "Dad?" The first mention of Earl, proof he's in the room listening to the discourse about his prodigal daughter.

It's Olympia who speaks. "Lucky, don't tell me what I can and cannot be okay with. And definitely don't try to tell me that I should pity her. You don't understand the challenge of raising a daughter like that."

Her words are a knife.

Cutting deep.

Cutting me open.

Forcing me into the room.

48

THE BOOTS ANNOUNCE my presence.

One by one, each member of my family turns to look at me. Take in my feral form in the dress from my dad.

The weight of their eyes is nothing compared to the suffocating pressure of my nightmare begging to be released from my skin.

It surprises me that the eyes I seek out first aren't Lucky's, my only defender.

Not Olympia, my greatest betrayer.

Not Sterling, the biggest shit-talker.

Not Earl, who failed me as a father.

It's Buck. His aquamarine eyes, hooded, with thick brown lashes. They've changed over the years, deepened their color, developed dark circles from bad sleep. But they're the same eyes that found me in the cabinet. The same eyes, their sadness a memory etched into the blue.

Buck and I have a history the rest of them can't understand. It's tucked between our teeth like a bridle bit, steering us where it wants us to go. I followed it all the way to this moment, gnawing at the metal until it drew blood in my mouth as I tore through the leather, broke free of the reins.

"I'm glad you're all here," I say, but still I only watch Buck.

This kitchen. They've remodeled since then, changed all the facings, put in new appliances, painted and upgraded, but the phantom scent of burning peanut butter cookies lingers in the air all the same.

Real or the nightmare. Memory or manipulation.

This house is its own box of horrors.

Lucky slides off the stool he's sitting on at the island. "I knew you weren't gonna bail."

"Where have you been?" Earl speaks over Lucky. It startles the rest of them. Even Lucky freezes midway to me.

"What do you mean?" I ask. Finally, I shift my eyes to him.

He knows. I don't know how he knows, what he knows, but the prick of fear like needles on the nape of my neck is a warning. *Earl knows.*

Why I came back to Friendship.

Not for the reason I gave.

But the truth.

I slide my eyes to Olympia. She's got her long blond hair spun up in a bun on her head. She's wearing denim that's dirty, like she was out working in the garden and came in before she was ready.

The box drops onto the counter between us.

Her eyes land right on it and fix.

"You can see it." Shock wrecks me, pinching my voice off to a choked whisper.

The first day I arrived in Friendship, there on the porch alone with her, for a second I thought she saw that aura spiral.

But that doesn't make sense. I am the only one who can see it. My box. My nightmare soul inside it.

"What are you talking about?" Buck asks.

"Mom," I say. The use of her name surprises her. Almost as much as it does me.

"I'd like a moment alone with Haven," Olympia says, her voice cold, her expression flat.

This is met with uproarious outrage from every single one of my brothers, but when Earl begins to walk out of the room wordlessly, without so much as a grunt, they take the hint and follow.

The only one who looks at me as he leaves is Buck.

Because Buck remembers the day with the cookies, I bet he knows who the man in the stable was. It's one of the things locked inside the gun case in his subconscious. It's at least part of the reason why he dreams about killing our father.

"Let's take a walk outside," she says, flicking her eyes toward where the men just exited. "Can't trust a one of 'em not to listen." She flashes her teeth in a smile. "And this should be just between us girls."

THE MOON IS high and bright, and this far out of town we can even see stars. We don't stop at the edge of the porch or the backyard, where the pool glistens ethereal blue. We keep walking, out the back gate, down the path toward the stable.

She's taking me to the scene of the crime. Somehow I know it.

Somehow I know that finally I want it.

"He thinks he knows better than I do, even after all these years, even after everything I've done to keep this family afloat." I keep my eyes facing forward on the path ahead, not on her. Whatever this show is, the pomp and circumstance, I have to let it play out even if I don't like it.

Olympia holds the reins; she always has.

"He was determined the right thing was to bring you back into the fold." She chuckles. *What a ridiculous idea*, the laugh seems to say. "Men have short memories. That's how they do what they do. Something will happen, they'll justify it in their minds, make up a whole scenario, and by the end of it—well, the truth doesn't matter. Truth is for us to worry about, for us to conceal."

She's looking at me now, a little side-eye glance that I sense as it runs over the planes of my face. I still don't turn my attention toward her. She carries on and I follow.

"I want you to understand. I explained it all to you when it happened. I explained everything. I don't like being held responsible just because you couldn't understand what you were agreeing to. It's not like I was asking anything of you that my mother didn't ask of me. We've *always* had to do this." She pauses. Her voice cracks.

I cave, glancing at her to see there's moisture in her eyes. Not quite tears, but close.

"What do you mean, 'we've always had to do this'?" I refuse to give her an inch, even if internally I'm cracking too.

"I know about the box, Haven." She stops moving, her hand gripping my arm. We are mere feet from the stable.

"How do you know?" I am not surprised. It comes out of my mouth as a question, but I already knew this. I've known all along but made myself forget it.

"I'm your mother. I made you. You think I couldn't teach you how to make *it*?" With her free hand, she reaches up to hold my chin.

Our eyes are the same eyes. And when they meet, hers tell me the whole story.

IT STARTS IN *the kitchen.*

Little girl me sits at the old breakfast table bench. It's upholstered with a tacky chicken-and-rooster-farm-animal print. Little girl me has been crying, my eyes almost violet from the tears.

Her mother sits across from little girl me. Her face is bruised.

Her eyes are swollen, there's blood on her lower lip, purple stains on her knuckles. Little girl me seems to know why. She's upset about it, she's hysterical about it, she's defensive about it.

Her mother doesn't want to hear little girl me cry anymore. She doesn't want to explain it, and she doesn't want little girl me to ask about it ever again.

"Can you do that for me, Haven? Can you forget this ever happened?"

She knows little girl me can't. She sees the way little girl me tries to pretend, her mind twisting around, up and down, performing mental gymnastics. Little girl me will want to get out of it later, when she's bored or when she's angry or scared. She'll use it against them, against Buck when he doesn't do what she wants, her father when he tries to make her behave.

Little girl me doesn't realize her mother only asks out of kindness.

Little girl me sees her mother's expression falter, a shadow passing across it, and in her eyes a cloud settles.

"There's something we can do. Something we women do best. You want to be a woman, don't you, Haven?"

Now, this is interesting. Because little girl me does want to be a woman. She wants it more than a new dress or a doll that can say "Mommy." She wants it in a way that makes her stingy, hungry, wild.

She'll do anything for it.

Little girl me nods.

"In your life, there will be things that happen that you don't ever want to think about again. Why should you? There will be nothing you can do about these things, no consequence to satisfy the pain these things cause you."

Little girl me listens, certain her mother is telling her the secret to what it means to be a woman, certain she can handle the job.

"As you get older, you'll see that it's better this way, better that you don't fight it, better that you learn to bury it. There's so many benefits to doing what is expected, to trusting they know better."

"Who's 'they'?"

"You'll see," her mother says. Sadness colors the words soot black.

Little girl me thinks she knows, and she doesn't like it. But she wants to be a woman, and this sounds like the only way.

"What do I have to do?"

Her mother takes her by the hands. Little girl me tries not to notice the scrapes and the bruises. She knows her mother doesn't want her to.

Her mother looks deep in her eyes.

"We're going to make a box. It's for you to put anything, everything, whatever you like inside, and then lock it up tight and forget it." Tears spring to her mother's eyes.

"Can it look however I want? Can I put a tree on the top? Can I make it pretty?"

"You can do whatever you want. It's your box."

Little girl me had always wanted something that was completely, totally her own, that Sterling couldn't break and Buck couldn't tell her was stupid.

And so she smiles. Happy she finally gets it.

I COME OUT of the memory on my knees, on the ground. Tears wet my cheeks.

Olympia stands above me.

A gun in her hand pointed right at my head.

49

"WHAT ARE YOU doing?" I push myself up from the ground and stumble back.

"I need you to know this isn't what I wanted." Funny. She doesn't look too broken up about it.

"I don't remember what happened that day, despite trying, I can't, so if that's why you're doing this–"

She shakes her head, chuckling. "Darling, we can't trust that, can't risk it." She pauses, looks me over. "We can't risk this *thing* getting worse."

"What do you mean, 'this thing'?" The words drop like lead between us.

"I wouldn't have taught you this little skill if I'd known this is what you would do with it."

"What am I doing with it?" I sound indignant and defensive.

But it is long-hidden sadness turning quickly to rage.

"You sound just like you did when you were a teenager," she says, disgust seeping off her tongue. "I found the police report about your boss, Roger–"

"There wasn't a police report." Fuck, I already stepped in it.

She smiles. "They investigated it even if it turned out to be an 'accident.'"

"Roger had a heart attack and hit his head when he fell."

She chuckles. "I remember those little incidents. They used to happen all the time when you were here, especially with Sterling. The broken arm, the nightmares about a man in his closet. In fourth grade, when those girls bullied the new kid and you invited them over for a sleepover, they all collectively walked out into the darkness in the direction of the train tracks."

"I don't remember any of this." I really don't, but it does sound like me.

"Well, of course not. You put it in the box. You put other things in there too. I know and I'm sorry for that, really. I tried."

I wish I knew what she was talking about, any part of it, to make sense of why she thinks the only solution to the problem of me is permanent sleep.

This is the cycle of violence. We are all a part of it now.

"This is my fault," she repeats, sounding a little deranged. "I'm fixing it. I promised him I would."

That's the thing that cracks it.

The box drops down between us and springs open wide.

I'M IN THE *stable.*

I look through my own eyes, feel the ground under my own feet.

But I am small. Little girl me once again.

I am her. I live out her memory.

I had been waiting for Buck to get done with his chores so we could play hide and seek. I went out to see Princess, take her an apple. I stole a knife from the kitchen to cut pieces off and feed them to her. Dad was always scolding me for plying her with treats, thought it made her see me as weak. Not the master I was meant to be.

I was six. I just wanted my pony to like me.

I'd fallen asleep in the hayloft, and I'd woken up to people shouting.

I'm here now. It is happening as if for the first time.

I peer down from my perch overlooking the tack room. I know to be silent.

The man, I notice him first. Tall and handsome, he wears sneakers and a tank top, a baseball cap, and a look of pure terror on his chiseled face. I'd seen him before, only when my dad wasn't home. I liked him, he was kind. There was this way about him that felt somehow different from other men I'd been near.

Dad stands across from him. He's got a hold on my mother. Grip firm on her arm. Her lip bleeds, her face bruised.

I'd seen my dad angry before, plenty. I feared him already, but this is different. The way he holds on to her, so tight she can't move, tight enough that when she tries, I can tell that it hurts her.

They argue about her, the man and Dad.

Dad has a gun. He points it from the man to my mother and back. "I won't let you take her," he says. "This is my wife, my property. This is my land and you trespassed."

I don't want the man to take her either, but I don't like the way she's begging my father to stop. Such sadness, such love, I can feel it. "Let him go." She sounds so weak. "Let him and I'll stay."

Dad likes it. I can tell. He is happy she's scared. Angry she would ever think she could leave him.

It happens so fast.

The flash of gunmetal, the crack of the bullet.

His blood and brain and skull spray the back of the stall.

Animals scream, revolting, terror a storm through the length of the stable.

The man drops to the ground. Red pools beneath him.

My mother is frozen, her face fixed, her eyes glistening.

My father turns the pistol on her. Now there is terror, her begging, and she lunges to break his grip on the gun. He is bigger and so much stronger; her struggle is useless.

He raises his arm and whips her face with the handle.

Crack *as the bone breaks in her cheek.*

I am wild with anger. I run from my hiding spot in the hayloft.

I have my knife from the kitchen. I have my small size as an advantage.

The man can't take her away, but neither can my dad.

I slide the blade into his side, through his muscle until it hits bone, and then I run.

I am fast. He's bleeding, she's screaming, but my lips tug up in a satisfied smile.

Years pass by . . .

I see the scar when he goes swimming. My mind revolts at the sight. It can't remember but knows somehow that it's bad.

Sometimes when I see it, I ask what happened. They brush it off, ignore me, so I will forget it again.

One day, it's lost–404 error page not found.

I COME TO in a cloud of black smoke.

The man was the moment I made it. The first moment I hid. Earl was the reason I kept on.

I turn over the box, spilling out memory objects, naming them all as they drop.

One, then another, and another, until the whole box is empty, the objects laid out like a puzzle.

My life put back together again.

The box sits on the ground between us. I reach out, knowing somehow that I have to save it, to take it.

Or she will do something to it. She will destroy it, and that may destroy me as well.

I can't see her. But I can feel the smoke twisting around and through her.

I don't know what to do. I don't know if I want it to kill her, so I do what I've always done.

I run.

50

THEY SPILL OUT onto the porch. Every one of them:

Earl, Buck, Sterling, Lucky.

Their eyes aren't focused on me. They look behind me.

At the smoke that must still surround our mother.

"Stop her!" Earl orders.

"What the hell is happening?" Lucky cries, eyes wide in horror. Sterling doesn't flinch, he takes the stairs two at a time, running for me.

I'm surrounded by smoke again.

A gunshot fires; the bullet narrowly misses me.

My nightmare is with me, running to help me, leaving her behind.

Lucky runs from the porch, screams, begs our mother to stop. She's gasping, the rasp of her breath still thick with smoke. She pulls back the hammer on the gun. Lucky jumps, putting his body between us just as Sterling takes me down. The wind is knocked from my lungs, and my arms fly up and over my head, sending the box flying out of my hands.

It falls at Buck's feet.

Lucky grabs Sterling by the shoulders, tries to pull him off, but he's unable to best him. Sterling is the bruiser, a strong brute without a mind of his own. For a second, our faces are close: his bright eyes, sea green, so like our father's. I stretch my lips in a smile.

"What the fuck do you have to smile about?" Sterling's spit drops onto my face.

"You're a coward." My words are venom. The nightmare tucks up through his nostrils.

"You're a freak," he says as the nightmare slides right down his throat.

"You're dead," I say without feeling.

I'm ready to do it, be the killer they all made me to be. I'll close every pore and airway until he's breathless, eyes bulging, tongue swollen—

Lucky's face appears beside his, struggling to pull him away from me even as smoke curls up from my body, around them, confusion and panic at war in his features.

Lucky would never forgive me. He'd never be a pea in a pod with me if I kill our brother.

I can't lose the one person I think might actually love me.

I pull the nightmare smoke back, my skin tightening as it slides up into my veins and recedes to the dark center of my soul.

I let them capture me. I give in but don't give up.

Sterling yanks me up from the ground and walks me back toward the house. I lose sight of the box.

I hear the call of my mother: "Don't trust her."

It's not Sterling who deserves my wrath.

It's my father. It's her. It always has been.

THEY SIT ME down in the den.

Earl and Olympia stand across from me together. Her face is kissed with soot, evidence of my nightmare still fresh on her skin. Lucky paces, eyes wild, searching each of our faces in turn. He keeps looking at me, then away. He knows now that I'm some kind of monster. He doesn't know how, and I hate that there's no way to save him from this. To protect him from the horror of whatever comes next.

Buck hovers in the doorway between the den and the hall to the kitchen.

Sterling seethes, restless to get on with it. Practically giddy.

"Shouldn't we tie her up or something?" Sterling asks our parents.

"You sick fuck," Lucky says. It stops his pacing momentarily.

"That won't matter," Earl says. "Will it, Haven?"

"So, we're doing this, huh?" I ask him, lifting my brow. His scowl is sour. He always hated my attitude. The bravado I come at him with.

I remember now how he used to slap me. Just hard enough that it would make me shut up. It's no wonder he didn't care if Tate hurt me. He was just like him.

A model member of the patriarchy.

"What are we doing?" Lucky asks. *Poor baby.* "Like, actually, this is insane."

"Maybe you should get out of here," I say to him. I try to sound casual, like this is no big deal, nothing I can't handle.

"I'm not going anywhere." My heart breaks, but I can't tell if it's from sadness or gratitude. Lucky deserves better than this from a family. Better than me, than them, than any of this.

I turn my attention to Olympia. "Where's yours?"

"My what?" She's stoic as ever. She crosses her arms. She's not going to give it up so easily, but I'm done playing her game and his.

"Your box." I hook my brow up, the corner of my lip following it. "I know you made one. You told me when you helped me build mine."

Olympia's expression is Machiavellian. "I'm sure I don't know what you mean."

"You said your mother taught you. And you taught me. This is what women do." I practically spit every word. It's verbatim. Amazing how my memory serves now that I can access it easily. "You said 'we' build containers to store all our trauma"–I cut my eyes from her to my father–"so they can go right on abusing their power."

"I never abused you." Earl prickles, his hackles immediately raised at the accusation.

Lucky stops moving. Sterling looks down at the ground. Buck shifts in the doorway.

The fear of our father is a tether from one body to another. A shared terror. A collective grief. For them, his torment was meant to turn them into men like him.

For me, it was to make me the kind of woman he told me to be.

Olympia was complicit. Earl held the power.

"Look at all of them, Earl." I hope his name on my tongue slices just like that blade in his side did. "They're terrified of you."

His eyes seethe. His face reddens.

"They hate you. You have to know that."

"*You* hate me, but my sons respect me." He eats up the floor between us, crouches down so he's eye level with me in the chair. Thick beard with gray, his tan skin, his deep voice. This is my father, who wants me dead. Always has and just didn't have the guts to do it till now. "I'm not scared of you, little girl."

I grin to mirror his. We have similar sadistic smiles. "You made Buck come and find me that day. What did Olympia tell you that made you believe you were safe?"

My brothers all listen with intense interest. None of them, with the exception of Buck maybe, understand what's actually happening, but none of them step in to stop it. They want the truth just as bad as I do, I think.

"Women have their ways of speaking to their kind. That was all I needed to know." Earl lifts his thick brows, heaves his shoulder in a dismissive shrug. "When you got out of line, I put you back. Easy to correct, just like a mare in a pen."

I hack a laugh-sob caught in my throat. "You're a sick motherfucker."

"You're weak."

I flick my eyes to my mother.

"She can't help you," he says. "She never could."

The smell of her perfume touches my nose. Deep dark violet. Green, green grass. But I was near her earlier, and I didn't smell it. Like so many times since I've been home, this phantom feels out of place and unreal.

A clue to something my mind reaches out to understand but still can't.

I can remember now how Earl would test the pen I built myself.

Every jab.

Every moment of fear.

The pain that I hid back inside the box, the way I slowly lost confidence to fight back.

"You must have been thrilled when Tate came along to fuck me up for you."

"Haven, you can make me the villain, but I'm not the one who keeps killing people." He gives me a *gotcha* smile.

He can't know about Keller or Tate—there's no way. Olympia must have told him about Roger.

Roger.

Buck's call came right after Roger. Olympia said she looked up the police report, but that doesn't mean it's what happened. They've gaslit together my whole life, kept the truth a secret, skewed the narrative when necessary, or even just for fun, and they've never cared if I noticed. No one believed me anyway, so what did it matter if I figured out the truth?

"You were watching me, weren't you?" Bitterness writhes in my stomach. "You had Buck call because of what happened with Roger, not—"

He smiles again.

I know I'm right. "You aren't sick, are you?"

"As sick as any man my age."

My skin reeks with rot and smoke seeps from my fingernails.

Lucky jumps and points. "What the hell is that? How is—"

"I think you need to let her calm down," says Buck.

When I look him in the eye, there is a split-second flash. He is my caring big brother again, who found us in forests after dark, in cupboards when we were scared, and tried to protect but never actually could. I can't trust him—I know that—but there's still some stupid small part of me that hopes he remembers that he once wanted me to.

He knows about the box. He knows everything.

"You just came to find me again," I say, my voice cracking, tears dripping. "Like that day in the kitchen. You were just delivering me right to him again."

Buck's face falls. "He said he wanted you back; I didn't think I could argue."

"And you all just went along with the lie?" I glance between all of them. "Lucky?" But I can tell by his face he didn't know; he's just as shocked as me. Is there a world where he survives this unscathed? I don't think so, but a girl can dream.

"You lied about being sick." Lucky's trying to make sense of it. "You told me you wanted to make things right with her because you wanted all of us together. Why would you do tha—"

"Oh my God, who *cares*? It's been a fucking nightmare since she came home!" Sterling says in a guttural groan. "It'll be better when you're gone."

Gone?

Gone.

"Let me go," I say through gritted teeth. I test them because, suddenly, I'm actually scared they don't mean to let me go freely. Leave the ranch and never return.

"We can't do that and you know it." Earl stands, looming over me.

"Dad, I still don't think this is necessary." Buck tries to be reasonable.

I start to hyperventilate, heaving breaths in and out.

They plan to kill me.

I won't let them.

I am a killer; I know that I can.

The nightmare unfurls from my skin.

It flies out in all directions. Covers Earl's face. Twists around Buck's wrists like handcuffs.

But Sterling moves toward me with new untethered rage, I have to stop him.

I wrap the smoke around his neck and twist.

It is a rope, a noose, a means to an end.

Lucky screams, "What are you doing?" He runs at us both. "Don't do this! You don't want to do this!"

And I almost, very nearly, for the sake of my little brother, stop.

Black coils around Sterling's throat, drawing tighter and tighter with every breath.

"Let him go," my mother says.

She raises the gun.

51

CRACK!

Buck shoves her arm up and away, sending the bullet flying off target. It buries itself in the head of the buck above the mantel.

Rage twists Olympia's features and she turns on her son. "What do you think you're doing?"

She spits flames. I swear I see them ignite on her tongue.

A thought breaks through everything. Quiet, a whisper, a truth that I know: *My nightmare is smoke. Is hers fire?*

My mother made me, made her own box, though she denies it, and carries generational horror locked up inside her body. She let torment unfurl all around her, her children trapped in its grip. She taught me how to hide my own secret nightmares inside a box with a lid.

"I'm not letting you shoot your own daughter!" Buck yells.

It's too late. It's too late and she knows it.

"Mom, look at what's happening. Look at what you're doing." Buck's voice is laced through with fear.

She takes aim at him.

I am distracted.

I am piecing her puzzle together–

Earl gets free from the smoke engulfing his face.

He yanks me up from the chair by the collar and slaps me across the cheek before he sends me flying. I crash into the coffee table, back flat, wind knocked out of me.

Smoke fills the air. I heave, pain severing my side with every inhale.

I don't have time to regroup before Sterling is on me, closing his arm around my throat.

I lost my grip, I lost my hold.

He drags me up to his body, squeezing the life out of me. My vision goes blurry.

Lucky sobs, and I think I see him running for me, but my vision isn't working too well.

I use every ounce of energy to send smoke to wrap up and around Earl's throat.

It fills his mouth.

Earl swallows it into his lungs, he coughs and he hacks, and screams. "Don't–let–" Earl pounds his fists against Sterling. "Go–" He drops to his knees.

This is what happens with the abuse of power.

Violence on violence on violence.

At this rate, we'll all kill each other.

Blood will cover all our hands.

A body slams into us, knocking me out of Sterling's arms. I fall to the ground, gasping. Buck's hands lift me up.

He's a little boy again, aqua eyes staring at me through the cupboard.

He's a grown man, living with all that he's done to become one.

"Call it off," he says to me. Olympia still has him in her sights. I can't trust him because he's only doing this to save himself. "Let Dad go."

"No."

Earl's body goes limp. His eyes fall closed.

I wither a little inside.

He'll be dead in mere moments.

"You'll kill him!" Sterling screams, a fire of rage in his eyes.

"Good." Pain slices through my throat from the grip Sterling had me in. "I have to do it. He'll never stop hating me. I'll never be safe. At least, now, this way, I can be done."

Buck isn't done yet. "You don't want to kill him. You don't want his blood on your hands." He's starting to shake. His eyes fill with tears. His body blocks me from Olympia and Sterling. "This isn't the way to stop this. You don't have to do this–"

"I do," I say as tears spring to my eyes. "He hurt her, hurt me, hurt you, and them."

Lucky sobs.

Sterling recovers and runs over to try to free Earl from the smoke that bleeds through his veins. He's shaking him, turning him over.

But it doesn't matter.

His veins turn his skin to an inkblot as the smoke becomes sludge and eats up his blood. Sterling squeezes his arms, trying to stop it, screaming for me to "Just let him go and you can leave."

"I am the bad guy." What a relief to say it out loud, to see how it scares him, and them, and her. "This is what bad guys do."

Buck shakes his head slowly. He closes his hands around my shoulders. Bends to peer right in my eyes.

"You're not," he whispers. "You never were."

"I'm everything they always said. I'm dangerous. I'm vengeful. I'm your worst nightmare come true."

The smoke lines on Earl spread out, all over, it's almost the end.

"You should be scared of me." I close my hands into fists. It hurts, stings like salt doused in an open wound, as the smoke courses up my veins. It is beneath my skin, tattooing the horror inside me.

I can end this. For me and for Earl.

Then I can finally be free.

Buck doesn't let go.

He nods. He keeps nodding. "I am scared of you, Sis." That word is such a small thing, but it cracks something open inside me. "I've always been scared of you." The ink sludge infiltrates through his fingernails. Pain washes over his face, eyes pricked with tears, skin flushed as it fills his veins, climbs his forearms on a path to his heart. "But you didn't get here on your own." The words are a struggle for him to get out.

The air between us goes still, like we're inside a vacuum.

A cupboard.

"I should have protected you." He's ready to give up. Exhaustion paints plum strokes under his eyes. All the fight, all that bravado depletes as color leaches from his skin.

I shake my head—wrong, right, not what I wanted. "You tried." There is fire in my voice. Rage that still wants to fight. "They didn't."

I can still control this. I can do something besides end it all here. I pull the nightmare back. As it clears, the pain twisting his features also contracts. He squares his shoulders, lifts his head.

He can still help.

"Is this what you did it all for?" He turns, looks at Olympia.

The gun hangs loose in her hand. Her eyes are fixed on my father.

"Do you want it to end this way, Mom?" he asks.

Earl's body twitches.

"Let him go, Haven," she says, ignoring Buck's question. She snaps back into herself and raises the gun. "I won't shoot if you let him go."

"I don't believe you."

Earl's face contorts. His eyes roll back in his head.

I'm killing my father. In the end, he was right to try to control me, but my will has always been stronger. Driven to survive no matter the cost, no matter the waste of my life, at least I kept going. But I am tired of running, and I can't forget anymore.

Lucky drops to his knees.

"Stop her, Mom. Shoot her!" Sterling begs.

"And then what? Bury her body beside the other one?" Buck asks.

This seems to penetrate. Sterling's lips clamp closed, shock resonant on his face.

"Dad is the reason. Always has been, and you know it." He sounds so certain. "You should be the one to do it." Buck wants him dead just like me. He knows, deep inside, it's what has to be done.

Olympia's eyes travel over the faces of each of her children. Her gun hand falls, smacking her side.

"Why?" Her voice wavers. "Because I didn't protect y'all like y'all wanted." As if it's our fault we needed a mother. But then her resolve seems to crumble. This powerful woman—who made us play games for affection, intimidated everyone, was the envy of so many other mothers in Friendship—suddenly trembles. "I didn't. I know it. I really did try." Her voice cracks, charred wood turning to dust.

We were trapped in her box with her. She was forced there by Earl, held captive by her fear, complicit and tormented at the same gruesome time.

She closes her eyes. Tears fall down her cheeks. "You don't have to do it, Haven," she says, blinking rapidly, her voice strong with conviction. "But someone does."

Someone does.

A sob catches thick in my throat.

"It's not too late." Her eyes are piercing. She swipes at her tears.

Tall, strong, beauty queen Olympia Powers. This is not who she had to become. This is not who any of us had to become.

She sets the gun down on the table.

I take a step toward her, allowing the rest of the smoke to pull back. It doesn't fully recede, it still cloaks the room with its haze, but it has let go of my father. He lies on the ground, unmoving. It won't be long before he comes to and comes for me again. But none of that matters right now. This is between my mother and me.

She doesn't reach out. I don't run into her arms.

"You asked about my box." Her voice drops low, almost a whisper. "This is it." Her gaze flits around at the house. "My little box on a hillside."

This house she made into a home.

It isn't just a house.

It's her nightmare box.

The smells that come from nowhere. The strange stretched spaces that go on too long. The closet where I saw that little Lucky apparition. The warp of the walls and the way everything feels here.

The silver card box. Those initials. I wonder if they were the man from the stable's.

It wasn't just triggers that started to change my box when it got here.

It was this place.

It was her.

I have so many questions, and somehow I know I've run out of time. That's what violence does. It steals everything good, every chance you wish you could take, all the potential, all the need to know more and do more and love and just simply live.

Tears fill my eyes. "I wish I knew before—" My voice breaks off with a sob.

"Don't waste time on that now." There's one final look just for me, a sad sort of smile, a tiny wink. "I had years to fortify the walls, etch my memories into each one. I tried to make it special." She flicks her gaze evenly between all of us now. "I failed you."

"You didn't fail," Lucky says in a small voice, like he can't quite believe it himself. He's moved up beside me.

"It's time for you to go." She turns her attention to Buck. "I'll take care of the rest."

"What do you mean?" Buck is bewildered, moves toward her, his arms outstretched. "We can go together, we can leave—"

"Oh, son, you know that we can't." She holds her hand out to stop him before he can reach her. He obeys. For a fleeting split second, she is our mother again.

She loves us.

She sees us.

She will protect us.

She snaps her fingers, and the shelf behind her ignites.

"Run."

And we do as she says.

One final time.

Buck drags Sterling screaming, feet kicking, arms reaching. I hold Lucky's hand, fingers tight, tears on our cheeks as, all around us, the house we grew up in is engulfed in flames. The smoke in our lungs isn't my nightmare; the heat that licks down our throats isn't from summer.

We fly through the door, down the porch steps, and out into the darkness together.

THE HOUSE BURNS behind me in the rearview mirror.

Faintly, the sound of sirens blare, speeding down the road from town. In the rubble, they'll find bodies, they'll piece together the whole gruesome story of this week in Friendship—the one we agreed we all want them to know, the one they'll want to believe, the one that leaves me all the way out of it.

The truth will stay our little secret. My brothers' and mine. All four of us Powers children.

We will contain it.

Tuck it away in a box we all see.

A shared nightmare we long to wake up from.

Epilogue

I DRIVE UNTIL I feel a tug to pull over. I'm far into the desert, somewhere between Texas and California, an alien landscape, a world of bleached colors, a sky of unending blue. The road seems to wind forever, curling around sandy brown hills, tucking into cavernous canyons, slicing through walls made of red rock.

I take the box in my hands. Sometime between the parking lot of Second City Title and Trust and the lawn at Powers Ranch, it turned solid. Separated from my subconscious, it became a real thing all its own. Not a cage, not storage. I touch the hinges, feel the coolness beneath my fingers. It's nothing now. No nightmare me lives inside it. No memories. Just wood, just metal, just a tree carved into the top. An object that holds nothing but air.

I set it in the dirt.

I keep walking. Sometime after the sky turns black and stars create a blanket above me, I lie down, listen for the wild things all around me: wolves howling at an icy-white moon, critters skittering, snakes slithering, bats circling. I am unafraid of them because I am one of them: an animal, a predator, a nightmare turned back into a woman.

I close my eyes.

It doesn't take long for me to find her.

The little girl with blond ringlets. Jelly sandals. Daisies on her T-shirt.

She's playing in the meadow of her own imagination, cocooned in sunlight, dew dampening her toes, a cool breeze lifting her hair as she twirls. I watch her dance, flitting around the green, laughing at nothing, singing some tune she made up.

She doesn't see me. She doesn't know I'm there.

It's better that way. She deserves to be left undisturbed, left to herself and this place. No shadow looms around her, no box sits open for her to spill secrets into.

Her story is over, her safety secured.

Here in this meadow. Held in my memory.

Finally free.

Acknowledgments

When I decided to write a book about a woman whose trauma becomes a weapon, I knew it would be challenging. At times during the process, it felt like I was the one boxed in. Haven's confinement became palpable, her desire for freedom intoxicating, and in order to better understand her, I had to pick apart the pieces of my own heart–a practice that was a lot harder than I ever imagined. At its core, this is a book about the abuse of power, systemically and personally, and how violence can create a cycle that *feels* impossible to break. While Haven's story cannot encompass all experiences, I hope that if you need to feel seen in these pages, you do. I hope it provides a cathartic release.

Thankfully, my editor and agent weren't too scared to let me write this book.

Kristine Swartz, I have to hand it to you. *What a Nightmare* wouldn't exist without you. You knew I had a horror side and even though you hadn't ever edited a book like this before, you jumped in with both feet and encouraged me to make it as gruesome as I wanted. I loved working on this with you; your vision helped me to realize my own and your willingness to go into the dark with me is a gift I'm unwaveringly grateful for.

Katie Shea Boutillier, there's no one like you. I'm the luckiest to have you as my friend and agent. Every time I pitch you an idea, or struggle with the reality of this business, or just need to talk it all out, your guidance and brilliance is there to keep me on my path. You get me and aren't afraid of me—which is good, because I have a feeling the scares are just getting started.

The book package you hold in your hand was made with the expertise and skill of some incredible talent. Vikki Chu, thank you for directing this cover to the most incredible place. The art, which has humbled me to my core, was created by the astonishing Andreea Dumata—you captured the energy of this book and our vengeful heroine perfectly. The whole team at Berkley Pub: Mary Baker, Chelsea Pascoe, Anika Bates, Christine Legon, Caitlyn Kenny, Will Tyler, Hannah Gramson, and Alicia Hyman, thank you for helping bring this wild story to shelves.

I am blessed with some of the best friends in the biz. People who have become more than colleagues, who I trust, lean on, and am endlessly inspired by.

Carlyn Greenwald: Your friendship is so dear to me. Thank you for listening to my voice messages, for the writing retreats, for the Phoebe snuggles, and for loving the dark parts just as much as I do. Emily Wibberley: I feel like I hit the friend jackpot when I met you years ago. Thank you for reading this book early and making me feel a little less scared to have it out in the world. Liz Parker, Gian Sardar, and Nika Serras: the most vibey writing coven around. I love our tarot chats and long dinners and sometimes murderous manifestations. Mallory Marlowe: Your Scorpio moon just gets it, gets me, and I am so glad we found each other in the romance world. Matthew Hubbard: I love being your friend. Cheering each other on is always a highlight. Veronica Bane: You're such a kindred spirit and I am constantly in awe of all you do. Gretchen Schreiber: Thank you for always being down for brunch and story talks. Forever and always, Beez: Liz Parker (again), Sara Biren, and Tracey Neithercott. Bridget Morrissey, Austin Siegemund-Broka, Emma Alban, Marie Cruz, Paulette Kennedy, Trish Lundy, Kirsten King: LA is full of talent, and I am honored to know some of the best.

To the new horror buds welcoming me into this space: Liz Kerin, Rachel Harrison, CJ Leede, Catriona Ward, Monika Kim, Amanda Mortlock, Justine Winans, Chelsea Conradt, Saratoga Schaefer, Chuck Tingle (just to name a few), you're all very cool and weird and I am honored to write alongside you.

I am overjoyed to have been welcomed into the thriller/horror bookish community through some amazing readers and reviewers. Thank you to every one of you who posted about this book, read, reviewed, told friends, bought copies, and helped champion my work far and wide. It truly means the world to me. Thank you to Lavender Public Relations and the awesome Brittani Hilles for working on this project with me.

Thank you to Olivia Burgher, my film agent, who loves my horror brain and is always pushing me to go dark.

Thank you to Jenn Levin for helping me understand better how the subconscious mind works.

Thank you to my parents. I know you did your best.

To my office mate James, the dog: Your company while I write softens every horrible thing I have to put on the page.

To my husband: Thank you for being a man that I can trust. Your love has been a safe place for over twenty years. Without it, I wouldn't be here and I know it.

To my son: You are the light in my eyes and the reason I don't float away. I am proud of who you are becoming.

This book exists because of a little girl who fought for a future that wasn't guaranteed. I acknowledge her fight and I hope she's happy with how things are turning out.

Author's Note

What a Nightmare contains depictions of emotional abuse, physical abuse, child abuse, self-harm, eating disorders, suicide ideation, alcohol abuse, gun violence, racism, homophobia, religious trauma, and graphic depictions of violence and gore.

Keep reading for a preview of Rebekah Faubion's contemporary romance

THE LOVERS

Available now!

KIT

SHUFFLING THE DECK is more than a nervous habit. The weight of the cards in my hands, the *swish swish swish* as they slide into each other, rearranging themselves based on the rhythm in my soul; it stops the spiral I so easily trip right into. I trust them more than I trust myself, and maybe that's part of my problem.

One flies out and turns over against the steering wheel.

Strength, a major arcana card, and not one I pull for myself often. It's a card that's all about flexibility, letting go of the status quo to transform again, truer and clearer than in the past. It's about courage, passion arising to spontaneously flow, washing through all your dead or dying places.

Okay, Universe, no need to paint with such a heavy hand.

It's only brunch.

Mom's birthday brunch, to be precise.

A Larson family tradition five years running. Location: the Polo Lounge, a Hollywood icon. The idea: my father's. Like he plucked it right out of one of his favorite movies and planted it in our life for cinematic flair—his favorite kind. He really loves a gesture—grand or mini, doesn't matter.

If Tom Hanks would do it to the tune of Jimmy Durante, so would Dad.

The Polo Lounge is located inside the Beverly Hills Hotel, a stunning pink palace right off Sunset Boulevard that is impossible to visit without feeling like the main character in a golden age romantic comedy. Even if you're wearing an off-the-rack dress du jour instead of couture and taking selfies alone instead of walking hand in hand with a hot, bronzed movie star to the *flash flash flash* of paparazzi light bulbs.

Last year I brought Gavin, the sculpted-from-marble veterinarian I was dating at the time. He was already on his way out of our relationship, but at least I had some arm candy for the photo op.

This year, I was supposed to bring my live-in boyfriend, David. The reservation is still set for four people, the split so fresh I hadn't had time to change it. It's going to get awkward when I have to sheepishly say "just three." Mom and Dad will look at me with wide eyes and furrowed brows and ask if everything is okay, and I'll have to tell them, "Yep, all is absolutely peachy. I'm just single and momentarily without a home again."

For the second time this calendar year.

I snap the mirror on my car visor closed and smack my glossy lips together.

David Young was everything I thought I wanted.

On paper, anyway.

He was quick-witted, tall, dark, and handsome, with long, perfect fingers, and hair the color of ink. He was also getting *that look* in his eye. The one men get right before they drop down on one knee with something sparkly. You'd think that a believer in rom-com-style happy endings would be gunning to put a ring on it, but the directive handed down from my screenwriter-in-progress father was not simply to "get married and settle down."

It was to "find love, the kind that lasts forever," just like Meg Ryan in *French Kiss.*

It was to "never settle for less than a guy who gives speeches," like Hugh Grant at the end of *Notting Hill*.

It was to "be the ingenue in your own life."

I liked David. We had the kind of chemistry that makes sex good, kissing great, and conversation easy, but he could go days without texting and I'd almost forget I was dating him until he called, *hey babe*, and asked me out for sushi or to go to some new swanky club. Because David liked the aesthetic of a manic pixie dream blond on his arm, and I liked how easy it was to be that blond when I was with him.

He also had the hookup with a lot of celebs I was hoping to convert to clientele. Celebs and semi-celebs who can pay more so I can hopefully work smarter, not harder.

Dad, however, *really* likes David. A lot more than me. Dad likes that he's a good dresser and is polite and smart, but he likes David's industry connections even more. Dad is a perpetually sleep-deprived orthodontist by day, and a screenwriter on the brink of his next great script by night. David is a successful TV exec. They talk about the biz, and in Dad's mind, that talking might one day lead to pitching, which could possibly lead to his big break.

On some level both Dad and me using David for his clout is what made me realize the relationship needed to end. Dad, however, wasn't let in on that train of thought, so I need to make sure he is at least one pink sangria in before I break the news.

The valet attendant, Robbie—a slim, nervous-looking barely-adult with a bright shock of red hair he's tried to tame with too much gel—passes in front of my car. Again. I told him I needed to use the Wi-Fi to finish my upload, so he let me idle in the drive.

But he's getting antsy.

My computer chimes to alert me the upload is complete. I check all the details one final time before closing the laptop. It's one of my "Choose Your Own Tarot Adventure" videos, which is just my way of doing a tarot card reading for the masses. It's a signature video on my channel, and always gets me dozens of new inquiries for private readings.

My subscribers hold firm at one million, slowly growing now that the initial publicity from my Kardashians appearance has calmed down. Before, I was Mystic Maven Kit Larson, YouTube personality and high-end event entertainer; now, I'm that, *plus* the woman who predicted Kim's most recent dating scandal.

My bestie, Nina, coined the name Mystic Maven in college when I got into tarot as a way to help curb my growing battle with anxiety and panic attacks. It stuck like glue, and before I knew it, I was giving readings at sorority parties, before finals, any time anyone wanted to know if their crush liked them back.

I stow my computer, pack up my tarot deck, and climb out of the car, waving Robbie over with a smile. He beams as he takes my keys, and I press a Hamilton into his palm as a thank-you. I flip my sunglasses up like a headband and check my watch. Mom and Dad are due any second.

Should I wait here for them?

Should I go ahead inside and get in front of this "reservation for four" drama?

My phone buzzes. I don't have notifications turned on for any of my apps—a mental health boundary my therapist and I set up after my channel reached five hundred K. It's a text from Nina. I told her about splitting with David before I begged to crash on her couch last night.

> **consider this a hug from the universe and a reminder that fate doesn't give us anything we can't handle**

Nina is an actress, mostly bit roles on TV and a few in movies, but with lucrative prospects on the horizon and a lot of faith in her divine path; she's going places. I may be the one with the spiritual brand who gives spot-on readings, but she's a lot better at discerning her intuition for herself than I am. When it comes to my own inner compass, I get lost more often than I get where I'm trying to go.

I send her a heart emoji plus the sparkly stars I associate with cosmic magic.

"Kitten." I hear my mom's nickname for me and look up to see she's stepped out of the driver's side of her Mercedes and is dropping the keys in the hands of the other valet attendant.

Seeing her driving herself to her birthday brunch, where she always, without fail, ends up on the other side of toasted, is an unnerving plot twist. Mom is a mediocre driver at her most sober. This does not bode well. I'm about to ask what's up when she reaches me, smacks air kisses to both cheeks, and tugs me in, saying, "Let's grab a selfie together before your dad arrives."

She attempts her normal toothy smile, but her newly "refreshed" (code: Botoxed) face is still a little light on dynamic movement. She raises her phone and begins searching for an angle that flatters both of us–mostly her–and settles on an above, left-of-center position. Her good side, but it's the side I part my hair toward, which means my cheek is shadowed by a curtain of blond waves.

She pulls the phone back to examine the shots. "The light is atrocious, but we can add some filters. Make it work." I regret encouraging Mom to get on social media. She needed it to build her life coaching biz, but she uses it to stalk me–tag me and then passive-aggressively prod until I reshare–almost as much as she uses it to sell her coaching programs and packages.

Dad's Mini Cooper pulls up next. Just a few minutes behind Mom. Were they coming from different locations? On her birthday?

The moment Dad steps out, I see tension etched into every one of his normally *relaxed to the point of sleepy* facial features. He shoves a hand in his pocket to pull out some cash for a tip, pushing his wire-rimmed glasses up his nose, and walks over with stiff shoulders. His eyes flick to Mom and then me before he leans in for a quick hug.

"Hey there, cupcake," he says, his voice tight. It's easy to read the energy racing back and forth between them. Easy and *uncomfortable.*

I swallow a few times. Clear my throat.

Keep it breezy, Kit.

"Did you have an emergency at work?" I ask Dad, letting my eyes trail to his car, which is now pulling away, driven by Robbie.

"They never call me on my day off," he says. It's not an answer. "You know that."

"Right," I say, no less confused.

My parents are the Nancy Meyers embodiment of Dad's long-deferred Hollywood dreams, right down to the kitchen in their South Pasadena Spanish Colonial and eccentric elderly neighbor with an Oscar hiding in his cluttered, dusty office. I'm the twenty-something daughter perpetually in need of guidance (and financial assistance) that they are somehow still ridiculously proud of anyway.

We each have our role, and we're all really fucking good at playing them.

We never go off script.

Am I somehow responsible for this improv session?

I rack my brain. They couldn't know about the breakup yet–it just happened. But neither one of them has asked about David, either. They may be too pissed at each other to notice my missing significant other.

"Shall we?" Mom asks, but she doesn't wait for our answer. Her chunky espadrilles hit the red carpet that forms the pathway into the hotel. She doesn't look back at either of us; Dad doesn't get any less chilly.

My parents have had plenty of spats over the years, and a lot of them have taken place in that Nancy Meyers kitchen over a bottle of merlot. I know they fight, thrive on it in some ways, but the ice always thaws quickly. Like rising ocean level thaw-out rates.

Dad exhales through his nostrils. "Too late to skip out, I guess."

Skip out? My thoughts want to untether, but this isn't my first rodeo, and I won't let my bucking bronco brain win.

He offers a small smile that doesn't reach his eyes before following behind her. I inhale a sharp breath, pushing it out with extra force. I've been handling my anxiety for years. I refuse to be weird at brunch no matter what sensations are happening in my brain and body.

No matter how unhinged my parents are acting.

Breezy as a motherfucking summer day, baby.

THEY DIDN'T RESPOND to my correction of the reservation with even a sideways glance. Mom was on her phone, typing like mad and ignoring the world. Dad was glaring straight at her like his stare could light her hair on fire.

We're seated at one of the Polo Lounge's iconic booths. The cushions are covered in deco-inspired lime-green palms, tucked into a pink stucco alcove that overlooks the lush patio. I take my seat on one end of the curved bench, and Mom and Dad slide into the other side, keeping a notable distance from each other.

The empty water glasses wink, taunting me. Panic makes me parched. Like a killer hangover or the end of a cardio blast.

I distract myself by perusing the menu, even if we always start with the same thing. Pink sangria and ceviche for Dad and me, and farmers market seasonal fruit for the vegetarian Mom. Our waiter arrives to pour the waters—bless his soul! I gulp down the whole glass. The cold liquid cuts through the heat spreading across my chest cavity like a wildfire.

"You need a second to look over the menu?" our waiter, Gary—per his name tag—asks. "Or are you ready to get this party started?"

"Any special apps we should know about?" Mom asks, leaning forward to beam up at Gary from what I'm sure she thinks is an optimal angle. Dad's mouth twitches. He covers the move with the rim of his glass, gulping deep.

Five years we've been doing this birthday brunch. Five years and the only thing that has changed has been my plus-one.

"Sick of your old standby?" Dad says through a loud crunch of ice between his teeth. Dad never crunches ice. Teeth are his livelihood, and he's a stickler for healthy dental practices of all varieties.

"I could recommend the artisanal bread and butter, a new butter flavor every week," Gary replies. "Something we're trying out on the menu this fall."

"That would be scrummy," Mom says, closing her menu. *Scrummy?* Jesus Christ, is she about to have a stroke? I have never heard her use the word *scrummy* in my whole life.

"Ceviche and a pitcher of pink sangria," Dad adds. He leaves Mom's fruit off, and she doesn't correct him. And with that, Gary is gone.

Mom exhales, leaning back against the booth. Only now, for the first time since arriving, do I see her eyes trail to either side of me in search of my plus-one.

"David couldn't make it, Kitten?" She pouts, reaching for my hand and squeezing. "Next time."

Just rip the Band-Aid, baby.

"There won't be a next time." Both of their gazes fix on mine.

"We broke up a couple days ago. I moved out of his place." *Took my two suitcases, Himalayan salt lamp, and bounced.* "I need to crash in the pool house if that's oka–"

"Oh for fuck's sake," Dad exclaims. "I can't take this anymore. Tell her or I will."

Mom's face stiffens. "We agreed to wait until after everything was finalized." Her lips are tight as she replies, and not just from the fillers.

"Fine," Dad says, nostrils flaring. He turns back to me, yanking his wire rims off dramatically. "Your mother is leaving me for a thirty-two-year-old British chippie she met coaching!"

My heart rate skyrockets.

Scrummy makes a hell of a lot more sense now.

My hands ball into tiny fists, which I shove into the fabric of the booth cushion.

"Chippie?" The word is the only question I can muster.

"She's incredible," Mom says. "So ambitious, so driven."

She???

Mom pulls out her phone and starts trying to show me the picture of her hot, barely-older-than-me girlfriend by swiping through an album on her phone titled "Lover."

I need a bag to barf into.

She's got wavy brown hair, tan skin, deep brown eyes, and a crooked but cute smile. I don't know what is more shocking, the fact that this album has hundreds of photos in it–some of which feature Mom and this woman kissing, snuggling, generally canoodling–or the fact that Mom is acting like this over a woman when I had no idea she was into women at all.

My brain immediately glitches and I see *her* face. Ten years ago, cheekbones already sharp, aquamarine eyes bright, lips pink and swollen from kissing.

No, not a chance. I will *not* think about her right now.

"Her name is Willa, and her Libra Moon really brings me so much balance," she says. *Swipe.* "She works at Erewhon as a health and wellness guide," she continues, "but her real passion is Pilates." This gets an eye waggle. "She wants to open gyms in Brentwood. She has investors–"

"Jesus Christ, Camille, I'm sitting right here," Dad exclaims, just as Gary returns with the pitcher of pink sangria and our appetizer. He makes quick work of dropping off the food and drinks as I watch Dad count down to an explosion.

Mom reaches for a glass, pouring her own sangria since Gary doesn't stick around for that part. Dad's brows twitch. His nostrils flare. She shakes the ice cubes into the glass and pours in a little more of the soft rose-colored liquid. Dad's hand curls around the hilt of his butter knife. She lifts the glass up to drink. He smacks the table and the dishes and silverware all clack in a metallic screech.

"Order your own pitcher," Dad says, yanking the glass from her hands. "This one is ours." He turns his eyes to me and then to my empty glass.

"I don't see why you're acting so immature about this. You're the one who ruined our plan, you're the one who spilled the beans right here," Mom says, yanking the glass right back and chugging it down. She hiccups, shrugging dramatically and swiping her thick, blond-laced-through-with-gray hair over one shoulder. "We were going to sell the house and get the details all sorted before we told her–"

"That plan is out." He looks at me. "I'm afraid you can't stay in the pool house, cupcake, because that's my current squat."

Mom reaches over the ceviche growing warm on the center of the table and cups my chin. "We can help get you a short-term rental, Kitten."

They had a plan.

I pull away from her grip. My chest grows tight. The steadily simmering embers in my belly ignite into flames that travel up my esophagus and into my throat. They lick the length of my neck and consume my eyeballs with their heat.

They had a plan to keep me in the dark while they packed up my childhood home and sold it to a stranger.

"Katherine." Dad says my full name. Mom immediately stills.

My throat is closing up and the only thing I can do is breathe in, out, in, out through my nostrils.

I push against the booth with my fists and stand, smacking my thigh on the underside of the table. I shake my head. I need a small, confined space where I can ride this out.

I BURST INTO an empty bathroom stall and slam it shut.

My eyes are frozen open. As much as I want to conjure my safe space from hypnotherapy, once I'm this far gone I can't risk dropping my focus to get there. That means finding something to visually hold the weight of my spiral. I pick the small spot of chipped paint on the back of the door, press my fingers to my pulse in my throat, and breathe.

It's been years since a panic attack took me by surprise in a public place. Hypnotherapy sounds very LA, I know, but I swear it's on doctor's orders. My *actual* therapist suggested it as a supplement to our sessions, a way to get off meds and reframe my triggers through my subconscious. It's been a game changer. But as my adrenaline begins to drop back down, a wave of sadness and shame sweeps over me, hard on impact, cracking through all my resolve.

And I have to give in.

Her brown hair fell across shoulders that were sun-kissed from spending all summer by the pool. I watched her walk away, her kiss still lingering on my lips, but my heart was already racing, running back over the promises I'd made as I fell asleep beside her.

I close my eyes and breathe into the feeling.

Let's go on a date. A real one. Like at a restaurant with fabric napkins, she'd said.

I'd said yes, and I had wanted to mean it.

In the sunlight, I knew that I couldn't.

I try to swallow the emotion down, down, down.

Still it bubbles up.

Hurting her almost destroyed me.

The one time I came close to dating a girl, it turned into a disaster tailspin of emotional confusion. Feelings got all jumbled and what I believed about myself–my *ideal* of myself–came into question. Sure, it all settled eventually, and I tried to write it off, move on without looking too closely at what the whole thing actually meant.

But the yearning never did go away.

In college there was Maia. She sat next to me in Western Civ. She smelled like citrus, saffron, and rose petals, and her hair was long, dark, shiny. When we weren't in class side by side, she occupied the space in my head between asleep and awake. Moments when my mind was vulnerable enough to wonder how the curves of her hips in her skintight jeans would feel cupped in my hands, or how her plump lips would taste, or what it would be like to make her laugh and then moan in the very next breath.

Midway through the semester I did the unthinkable and moved seats, causing a disruption to the implied structure of our auditorium classroom. I couldn't take her passing in front of me to get to her chair anymore. She'd brush against me; she'd whisper responses and critiques of the lecture, her necklace would taunt me from the dip in her clavicle, the pendant dropping down to disappear between the mounds of her breasts, and my eyes would drift, my pulse threatening to give me away.

My TA called me out on the move. Maia took it personally, and not for the right reasons. I almost flunked out of the class rather than attend in a cloud of embarrassment. Another massive mess, only that time I didn't even let myself kiss her.

I blink, squeezing the bridge of my nose, exhaling a sharp puff through my nostrils.

I've had oodles of crushes on women, but I'm still not brave enough to take my yearning outside the safety of my daydreams.

I'm not straight–not even close. But, wow, the undeniable existence of my queerness doesn't make it any easier to *be*. How do you take a secret you've kept hidden away for all of forever and make it public? How do you say it out loud and have it not become the only thing anyone ever sees again?

Acceptance doesn't mean it's comfortable.

Or easy.

It doesn't make you ready to process other people knowing; it doesn't make you willing to change your life–because it does change your life. There's no way it doesn't. Maybe for the better, but then, I cite my previous experience and Exhibit *Mom's B-Day Brunch* as evidence to the contrary.

So . . .

I daydream. I yearn.

But my reality stays the same.

Why the hell does Mom have to shake everything up?

The Ideal Rom-Com Life Path is just fine. It's a path Mom and Dad always made look iconic. It's a path that was supposed to ensure that all-important Happily Ever After. Hugh Grant in a ruffled button-down, Tom Hanks at the top of the Empire State Building, *insert your favorite rom-com hero here*, that's what we're going for.

That's the path.

Your mother is leaving me for a thirty-two-year-old British chippie. Dad's words ring again in my head. They land, a lead weight in my gut. The perfect Nancy Meyers couple is splitting up.

Maybe the path is fucked.

Photo by Chandra Wicke

REBEKAH FAUBION is a queer author and screenwriter living in Los Angeles. Her books include the YA thriller *Lost Girls of Hollow Lake*; the sapphic rom-coms *The Lovers* and *The Sun and the Moon*; and her forthcoming adult horror debut, *What a Nightmare.* She enjoys reading tarot, bingeing horror novels way past her bedtime, and thinking up places to bury the body—for the plot, of course.

VISIT REBEKAH FAUBION ONLINE

RebekahFaubion.com

RFFaubion